JACKSON'S *Rise*

TIELLE ST. CLARE

ELLORA'S CAVE
ROMANTICA®
www.EllorasCave.com

An Ellora's Cave Publication

www.ellorascave.com

Jackson's Rise

ISBN 9781419965685
ALL RIGHTS RESERVED.
Jackson's Rise Copyright © 2009 Tielle St. Clare
Edited by Briana St. James.
Photography and cover art by Les Byerley.

Electronic book publication October 2009
Trade paperback publication 2012

JACKSON'S RISE

298

Prologue

ဢ

"Ballroom full of people—designers, models, me and a few other photographers and of course, the press."

Jackson kicked his feet onto the end of his couch and relaxed. Holding the phone to his ear, he listened to his brother Max set the stage for his latest adventure.

"I'd been dodging her all night. Did *not* want to deal with her. She finally catches me."

Jackson made a noise, just to let Max know he was listening.

"You know me. I don't want to cause a scene."

The sentiment clogged Jackson's throat and he coughed. If Max heard it, he ignored the sound.

"I'm trying to be polite, trying to get her to just move on but damn, whatever I said, it was the wrong thing. She just snapped."

Jackson laughed, the sound almost a sob, anticipating the punch line but knowing this wasn't going to be good. "What happened?"

"She grabs the front of her *very* expensive designer dress and yanks. Rips the thing in half. Glitter's flying everywhere. She pulls back the edges and screams 'Are my tits too small? Is that why you won't fuck me'?"

"You're kidding." How did Max manage to get into these situations?

"No lie."

"What did you do?"

"I looked at her tits. What else was I going to do?"

"And..." he prompted—because there was more to the story. There always was with Max.

"She's right. They're a bit on the small side."

Jackson covered his eyes with his forearm. "Tell me you didn't say that."

"No. I said, 'Lady, it's not your tits that are too small, it's your IQ.'"

He didn't know whether to laugh or cry. For all that Max was the charming twin, his mouth got him in trouble.

"Max, you didn't."

"Yeah, it just kind of slipped out. But she only got in one good punch before I escaped."

"She *hit* you?" Jackson sat up. Every defensive instinct he had tore through his muscles. Logically he knew Max was more than capable of protecting himself against one practically anorexic model. But that didn't silence the wolf. The creature snarled inside his head, ready to face any threat to its pack mate.

"Don't worry." Max paused. Made him wait for it. "She hits like a girl."

He chuckled and shook his head. "Don't let our sisters hear you say that." Bridget and Kiki were small but damn, they were fierce.

"God no," Max said.

The image of Max standing in a crowded room with a naked woman taking a swing at him wouldn't leave Jackson's head.

"So uh, what happened to her, standing there, you know, topless?"

"Ah, it's Vegas, baby. Topless women aren't that unusual."

And how his brother had ended up in Vegas while Jackson exiled himself to Alaska was still a mystery to the family. Everyone assumed—including Jackson—that he and

8

Max would end up at least in the same state if not living next door to each other. He missed his family — Max in particular — like hell.

"Only you, Max. This kind of shit only happens to you," he said, taking a sip of his gin and tonic, the bite of alcohol a comforting burn in his throat.

"I don't know why. It wasn't like I egged this girl on."

In his mind, Jackson could see the confusion on his twin's face, lines crinkled around his blue eyes, the little grimace, shoulders shrugged.

"Mom always said you just fall into trouble."

"And you rise above it."

Their matching laughs combined in the phone lines and Jackson resettled on the couch.

"So what's going on with you?" Max asked. The tone of Max's question came across too casual, alerting Jackson he hadn't done as good a job as he'd hoped in hiding his stress.

He sighed. If anyone was going to notice, it would be Max.

"Nothing much."

"Jax." With one word his brother managed to communicate the perfect warning — he *wasn't* going to let this go.

But Jackson couldn't reveal what he didn't know. Yes, he was vaguely discontented, some kind of lingering ache that wouldn't leave but he couldn't pinpoint the source. Whining about it wasn't going to help.

"Max, I'm fine. Just helping out a friend on a project." It was a little more than that but he wasn't quite ready to share with the family. "It's nothing big." Just a game of cops and robbers — with real bad guys.

He hoped that would put his brother off but knew better. Once Max had his teeth into something, he didn't let go. He was more pit bull than wolf. Unless Jackson could redirect him.

"How's Dani?" Jackson asked, hoping the topic of Max's gorgeous, showgirl fiancée would be a distraction. At least Jackson assumed she was gorgeous. He'd never seen her but Max didn't date plain women.

He waited, expecting his brother to launch into their latest plans, like maybe picking a date. They'd only been engaged a few weeks but already their mother was asking if *he* knew when the wedding would be.

"Uh, fine."

The response echoed hollow across the phone.

"Doesn't sound fine."

"No, she's good. Really." False energy infused his words making Jackson's teeth ache. Something was going on. That was the problem with the phone. He couldn't look at his brother. Couldn't read his eyes. He needed to see Max. The wolf inside him rumbled its agreement.

He thought about the next time he would see Max face-to-face. Their brother's wedding a month away.

"When are you heading to Mik's wedding?" Max asked as if he'd heard Jackson's thoughts. "Dad called tonight and asked when we were arriving."

Jackson groaned. He loved his family—he really did—but spending concentrated time with them and at a wedding no less—he wasn't looking forward to it. His father would start in on him about moving back. Mom would turn her attention to him now that Mikhel was getting married and Max was engaged. "The Thursday before," Jax said. The wedding was on Saturday. He could leave on Sunday and be back at the office on Monday.

"Cool, that's when I'll arrive as well. You bringing a date?"

"Right." Jackson laughed. The only woman he could even think to bring was Mandy and that had disaster written all over it. "None of the women I know would exactly blend with our family. You bringing Dani?"

He wanted to meet this woman. Wanted to see if she was good enough for his brother. "Probably not. She's got a new show starting. Bad time for her to be gone. Listen, I'd better go."

Hmm, Max *really* didn't want to talk about Dani.

"Yeah. Have a good night," he said, letting his brother escape.

"You too, Brother."

He hung up the phone and sighed. Max didn't sound right. Didn't sound happy. But there was no way to pry it out of him on the phone.

He looked around his living room, his eyes not really seeing tidy bookshelves or light brown carpet. He mentally flipped through his calendar. Nothing much coming up. He could take a few days. Not letting his natural common sense interfere, he walked upstairs to the room he used for his office and flipped on his computer. A few key strokes and he had a flight to Vegas.

Chapter One

❧

Jackson slung his carryon over his left shoulder and reached for his phone as he walked through the Vegas airport. Busy didn't even begin to describe the overwhelming press of people and bodies and things. His wolf snarled its discontent. After three years in Alaska, these infrequent visits to the Lower 48 stressed his wolf. And him. He'd grown used to a little distance between him and his neighbor.

He dug into one pocket, came up empty and reached into the other. Nothing. Lugging his carryon forward, he patted the outside pouches. None revealed the hard case of his phone. Damn, he'd left it at home. He sighed, almost able to picture it sitting on his kitchen counter. Only a few people called that number anyway. His clients called the office and he'd be able to retrieve messages. Thankfully it wasn't tax season so he had few clients in crisis.

A woman bumped into him and he stepped out of the way, into the path of an oncoming gaggle of young women, all talking and laughing. A few eyed him with interest as they split and moved in a wave around him. One even winked. He ignored it and focused on the tense wolf pacing inside his brain.

The animal's flight instincts sent ripples of panic through his muscles. He clamped down on the impulses. Letting the wolf lead now would be a bad idea. His gum line ached, his teeth strained to plunge down. He took a deep breath and blocked out the turmoil. He mentally petted his wolf, silently assuring the animal it was safe.

Everyone in his family had their method of containing or calming their wolf. Max locked his in a mental cage. He'd found a different method. He tended to pet and soothe, almost bargain with his wolf. If he tried to lock the animal away, it just became more determined to gain its freedom. He'd lived through that once before. Never again. Control was his only option.

He avoided the crowd and moved straight to the taxi stand, knowing the fresh air would soothe his wolf and avoiding the crowd converging on baggage claim. Fumes and whistles clogged the "fresh" air he'd been seeking, noises and smells foreign to his wolf. The animal voiced its protest but the panic was gone.

Jackson sped through the taxi line. He considered renting a car, but decided against it. Max didn't mind driving him around. And he was here to see his twin.

Plus—he grimaced as he climbed into the taxi and gave the address for Max's apartment—he was directionally challenged. He routinely got lost in a city a quarter of the size of Las Vegas.

The taxi driver turned out of the airport and headed away from the Strip. Jackson stared out the window. Even without the gaudiness of Las Vegas Boulevard, much of the town was lit up with neon and way too much light. The driver turned into a quieter neighborhood, dropped him off in front of Max's building and left.

He took a deep breath, letting the scent of warmed flowers sink into his lungs, clearing out the fumes and rank human smells left behind in the taxi.

He glanced at the parking lot. Max's car sat two spaces down, front row. That didn't mean much. Finding Max home at eight o'clock on any night was unlikely. He was probably off with the lovely Dani.

Despite his brother's assurances that she was the perfect woman, Jackson wanted to meet her, see if she was the *right* woman for his brother. Not that he doubted Max's judgment but sometimes he was swayed by large breasts and a tight ass and wasn't overly concerned with the woman's ability to hold a conversation. That was fine for a few nights or even a few months but not the rest of his life. And if Max brought a bimbo home, Mikhel and their sisters would brutalize him. They'd be nice to Dani but they'd hassle Max endlessly.

Better that Jackson check her out now.

He hefted his bag over his shoulder and went inside the main building, following the short hall to Max's apartment. He knocked on the door and waited. No answer. He wished again for his phone. Max obsessed about having his cell on him. The only time he didn't answer his phone was when he was in bed with a woman.

Jackson tapped on the door again but didn't hear anything coming from the other side. *Okay, so the likelihood you'll interrupt your brother while he's actually having sex is slim. It's too early for Max to be home.*

With that logic, Jackson pulled out the key ring Max had sent him. It didn't matter that they lived more than a thousand air miles apart, they still swapped keys. Max said if anything ever happened to him, he wanted Jackson to be the one to clean out his place. Hide any embarrassing photos or videos before Mom saw them.

The memory made him smile. He doubted his brother had made any sex videos but with Max, it was hard to say.

Jackson stuck the key into the lock and turned it, knocking as he opened the door and stepped inside.

"Max? You around?" Again no answer. He walked into the living room and listened upstairs. Nothing.

He scanned the living room. Max hadn't inherited their mother's need to tidy like Jackson had. It wasn't dirty or cluttered. There were just bits and pieces he felt compelled to put away. An orderly world helped manage the wolf inside him.

Today's newspaper was tossed unread on the recliner. He walked into the kitchen. Small. But then Max didn't like to cook. They'd eaten out whenever he visited. Not that he was much better but he at least tried to eat a meal in his house a few times a week.

He grabbed the wireless phone and dialed his brother's cell. It went straight to voice mail. Max's message finished and the beep pierced Jackson's ear.

"Max, where are you at? Listen, I left my cell at home and I'm, uh, out of town so I'll have to call you. Step away from the woman and pick up the phone next time. Talk to you later, Brother." Jackson winced as he hung up the phone. Max wasn't with "a woman". He was with Dani. The distinction was clear. Dani was his fiancée and not just a random hookup. He had to get used to the idea that Max was part of a couple.

While I'm still alone.

Oh, good. Self-pity. Just what I need. He sighed. He'd assumed he'd be the first to get married. It seemed unlikely that Max would ever settle down. Jackson, however, was the settling down type of guy. Just ask any of his friends or past girlfriends. They'd called it being stable or solid. Boring was another word many of them used. He pushed the thoughts aside. Didn't do him any good to dwell on it.

"Might as well make myself at home," he announced to the empty room.

He carried his bag upstairs and dropped it into the second bedroom. Nice apartment. Lots of room.

Jackson glanced into his brother's bedroom just to make sure Max wasn't passed out on the bed. Empty. He headed back downstairs, hopeful there was something edible in his brother's kitchen.

* * * * *

Dinner turned out to be a frozen pizza and the gin Max stashed in his cupboard for when Jackson visited. At about eleven, he trudged upstairs, made up the couch in Max's spare room, stripped off his clothes and stretched out on the cool sheets. He hadn't heard from his brother but he wasn't worried. Max was likely out with his woman, spending the night at her place. They'd meet up in the morning. If Max didn't show up by then, he'd call him again.

Jackson stared up at the ceiling, his mind surprisingly quiet. Maybe he'd just needed to get away. A few days of playing in Vegas with his twin would probably set him right, get rid of the weird, low level hum in his head. The vague sense that something was missing. If he were female, he'd think it was his biological clock ticking but that was unlikely. Werewolves came into their maturity a little late. He still had plenty of time to find a mate and have puppies, if he wanted them. Wasn't sure about that.

Maybe it was the fact Max was engaged. That he'd soon be mated. While he knew he and his twin would always be close, once one of them mated, the bond between them would break. He understood that, even accepted it. But he didn't like it.

He took a deep breath, closed his eyes and allowed his mind to clear. He pictured the forest near Mik's home—the trees, the lake, the wild rabbits. The wolf inside his head growled in approval and Jackson felt himself sliding into sleep.

He wasn't surprised the dream was there to greet him.

He ran. The forest alive beneath his paws, the scents of earth and rain filling his head. The wolf brain catalogued each smell, searching for food, threats or another like him.

He raced down the pathways, a growing awareness that another creature ran beside him. His mate. His wolf growled its greeting and the creature answered back. It wasn't a wolf's reply.

His subconscious rose to the surface, observing the strange response and pulling him from the dream. He'd always imagined he'd end up with a female from a neighboring Pack. But this creature wasn't a wolf. Human? No, if she were human, he would have converted her. Coming

16

inside her would start the process and he'd finish it by sinking his teeth into her flesh.

The dream seized him and dragged him back below the surface. *He was there, kneeling over the female's body. He couldn't see her, her shape still mist but he felt her, felt her body ease and accept his penetration – his cock in her pussy, his teeth piercing her skin.*

The world shifted again and he found himself on his back, the sweet cool grass beneath his skin, the warmth of his female above him. He groaned as wet heat engulfed his cock. He scraped his hand through her long hair. Yes, he'd always imagined his mate with long hair. She lapped at the head of his cock, teasing strokes and contented murmurs against his skin.

She rose up, her hair shielding her face, the tips of her breasts teasing his skin as she whispered kisses across his chest, avoiding his nipples when he craved a hard bite.

"*Hmm Max…*"

The voice pierced the fog of the dream. His eyes drifted open and he stared at the beautiful woman straddling his hips. Beautiful *naked* woman. Her hair was black, straight and long, hanging down past her shoulders, the ends meeting her nipples. Her breasts were large and firm and Jackson's palms tingled, imagining cupping those beautiful mounds, holding them as he sucked and bit her tight nipples. They'd cuddle his cock close as he fucked himself between those nice round breasts.

His wolf growled inside his brain, approving of the female, mentally licking his lips, trying to taste the delicious scent that floated from between her legs.

Her hand wrapped around his cock and she guided the tip into her pussy. *Yes, that's it, baby. Put me inside you.*

Slick and hot, her pussy juices coated the head of his cock. Heat spiraled through his dick and converged in his balls. She moaned as she started to sink, her tight opening stretching around his cock.

So good. So real. Real.

The truth slammed into his brain. This was no dream. There was really a gorgeous woman straddling his thighs, sliding his cock in her pussy...and she thought he was Max.

"No!" He lifted her up, moaning as the heat from her pussy left his shaft, and pushed. Adrenaline gave him extra strength and she flew, tumbling off the couch, landing on the floor beside him.

Sprawled across the carpet, she flipped her hair away from her face and glared up at him, indignant and pissed. She shook her head, her mouth hanging open as she stared up at him. He blinked, trying to clear his mind. The vision before him didn't evaporate. A beautiful woman had been seconds away from fucking him and he'd tossed her to the ground. His cock twitched, hard from the teasing caresses of her mouth and her hand and, fuck, the heat of her cunt.

As if the word controlled his gaze, he looked down. Her legs were spread and he could see the deep pink flesh of her pussy. It was almost bare, with a just narrow strip of hair, nothing to hide the beauty of her cunt. The wolf inside him growled as he inhaled, capturing the delicious perfume dripping from her pussy.

She snapped her legs shut and the movement yanked his eyes upward. She brushed a few stray hairs from her face.

"Sweet heaven, Max, I know you're not crazy about 'woman on top' but this is a little extreme."

"No, that's not—"

She rolled over and stood up. The movement sapped all thought from his brain. Every sense focused on the sweet sway of her breasts. She bent down and he fought to suppress a groan. God, her ass was gorgeous. Tight and round and it would fit perfectly again his groin when he fucked her from behind.

She glanced back, saw the path of his eyes and grunted as if she'd expect nothing less from a man. She grabbed a bright red lace bra, what appeared to be a blouse and maybe a skirt. Clutching the clothes to her waist, leaving her breasts bare, she looked down at him.

"I realize we're officially on a break, but how many times have you crawled into my bed at two a.m. because you were horny? I do it once and you act like you're being raped." She spun away and stalked out but not before she muttered "asshole".

He stared at the empty doorway, his mind racing to process what the hell had just happened. One thing was clear. She was leaving. Pissed and leaving. He had to explain. He rolled off the couch and dragged on his jeans, wincing as he eased his erection behind the button fly. A scrap of red caught his attention. Her panties. He snagged them, cramming the silk into his pocket as he ran down the steps.

Dark hair swung across her naked back as she juggled clothes, a purse and high-heeled shoes while trying to turn the doorknob.

He ran across the room, arriving just as she managed to open the door. He slapped his palm against the wood, slamming it shut.

"Let me out," she said, though she barely opened her teeth when she spoke.

"No."

"Max..." Her voice hummed with a warning that every male recognized. He swallowed and ignored the instinctive response to protect his balls. "Get out of the way."

"No. One, you're naked and two, I'm not Max."

She scoffed and shook her head, flicking her hair over her shoulder, enough to glare at him. "I'm not in the mood for role-playing. I wanted a simple fuck but don't worry, that desire's gone. For good." She yanked on the door and managed to open it a few inches before he slammed it shut again.

"Please don't leave. You're still naked and I really am not Max. I'm Jackson, his twin brother." She rubbed her tongue across the front of her teeth as if she was physically holding back words he was pretty sure he didn't want to hear. "Would seeing my driver's license help?" he asked.

She tipped her head to the side as if considering the offer. "Sure."

Relief came out as a sigh. "Okay. It's upstairs. Please don't leave. I'll go get it and—" He did his best not to look down—he'd ogled her enough upstairs. "That will give you a chance to get dressed." He slowly backed away, prepared to lunge forward if she reached for the doorknob.

Her suspicious eyes watched him and then she sighed. "Never mind. I believe you." She shook her head and laughed softly. "I don't think Max has *ever* told a woman to put her clothes *on*."

He grimaced and nodded. She obviously knew his brother well. She turned her back to the door and shifted the clothes in her arms, using the mismatched bundle to cover her breasts.

Of course, now she realized she wasn't naked with her lover but a stranger.

"Sorry." Jackson turned away, giving her time to dress. He stuck his hand in his pockets as he listened to the rustle of her clothes, imagining them sliding across her soft skin. He rubbed the silk panties between his fingers and knew he should give them back to her. He *should* but he also knew he wasn't going to. He had the vague notion that he wanted something with her scent on them. It was insane, stupid. She belonged to Max. Even if they were "on a break". And what the hell did that mean? She obviously thought it meant they could still fuck.

Is Max of the same opinion?

What am I thinking? Doesn't matter. You can't fuck the woman Max once planned to marry. Hell, he might still be planning to marry her. Being "on a break" didn't mean broken up and even if it did, could he actually fuck his twin's ex-girlfriend? And why was he having this conversation with himself? Because he wanted to. His cock was still hard, pulsing with the need to fuck, to ride between those long sleek legs, feel her heels dig into his ass as she pulled him deeper. Stop it, he told himself, but couldn't quite break the cycle of the fantasies.

The wolf wasn't helping. The creature used its heightened senses to gather as much information about her as possible, returning time and again to her scent. Needing what the wolf craved, Jackson took long slow breaths, trying to ease the hunger of the animal and the human, almost wishing he'd let it go a little farther upstairs. But he couldn't have done that—couldn't have let her fuck him not knowing he wasn't Max. That would have too underhanded.

"All done."

Jackson turned around. His cock twitched and he fought the urge to moan. Dani dressed was almost as potent as Dani naked. Maybe because he knew her pussy was bare beneath that short skirt and her nipples made tiny dents on her silky shirt. Because he couldn't stop himself, he licked his lips and forced his gaze down her body. He had to get used to seeing her. Showing up at Max's wedding with a hard-on was bad on so many levels.

Chapter Two

ℰ

Dani tried to hold still while he scanned her body. She was used to men looking at her. Hell, that was part of her job.

Jackson was faster than most and the high lines of his cheeks turned red. She didn't think she'd ever seen Max blush.

And she knew *he* wouldn't have stopped her storming out of the house naked. He'd have watched and laughed. Wouldn't that have given Max's neighbors a thrill?

Fury mutated into embarrassment and her cheeks heated up. What must Jackson think of her?

"I'm Danika," she said, realizing she hadn't introduced herself. Had Max spoken to his family about her? Awkwardly, she offered Jackson her hand. "Everyone calls me Dani."

"I've heard a lot about you."

"Really?" she asked, unable to keep the surprise from her voice. Or maybe that was her guilt talking. She hadn't mentioned Max or their brief engagement to her family. After three failed engagements, she'd wanted to avoid the uncomfortable platitudes from her sisters.

"Well, not a lot—you know Max. Basically I got a description." He grinned.

"Description?" The hair on the back of her neck stood.

"He was light on details..."

The adorable blush returned to his cheeks.

"But he did mention you were tall, with black hair and absolutely gorgeous." The last words were spoken low, almost under his breath. She sank down into one hip. This was something she could handle. Men admiring her. Lusting after her. Jackson would be no different. A little tease, a little flirtation—and she could blow him off. Just like she had his brother.

"Thanks." She snagged a strand of hair and twirled it around her finger, wondering if Jackson's gaze would follow the slow circular movement. His eyes stayed locked on hers.

"I know you must think I'm a total slut." She dropped her voice, making it husky and teasing, and waited for him to flirt in return.

"I don't, no." The serious reply sapped the laughter from her chest and the truth came tumbling from her mouth.

"It was just...I was out with some friends and we were dancing and drinking and a couple of them hooked up with some guys at the club and after a few more drinks, coming here seemed like a good idea." She winced. "Great, now I'm not just a slut, I'm a drunk slut. I'm sorry. I—" She braved a look at Jackson, stunned by how much he resembled his twin. Until she got to the eyes. Same shape, different color. But the deep green staring back at her was a minor difference compared to the light inside. The serious glint in his stare reflected divergent personalities.

Jackson shook his head and stepped closer. "I don't think any of those things," he said, his voice low and strong. Commanding without intimidation. Unexpected tears formed in her eyes.

"I think you're a beautiful, sexual woman who came here tonight expecting a welcome from her lover." Jackson looked into her eyes—a straightforward stare that tugged something in her chest, made her want to believe. "And under any other circumstances, I'd love to be the one you crawled into bed with."

His tone reverberated power, subtly convincing her she could trust every word. That he would never betray her. The wave of lust that had driven her here returned with a surge, a light flicker in her pussy. The memory of his response as she'd licked him distracted her for a moment. He'd been asleep for most of it, true, but damn, his cock had been ready, hard. Thick. Heat flooded her pussy. The fact she'd forgotten her panties upstairs made the sensations more intense.

Hunger flared in his eyes, as if he knew what was happening between her legs.

She pressed her knees together and tried to think good-girl thoughts. She'd climbed into one bed naked already tonight and wasn't going to risk it again.

No matter how her body responded to the man before her.

So different from his brother. She'd rejected Max for a month before agreeing to go out with him. Then she'd waited another thirty days before she'd slept with him.

Yet she wanted to throw Jackson down and mount him right there in the living room.

Fighting that urge, she folded her arms over her chest to hide the fact her nipples were still hard.

"And I guess this answers one question." Jackson stepped back, his chuckle deliberate, diffusing the sexual atmosphere.

"What's that?"

"Max isn't with you."

"Did you think he was?" Her mind snapped to the most logical explanation—Max was using her as an alibi?

Jackson laughed. "No. He wasn't expecting me. I just showed up. He's not answering his phone."

"Ahh." She knew what that meant. The only time he didn't answer—even if it was just to say he'd call back—was during sex.

"He's probably on a date or—sorry. I guess he wouldn't be on a date if you're here..." He winced as his words trailed.

"Don't worry. Max and I are 'on a break', whatever that means, so if he wants to go on a date, he's allowed. But he usually takes his car when he goes out." She rolled her eyes upward and couldn't resist flashing Jackson a teasing smile.

"Gives him a chance to make a clean getaway in the middle of the night. Oh, sorry," she said, realizing it had come out bitchier than she'd intended.

Jackson laughed. "Don't be. I love my brother, but I also *know* my brother."

"Well, it was nice meeting you. I'll just catch a cab and get myself home." She opened her cell phone and hit the first number. Working on the Strip, she tended to take cabs to work and knew one could be there in moments to get her.

"Why don't I drive you?"

"Oh, that's not necessary."

But it would be cheaper. Max lived on the opposite side of Vegas. *And then you'd get to spend more time with the* sexy *brother.* The thought jolted her subconscious. It made no sense. Max dripped sex appeal. That had been one of the reasons she'd resisted him for as long as she had, knowing he would be too tempting. But something about Jackson made her think his appeal went deeper than just sex. Though at this point, that's really all her body was interested in.

She gave herself a mental shake.

"It's the least I can do," Jackson said. The exaggerated grimace made her smile. "After all, I did throw you on the floor."

She sank down into her hip and tilted her head to the side, offering him a considering look. "Yes, and I can honestly say I've never been thrown out of a man's bed before."

"I don't doubt that," he muttered.

Another wicked shiver ran through her pussy and she grinned. Sweet, sweet heaven. What the man could do with a few words. "Well, when I was six, my sister kicked me out of bed because I wouldn't stop talking and she was trying to sleep."

"What happened?"

"I climbed back in bed and bit her." She sighed dramatically. "Yeah, that didn't go over well with the parents."

"Or your sister, I should think."

"Oh, her too."

The corner of his mouth kicked up in an endearing half smile and she had to remind herself there were really good reasons why she shouldn't throw herself at this man. Like—he looked just like her ex and wouldn't that be creepy?

Except when he gave her that sweet smile, he looked nothing like Max.

"Well, since you didn't bite me in retaliation, let me give you a ride home." He cocked his thumb toward the stairs. "I'll grab my wallet. And a shirt."

"Yeah, probably best not to go outside half naked."

The smile got a little wider. "Probably best," he agreed. He turned around and jogged up the stairs, too fast for her to get a good look at his ass. Drat. He came back down moments later—with no indication that he'd taken time to brush his teeth or slip condoms in his pocket. Was it possible he wasn't even related to Max?

He grabbed Max's keys off the ring by the door and led her into the hall.

"Just tell me where I need to go and don't let me leave without directions to get back here."

"You'll just do the reverse of how we go there," she said. Kind of obvious, she thought.

"Won't work. I'll get lost." He opened the passenger door and helped her in. It seemed old-fashioned, almost chivalrous. Something she'd never expected from Max, except maybe for a chance to look up her skirt. Jackson kept his eyes trained above her neck.

He climbed into the driver's seat, started the car and waited. "Which way?"

"Go south."

He shook his head. "I have no sense of direction."

She pointed to her right. "That way."

"That works." He pulled the car onto the main drag.

"From where we are, the Strip is west."

Jackson shook his head again. "I'm not kidding when I say I have no sense of direction. I once had a meeting at the university in Anchorage. When it was over, I couldn't figure out how to get to my office. Anchorage isn't that big."

She laughed, enchanted a man would confess such a flaw. Especially one related to Max. "What did you do?"

"I could get from my house to the university and from my house to the office." He shrugged. "I went home. Once I got there, I could get back to my office."

She giggled and Jackson flashed a mock glare at her. "I'm sorry but having a man, *any* man, admit he can't find his way around his home town is pretty funny," she said.

"It's embarrassing."

"It's kind of cute." His eyes flashed with surprise and Dani winced. She shouldn't be flirting with him. He was Max's brother. A definite no-no in her book—you didn't date friends of ex-boyfriends and that went double for brothers.

She directed him toward her house, the conversation light and easy.

"Do you like living in Vegas?"

She laughed. "It's okay. Kind of hard to be a Vegas show girl in many places you know?"

"I guess that would limit where you could work. Hmm."

"What?"

"I just never thought about it. What do you do when you can't be a dancer?"

She shrugged and looked out at the lights of the city, trailing her fingernail across the glass. "I'll find something. I'm interested in photography."

"Like Max?"

She cringed. She didn't want to bring her sort-of fiancé back into the conversation. "Not really like Max. I like portraits and faces." She took a deep breath and spun around to look at Jackson.

"What about you? You live in Alaska, right? What's that like?" Her questions carried a little too much force, making it obvious she wanted to change the subject but Jackson seemed to go with it, telling her about his life and work. Somehow the way he spoke and the deep timbre of his voice made even accounting sound interesting.

He pulled into her parking lot and shut off the car. She thought he'd say good night but instead climbed out. He opened her door and took her hand. She appreciated the gesture. Exiting a low-slung car in a miniskirt wasn't the most ladylike endeavor. And she wasn't wearing underwear. Somehow she'd missed collecting those from the bedroom floor.

Of course, he'd already seen her. Sprawled across the floor. Her cheeks heated up just thinking about it. And he'd looked. No way he could have avoided it. Her one consolation was that he'd responded as well. His cock, already hard, had lengthened even more.

Need weakened her knees. Wow, she'd forgotten what it was like to feel this strength-stealing kind of desire. Hunger, really. Like she wanted to eat him up. She licked her lips, imagining doing just that. His cock sliding into her mouth. Yeah. That would be—

She shook her head. What was she doing? She was thinking like a guy—all sex, no substance. She blushed, trying to blame her reaction on the third and fourth cosmos she'd downed at the club.

"Thanks," she said, conscious she was breathless. Turned-on and he hadn't even touched her. He'd been very specific not to touch her, as if he felt the same restrictions between them. "Uh, well, thanks for the ride home."

"I'll just make sure you get safely to your door."

With any other man she'd have suspected he was angling for an invitation inside, but not Jackson. She'd known him less than an hour but knew she could trust him. Rely on him.

Strange.

Not that Max hadn't been trustworthy or reliable. She could always rely on him to try to get into her bed. Even when she was tired or crabby, he'd seduce her into sex.

She looked at Jackson, amazed at how much he looked like Max. But she'd never again mistake one for the other. The light in his eyes reflected a different energy, steady and calm but humming with an excitement she felt in her core.

They zigzagged through the condos until they reached Dani's. It wasn't huge but it belonged to her. That little bit of independence went a long way in making her feel grown up.

"This is it." She lived a few buildings away from the condo pool and had good neighbors. They all watched out for each other.

"It's nice."

She shrugged. "I like it. And it's mine." She smiled. "You know, no roommate." Now why had she felt compelled to mention that? She never would have if this had been a normal first date but it wasn't a date. And this was Max's brother. The reliable, slightly boring brother if Max's description could be believed. But nothing about Jackson struck her as boring. He was funny and sweet. And he had this power in him — completely different from his brother's energy — that just seemed to radiate calm and strength. Protection. With an undercurrent of sex.

Still, that didn't give her leave to drop hints.

29

She dug her keys out of her purse and unlocked the front door. She turned to Jackson. A low sexual spark fluttered beneath her skin. Even before she spoke she knew it was a bad idea. Way too tempting. But none of that stopped her from speaking.

"Would you like to come in for coffee?" She hadn't intended her voice to sound seductive...or maybe she had. Heat flared in Jackson's eyes and she knew he recognized the hunger.

"I would love to come in for coffee." He came forward, his hand gripping the doorframe, physically holding himself outside. "But I'm sure that's not a good idea."

She nodded but moved closer, pressing up on tiptoes. She figured she had one chance to kiss Jackson and she wasn't going to miss it. She tipped her head to the side and parted her lips. If he moved back, she could peck his cheek and claim it was a "thank you for driving me home" kiss.

But Jackson didn't back away.

He bent forward and met her, accepting the subtle invitation to taste her. His lips whispered across hers, the gentle touch at odds with the power she sensed inside him. He repeated the delicate caress, as though giving her a chance to back away. Or himself a chance to rethink what he was doing.

She moved a fraction of an inch closer. The need to press against him flowed through her muscles. She struggled to stay still, letting him lead.

He returned, his lips meeting hers, soft but strong. His tongue eased between her lips, without force, gliding inside her mouth as if it was his right, his territory. She moaned, savoring the spicy taste of him underlying the hint of toothpaste that lingered in his mouth. He shifted and her skin tingled, anticipating the hot press of his body.

But it never came.

Torturously slow, he pulled away, as if his lips were reluctant to leave hers. She licked her lips, capturing the faint taste of his mouth, enough to tease her into wanting more.

"I should be going."

She nodded, echoing his unspoken comment. Neither wanted him to leave but they both knew he had to. Neither was willing to cross that line. Not yet.

"Thanks for driving me home," she said, suddenly shy. She stepped back and started to close the door.

"Wait."

Her heart missed a beat. What would she do if he changed his mind?

Then his eyes crinkled. "You need to give me directions back to Max's."

He said it with such seriousness that she forced herself not to smile. A man who asked for directions. A phenomenon she'd never expected.

She grabbed a pad in the basket by the door and jotted down instructions to Max's place. She ripped out the page and handed it to him.

"Oh wait." She snatched the page back and wrote her phone number on the bottom. "Call me if you get lost or need...anything."

Jackson fingered the paper as if he was running through the list of "anythings" she could help him with.

She closed the door and sighed, a mixture of contentment and frustration. A wonderful kiss. The kind of kiss that said "this man knows how to fuck".

She licked her lips, remembering each stroke of his tongue. God, it was easy to imagine that same kind of seductive attention on other parts of her body. *Did he like to eat pussy?* She wondered. *Fuck with the same attention with which he kissed?*

31

He'd seemed almost tentative but Dani could tell it wasn't from fear or lack of confidence. It was from too much strength. As if he was restraining himself, constraining a wild animal inside him. She smiled at the thought. Right. Jackson was the civilized brother. She wasn't sure there was an animal inside him.

A giggle tickled the inside of her throat as she pushed away from the door.

But it would be fun to find out.

*   *   *   *   *

"Take fifteen, ladies, and then we'll do it again. From the top."

Dani groaned in unison with the rest of the girls. A little over a week from opening night and rehearsals were taking on a desperate, vicious tone. She bent down and rubbed the back of her calf. Two weeks off work and her body had forgotten what spending hours in three-inch heels felt like.

"So, how did last night go? Was the hot and studly Maxwell hard and ready?" Jessica teased as she offered Dani a bottle of water.

She winced. Those hadn't been her precise words last night but close enough—she might have mentioned that Max was always ready to fuck.

"He wasn't there."

"Oh shit, we just dropped you off. Were you standing outside for long?"

"Uh, no. I have a key still."

"Oh that's good. That way you could...wait, why are you blushing? Did you search his house or something? Burn his clothes?"

"No." The break up hadn't inspired that kind of anger. "I kind of, almost, seduced his twin brother."

32

"What?!" Jessica's shout drew the eyes of the other dancers. "Twin brother?"

"Identical."

"Oooh, another one? Just as hot and studly?"

"More." As the word slipped out of her mouth, she knew it was a mistake.

"More? Oh no, now you have the hots for his brother?" Jessica's moan straightened Dani's spine.

"I don't have the hots for him."

Jessica's eyebrows popped up.

She sighed.

"Well, okay, maybe, but he's made it very clear he considers me off limits. And really, I mean, he should be off limits, right? I dated his brother. I *slept with* his brother. I shouldn't even be considering Jackson."

"But you are?"

"No. Not really. It's just—" She shivered as she thought about their kiss. One kiss and she'd been ready to drop to her knees and beg him to fuck her. That just wasn't normal. Not for her.

"Yes?"

"Nothing. He was just a nice guy. I mean, not that Max couldn't be nice."

"There's a difference between being nice and being a nice guy."

"Exactly. Jackson was..." She shrugged. "He was almost sweet." *So* not the kind of guy she usually dated. Nice men were either too intimidated to ask her out or too much the puppy-dog to be interesting for long. She laughed. Right. Jackson may have been sweet, but there was nothing puppy-dog about him.

"I think you should call him," Jessie said.

She looked up. "Jackson?"

"Yes. Call him and take him to dinner."

"Jessie, I can't do that. That's weird."

"Listen, your eyes have this kind of dreamy distant glow from just *talking* about the guy. That's the look of a woman in love."

She coughed. "I met him last night." And thought about him all morning.

"So it's the look of a woman who's *hopeful* about love." Jessie shook her head, her upper lip pulled up in a sympathetic grimace. "I never saw that kind of look when you talked about Max. I mean, you always seemed to be waiting for the right moment to dump him."

Jessie was probably right. She hadn't expected her relationship with Max to last. Even their engagement seemed somewhat temporary. But did that mean she should go after his brother? A man who'd only be in town for a few days?

God, just think of the two of them talking. Comparing notes. Her stomach turned a slow flip. She couldn't do it.

"Listen. Call him. All you've got to lose is a little pride."

That was Jessie's view of the world.

"And I can afford to lose some of that."

Jessie shrugged and limped away, found her water bottle and bent over to stretch the muscles at the backs of her legs.

Jackson's kiss, his smile, the honest way he'd admitted he couldn't find his way home melded in her mind and before she could think better of it, she turned on her phone and hit the speed dial for Max's house. If Max was there, this was going to be embarrassing. Hell, might be embarrassing even if Max wasn't there. Jackson would likely think she was some bimbo chasing after every sexy man she met.

Even with those grim thoughts, she listened to the phone ring and couldn't find the strength—or desire—to disconnect. When the answering machine picked up, she took a deep breath.

"Uh, hi, it's Dani. Max, if you're there, uhm, ignore this call. Jackson if you haven't found your brother and you're on your own tonight, I thought maybe you'd want to have dinner or something." She winced as she thought about what that "something" could be. She had a whole list of ideas. "Uh, don't worry. I'm not intending a big seduction scene or anything." *Great, remind him about the kiss last night. This is just a friendly meal.* "I just thought you might, you know, not want to eat alone. Max, if you're listening to this, ask your brother about the seduction scene comment. You'll get a laugh out of it. And Jackson, if you want to do dinner, call me."

She clicked the phone closed and breathed. She'd done it.

The rehearsal director called them back and she stuffed her phone back into bag. She'd have to wait to see if he called back.

* * * * *

"Yes, Jackson, just like that. Oh, again."

He arched his hips up and drove his cock deeper into the hot slick sex. She tightened around him and pressed down, meeting him, taking him, as if she truly needed his cock inside her.

His fingers bit into her hips, guiding her as they fucked. She tipped her head back, her long black hair hanging down to her ass. Her breasts pushed forward and he couldn't resist. He reached up and slid his fingers over the full ripe mounds. He flicked his thumb over the tight nipple. Her pussy contracted around his shaft, gripping his cock a little more. Jackson ground his teeth together and pushed the rising orgasm back. He didn't want this to end, not yet. He needed to be inside her, to fuck her just a little longer. He pumped his hips up, sinking fully into her. Her cry rang in his ears, driving him on.

"Dani."

The sound of his own voice jolted him awake, his mind coming alert moments before his body. His hips moved, rubbing his cock against the soft couch cushions.

He groaned and rolled on his back, his eyes open, staring up at the ceiling. He had the damn thing memorized by now. He'd looked at it all night. Except for those moments when he'd forced his eyes shut struggling to convince his body to sleep. The wolf inside him was too wound up to rest. Strange. He'd always battled the wolf, struggled to control the beast. More than his brothers or father. Maybe it was his fear of losing control that made him so aware of the animal's power. Over the years he'd learned to contain the beast.

Last night, the wolf just wouldn't calm. Jackson groaned. Normally when his wolf clamored to get free, he'd take a run. That soothed the animal. But here, in the middle of a city in the middle of a desert, he couldn't imagine a safe place to release the wolf.

And somehow he didn't think a run was going to satisfy the animal this time. The wolf wanted to fuck. It wanted Dani.

Without any specific mental command, his hand slid down his body, finding his cock hard and pressed against the sheet. He'd been like this most of the night, unwilling to bring himself off because he wouldn't, *couldn't* use his brother's fiancée as his jerk-off fantasy. But nothing else seemed to do it. His fingers curled around the base of his cock and he slowly stroked up, keeping the touch light, remembering the heat of Dani's mouth, her pussy. God, it would be so easy to come.

He jerked his hand away, draped his arm across his eyes and took a deep breath. The faintest trace of her scent lingered in the room but Jackson took it in, savored it.

This was so screwed up. He couldn't want Dani. She belonged to Max. They were engaged.

They're on a break.

Didn't matter. Max was his brother—hell, he was his best friend—and Jackson couldn't poach on his woman.

They're on a break.

"Arrrgh." The sound echoed through room and came back to him reverberating with his own frustration. Damn, he needed to talk to someone. He smiled. This was the kind of thing he could talk to Mandy about. She was practical, logical, down to earth—the female version of him.

Of course, he didn't need to call Mandy to get her advice. She'd tell him what he already knew—*Dani belongs to your brother.*

Besides, she had enough stress, trying to clear her father's name. *And you were supposed to be helping her.*

Jackson groaned. Fuck. He'd been scheduled to go to dinner with Mandy and her "friends" last night. Shit. He'd spaced it, so intent on discovering what was bothering Max.

He rolled off the couch, tugged on his shorts—in case his brother came home—and ran downstairs to the phone. He dialed Mandy's cell, though he was pretty sure she wouldn't answer. She didn't pick up unless she recognized the number.

He glanced down. The answer machine flashed with a message. When had he missed a call? As he listened to the phone dialing, he hit the button, thinking it might be a message about Max.

It was from Dani. Inviting him to dinner. His cock jumped and he groaned. Damn, just her voice was enough to make him need.

"Leave a message after the tone," the mechanical voice said in his ear. Message? Oh, right. Mandy.

"Hi, Mandy—"

"Jackson, if you want to do dinner, call me." *Dani.*

Silence hung in the air and he realized he was supposed to be speaking.

"Oh, Mandy, sorry just listening to another message." Great, his mind and his dick were focused on Dani and he had to find a way to apologize and sound coherent. "Uh, anyway, listen, I wanted to call and apologize for last night. I'm really sorry. I hope I didn't screw things up completely."

Lame, but the best he could do on a machine.

37

"There is a really good explanation—or at least, it's some kind of explanation. I just...I'd rather talk to you in person. Anyway, I'm sorry about last night and I'll call you later."

He clicked the phone off. Mandy was adaptable. She'd have figured something out.

His gaze fell and he stared blankly at the answering machine. The light was no longer flashing. Dinner with Dani. A bad idea all around but the other option was spending the night here, alone. Max must be out of town and Jackson should call him, leave him a message. Tell Max where he was.

But for the first time in years, Jackson had little desire to talk to his brother. Max was damn perceptive—at least where Jackson was concerned—and he wasn't entirely sure Max wouldn't be able to tell something had changed. Like the fact that he lusted after Max's woman.

The best thing for him would be to hide in Max's apartment or go home. His intention in coming to Vegas was to check on his brother. Max wasn't here. He was obviously fine. Though why he hadn't mentioned he'd broken up with Dani...

"They aren't broken up," he said aloud, just to make sure every part of his body heard. "They're on a break. Whatever the hell that means."

The phone rang and Jackson compulsively picked it up and answered.

"Jackson?"

His cock perked up. Any softness created by calling Mandy disappeared. He thumped his dick, hoping the shock would make the damn thing back down.

"Dani. Hi."

"You okay?"

"Yeah. Sure." *Fuck. Why did I answer the phone?*

"I'm calling back—I'm not stalking you or anything—but I realized I didn't leave my phone number."

"I didn't hear the phone ring earlier. I must have been asleep." *Just tell her the truth. You were so wrapped up in the fantasy of fucking her that you didn't hear it.*

"No stress." She laughed and he closed his eyes, trying not to groan. Damn, if the sound of her voice and laughter could make him this hard, he was going to be rock solid when she finally touched him. "Did you find Max?"

"Not yet."

She hesitated for a moment and he imagined her biting her lip, thinking before she asked...

"So, do you want to do dinner tonight?"

"I'd like that."

The words fell out of his mouth but he couldn't regret them. He wanted to see her.

"Great." She gave him the details and directions again to her condo before they hung up.

Jackson put the phone down and shook his head. If going home was the best thing he could do, going out with Dani was the worst.

So why did it feel so damn right?

Chapter Three

ഌ

Jackson looked at the door but stalled. All he had to do was knock, let her know he was there. Or he could take the coward's way out, retreat back to his car and call. Tell her something had come up. That aliens had landed in the desert and he needed to go investigate. Anything.

He shouldn't have accepted in the first place.

It's just dinner. Nothing more. Two casual acquaintances enjoying a meal. Right? Nothing sexual about it.

As long as he didn't think about last night.

Which immediately took his brain to last night.

His cock twitched. Damn, it didn't take much to recall the memory of her on the floor, legs spread, her deep pink pussy wet and open. Fuck. But that liquid lust hadn't been for him. And he wasn't fucking a woman who wanted his brother's cock between her legs.

But even as he listened to his own mental diatribe, he remembered the way her lips had glistened after their single kiss. Damp and soft. That kiss was for him, not his brother. God, he wanted to kiss her again, let his tongue fill her mouth and taste. Then he wanted all of her.

She's your brother's woman.

But they were "on a break" and Jackson knew his brother. When he took a break, he never returned. Max was probably even now fucking some sexy blonde with legs that stretched for miles.

Probably.

And it was that small percentage of doubt that had Jackson hesitating. If only he'd been able to connect with Max.

He'd talked to their sister Kiki, who'd spoken to Max today and seemed to think he was alive and well. Though she did say he sounded odd. She actually said he sounded guilty. So, he could be fucking another woman. Which would explain why he wasn't answering whenever he called.

It wasn't like he could leave a message on his twin's phone asking permission to fuck his woman. Not the kind of thing you left on a voice mail.

You're not going to fuck her. You're just going to have dinner with her.

Right. No sex. Just dinner.

So why did he have a condom in his pocket?

Before he could justify slipping into Max's bedroom and grabbing an extra condom, or two, the door opened and Dani filled the space.

Every male instinct — human and wolf — went on full alert. She looked positively edible. Her shiny red skirt hung to mid-thigh, leaving the luscious expanse of her lower legs bare. The top was a halter, slick material draping across her curves, molding to her breasts and defining each perfectly rounded edge. The bottom half fell away in loose folds that made him imagine her mounted on him, dressed, the skirt teasing his skin as she rode him, his cock sliding in and out of her pussy, hidden from sight by the soft material.

The outfit and the body in it was the perfect temptation. Sexy without being overt. Flirtatious. Enough that he wanted to strip it from her body and take her to the floor.

God, it was going to be a long evening.

"Jackson? You okay?"

He blinked and found his voice. "I'm fine." The words came out strained. "You look lovely."

She smiled, like he'd given her a gift, and ran her fingers along the skirt. "Thank you." She hesitated for a moment then shrugged, the tops of her cheeks turning a delightful shade of pink. "I saw you walk up but you didn't knock. I didn't know if you'd forgotten which unit."

He grimaced and shook his head. "I wrote it down." He pulled out the piece of paper with the specific directions just to complete his confession.

Her smile broadened and the tension in the center of his chest eased.

"Well, I'm glad you found me."

So am I. He didn't say the words out loud, knowing they would come out much more serious than she was prepared for. Hell, it was more serious than *he* was prepared for. But somehow it seemed right. He'd found her. And he was keeping her.

The sentiment should have shocked him. Instead a strange calm invaded his chest. That nagging voice in his head again reminded him that she belonged to his brother, but it had no influence on the certainty of his conviction.

"I'll get my wrap and we can go." She disappeared and returned moments later, a black lacy shawl draped over her bare shoulders. The tiny triangles in the filmy material revealed hints of her pale skin, creating a shimmer of light and dark.

She stepped outside and locked the door. A strange tension rattled between them as they walked toward Max's car. They'd been so easy with each other last night but then they hadn't been on a date.

They stopped at the car and Dani turned to him, blocking the door so he couldn't open it.

"Are we okay? I don't want to make this weird for you and your brother."

She'd given him an opening. He could gracefully back off, get a hold of Max and then come back to Dani with a clear conscience. But he wasn't prepared to leave her for the night.

"We're good," he said, forcing his lips into a smile. She raised her eyebrows. Damn. She'd seen right through his false charm.

"It's not like we're doing anything wrong."

"Right. Just friends going out to dinner."

"Right."

"So we're good?" he asked.

She smiled and it turned his false grin into a real one. "Yeah."

He opened her car door because even if this wasn't a date, his mother had reared him right. She settled into the front seat and the skirt rode up her thighs.

He jumped back and closed the door with a heavy thud. As he walked around to the far side, he pushed the wolf further back into his brain. He didn't need the animal's heightened senses. Didn't need to smell her arousal or hear the tiniest catch in her breath. He needed to go full human for the evening.

The wolf grumbled its displeasure but retreated. Jackson's relief eased the strain his chest.

He settled into the driver's seat and turned the key in the ignition. The engine came to life, growling. The animallike sound reverberated in his chest. He took a deep breath, the faint floral scent of Dani's perfume filling his head. The wolf responded, releasing a growl of warning.

So far, the animal remained in the background. But Jackson knew that wasn't going to last.

* * * * *

If at some point later Dani thought about when the evening changed — when it shifted from a friendly dinner to a date that would end in bed — she'd be hard pressed to pick the exact moment.

It could have been during the meal. They'd started with drinks and dinner at one of her favorite restaurants. Like Max, Jackson had ordered the largest, rarest cut of meat they had. But that was where the similarities between them ended. They'd found plenty to talk about—books they agreed on, politics they didn't—and soon they'd consumed dinner and dessert and were lingering over coffee.

Or possibly it had happened after dinner. They'd decided a walk would help dinner settle and she guided him downtown to Fremont Street. The crowds were different there, less focused than on the Strip. People walked and talked, stopping to watch the light show overhead.

The conversation remained friendly, even when she'd told him about the tattoo on her ass. He'd stared at her butt for a few seconds as if trying to see through the shiny material of her skirt. Heat bounced between them but then she wiggled her ass and the mood snapped. Jackson laughed and they started walking, heading back toward the car. He'd taken her hand as they strolled down the street.

Or maybe it was the drive out to Red Rock Canyon, where they'd parked away from the city lights. Mellow and a little lazy, they got out of the car and leaned against the front hood, staring up at the stars. His shoulder touched hers. The slight breeze had been too much for her lace shawl and she shivered. Jackson had taken off his coat and draped it over her shoulders, then pulled her close to add his warmth. The heat from his body melted the layers of clothes between them.

Definitely by the time they headed back to her condo, the best intentions of a platonic evening were gone and it was all she could do not to slip her fingers under her skirt and stroke her pussy. Her panties were soaked, slick with her pussy juices. She pressed her knees together, trying to keep a ladylike pose during the final few minutes of the drive.

Jackson turned the car into the parking lot and stopped. Her heart started to pound and for one breathless moment she thought he might wish her good night then and there and drive away. Was she the only one to feel their connection?

He opened his door and came around to her side of the car. She stood, fighting the urge to rub up against him and purr as he helped her out. Before she had a chance to press forward, Jackson took a step back, the tension between them returning. They strolled along the walkway toward her condo, the conversation slowing with the silence surrounding them.

It was as if the closer they got to her house, the faster reality returned. And with it all of the reasons for not sleeping with him. Still she didn't want the night to end. Even if all he offered was just another kiss on her doorstep, she wanted — needed — a few more minutes with him.

They stopped on her front step and Dani fumbled with her purse, digging to the bottom to get her keys. Her hands shook, unexpected nerves making her tremble. Clutching the metal ring in her fist, she pulled the keys free and looked up, her gaze landing on Jackson's mouth. She was assailed by the sweet memory of their one kiss. Her pussy clenched and the low heat that had built in her core all evening blazed at the memory and the possibility of more.

"Would you like to come in?" She forced the words out through a tight throat, the effort making them sound husky and deep. "For coffee?" she clarified, though unsure herself what she was offering.

A moment passed, long enough she was sure Jackson would say no. They'd both agreed it was a friendly dinner and he considered her off limits.

"I'd like that."

His voice was low and strong. She hoped the surprise — and the lust — didn't show on her face. God, did he know how sexy he sounded? Probably not. It seemed to be instinctive. *He isn't trying to seduce you. He doesn't intend to take you to bed and fuck you until dawn.*

It was better to let her hormones hear the message directly. She couldn't and wouldn't expect anything besides coffee and more conversation when she let him inside. Ignoring her disappointment, she led the way inside, tossed her shawl over the back of the dining room chair, dropped her purse on the table and headed to the kitchen. Jackson didn't follow. He wandered through her living room, making comments on how he liked the room, liked the style.

That made her smile. She'd worked hard on her condo. It was small, but elegant in a way that still felt comfortable.

She scooped coffee into the French press and placed cups on a tray. She worked quickly, wanting to spend as much time with Jackson before he felt the need to leave.

Letting the water heat, she went back into the living room. Jackson stood to her right, staring at one of the paintings on the wall. A violent mixture of colors that should have been offensive but somehow blended together. Power radiated from it.

Like the man standing in front of it.

Bad idea. You're still semi-engaged to his brother.

She glanced around the room to distract her thoughts. The message light on her phone blinked with an even pulse. She hit the button and waited. She hadn't moved yet to electronic voice mail. Everything else in her house was pretty high tech but she'd kept the answering machine. She liked being able to walk in and see that flashing light. Few people called her house anyway. They usually found her on her cell.

The tape wound back and Reign's voice filled the room. Detective Reign. She didn't know his first name. Everyone just called him Reign. The image of the man attached to the voice flickered through her brain. Tall, blond and freakin' gorgeous. She glanced over her shoulder to Jackson. He'd be a little shorter than Reign and darker, but God it would be a panty-creaming experience to have both men in the same room.

In the same bed. With her. She suppressed a chuckle, keeping the thought in her head. That's what fantasies were for, yes? Funny she'd never imagined Max and Reign in bed together with her.

She shook her head to clear it and listened to the message.

"Dani, it's Reign." She sighed, loving the mellow sound, the slight accent. "I just got word that Winston's back in town and he's doing business at a party tomorrow night. Are you still up for this?" Though the effect was muted—not nearly as powerful as Reign actually being there—the sound of his voice made her toes tingle. From their first meeting, even though she'd been dating Max, she'd flirted and teased Reign, had wanted him. Something just clicked inside her when he was around. When she'd been mad at Max, Reign had been the perfect fantasy revenge.

"Listen, it looks like Max is out of town but I can't miss this chance. I'll come by tomorrow morning, maybe around eleven? It's a little complicated and we need to talk about it. Have a good night." His voice dropped low, the seductive sound more instinctive than directed at her, she was sure.

She sighed again and realized Jackson had grown still listening to the message as well. She looked up and saw him watching her, his eyes curious.

"Friend?"

"Sort of."

"Lover?"

"No." *Not yet.* But maybe now that Max was out of the picture. And who knew if Jackson was going to stay around beyond a few days.

"Not yet," he said, echoing her thoughts. The lines at the corners of his eyes deepened. He crossed his arms on his chest. "But you're thinking about it."

"Why do you say that?"

This time the change in his eyes was accompanied by a slight smile. "Your body. I've spent all night watching you and

I know when you're thinking about sex. Or something sexual at least." A neutral tone filled his voice sparking a hint of defiance in her chest.

"I'm not sure I like being read so easily." She strolled forward, feeling the sensual atmosphere invade her body, giving her hips an extra sway. "But yes." She lifted her chin and met his eyes. "There is something about Reign." She stepped close. "I get around him and I have the urge to rip off his clothes." She leaned in, her lips close to Jackson's ear. "Toss him to the ground, climb on and ride." She stretched out the words, making them last, letting her lips brush his skin. "Long and hard, all night."

Tension rippled through his muscles and Dani couldn't contain her smile. Feeling just a little smug that she'd shocked the hell out of him, she took a step back, intending to use the excuse of coffee to make her exit.

She didn't get far. Jackson reached out, wrapped his hand around her waist and pulled her back. She landed hard against him, chest to chest, their faces inches apart.

"Now, a visual like that would almost be worth letting another man fuck you."

She mentally gasped but did her best to contain the sound. Jackson would watch her having sex with someone else? She wasn't sure how she felt about that. And what did he mean "let" her? He didn't "let" her do anything. She opened her mouth to explain that in clear precise terms but the screeching of the teakettle interrupted her.

The piercing sound wailed above them but neither moved.

"I should get that," she said when it was clear Jackson wasn't going to release her on his own. He stared into her eyes—the strength of his embrace sending shivers over her skin, a subtle warning that he wasn't a mild-mannered accountant she could control. She was about to ask again—the screaming kettle grating her nerves—when he stepped back, his hand sliding away, fingers trailing off her waist in a slow caress.

Confused as hell she stumbled into the kitchen. This had gone from being a friendly evening—though if she were honest it was never quite that—to some strange sexual game. And she wasn't sure who was playing who. Or who was winning.

She took a deep breath, trying to regain her center before she went back to the living room. Jackson was alternately sweet and sexual and she wasn't quite sure how to deal with that.

She poured the water in the carafe and carried the tray into the living room. He came forward and took the tray, placing it on the coffee table. The material of his trousers pulled across his ass adding definition she hadn't expected. The heated sexual discussion from moments before seemed forgotten. It was all very civilized and elegant...if Dani could get over how good his ass looked and that with one good shove she could have him on his back and be on top of him.

She flexed her fingers, keeping them busy so they didn't reach out and touch.

Touching is bad.

Jackson stepped to the side, giving Dani space to sit. The faint scent of his aftershave teased her nose and she wanted to snuggle close, breathe him in deep. God he smelled good. Her nipples tightened and she knew they were pressed against her top. She could have chosen something a little more modest but the devil in her won. She had a good body. She worked damn hard to keep this body.

But that doesn't mean you have to behave like a slut. The mental reprimand seemed to help and she lowered herself to the couch in her most ladylike fashion, knees closed, the hem of her skirt down. Not that it helped much. The skirt only reached mid-thigh when she was standing.

Maybe this wasn't the best outfit to sit and talk in. She had a whole closet full of clothes upstairs. Something would be appropriate. She'd just pull the old "slip into something more comfortable" routine. Except she needed to slip into something that covered more flesh.

She lifted her head to say she was going to change. She expected to meet Jackson's gaze. Every time she had looked at him tonight, he'd met her eyes. He didn't have to stare at her chest before finding her face either. Another reason she liked him so much.

But this time, he wasn't staring at her eyes. He wasn't even staring at her breasts. He was looking at her legs and the line of her skirt stretched across her thighs. His eyes glowed with an unnatural light, looking almost red in the soft illumination of her living room. The heat from his stare warmed her pussy, making her already wet sex ache. His chest expanded and contracted in quick succession, as if he fought to control his breathing, to control himself.

Part of her recognized the danger.

Feeling strangely like a mouse being hunted by an eagle, Dani's first instinct was to freeze but she shook off the sensation. She shifted, leaned more on one hip and turned toward him. The subtle movement seemed to jolt Jackson and he straightened, looked away and blinked before finally turning back. The weird light she thought she'd seen in his eyes was gone as was the sensation of being hunted.

A heavy tension hung between them that hadn't been there before.

"Have a seat," she said, tipping her head toward cushion beside her. He nodded but didn't sit. Though she knew she'd regret it later, the flirt in her wouldn't let her ignore the opportunity. She leaned forward, knowing what it did to the top of her dress. She pressed her breasts against the silky material so they were clearly defined. Jackson followed the direction of her body and looked down. She lifted her right shoulder and draped her arm across the back of the couch. The movement raised her top and revealed a few inches of skin at her waist. It was a wicked sensation — to feel like the seducer.

For a minute she thought he'd back away but then the corner of his mouth kicked up. "Tempting."

She waited for the rest of his statement but nothing followed.

Instead, he sat down beside her, leaving mere inches between their bodies. He moved with a vibrant energy, as if danger had become a force inside him. The contradiction fascinated her. The polite gentleman who'd given her his coat when she was cold was as real as the wild animal that seemed just below the surface.

Another shiver raced down her spine. The delightful tingle settled into her pussy and she pressed her knees together, trying to keep the sensation under control.

Jackson's gaze wandered down her body, pausing at her pussy and then moving on, lingering at her knees. The edge of his mouth pulled up into a half smile.

"That won't help, baby," he said, his voice low, compelling.

She swallowed. "What?"

"Squeezing your legs together." His fingers wiggled into the tight space between her knees. Dani shifted, willing her legs not to open but knowing she'd just made it easier for him. "All that's going to do is make the hunger worse." The smile grew a little deeper. Every nerve in her body came alive. She gasped. All he'd done was touch her knee and her skin was humming. She didn't look down, didn't dare. The sight of his hand on her skin would be too much. Instead she stared into his eyes. Not much better. The beautiful green darkened, almost to black.

She gulped. "Hunger?" she asked trying focus on his words, not on the heat radiating from his touch. Subtle but the intensity made her shiver. He didn't try to grab up under her dress, wasn't even trying to seduce her into opening her thighs. He just stroked the inside of her knee, as if warning her that she would be spreading her legs soon.

The center of her stomach fell away. Damn. She was seducing herself.

Jackson nodded, leaning a little closer. "Hunger. So strong, you can't resist it."

As if a string pulled her forward, she leaned into him. Jackson bent toward her, their lips meeting in a light kiss, the delicate contact drawing out a moan. The warm addictive flavor of his lips drew her closer. He didn't pull away, nor did he deepen the kiss. She tried to hold back but every sexual thought she'd suppressed throughout the evening came flooding back. She needed to taste him. She opened her lips and flicked her tongue out, teasing the peak of his upper lip. He brushed their lips together and then pulled back. Quick samples that made her crave more.

She dug her fingers into the couch cushion, holding her body in place. Her head spun as she tried to understand what was happening. A few simple kisses and her body was vibrating. His fingers lingered on her knee, delicately stroking the soft skin. He didn't touch her anywhere else. Her nipples scrunched to peaks so tight she was tempted to grab her own breasts and squeeze just to get some relief. She tightened her knees but Jackson was right—that only made the ache in her pussy worse. She needed to open her legs and have him between them.

Fighting for each breath, she squirmed in her seat but each time she moved closer, he subtly retreated, not taking away the magical kisses but keeping his body out of reach.

He pulled back, leaving her lips wanting more. Her cry was more whimper than moan. His lips bent into a slow smile. He skimmed his mouth along her jaw, fire kisses that left a heated trail. Her pussy warmed with hot liquid. His teeth nipped her earlobe, a bite just a little too hard to be pleasure. She gasped but the sound turned to a sigh as he sucked gently on the site, teasing it with his tongue.

"Where's your phone?"

The question was followed by hot kiss beneath her ear.

"Hmm?"

"Your phone, baby. Where is it?"

Clarity inserted itself for one moment. She tingled from head to toe, her brain spun with the need to fuck. He had his hand on the inside of her thigh, his lips on her neck and he wanted to use the frickin' phone?

"You need to call someone *now*?"

Chapter Four

ഗ

Her sex-drugged brain struggled to process his question. Admittedly, neither of them was naked and they'd barely kissed but who could he possibly need to call *now*?

"You need to make a call now?" She drew back and stared into Jackson's eyes, assuming he was kidding, that this was a joke she didn't get.

No laughter stared back at her.

"I don't. You do."

"Who am I calling at two in the morning? When we're about to..." She let the words trail because maybe she'd mistaken about what was going to happen and they weren't actually going to bed. Desire flared in Jackson's stare. No, she couldn't have been mistaken. They were certainly headed to bed and he thought she needed to call someone?

"Max."

Dani's stomach dropped.

Jackson reached up, stroking one finger down her cheek. "If we're going to take this any further, you need to break up with him." Dani nodded. Jackson was right. She couldn't sleep with Jackson without making a clean break from Max but was she prepared to do that?

"Is that what you want?" she asked, not sure which part of Jackson's statement she was addressing.

He nodded and that strange light glowed in his eyes once again. He leaned forward, cupping her cheek in his palm as he kissed her lips. "Once isn't going to be enough." He breathed the words into her mouth, calling her lips to move with his until she felt herself speaking them back. "I'm going to need you again and again."

"Yes." Her whispered reply echoed through the room, growing in strength until it was almost a scream by the time it returned to her.

"Call Max."

Her stomach flip-flopped again. She wanted Jackson, wanted what he was offering and truly if she was this into him, then it was obviously over with Max, but still, it was frightening to give up a man who offered to marry her. Even if that engagement was on hold.

"It's late," she offered in weak protest.

"It's Max."

Jackson had a point. Taking a deep breath, she turned away and stood. Her cell phone was in her purse. Jackson followed. Taking a deep breath, she touched the screen on her phone. *Here I go. I'm going to do it.* Hesitating just a moment longer, she turned and looked at Jackson. He stood one step away from her, calm and strong. No pressure. It was her choice.

She tipped the phone over in her hand.

"Am I doing this for a one-night fuck?" She didn't doubt that it would be a great night of sex.

The corner of Jackson's mouth kicked up but his eyes remained serious. "Doesn't feel like one night to me."

Dani nodded, appreciating his honesty. He didn't vow eternal love. *That* she wouldn't have believed. And if she was honest, she knew it wasn't going to work with Max. Might as well get out now. Grabbing her courage one more time, she turned away from Jackson as she touched Max's name on the screen, tensing at the first ring. Max always answered his phone. Unless he was fucking, he answered.

It rang a second time.

Jackson's arm slid around her waist, easing her back against his chest. Heat flowed into her body, shoring up her strength. The ring repeated in her ear.

Max wasn't answering. That made her feel better. Max was taking their "break" seriously.

His voice rumbled through the phone instructing her to leave a message.

Hot lips pressed against her neck and grabbed her attention. She tipped her head, inviting more. Jackson's lips curved on her skin but he accepted her invitation, trailing kisses up to just below her ear.

"Talk, baby," he whispered, the words painted with lust and teasing.

"Huh?" She'd missed the beep. "Oh, Max, it's Dani." That was inane. He knew her voice. Or he should.

Jackson nipped at her earlobe. She jumped but the arm around her held her in place, easing his erection against her backside. She squirmed, pressing her ass back, needing more. Again he responded, giving her what she craved. He shifted his hold, placing both hands on her hips and pulling her back, snugging her tight against his body.

His right hand slid forward, moving below her waist, fingers teasing the crease between her thigh and hip. Breath caught in her throat and she held herself still, not wanting to miss a single touch.

"Talk, baby."

Damn. "Uh, Max, it's Dani. Oh wait, I already said that." The hand moved farther south, fingers tripping across her pussy, light brushes that sent delicious sparkles into her sex. Heat rushed through her body, weakening her knees. "Listen, I think we should—" Jackson rocked his hips forward, grinding his cock against her ass. "Oh God, uhm, sorry, Max, right." Jackson eased away. Cool air rushed across her bare back. Moments later his fingers stroked her skin, lingering caresses that moved up to her neck. "I think it might be better if we—"

He fiddled with the strap around her neck. Her mind figured out what was happening moments before gravity took over. Tiny trickles raced across her nipples. Her uncoordinated fingers reached for the material but it was already gone. Dani gasped and her top slipped away, flowing into a glittering pile at her feet.

Leaving her topless. With one hundred degree heat outside, she'd left the air on as they'd gone to dinner, giving the room a nice chill. She shivered as the cold swirled across her skin.

"What the—?" Before she could get the question out, Jackson cupped one breast, his other hand continuing the delicate strokes to her pussy, muted through the material of her skirt. The hand holding her breast gave a quick squeeze then the fingers slipped down gripping her nipple in an almost painful pinch. *Almost* painful. The shock raced into her core. She wasn't overly fond of having her breasts played with—her nipples had never been sensitive—and if she was going to get any pleasure from it, she needed a firm touch. And Jackson had found it. With one caress. He reached across her body and tweaked her other nipple.

She anticipated this one but it only made it worse. Or better. "Oh fuck." Her knees wobbled and she placed her hand on the wall to keep from falling. The rush of air on her skin battled with Jackson's hot touch and left her feverish.

Jackson reached down and grabbed the hem of her skirt. "Yes." She arched her back, pushing her ass toward him, subtly helping him raise her skirt. He trailed kisses along her neck, laving the hot skin with his tongue.

"The phone, baby."

Phone? She looked at the phone. Why did she have it in her hand? Oh, right. Damn. "Oh, right, Max." Jackson's evil chuckle jerked her from the sensual fog he'd created. She jabbed her elbow back and was rewarded with a grunt as she connected. "Listen, I think we should just consider this break permanent."

Jackson turned her, facing her into the wall, using both hands to pull her skirt the rest of the way up. Heat washed over her ass as he pressed against her, the hard line of his cock snuggling into the split between her cheeks. He trailed one finger down the front of her pussy, teasing the silk of her panties. The isolated caress created an intense streak, stopping at her clit. He didn't rub hard, just a little touch that made her move, wanting more.

Oh yeah.

"It's definitely permanent." She blinked and stared at the wall, her body already moving beyond the phone call but innate politeness made her finish in some normal way. "Well, have a good night." The forced perkiness to her voice made her cringe. "Bye."

She killed the call and slapped the phone onto the table.

Then she felt it. The pulsing of Jackson's chest as he laughed. No sound came out but she felt every chuckle.

"It's not funny," she snapped, jerking her elbow backward again. This time he was ready. He grabbed her arm and trapped it against her body, holding her in place. Irritation put a huge damper on her lust and she stared at the wall thinking she might have made a huge mistake.

"You break up with a guy then tell him to have a good night?" The laughter tainted his voice but affection lingered behind the sound. He tightened his hold around her waist and whispered. "I think you pretty much screwed up his whole week."

She looked over her shoulder, trying not to smile though she could see the humor in it. Jackson's eyes met hers.

"Really?"

The serious glint returned to his gaze and with that the mood in the room shifted. "Yes."

The lust and hunger that had vibrated between them all night returned, slamming into her chest, making it hard to breathe. Every nerve in her body fluttered but it was beyond the physical. She believed him.

"How do you do that?" she asked, trying to focus on her question even as she succumbed to the slight pressure from Jackson's chest to lean forward. Following his silent guidance, she put her other hand on the wall.

"Do what?" Curiosity laced his question but she could tell his attention was focused elsewhere. Like maybe on her ass. She pushed her hips back, rubbing against his erection. The low grunt-groan combination made her smile. Gave her a little power. He wasn't as in charge as he appeared.

She swirled her hips again, loving the heat against her ass. It sank through her skin, warming her core. "Somehow when you talk, I believe you."

"You can believe me."

She giggled, repeating the slow swirl against his groin. "Right. Nothing personal, Jackson, but no woman in her right mind believes everything a man says. Especially when they're fucking."

She felt the silence. Then the world spun as he whipped her around. Her back hit the wall, a subtle shock to her already strained system. His hand cupped her head, making sure it didn't bounce against the wall.

"What the—?" She looked up. The red glow in his eyes had returned and his teeth looked big and white. Her chest rose and fell in harsh breath. She couldn't move, trapped by his stare and the weight of his body caging her.

"Listen to me, Dani. I will never lie to you."

All oxygen disappeared from her body and her stomach dropped. For a moment, she considered that she should be afraid. She wasn't imagining the red light in his eyes. And there was no denying the power that radiated from inside him.

But there was no fear. Desire yes. Even without looking she knew her nipples were tight and straining. Her pussy clenched and the muscles in her body tensed, wanting to move, to press against him.

His nostrils flared as if he could smell her pussy juices. She blinked, trying remember what had brought them here.

Right.

He would never lie to her. Her logic tried to scoff at the statement but instinct silenced the mockery.

"Do you believe me?" There was an edge to his voice that warned this wasn't a negotiable point.

"Yes," she answered with complete honesty. Since she'd caught her first boyfriend holding hands with her best friend, she'd never allowed herself to fully trust a man. Something about Jackson made her want to try.

Jackson nodded, the red contracting in his eyes to mere pinpricks. Not quite disappearing but moving to the background.

Dani dropped her gaze, knowing she'd kind of killed the mood. Not quite used to a guy who actually listened to her, even during sex. So maybe it was her job to entice Jackson. Despite the up and down tension of the last five minutes, her body still hummed, still reacted to Jackson's in a way she'd never experienced before.

And she needed to see where it went.

She arched her back, pushing her breasts forward and up as she reached behind her to the skirt zipper.

She'd learned through the course of the evening that Jackson didn't spend all his time staring at her tits but even he couldn't resist when she so blatantly presented them.

His stare fell and she felt the red flare in his eyes even if she couldn't see. She squirmed a bit, probably a bit more than necessary, knowing it made her breasts shimmy just enough. Her fingers found the tab for the zipper and pulled it down.

Unlike her top, the skirt didn't fall. It clung to her hips. Which actually worked out well, Dani decided. She hooked her thumbs into the waistband and wiggled, working the tight material down, over her ass. She leaned forward, just a little, just enough to brush her nipples against the white material of his shirt as she pushed the skirt down, holding onto it until it reached her knees. Then she let go, straightening.

She left the silk panties on. They made her ass look great and leaving a little hidden was always a temptation.

She raised her eyes but Jackson wasn't looking at her face. His eyes tracked down her body. Knowing that he watched, *loving* that he watched, she lifted her left foot and stepped out of the skirt, planting her high heel inches away, just enough to tease him with the idea of spreading her legs.

The change in his body was so subtle she almost missed it. His chest rose in a longer breath and the muscles in his arms tightened.

His gaze made a long trek up her body, fevered caresses across her skin until he met her bold stare. Hunger flickered in his dark gaze igniting a new kind of fire in her chest—that she could seduce a man like him—but even as she watched, laughter shone in Jackson's eyes. Ooh, Jackson liked to play.

"You dropped your skirt," he said, his voice casual, as if she'd left her purse on the store counter.

She could play that game. She shrugged, the movement slow and again gave a little sway to her breasts.

"I was hot."

His lips bent upward. "I can see that." He stretched one finger out, traced it down the center of her chest, a curvy path down around her bellybutton and then skimming off to her hip. She shifted, her body reacting to the surface touch, wanting more.

Jackson tapped the thin strap of her panties, resting low on her hip.

"You left these on. Does that mean you're still feeling a chill here?"

61

The pads of his fingers traced her skin, following the waistband across her stomach.

"Maybe."

There was that smile again.

"Maybe I should check. Warm you up a bit."

The possibility that she could be *any* hotter made her voice disappear and she nodded. She didn't think it was likely but dang she wasn't about to say no.

The red returned to his eyes, flaring before fading away. Jackson stepped back and did a long slow scan down her body.

She sucked in her stomach and struggled not to squirm. Men stared at her body all the time. Night after night they looked at her skin, her bare breasts, but that was with the distance of the stage.

"So beautiful." The compliment slipped out low and soft, moving like fire across her skin. Every word from the man's mouth made her heart pound. She didn't understand it.

He came closer, hooking his thumbs in the sides of her panties and inched them down. Her legs were spread making the material cut into her skin. She straightened and tried to bring her thighs together.

A quick tap of his palm against her bare ass made her freeze.

"Don't, baby. I like those pretty legs spread."

She gasped, the sting of his hand shocking her into silence. *He does have a touch of the dominant in him.* The center of her stomach dropped away as she imagined him standing over her, spanking her. She liked to play that way but she wasn't going to make it easy for him.

"I don't want them to rip." She didn't buy cheap lingerie.

"I'll buy you more."

Before he could stop her, she wiggled and nudged the panties down. They dropped to the ground, landing on her shoes. She lifted one foot out and bent the other knee, carrying the fuchsia silk material up to her waiting hand. She slapped them into Jackson's open palm. The scent of her pussy wafted through the air, released from the panel in her underwear. She might have cringed if it weren't for the hungry look on Jackson's face.

He raised the panties, tipping his head to the side in question.

"So you'll know what size to buy." She smiled, unable to remember the last time sex had been *fun*. She pursed her lips and lifted her chin, daring him to make a smart comeback.

He rubbed the silk between his fingers, as if transferring the scent to his skin.

He opened his fist and let pink silk tumble to the ground.

Dani felt her mouth drop open. Jackson smiled.

"Don't need 'em." He winked. "I have the red pair from last night."

Her gasp came out like a squeal. He'd kept them? Her mouth dropped open.

"They touched your pretty cunt, baby. I'm not letting them go."

The laughter between them disappeared and a heavy sexual atmosphere settled on the room.

Red sparked in his eyes. His eyes were glowing. She blinked, expecting the vision to disappear with a shift in the light but the wicked fire remained. Dangerous shivers ripped across her skin. The roller coaster of tension ran to the top of the tracks again and Dani couldn't catch her breath. He sank down to one knee, his face inches from her stomach, his breath another delicious caress to her skin.

"Those pink panties, such a delicate decoration for your pussy," he said. He focused that intense stare on her sex, reaching up and letting his fingers trace the smooth skin of her pussy. She waxed religiously, leaving her smooth, sleek. She did it for work but it was sensual to have a man appreciate the effort. "It's so beautiful on its own. It doesn't need any adornment."

He leaned forward and placed a single kiss at the top of her slit, holding his lips there as he flicked his tongue out and dipped into the wet space between her pussy lips. The subtle touch shimmered through her core. He hummed his approval and Dani gripped the table, fighting to keep her legs steady. He pushed his tongue into her slit again, rubbing against her clit with the shallow penetration.

Sensation overwhelmed her. She dropped her head back, pressing against the wall behind her, and closed her eyes, her awareness arrowing down to the slow slide of his tongue. He dipped deeper, murmuring words she could almost understand as he eased the hard tip of his tongue into her passage. Pushing in and pulling back. The slight penetration jolted her system but it wasn't enough.

Jackson moaned, the sound vibrating through her cunt sending shivers deep into her core.

She rolled her hips forward to meet his shallow thrusts, wanting him deeper, harder, longer.

Oh please...I need...fuck me.

The sounds swirled through her head but making them form words was beyond her.

"Jackson." His name seemed to communicate every need coursing through her body. He lifted her left leg and draped it over his shoulder, opening her, giving him access. He sank his tongue long into her pussy, tongue fucking her. Her hips canted forward, pushing against every thrust.

She loved to have a man go down on her, loved the subtle play of tongue against clit and wet flesh.

It was so good.

But tonight it was not enough. She needed to be fucked.

"Jackson!"

His head snapped back and she saw the red in his eyes. A growl erupted from somewhere deep inside him. A distant corner of her brain tried to point out that wasn't a normal human sound but her need shouted it down, absorbing the noise into her body, letting its hunger reflect inside her.

Her pussy juices glistened around his lips. She ran her tongue along the inside of her lip, wanting to taste the two of them together.

He stood up, the movement abrupt and sharp, pressing her into the wall. He cocked his head to the side and claimed her mouth. The warm flavor of her pussy tingled on her tongue and combined with the wild taste of Jackson. Like fresh berries, washed by the rain, straight from the vine.

"Your pretty cunt tastes as good as it looks," he whispered against her lips. His hands moved across her skin, hot and smooth. "Makes me want more."

"Yes."

"Later."

"Fuck, yes."

She felt him smile.

"Baby, I'm going to spend hours with my face buried between your legs." He kissed along her jaw. She leaned into the caress, wanting more. "I need to be inside you." The sharp bite to her earlobe was too much.

"Yes!" The moan was soft, spoken against his neck. She licked his skin, the salty flavor clinging to her tongue. The ache built in her sex. She scraped her teeth across his shoulder, biting down.

A dangerous growl filled the room.

He pulled back mere inches and spun her, turning her to face the wall, placing her hands high against the dry wall. She spread her fingers apart, supporting her weight as he adjusted her hips. She glanced over her shoulder. Jackson worked fast, pulling a condom from his pocket and sliding it on, grabbing her hips to hold her in place as he aligned his erection to her pussy.

She braced herself against the wall, prepared, trying not to tense as he pushed the tip of his cock into her. Heat invaded her pussy, the long slow penetration stretching her, the thick cock almost too much—but the slight pain was delicious. She forced her lungs to breathe and tried to relax, wanting him inside her. She leaned her forehead against the wall, needing the solid surface beneath her as his cock filled her pussy.

"Sh, sh. It's okay, baby."

She bit her lip, not realizing those whimpers belonged to her. The steady, hard press of heat into her pussy made her crave more. Her body no longer under her control, she pushed her hips back, sinking Jackson's cock a little deeper. Hours of teasing had left her slick and she needed him, her pussy both accepting and fighting the heavy entrance.

His fingers gripped her hips, holding her in place as he pressed forward. She took a deep breath and her pussy relaxed around him, letting him fill her until his hips settled against her ass.

"That's it." She nodded, silently accepting his penetration, his ownership of her pussy. He didn't move. Just held himself inside her. Dani closed her eyes and breathed, letting her body adapt to the feel of him inside her. It wasn't that he was bigger than her previous lovers, just that he was there, solid, hard. Not just his cock but the presence that surrounded him, that innate honesty, no matter how hard the fucking became.

Her heart fluttered, recognizing this as so much more than sex. So much more than one night of fucking.

The urge to feel him, to touch him sent her arm back, grabbing behind her head to pull him close. Jackson moved in, turning and kissing the inside of her wrist, his lips and tongue lingering on the soft skin.

"I'm here, baby. Inside you."

"Yes."

He turned his head and pressed kisses on her neck. "Fuck, Dani, I need to move." His teeth scraped along the curve of neck and shoulder, the delicate pain sending delightful zings into her pussy. "Can I have you, baby?"

She nodded. Individual nerves vibrated with need. "Please."

"Damn, baby, you are so sweet." He pulled back, easing his cock from inside her. She braced her hands against the wall, knowing he wasn't finished with her. He retreated until just the head of his cock rested inside her. A breathless pause sapped the air from the room and he pushed forward, driving deep into her pussy.

His hands covered her breasts, holding her in place, a brief hard squeeze as he fucked her deep and hard. She curled her fingers, almost wishing for claws to grab the wall as she held on, her body absorbing every stroke as he drove his cock into her. She shoved her ass back, loving the hard solid thrusts, wanting him deeper, faster.

"Not yet, baby. I want to feel you."

Her body was on the edge, so close. "Please, Jackson." The words were more groan than spoken sounds.

He pulled back, his cock almost leaving her, holding her weightless for one moment before driving back into her pussy. She cried out and moved against the heavy thrust, her pussy clenching around his cock trying to hold him inside her. He groaned and his hips slammed into her ass, pounding his cock into her. The iron control seemed to be wavering.

She moaned, making the sound deep and husky, wanting him to move beyond thinking. "Yes, harder. Fuck me. Harder."

Her words seemed to enflame him, giving her what wanted. Faster and deeper he fucked her until words were gone from her head. Sounds reverberated through the room—masculine groans and feminine cries. She pushed against the wall, bracing herself, taking everything thing he had. He

67

opened his mouth and bit down on her shoulder, the sharp points almost painful. A shiver raced into her cunt, like a tongue twirling around her clit.

He reached down, sliding his hand between her legs, cupping her pussy, pressing his fingers against her clit. He rubbed slow sweeping circles countering the pounding of his cock inside her.

Breath caught in her throat. She was close, could feel the climax rising inside her.

"That's it, baby. Come for me. Let me feel it." His harsh breath washed against her back as he stroked one finger between her pussy lips, sliding by her clit. Luscious little sparkles zipped from her clit and spread through her pussy. She might have cried out but her mind was beyond processing individual senses.

He growled, the sound vibrating her hair as he grabbed her hips and pounded into her, hard fast thrusts that drew out her climax. His fingernails bit into her hips but her body translated the touch into pleasure and a second delicate orgasm zipped through her pussy. He tensed behind her and pushed into her one last time, groaning as he leaned forward, pressing his chest to her back, leaning against the wall as he caught his breath.

"Damn," he whispered, his tone amazed and mirroring the sentiment in her own mind.

Chapter Five
ℬ

She turned her head, pressing her cheek against the wall. It was cool, soothing her hot skin.

Jackson placed a kiss on her shoulder and eased his hips back, pulling his cock from inside her body. She moaned at the loss, feeling strangely empty. She felt him moving behind her, knew he was cleaning up. The practicalities of sex that sometimes just blew the mood. Max had always been religious about using condoms, safer sex practices. Dani was thankful that Jackson had thought of it because she'd been a little too concerned with actually fucking him to think.

Chilled air swirled about the room, cooling her heated body as he walked away, heading toward the downstairs bathroom.

Naked except for the black strappy high-heeled shoes she wore, she turned around and waited. She'd known the man just over twenty-four hours and they'd had sex — but still — her body hummed with the aftereffects of her orgasm, and the feel of Jackson's body pumping inside hers.

The light to the bathroom flicked off and he strolled out, his clothes adjusted, leaving her feeling very naked. The white shirt he wore looked crisp and pressed. She'd never known a man could look less disheveled after sex. If she hadn't been the one he'd been fucking, she would have thought he was merely an appraiser checking the house.

Very controlled. That was how Max had described his brother. And she could see it.

Jackson walked across the room and picked up the suit jacket he'd draped over the back of the couch.

He's leaving?! Shock rattled her teeth. The man had just fucked the strength out of her legs and he was leaving.

Just like his brother.

She dismissed the snide remark in her brain. He wasn't like Max. And if he wanted to leave, she wasn't going to stop him.

She shook her head, swishing the bangs out of her face. Her gaze landed on the French press and cups she'd placed on the coffee table. That seemed so long ago.

Jackson turned, following her stare. "We never got to have our coffee," he said, his lips curling into a tired smile.

She sniffed. "Well...next time, huh?"

He faced her. "In the morning." He draped the suit jacket around her shoulders. The satin lining cold against her skin before heating and warming.

"The morning?"

Jackson nodded. "I like mine black and as strong as you can make it." Before she could react, he covered her mouth with a kiss, distracting her from any thoughts of leaving or staying. She draped her arms around him, his jacket dropping to the floor. She didn't need it anymore. He was hot enough. She snuggled close. The hard line of his erection pressing against her groin. She moaned and pressed her hips forward. Jackson's hands landed on her ass and lifted her — no small feat being that she was almost six feet tall in her heels. Dani squealed and wrapped her legs around his waist.

"Jackson?"

"I won't drop you."

His shoulder muscles flexed beneath her hands and Dani knew she could trust him.

"I can walk," she offered anyway, feeling off balance — physically and mentally.

"I know. I like to feel you." His fingers slid together, teasing the split between her ass cheeks, moving deeper until one finger slipped into her cunt, pumping in and out.

She moaned and nuzzled his neck, licking that tasty skin. She squeezed her heels closer and rubbed her pussy against his stomach, slow circles that massaged her clit against those hard muscles.

"Fuck, baby, I can feel you through my shirt," he said, turning his head and taking a biting kiss.

She smiled against his lips. "Is that bad?"

"I want you against my skin."

She lifted her head, flipping her hair back away from her face, feeling solid in his arms. He didn't even seem to be straining to hold her.

"Hmm, does that mean you're going to fuck me again when we get upstairs?" It was just a tease and she expected a flippant response—Jackson knew how to make sex fun.

Instead, he nodded and locked his gaze with hers. The red flared again in his eyes. "Damn straight."

There it was again. That serious tone that tugged at her heart. His words were a promise.

And this promise made her pussy clench. She didn't doubt him for a moment. She was in for a long, hard night.

* * * * *

Jackson groaned, the hot wet mouth sliding over his cock invading his already sexual dreams. Dani. He let the fantasy play out in his dream, even as mind processed how he'd gotten there.

He'd carried her upstairs, hard and ready by the time they'd reached the landing. He'd barely made it into the bedroom before he'd been inside her again. As if the fucking downstairs had just made them both ready for more, the frenzied lovemaking had been hard and fast and Dani had dropped off to sleep while Jackson had been in the bathroom cleaning up.

He'd held her, tracing patterns on her smooth stomach, absorbing the serenity in his head. He'd opened up his wolf senses and indulged the animal—the perfume of her cunt on him, his scent covering her skin. It was barbaric but Jackson loved that his scent marked her as belonging to him. It would warn other werewolves and shifters that she was protected. The idea seemed to comfort the wolf and he'd finally retreated, giving Jackson the chance to sleep.

Dream.

Another long lick started at his balls, teasing before sliding the full length of his dick. Strips of fire moved across his skin. He shifted, his hand sliding down, cupping the back of her head, holding her closer. The wolf inside his head growled its pleasure, the sound more comforting than startling.

The human side of his brain struggled to wake but the animal took advantage of his sleep state and seized control. He felt his teeth lengthen and knew his eyes had to be glowing. Reality scratched at his brain, telling him this wasn't a dream and he had to stop her. But he couldn't remember why. Couldn't find the strength to pull that wicked mouth away from his cock.

She hummed and murmured words against his shaft, flicking her tongue against the base then leaving a hot wet trail up the full length until she reached the head. Fire encased his cock as she took him into her mouth, driving him to the back of her throat.

He cried out and his hips punched upward. Dani flinched and jerked back.

"Sorry," he muttered. "So sorry."

"Don't worry, babe." She whispered the words against his skin, binding him closer. "I love the way you taste." *Taste. Yes, good.* "Hmm, sweet." The word snapped his eyes open. She was actually tasting him. Without a condom.

Every lecture his father, his father's Beta and his older brother had ever given him came shooting back into his now awake brain—dire warnings of what could happen.

He couldn't come in her mouth. *Couldn't.* But neither could he find the strength to pull away.

She moved back to the tip of his cock and once against swallowed him deep. He fought the urge to thrust, grabbing the sheets beneath his hips, holding himself on the earth, allowing her to do whatever she wanted, enduring and exulting in every stroke, every whisper of her tongue and lips.

He lifted his head and watched, fascinated and amazed by the picture before him. Dani, gorgeous and sexual, hot and loving every inch of cock that slid into her mouth. She pulled back. Her lips were red and swollen, but her eyes were bright, glittering with hunger and pure devilish lust.

Holding his gaze, she opened her mouth and put the tip of his cock between her lips. Her moan vibrated his cock as she sank down fast, swallowing him deep and then drawing back. Her cheeks hollowed out as she drew back. God, the sight of his dick sliding into her mouth was too much. He could come just watching her. He had to stop this.

He groaned and pushed her shoulders, forcing her away from his cock. He rolled away, shifting his hips to the side, his body, his wolf screaming in his head, almost blocking out Dani's outraged gasp.

"I'm sorry, baby. So sorry." He reached for her, dragging her up the bed until she lay beside him. Her eyes were filled with confusion and hurt.

She pushed up on one arm, her eyes flashing with irritation. "You didn't like it?" Her tone indicated she never would believe him if he said yes, no matter how sincere he sounded.

"Loved it, baby. You made my eyes cross."

"Then why —?"

He shook his head. He couldn't answer her. What was he going to tell her? *If you swallow my cum you'll become my sex slave for twenty-four hours?* It wasn't exactly that bad but some ingredient in werewolf sperm had an interesting effect on human women, keeping them aroused and hungry. And while he would love nothing better than to spend the next twenty-four hours satisfying all of Dani's desires, he couldn't do that to her. Not until he explained it to her. And wouldn't that be a fun conversation?

"I just need to fuck you, baby," he said, hoping to stall any more discussion. He traced his finger along the lower edge of her lip. "I didn't mean to be so rough. Your mouth was making me insane." His confession seemed to ease some of her concerns but when she opened her mouth to ask "why" again, he kissed her. "I want to be inside you." He slid a hand between their bodies. His fingers dipped into her slit and wet, hot liquid slid over his skin. She was ready to fuck. Perfect. Because while he'd found the strength to not come in her mouth, he knew he didn't have the control for a slow leisurely fuck.

She closed her eyes and pumped her hips, driving his fingers in and out of her pussy. His teeth stretched in his mouth — the creature inside him coming alive. Every instinct screamed to flip her over and mount her, claim her. The human side fought for tenuous control. She leaned forward, her hair shielding her face as she fucked his fingers. The rise and fall of her ass made his dick impossibly harder.

The memory of last night flooded his thoughts, her straddling him, ready to slide his cock into her pretty cunt. The image filled his brain and wouldn't release him.

Her lips opened as she moved against his hand. Fuck. She wasn't coming like that. He wanted to be inside her.

Hating to lose her heat, he dragged his fingers from between her thighs.

Her head snapped up and the previously languid gaze flashed.

"What—?"

He carried his hand to his mouth and licked, sipping the slick cunt juices from his fingers. Dani's eyes locked on his lips.

"You taste good, baby." He pulled her up to him, easing her across his body and taking her mouth in a kiss, sharing the taste of her pussy. Jackson rolled onto his back, his cock hard and straining, pressed up against his stomach.

"Ride me, Dani."

Her lips spread into a predator's smile that the wolf inside him recognized. "Really?" The sexual tone made him groan. Self-preservation recommended one answer but he'd told her he wouldn't lie to her.

"I can't wait to have you on my cock."

Her tongue touched the inside edge of her upper lip as she looked down his body. His cock twitched as if wanting her attention. The pressure of her stare sparked a rebellion in his mind.

He grabbed her, lifting her, the wolf's power coming through, lending him strength. He raised her up and settled her over him, her knees on either side of his hips, his hard cock against his stomach, the drops of pre-cum wet against his skin.

She raised her stare—challenging him with her gaze before looking down. She skimmed her tongue along the inside line of her upper lip as if she was remembering the feel of him in her mouth.

"Careful, baby."

Sensual lights flickered in her stare. But the saucy flirt had returned.

"You taste good."

He closed his eyes and groaned, grabbing hold of the animal inside him. The instinct to take control and mount his mate gripped his muscles but Jackson pushed the creature back.

"You're about to find yourself flat on your back," he warned.

Dani smiled. She leaned down, meeting him in a hot opened mouthed kiss. "But you said I could ride."

"Yes, baby. Ride me."

She pushed back, going up high on her knees. The sleek lines of her body were glorious in the pale light coming through the window. The full moon was tomorrow night and he could feel it in his bones. The need to justify his own guilt at taking his brother's ex to bed flashed through his head. He could blame his hunger for Dani on the full moon so close but that would be a lie. He wanted her—human and wolf.

She arched her back and stretched, fluffing her hair, fingers slipping through the straight black strands, her eyes twinkling. Her breasts swayed, the tips hard and eager. Even in the weak light he could see her pussy juices coating the insides of her thighs. Confidence and sex emanated from her soul like a goddess rising. She ran her hands down, cupping her breasts, her fingers tweaking the tight nipples. A rush of heat flowed from her pussy but she made no move to fuck him.

"Dani." He infused the word with warning. The wolf clawed at his control—and tonight he had not patience to soothe the animal.

His caution must have reached her. Her laughter trickled through the room and she reached down, both hands wrapping around his cock and stroking, sliding down and cupping his balls, squeezing just hard enough.

She hummed, lost in her touch, her fingers caressing his shaft. "You sure I can't suck you off?" she asked, her voice husky with need.

"Later, baby." *Soon.* As if his conscious mind and wolf came to a mutual decision, Jackson vowed it would be soon. Dani belonged to him.

But she had to be warned what would happen when he bit her, came inside her. Until then, he would be safe.

He stretched over and grabbed another condom off the bedside table, opening the packet and handing it to her.

She took it and smiled. Wicked light flared in her eyes.

And Jackson knew he'd made a mistake.

She eased the condom over the head of his cock and smoothed it down, taking her time, running her fingers up and down his shaft until he couldn't hold still, his hips pumping up to meet her touch. She hunched over, her hair caressing his thighs as she sucked the head into her mouth.

He ground his teeth together and pressed his lips shut, knowing he no longer looked quite human. Hopefully the semidark of the room would hide the truth. She continued to stroke the condom onto his cock with her fingers, working the head with her lips and tongue, sucking hard.

"Damn it, Dani."

His cock popped out of her mouth and she giggled, the sound happy and sexual in the same moment. "You're not letting me play," she pouted.

"You can play later, baby. When I'm not about to flip you over and fuck you until you can't walk."

"You keep threatening that like it's a bad thing."

"Only if you want to ride me, baby."

"I do."

"Then do it."

For a moment he thought she might ignore his command — and fuck, he couldn't stand another round of teasing — but slowly she pushed up, brushing the tips of her breasts against his hips as she leaned forward, kissing him. The faint taste of latex offended the wolf but Dani's flavor overcame it. She sucked on his tongue, drawing back and raising up on her knees.

She raised his cock and guided the tip to her entrance, spreading her legs wider, sinking down. Heat singed his cock—encasing him in liquid fire. The wolf howled in his head, screaming for more. But Jackson was determined to let her lead. She eased the first inches inside and stopped, hissing in a breath.

"Sore, baby?"

She bit her lip. "A little but still good."

She took another breath and pushed down another inch. Jackson slid his hands around her thighs, holding her, giving her something to lean against. She had a dancer's body and the muscles in her legs were sleek and solid as she continued to sink down, taking him into her body. The tight clasp of her pussy squeezed his cock. His muscles strained, fighting the urge to grab her and thrust, to hold her in place as he pumped between her thighs again but this was her ride.

He closed his eyes, sure that they were turning red or worse, lupine. Claws erupted from the tips of his fingers, painful little bursts that actually distracted him from taking control. Careful to keep the sharp tips away from her skin, he dropped his hands back to the mattress.

Fire invaded his cock as she settled to the hilt. Unable to resist, he opened his eyes and looked at the place their bodies were joined. The pretty flesh of her cunt surrounded his cock, holding him inside her.

"Fuck, baby. You're beautiful."

A purely sensual smile curved her lips and she shifted her hips, rocking back and forth, creating shallow little contractions around this cock. She repeated the motion and stopped as her breath caught. This time the delicate gasp wasn't pain. Her hands spread out across his stomach as she raised her hips, sliding almost off his cock before returning, the return faster and a little harder than the first penetration.

Her tongue peeked out licking her lips as she did another slow retreat and return. Her hair fell forward, the tips of her breasts peeking out between the dark strands.

Jackson knew he should look away, give himself *some* chance at control but she was too beautiful—not just in the physical aspects. Her sensual nature radiated through the surface beauty.

She rose and fell, riding his cock as he'd imagined, dreamed of last night, her body locked in the pleasure. She looked like a Valkyrie riding to victory, a feminine warrior claiming her prize. Every downward stroke sent him deep into her heat, her pussy tight and slick around him. He wasn't going to last long but he had to wait, let Dani find her pleasure.

He grabbed the sheet beneath his hips, fighting the urge to grab her. His claws dug into the cotton material. The "rip" rang loud in his head but Dani was too gone to hear it. She leaned forward, bracing her hands on his shoulders, her hips pumping, using him to reach her climax. She panted and fucked herself onto his cock, her thrusts growing shallow, fast and hard. The pressure squeezed the head of his cock until he thought he'd explode.

"Jackson!"

That she would scream his name as she came triggered his own climax and he groaned, giving into the need to move and driving his cock hard up into her. Her pussy contracted around his dick and he came, flooding the condom.

She lifted her head and shook the sweaty strands of her hair back away from her face. A delicious calm flowed through her muscles and she crumpled forward, landing on his chest in a satisfied heap. Her breasts pressed against his muscles, the nipples still hard. She nestled against him, her mouth open, kissing and licking his shoulder as if she loved the taste of him.

With a moan, she slid off him, rolling to the side, her leg curled between his thighs as she cuddled against him.

He wrapped his arm around her waist and pulled her snug up against him, his cock cradled between her legs. He was going soft for the first time in hours. It felt like days. Maybe it had been. He was pretty sure he'd been hard since he'd met Dani. He'd have to get up in a few minutes and get rid of the condom, but not yet.

She moaned and shifted with him.

"Jackson?" she murmured through swollen lips.

"Sleep, baby. It's okay."

Another soft moan and her head fell forward, resting on his chest.

The wolf in his head rumbled its approval, a soft snuffling sound. The animal was content—its mate close and sleeping, exhausted by their fucking. Nothing satisfied the wolf more.

Chapter Six

ℬ

Alastair Reign—known as Reign to almost everyone—
looked at the scrap of paper in his fingers. *Thursday night.
Spirits.* The bastard was going right for the heart of his market.
And damn it, Reign intended to be there.

The phone on the desk rang but he ignored it. He nodded
toward Charlie, silently telling him to get it. Charlie balked
and the two of them indulged in a staring contest, neither
willing to give in. Finally the phone stopped ringing. Charlie
laughed and Reign shrugged. That was one way to avoid
work. Of course, if that had been the boss, they were all in
trouble.

But Reign didn't have time to take on another shit case.
He had a major asshole to catch. And unfortunately, this
wasn't something his department could be involved in. It came
too close to the Cat Community to allow any interference with
the police. He didn't worry about exposure to the Community.
Cats were notoriously quick about protecting themselves. And
that was the danger. He couldn't risk the Cats taking out a few
cops just to protect themselves.

He took a deep breath and looked at Charlie. He'd had
Reign's back, good man to have in a crisis. It might be smart to
bring him in. Except he was full human. Again dangerous for
the Cats and for Charlie.

Besides, Reign had Max as a backup. Little good it would
do him tomorrow night at Spirits. No way was Max getting
inside. It was a Clowder, a gathering of Cats—no dogs
allowed. There would be a few humans in attendance—pets
kept by various Cats. That's how Reign would get Dani inside.
Reign smiled thinking about the Cats' reaction if he showed up

tomorrow night with a wolf in tow. They'd think he'd gone off the deep end. God knows what they'd do to Max.

Cats were easily offended and their retribution came fast and vicious. Most days, Reign wouldn't mind. He didn't exist or even socialize within any of the Prides. But he needed access to the Cat community...at least long enough to save them.

No, the wolf couldn't go and that was going piss Max off. Reign sighed preparing himself for the fight.

"You okay over there?"

Reign looked at his partner. "Yeah, why?"

"First you're grinning like a Cheshire cat." Reign's ears twitched at the reference. "Then you're sighing like a teenager in church."

"It's nothing. Listen—" Reign wiped his hand across his chin. "I've got some stuff I need to do tomorrow so I'm going to take the day off. Cool?"

Charlie shrugged. "Fine by me." He paused and looked across the desk that separated them. The intent look in his eyes warned that Reign hadn't been as discreet as he'd thought. "Anything you need help with?"

"Naw. I got it. Just some errands."

"Right. Errands. Don't let those errands get you killed."

Reign nodded and flipped open the file folder on his desk. He scanned the contents but his mind was tracking the clock. Off duty in forty-five minutes and he could call Max. Max would balk about not being inside the party but it would be better if he remained outside anyway. Someone to rescue Dani if things went south. Reign scoffed. *Right. Like the wolf is going to accept that.* Still, it was his best argument so far. Not that he expected the wolf to be logical. They relied too much on instinct.

A meeting with his lieutenant took up most of the rest of Reign's day and when he was done, he grabbed his jacket and headed for the door. Being that it was Vegas in the midsummer, he really didn't need a coat but it helped hide his shoulder holster.

He dialed Max's cell phone and it immediately switched to voice mail.

Reign closed the phone and headed home. By the time he'd cooked dinner and paced around the living room, thinking up possible scenarios, outcomes and trying to decide the best place to station Max, two hours had passed and he tried Max's phone again.

This time it rang. Twice. Then Max growled, "This is Max."

"And don't you sound cheery," Reign replied. He liked to tease the wolf. Hell, teasing any of the dogs was fun. That's what Cats lived for.

"Reign, what do you want?"

"So polite. Does your mama know how you answer the phone?" he taunted, knowing how protective dogs were of their families. Cats, whatever. Once the kittens were old enough to be on their own, their parents shoved them out.

"Leave my mama out of this. Now I'm busy. What do you want?"

Reign rolled his eyes. And people said Cats were rude.

"I have no idea what Dani sees in you."

"A better fuck than you'll ever be."

"In your dreams, wolf-boy."

"Listen, Cat, is there a reason you're calling me? Or did you just want to jack off to the sound of my voice?"

Reign felt his lips pulled back into a snarl. Damn the wolf was an irritating bastard. It amazed him that a woman like Dani intended to marry him. She was too fine to be locked into a one-man relationship.

"Bite me." It wasn't the cleverest of comebacks but it worked.

"And risk turning you into one of mine? Not a chance."

"Asshole."

"You know it." Max laughed and the tension between them disappeared. That's how it was with dogs. From growling to tail wagging in seconds. Reign thought about pointing that out to his wolf friend but they needed to move onto actual business. "So what do you want, Reign? I have a friend here," Max said.

Reign sighed. "I got word the bastard's back in town. There's a party tomorrow night. It's all set. Invitation only. I'll take Dani and you station yourself—"

"Can't do it."

Reign squeezed his hand in to a fist, wanting to punch the wolf or the wall. Instead he forced oxygen into his lungs and said, "I know it's not your first choice but you can't walk into a Clowder." Max tried to interrupt but Reign talked over him. He needed to get his argument out. "You'll be ripped to shreds. I'll position you close. You'll have Dani within hearing at all times. Let's meet tomorrow—"

"I'm not in town."

"What? Where are you?"

There was a pause. "I'm in Alaska, visiting my brother." He paused. "Sort of. Either way, I'm not there. It can't happen. You'll have to wait until the next time he comes through."

Reign shook his head. He couldn't wait. Too many Cats would die if they didn't act now.

"I'll just take Dani myself."

"Alone?"

"No. Charlie would act as backup."

"A human? No fucking way. Dani is not going to one of your Cat orgies without someone who can actually protect her."

"I think that's her decision, don't you? She knows I'll take good care of her."

"You stay the fuck away from her."

Reign grinned. He loved riling the dog. Strange, Max had never been possessive of Dani before—at least not what Reign had come to expect from wolves and their mates. Max had to be blind not to have noticed the energy that hummed between him and Dani. They'd never done anything about it but the few times they'd met, it had been like someone had electrified his dick. And Max appeared oblivious to the situation.

Reign would have acted on it—if Dani wasn't engaged to the big bad wolf. If Max had been a Cat, Reign wouldn't have been concerned about moving in on her. Cats did that, they accepted that only the strongest got the mates.

The wolves were a little more traditional and once a mate had been claimed, she stayed claimed. And while Reign wasn't sure he agreed with that theory, he respected the dogs enough to stay back.

But that didn't mean he couldn't tease the wolf just a little.

"Again, that's her decision," he drawled.

"I'll be back in town in a few days. You stay the hell—"

Reign opened his mouth to defend his case but noises on the other end of the line stopped him. Or more, the lack of noise. Like Max had stopped breathing.

"Damn."

The word came out low and sexual. Just the tone made Reign's cock twitch. He could only imagine what Max was doing to cause that kind of sound. Was Dani with him? Or was he fucking around on her?

"Hello? Max?"

The phone clicked and Reign knew he'd been hung up on.

He sighed and stared at the phone. Damn dog.

Well, Reign couldn't wait. Tomorrow night was his best chance and Dani had to be there.

He hit the speed dial for Dani's number, smiling grimly. Did Max even know that Dani was on Reign's speed dial? Or that he was just waiting for Max to bail before he made his move?

Dani's voice mail picked up. *Damn, am I the only one without a life?*

When she finished her recorded greeting, Reign spoke. "Dani, it's Reign. I just got word that Winston is back in town and he's doing business at a party tomorrow night. Are you still up for this? I know Max is out of town but I don't want to miss this chance. I'll come by tomorrow morning, maybe around eleven? And we can talk about it. Have a good night." His voice dropped, hoping Dani could hear the hunger in his tone.

He closed his phone and stared at the little silver box. He had work to do. If Max wasn't there, it almost made it easier. Dani was as anxious, if not more so, to get Winston out of the picture. But with no Max, Dani would be vulnerable. If Reign had to go after Winston, there was no way he could leave Dani unprotected. Not in a room full of Cats.

Individually the Cat Community was reasonable, not quite trustworthy but not dangerous. When they got together in a Clowder, the human traits they tried to assume disappeared and they turned feral. The atmosphere was sexually charged and inhibitions were thin-edged lines. It could be a dangerous situation. Particularly with a human like Dani as the instigator.

* * * * *

Dani skipped downstairs, her body alive and tingly. And the man upstairs was the cause. She licked her lips and couldn't hide her smile. She'd definitely been dating the wrong brother for the past five months. Thank God she'd realized it in time. Even after a night of great sex with Max—and she had to admit there were more than a few—she'd never felt like this. Of course, Max never stayed over. Ever. He always had a reason for slipping out in the middle of the night.

Not Jackson. He'd stayed and cuddled and loved her. The center of her stomach dropped away at the sexual memory. He'd held her, touched her, whispered delicious words to her — and when she would have expected him to seduce her into more sex, he'd lulled her to sleep, never leaving. *She* had been the one to wake up in the middle of the night, hungry and wanting more. She moaned, remembering the sleepy way he'd come awake, his cock in her mouth, on the verge of coming. He'd been stunned, she'd been thrilled. From their short acquaintance she could tell Jackson was used to being in control. He'd managed to pull back but it had been close.

She licked her lips, remembering how it felt, tasted to have Jackson's cock in her mouth. He'd been downright yummy. Of course it had been months — maybe a year — since she'd sucked cock. Max, for all his sexual needs, wouldn't let her mouth near his dick.

She liked sucking cock — liked the tastes and textures, the thrill of power at making her lover groan.

Hmm, now she wanted more. Wanted Jackson.

He'd tasted delicious. It wasn't a word she usually used when she thought about sucking a guy off, but Jackson...hmm, almost sweet. She wanted more.

Her pussy tingled and she giggled. Last night the lust had been overwhelming, now it lingered in the background, teasing and tempting her.

Jackson was up in the shower. She had a couple of hours before rehearsal. There was time for breakfast. Assuming Jackson was planning on staying. Of course, she had promised to make him coffee. Strong and black, he'd said. She smiled as she threw an extra scoop of grounds into the basket. She had an espresso machine but somehow Jackson didn't strike her as the espresso-latte kind of guy. He was a little too practical to spend four bucks a day on a cup of coffee.

The drip machine bubbled happily along as she opened her refrigerator. And groaned when she saw what was inside. Or what wasn't there.

She had no food. Leftover Italian and bagged salad didn't qualify. This is so not how she wanted Jackson to see her apartment. Max—no problem. He hadn't cared. But somehow she just imagined Jackson as having the perfectly tidy house with a full pantry.

She slammed the fridge door shut and leaned against it.

New plan. Breakfast out. Before she could slip upstairs to see if Jackson would be interested in making a run to the café down the street, her doorbell rang.

She hurried to the door, the energy in body moving her quickly across the carpet. Hand on the doorknob, she peeked through the curtains beside the door.

Reign? Oh, that's right. He'd said he was coming by today. Was it already eleven?

Unable to resist, she took another look between the curtain slats. Her body reacted as it always did seeing Reign—like she'd been dipped in honey and was just waiting for him to lick it off her body. It had been like that from the first meeting—sexual sparks had ricocheted between them. If she hadn't been engaged to Max at the time, she might have pressed the issue to see where it might go.

She glanced toward the stairs. Her reaction to Jackson had been as intense though considering she'd thought he was Max the first time they'd met and that she'd been about ready to fuck him, she hadn't really recognized it then. Her body sparkled with a similar anticipation.

This could be interesting. The two men who made her turn into a sex kitten in the same room.

Knowing she'd left him standing on the porch for too long already, she scraped her fingers through her wet hair and tugged on her cropped shirt. It hung midway between her breasts and her bellybutton. Leaving most of her stomach bare.

It was one of her favorite outfits, comfortable and sexy. She'd hoped to inspire Jackson to return tonight.

Oh, what was Reign going to think when he saw Jackson?

That she was a slut. Working her way through the males in Max's family. She closed her eyes and took a deep breath. It didn't matter what Reign thought. *And you really need to let him in.*

It took her another dozen seconds before she found the courage to open the door.

"Reign, hi!"

He looked at her and those sparks that had previously bounced between erupted into a full-grown fire. Oh, this was bad. She had one man upstairs in her shower. She really shouldn't be lusting after another. Particularly not when she'd just spent huge chunks of the previous night having incredible sex. Her body should be beyond wanting to fuck.

Somehow that didn't seem to be the case. Her pussy warmed and she had the urge to rub against the door, needing pressure to her clit. She let her eyes wander down his body, stopping just below his waistband. The worn jeans did nothing to hide his erection. The heat from her pussy spread and she pressed her knees together.

"Good morning, Dani."

The sound of his voice skipped over her skin like hot fingers. Her body moved with the sensation. She looked into Reign's eyes and saw a shimmer of gold so strong it almost glowed. Pure undiluted lust flowed from that stare and it was all Dani could do not to fling open the door and throw herself on top of him. *Jackson had said he wouldn't mind watching.*

She grabbed the door tighter, bracing her body against and using it as a shield against the wild thoughts going through her brain.

"What's going on?" she asked, trying to keep her mind off sex. God forbid that Jackson come downstairs while she was lusting after another man.

Her question seemed to stabilize Reign as well. The golden glow from his eyes faded.

"Did you get my message?"

"Yes, I just didn't know it was so late." Realizing she'd left him standing on the front step, she released the death grip she had on the doorknob and stepped back. "Come on in."

As he stepped inside, he took a deep breath. And for a moment the heat in his stare turned to confusion. Cautiously, Dani inhaled as well. Did her house smell funny? Was it possible he could smell the sex from last night? She really needed to open a few windows.

He sniffed the air and looked around, as if trying to catalog the strange scent.

When he turned to look at her, the heat had returned to his eyes—so strong it almost burned her. Dani's body moved through instinct, wanting to be closer. She took two steps and stopped. What was she thinking? Jackson was upstairs.

She pulled back, stepping behind the couch, needing some distance between them. She shoved a strand of hair behind her ear and noticed that her fingers were trembling. She needed to get back in control. *Reign is here so you can identify a killer.*

That did it.

"So you said he's back in town."

Reign's eyes popped up toward the stairs then back to her. "That's what my source says. Tonight—"

He stopped in mid-sentence. The tension radiating from his body infiltrated her body until she reflected his stress. He froze and looked up at the stairs. The muscles in his shoulders rolled backward and shifted, straining the material of his shirt. His eyebrows dropped low followed by a deep warning growl.

Jackson came down, slowing as he reached the bottom.

"Dani?"

Already she could hear the differences in his and Max's voices. She opened her mouth to introduce him but never got the chance. Reign stalked forward, his arm snapping back and forward in one sharp punch. Fist connected with jaw and Jackson flew, groaning as he hit the wall. Pictures rattled on their hooks as his skull dented plaster.

"Reign, what are you—?"

"Listen, asshole, we don't have time for this shit. I have less than twelve hours to put together a reasonable plan because you wanted to spend the night fucking?" Reign's voice rose and Dani started to worry her neighbors might call the police.

"Reign, that's not—"

Again her explanation was interrupted. Jackson moved—faster than she'd thought possible—jumping away from the wall and landing a punch on Reign's jaw, mirroring the hit to his face. Reign's head snapped back and he stumbled under the force of Jackson's fist.

"I'm not Max, asshole." Jackson straightened and took a deep breath. The crinkles around the edges of his eyes deepened. "Oh this is just perfect," he said in disgust. "I got sucker punched by a *pussy*."

"You know it, ball-licker."

Both men seemed to condense. Their bodies pulled in tight, preparing to attack. Dani didn't think her furniture could handle a full-out battle between these two. Jackson's lips pulled back from his teeth and Reign rolled his shoulders back.

And all thoughts of her furniture disappeared. Her pussy clenched and creamed, sending a violent jolt into her core. What the hell was that? She was not a woman who got off on men fighting over her—tended to think the men were idiots—but something about the way they stood, ready to battle. God, all that power, strength. She squeezed her knees together trying to contain the sensation. Or at least stop it from getting any worse. It really didn't make any sense. Yes, she was attracted to Jackson—obviously—and she'd always had a lust crush on Reign but this was ridiculous. Particularly after last night. She should be completely immune to desire.

But all she could think of was turning the aggression of the two males and directing it toward her. In bed. Naked. Oh yeah.

Jackson shifted right and Reign followed, they started to circle each other.

Oh no. This wasn't good. She had to get control.

"Stop it." She stepped forward, physically placing herself in the space between them. They looked ready to ignore her. She took a deep breath and both sets of male eyes dipped down to her breasts. They stopped and stared at her nipples pressing against the thin material of her shirt.

Men, she thought with a mental sigh. But it worked. Jackson's gaze snapped back up and he had the courtesy to look a little embarrassed. Reign's stare lingered before he finally looked away.

"Now, can we discuss this—" whatever the hell *this* was "like rational adults?"

Both men nodded but neither spoke.

"Reign, this is Jackson, Max's twin brother. Jackson, this is Reign. He's a friend of Max's…" She paused. "And mine." Neither moved. "Shake hands," she ordered.

She almost moaned when they both stayed locked in position. Suddenly the reasonable, practical Jackson wasn't so reasonable or practical. He'd turned into a macho asshole like Max. And Reign. Hopefully, Jackson's residency in that world was temporary. After long seconds that wore on Dani's nerves, Jackson sighed and offered his right hand.

Reign nodded and met Jackson's hand with his own. The muscles along Reign's jaw twitched like he was going to speak but he seemed to change his mind. The two men shook and then released each other. The tension between them still hummed and Dani felt compelled to insert herself into it.

"Reign is a cop and he's kind of been working on a case." She shrugged. "And I guess I'm working with him. And Max." Despite Jackson's assurances that it didn't make a difference to him that she'd been with his brother, she still felt uncomfortable bringing up his name.

Jackson just nodded, the macho strain on his muscles hadn't diminished. He stared at Reign like he was assessing a threat.

Reign returned the glare.

Great. Warring animals in her living room.

"Reign." He didn't acknowledge her. She tugged on his arm. "Reign? You're here to talk to me, right?"

He nodded, letting his gaze linger on Jackson before turning his attention to her.

"There's a party tonight. Full of his—" He paused "Target market. If we're going to get him, it's going to be tonight."

Dani's stomach dropped and she could feel the blood drain from her face. She'd agreed to do this. She had to do this. This asshole drug dealer had killed someone, shot someone right in front of her.

And Reign was hoping she could help lock up the bad guy.

The hollowness in her stomach sank into her legs and her knees started to wobble. She reached for the back of the couch to steady herself but Jackson was there, the arrogant masculine posture disappearing as he wrapped his arm around her back and he pulled her to his front. His attention had shifted, leaving Reign behind and focusing on her. Warmth and strength poured from his body and covered her, comforting her. She turned into him, her body craving the closeness.

"It's okay, baby. I won't let anything happen to you," Jackson vowed, whispering the words into her hair.

The instinct to stay protected in Jackson's arms was strong, but she knew she had to face whatever was out there.

She swallowed, trying to clear the tightness in her throat, and looked at Reign. "What do you need me to do?"

Reign stared at the slim, frightened woman wrapped in the wolf's arms. Even though she was almost six feet tall, she looked tiny. The wolf was big. An exact copy of his brother, except for their eyes. Max's were blue. Jackson's green.

The Cat inside Reign rebelled at being so close to one of the dogs but he had enough control, had lived a human life for long enough, that he was able to control the urge to slash his claws at the beast's face.

From a purely male standpoint, Reign wanted to grab her away from the wolf and comfort her. Let her use *his* body. But damn, somehow he'd missed again. He'd always had the thought that once Dani and Max had broken up, he could slip in. Despite the fact that they were engaged, he hadn't expected it to last. The two of them had been hot together but it hadn't been stable. Not the kind of forever relationship a wolf was looking for.

But somehow she'd transitioned from one brother to the other. Jackson stood with her, providing support. After maybe ninety seconds in their presence, Reign could tell there was something solid between these two.

Fuck, he'd missed his chance to have Dani.

There was no doubt in Reign's mind they'd had sex. The scent was all around them and there was a sensual glow about Dani that he'd never seen before. *Bet that pisses Max off. Seems his brother is a better fuck than he is.*

Reign held back a smile and tucked that information into his brain. He might need it later. Something to torment Max with.

"What do we have to do?" Dani asked bravely.

"Should be fairly simple," he said putting a shiny polish on an ugly situation. Besides, without Max here, he was going with Plan B. Just get Dani in. She'd identify Winston and he'd take it from there. "We'll go to the party and you just have to—"

Dani nodded. "Point him out to you."

"Yeah."

"Wait."

Reign felt his eyeballs begin to ache. He should have expected this. The werewolf was throwing himself into this.

"Catch me up."

Reign almost told him to stay out of it but Dani looked a little fragile and she was taking some of her strength from the wolf.

She flicked her hair back and took a breath. Reign could see the painful memories work into her muscles. The sadness made his heart ache.

It was strange. He was a Cat. By nature, he didn't form relationships—at least not lasting ones. But something about Dani drew him closer, made him wish he could be the kind of guy who stuck around. Someone who could marry and have kids. The whole white picket fence thing.

"A few months ago I was at a party with some friends. I was tired and decided to go home. I got turned around and ended up going out the wrong door of the club. Ended up in this back room but it had cell service so I decided to call a cab from there. These guys came in and I hid out—because I wasn't supposed to be there. I saw this guy, this Winston, shoot someone."

"Oh, baby." He put his hand on her cheek and eased her head onto his shoulder. Over her head, he glared at Reign.

Reign suppressed the growl that scraped the inside of his throat. Part of his irritation was the interference of the wolf—who was going to complicate things—and the other part was the desire to comfort Dani himself. To be the one who protected her.

"If this guy is in town, pick him up."

"We can't."

"Why not?"

"We don't know what he looks like."

"What?!" Jackson's shout jolted Dani from her comfortable position snuggled up against his chest. "I'm sorry, baby." He patted her shoulder but she forced herself to straighten up. "What do you mean you don't know what he looks like?"

Reign's lips tightened and for a moment Dani thought he might not explain but finally he said, "We know his name. We know his product but we have no pictures of him. He's a full-on ghost."

"But Dani can give you a description, can't you?"

She shook her head. "No." Guilt and regret made her step back, putting distance between them. "I know what he looks like, I can see him in my mind but I couldn't work with the police artist. I can't figure out how to describe him." She shrugged. The officer that worked with her said it was rare but admitted that sometimes a person just couldn't provide the detail for a sketch.

"I need her to point him out."

Energy blasted from Jackson's body as he straightened, pulling himself to his full height. "And you want her to walk into a party alone and just point to a murderer?"

"Of course not. She won't be alone. I'll be there." He turned to Dani. "The party is very ritzy, lots of security."

"Sounds like fun," she said weakly.

Jackson nodded. "Yeah, sounds like something I might like to attend." The sarcasm wasn't lost on Dani or Reign.

"Not happening, wolf-boy. These aren't *your* kind of people."

Jackson stepped forward, planting himself in front of Reign. "She's not walking into some Clowder unprotected."

"I'll be there."

"She's not going."

"That's not your call."

"It became—"

Dani stared at the two men, their bodies aggressive, challenging. Damn, they were going to start punching. Again.

Reign she could almost understand. He'd always had that aggressive tendency, even around Max. But Jackson had seemed so civilized last night. *Well, until he fucked you against the wall.* She had to admit the veneer of civilization had tarnished just a bit. Still, she never would have expected this kind of physical aggression.

And damn if all that energy wasn't surging through her body—only as sex. It would be so delicious to step between them, pull them both to her, one cock rubbing her clit, the other against her ass. Her pussy creamed and she had to open her mouth to get in enough air.

"Arrrgh!" She wasn't sure if the noise she made was from frustration over the men's behavior or her own unsatisfied desire but it worked. Both men jerked and looked at her. She flipped her hair away from her face. "Now that I have your attention…" She drilled Jackson with a stare. "I appreciate you wanting to protect me but Reign's right. This isn't your call." Jackson opened his mouth to reply but she held up her hand, stopping the protest. Smart man that he was, he backed down. "And Reign, I want to help but I'm also scared so if there's a way to have Jackson there, I'd feel more comfortable."

The two men looked at her, then she saw surreptitious glances toward each other.

Neither nodded. Neither agreed.

"How about this? How about we sit down, have some breakfast—because I'm thinking you'll both be a little more reasonable once you've eaten—and talk about this." Again neither man responded. "Okay, that wasn't really a suggestion. It's what we're going to do."

The corner of Jackson's mouth bent up into a small smile and eased some of her tension.

"Works for me," he conceded then flashed a challenging stare toward Reign.

"Fine."

"Great. I also have no intention of cooking for both of you and don't have any food in the house anyway, so, Reign, you know where the Cozy Corner Café is?" Reign nodded. "We'll meet you there. I need to change and we'll head there." And it would give her a few minutes to lay down the law with Jackson. Not that she didn't appreciate his attempts to protect her but she was a big girl and she had agreed to help Reign catch this guy. The memories of the sounds—the shot, the man's groan and the thud of his body hitting the ground—still crept into her dreams.

Reign hesitated. He tossed a final glare at Jackson then walked away. Dani sighed with relief when the door closed behind him. That left only one pompous male she had to deal with.

"You're not going anywhere with him alone."

Jackson's bald statement made the hair on her neck stand up.

"Excuse me?" She stepped out of Jackson's reach, not wanting to risk the temptation of his touch. Her body hummed from the brief fantasy of being trapped between their bodies but thankfully her mind still functioned. "You don't get to decide that."

"Dani, how well do you know him? Or his friends?"

"I know him well enough. And I trust him."

The edges of Jackson's eyes squinted down. "Are you lovers?"

"I told you 'no' last night. Just because I fell into bed with you, you assume I do it with every guy I meet?" It was a kind of bitchy response but Dani was having a tough time focusing. Between the steady desire to have sex, which wasn't going away even though she was out of Jackson's range, and the fact that she really had fallen into bed with a guy she didn't know, who happened to be the brother of her ex-fiancé, yeah, she was feeling a little tense.

Jackson shook his head. "You didn't exactly fall into bed with me. The first time was up against the wall if I remember correctly." Dani gasped and knew her mouth fell open. In her shock, she wasn't ready for Jackson to move. He took two fast steps and was in front of her, his arm around her back, holding her plastered against his body. Pissed but unable to resist the need of her body, she straddled the thigh he shoved between her legs and moaned as he clamped down on her ass, forcing her clit against the strong hard muscles in his thigh. She groaned and moved her hips, rubbing a fast hard circle with pussy. "That's it." She heard his encouragement and knew she should be mortified. This was exactly the behavior that was going to get her into trouble. But she couldn't stop. He held her hips, following her movements, guiding her a little faster, harder, his mouth on her neck, kissing and licking and whispering those hot sexy words.

The climax hit her hard and fast and she cried out, clinging to Jackson. Using his strength as he worked her through the sweet after-tremors.

Unable to look him in the eye, she dropped her head forward, landing on his shoulder.

"You okay, baby?" She nodded but didn't look up. "Look at me, Dani." The command in his voice made it impossible to resist and she forced her eyes upward, expecting laughter, humor, even a little mockery. After all, she'd just tried to claim she wasn't a slut and then humped his leg like a bitch in heat.

All that stared back at her was lust and heat. And maybe a hint of affection. After a moment that made her body ache to have him inside her, the lust in his eyes eased. It didn't disappear but the logical controlled man she'd had dinner with returned.

"I don't think you're a slut. At all." She took a breath, ready to point out the obvious that she had fallen into bed with him after way too short an acquaintance. But he shook his head, stopping her words. "The reason I wanted to know if you and Reign were lovers is sheer jealousy on my part." She felt her cheeks turn red at the heat in his voice.

She shrugged. "I told you there was some attraction between us," she reminded him, her confidence returning.

"I expected a little heat. I almost got burned just standing next to you."

The wry tone of his voice made her smile. "It was particularly strong today." She looked to where Reign had been standing and shook her head. "I mean, I think he's attractive but today, wow."

"Felt like you wanted to jump him in the living room."

She gasped but nodded. Confusion crinkled the edges of his eyes.

"We okay?" she asked, tapping her finger against the button of his shirt.

"We're definitely okay."

"We should go. I need to change and then we'll find out what Reign has in mind for this party."

"I can hardly wait."

"Ooh, sarcasm. Be nice."

The edge of Jackson's mouth kicked up. "Baby, this is me being nice."

She laughed and felt the tension between them disappear. "I'll just go up and change."

Jackson nodded but she noticed that he followed her. Secretly, she smiled. The quick orgasm from downstairs seemed like an appetizer, a taste that made her want more. She shook her head. She enjoyed sex, sometimes even craved it, but never anything like this. Her cheeks felt warm and flushed.

Her nipples remained tight and sensitive. And when she got upstairs she was going to have to change her underwear.

She strolled into her bedroom. Jackson came right behind her. Her heart started to pound, distinctly aware that Jackson didn't have a reason to be here. He didn't have clothes to change into. He wore the suit from last night, without the jacket, which was draped over the couch downstairs.

Maybe he's going to finish what they started downstairs. Oh yeah. She glanced at her rumpled bed. Jackson hadn't come downstairs and that hardly seemed fair.

Reign. Damn. His name popped into her head, her conscience still alert even while the rest of her focused on sex.

Reign is waiting. Waiting to talk to you about identifying a killer.

There. That little reminder distracted her.

She undid the button at the waistband of her skirt but didn't pull it off, leaving it hang low on her hips. She flipped through hanger after hanger looking for what she wanted. Something cool and light. She needed the possibility of a breeze against her legs to keep her body temperature down.

She came out of the deep walk-in closet—the best feature to her condo—and found Jackson waiting, a serious, thoughtful expression on his face.

"What?" she asked, clutching the floral printed fabric in her hand. He stared at the skirt, his gaze intent, possessive.

"What are you wearing?"

She waved the skirt, trying to laugh off the question. She was all for a little dominance in bed—that was sexy—but no way was a man, *any* man, no matter the size of his cock or how well he used it, going to tell her what she could wear. "This."

"Let me see it."

With a sigh, preparing for the battle ahead, she handed him the skirt. It was conservative compared to what she normally wore. It actually reached to the midpoint of her thighs. Every other skirt stopped just short of her ass. She had a good body. It took work and denying herself dessert and pasta but she kept herself in good shape. And she had no problem showing off her body. If she did, she'd picked the wrong profession.

Jackson held up the skirt and nodded.

"I have your approval?" She said it with enough sarcasm that there was no way he could miss it. He was a smart guy after all.

"Skirt's fine, but I want you to wear these." He stretched out his hand. Pale blue cotton was crunched in his fist.

She looked at it for a moment. It was vaguely familiar. Like she used to have...she noticed two of her drawers were open. It looked like a pair of panties she had.

She pulled the underwear from his grip. "Been digging through my underwear drawer?"

"Yes." He appeared unrepentant.

She stretched out the panties. They were blue and big. Full-sized briefs that her mother must have given her years ago. And they were cotton. She was pretty sure the last time she'd worn them she'd had the flu and wanted comfortable and warm. "Those are granny panties."

"Yes."

"And you want me to wear them?" This made no sense. Every other man she'd ever known—Jackson's brother included—loved to see her in skimpy underwear.

"Yes."

"Why?" With a teasing look, she lifted the bottom of her shirt, flashing him the bikini-cut tiger-printed panties she currently wore. She wiggled her hips. "Aren't these better?"

Jackson didn't smile. "They're lovely. But I'd still like you to wear those." He nodded to the cotton underwear, his voice implacable.

"Why?" she asked again.

Now he flashed her that wicked smile. "Because I want to know that your sexy little cunt is well covered." He stepped forward and slid his hand down around her hip, cupping her backside and cuddling her close to him. Warmth flowed into her body, pooling in her core and she moved closer to the source. "I want to know that I'm the only one who gets to see your pussy, the only one who has a right to touch it, taste it." Her body sagged against his, melting into his heat. "It's not so much to ask, is it, baby? You're so sexy that I want to know this one piece is mine and mine alone."

She knew that after one night, she shouldn't allow this but damn, he was seducing, convincing her. He didn't wheedle or whine. He just stood there, those bewitching green eyes watching her, his stare convincing her. Finally she sighed.

"Okay."

His hand tightened on her ass. "Thank you, baby."

"Now, we'd better go. Reign is waiting."

"Yes."

Though she hated to leave the warmth of Jackson's arms, she knew they had to get moving.

"That means you have to let me go," she teased.

"Right." But neither of them moved, except to move closer. Jackson turned, guiding his cock against her stomach. Teasing her. Dani stretched up on her tiptoes. Wanting that hard erection inside her. Downstairs had been sweet but she needed him to fuck her.

The sexual heat erupted in her body, flooding her pussy, making her nipples ache. Even as her thoughts nagged that they didn't have time, she wrapped her arms around his neck and pulled his lips down to hers. He didn't resist, following her guidance and taking her mouth in a commanding kiss. Her body chimed like he was licking her pussy. She might come just from his kiss and the sweet brush of his chest against her nipples. A little pressure and she'd be there.

"How close are you?" Jackson asked, speaking the words against her mouth.

"Very."

"Good, because I don't think I'll last long." He grabbed her hips and lifted her, carrying her to the end of the bed in three fast steps. As he put her down, he grabbed the thin strap of her panties and pulled, yanking them down.

While he fought with her underwear, she rolled halfway over, reaching for the bedside table. Her fingers closed around a condom and she almost groaned in relief.

Red heat from Jackson's eyes glowed as she turned back, her skirt tossed up above her waist, her legs bare. She slapped the condom in his hand and sat up, pulling his mouth back to hers. He groaned into the kiss, his fingers working between their bodies to free his cock and slide the condom on.

God, he tasted good. She licked inside his mouth, flicking her tongue against his. He growled and turned his head, driving his tongue deep, making her head spin.

"Hurry, Jackson," she moaned against his lips, unable to separate from him.

The growl turned to a snarl and he clamped his lips down over his teeth. Teeth that felt bigger than they should. He dropped his head and concentrated on the condom. His fingers fumbled with the wrapper. Fuck, what was wrong with him? He never lost control. Not even during sex.

But something about Dani—it ravaged the animal's patience and tore at Jackson's control.

And that Cat. The way he'd looked at Dani, like he wanted to fuck her. Right there. In front of Jackson. The image slammed into his brain and Jackson tensed, waiting for the wolf to go insane.

Instead his cock twitched and the wolf howled its approval. He shook his head, wiping the visual slate clean, and focused on getting the damn condom on. Dani's breasts brushed against his arm as she kissed and licked and sucked at his neck, making it almost impossible to function. His body was primed to fuck and this interruption strained every bit of control he had. He slipped the latex over the head. Dani's fingers joined his, rolling the sheath up.

Unable to look away, Jackson watched as she stroked the condom up, covering his cock, her slim fingers and bright red nails glowing against his skin. A soft hum and moan floated through the air as she leaned forward and sucked the tip of his cock into her mouth. Heat swallowed him as she sank forward, not pushing deep, just enough to tease. Her tongue fluttered against the underside.

"Fuck." He wasn't sure if that was a command or curse. He pushed Dani back, using a little more force than needed but she didn't seem to mind. She landed on the mattress, her long legs bending, wrapping up and around his back, her skirt crumpled up around her waist, the dark pink of her cunt so pretty against the tanned skin. His mind registered that she had no tan lines and the wolf growled its displeasure.

Jackson vaguely acknowledged that his wolf was more upset by the thought of her tanning nude than fucking Reign, but the thought was gone almost as fast as it appeared.

"Jackson." Dani shifted, arching her back, pressing her breasts up, straining her tight, tiny shirt, her nipples imprinting on the soft material. Her hands slid down her sides, stroking the inside of her thighs. Human and animal attention narrowed down. The room around them disappeared. All thoughts of Reign vanished. There was just Dani—sleek and wet, the hot taste of her pussy a sweet memory on his lips.

Jackson placed the tip of his cock to her opening, giving her one breath to anticipate before he drove in. Her cry ripped through the air but he was familiar with the sound now— pleasure not pain drew the soft scream. Wet heat surrounded his cock and he groaned, pushing just a little deeper before he pulled back. Dani's pussy clung to him as he retreated, dragging him back in. She dug her heels into his back and tried to pull him forward.

He scooped his arms under her knees and guided her legs up, putting her heels on his shoulders. This wasn't going to be a nice, easy get-to-know-you fuck. He grabbed her hips and held her in place as he slammed back into her. Her body tensed, almost visible shivers running across her skin. Yeah, she was feeling it. His body took over, driving into her, his mind absorbing the sweet cries turned to screams and pleas.

"More, please. Jackson!"

He loved the way she called his name. Never any hesitation.

Her long strong body strained as he worked to give her more, find the touch that would send her flying. He gripped her legs and pushed into her, deep and hard. Every stroke a shock to his cock. He ground his teeth together and thrust, working the angle to stroke her clit as he rode inside her. Her back arched, her breasts pushed forward and a low scream-gasp-moan tore from her throat. Her pussy clenched, squeezing his cock as the orgasm ripped through her body. The wolf growled inside his head and he slammed into her one more time, filled the condom with his cum, wishing he was pouring himself into her.

He propped his hands on the mattress, leaning over her, barely supporting his own weight as he stared down at the sexual sated woman beneath him. He licked his lips, tasting the scent of her orgasm.

Soon, he thought, as he slipped his softening cock from her pussy. Soon he would be fucking her with no barrier, marking her as his.

Chapter Seven

ℬ

They walked into the crowded diner and quickly spotted a rather irritated Reign sitting near the wall. Jackson didn't bother hiding his smile. With the Cat's heightened senses, there would be no way to miss the smell of Dani on him. And smell him on Dani. Didn't matter that he hadn't actually come inside her, his scent was all over her. It was primitive but he liked having her marked in this basic manner. Humans wouldn't notice but Reign...it was going to drive the pussycat crazy.

Dani gripped Jackson's hand as they wove through the tables crushed together. He didn't know if she was afraid he would bolt or if she just needed the reassurance so he held tight. He had no intention of leaving her. Of course, after one night, it was probably too soon to announce he intended to spend the rest of his life with her. She'd asked if last night was one night of fucking. That didn't mean she was ready to be a werewolf's mate. Strange that Max hadn't told her about their family history.

Before last night, he'd never been a big believer in his wolf selecting his mate. He spent the majority of his life in human form, he would find a wife for the human. The wolf would have to accept her.

Except it hadn't worked that way. His relationship with Mandy at home was a prime example. Jackson and Mandy were great together. Worked together, liked the same things, enjoyed each other's company, but there was no spark. His wolf was indifferent to her.

The animal's reaction to Dani was the complete opposite. The wolf filled Jackson's head with growls, snarls, whimpers if she got too far away. Thankfully, his human side enjoyed her as well. The male in him certainly did, he thought watching her ass sway, the short skirt flipping back and forth with each step.

He smiled again, knowing what she wore beneath that skirt—full ass-and-pussy-covering panties. She could change back into the tiny scraps of silk once they were home again. Not that Jackson needed the visual stimulation. He knew what she looked like beneath her clothes and that memory was enough to grab him by the balls and drag him forward.

"Hi, Reign. Sorry we took so long." If Jackson's scent on her hadn't given away what they'd been doing, Dani's blush would have.

Just to nudge the Cat a bit, Jackson nodded. "Yeah, sorry we're late."

The pussycat's eyes squinted down.

"Right."

Dani slid into the booth and picked up the menu. Jackson took the space beside her. She offered him a menu but he shook his head. It was a diner. They'd have what he wanted. Instead, he reached for Dani, sliding his hand on her knee and sliding up, inching the hem of her skirt higher, pushing until his hand was under the soft material and cuddled between her sleek thighs. Dani looked at him, the smirk on her face warning him she recognized he was staking his claim in a barbaric way. But she let his hand stay so he grinned back.

Reign shifted in his seat and Jackson felt a jolt of sympathy. Dani looked flushed and well fucked, even if she had taken the time to brush her hair and put on lipstick before they'd left. The air of sex surrounded her. With the Cat's extra senses, Jackson didn't doubt that every nerve was on alert. And he didn't doubt the pussycat's dick was hard.

The harried waitress came by and asked for their orders. Dani ordered fruit and an English muffin. Jackson listened as Reign ordered the biggest breakfast on the menu. With his wolf so close to the surface and the full moon tonight, Jackson's cravings were for meat and a lot of it. He ordered eggs and bacon with a side order of bacon and sausage.

Once the waitress was gone, Dani dropped her hands under the table and leaned forward, her knees bouncing up and down. Jackson eased his hand from between her legs and placed it on her knee, going for comfort instead of sex. She offered a weak smile and took a drink of water before she said, "So tell me what happens tonight." Her voice trembled just a little and Jackson wanted to grab her, carry her away. But she was determined to help. And he had to admire that.

Reign sat forward. There was no competition or humor in his stare. He was all cop.

"Word has it Winston is going to be at this party tonight. He's meeting with some of his buyers."

"Seems strange that he'd do something like this in public," Jackson said. "Don't things like this usually happen in back alleys?"

"Not when you're dealing with this kind of high-end shit."

"High-class drug dealer?" Jackson wanted to know what Dani was up against.

Reign shook his head and met Jackson's eyes. The serious glint gave Jackson confidence Reign was solid but it also scared the hell out of him. Anything that frightened a Cat this badly was something to be worry about.

"Wouldn't go that far. Designer drugs." He paused, making sure Jackson was listening. "Targeted market. Doesn't affect some *people* at all. Others? Instantly hooked and it kills fast."

"That bad?"

Reign's mouth went flat, his eyes turned gold. "Yeah. It's that bad."

Jackson felt a tug of sympathy. It wasn't that he particularly liked the Cats—they thought they were superior to wolves because their shapeshifting ability was part of their genes. With werewolves, it was more like a virus, transmitted through the blood or through a bite. So yeah, he didn't feel much camaraderie with the pussycat nation, but still, a drug like this, targeted at one community...it was dangerous.

"This guy Winston has made friends with some of *my friends.*"

Jackson nodded, understanding that Reign meant the Cat Community.

"From what we can tell, he bought off a few of them and now they work for him like guard dogs." The disgusted spat of his words wasn't lost on Jackson. Cats weren't particularly loyal to anyone, except maybe their own Prides and to have a Cat protecting a human would be the ultimate insult. "And they're spreading the wealth. My friends are either getting hooked on this crap and dying a few months later or dying outright.

"This party's big. He'll be there to meet new clients. My source says he's tripled his supply and now he's looking for markets."

"He's creating demand."

"Exactly."

Dani shuddered. "Okay, so what do I have to do?"

She was trying to be brave but this had to be scary as shit. Jackson squeezed her knee again and shifted, turning just a little, his body moving to shield hers.

"Since you're the only one who knows what he looks like, except for his guards—" He looked at Jackson. "And they aren't talking."

Funny, that had been his next question.

"I just need you to point him out." Reign drilled Dani with his gaze, holding her eyes until she nodded, her breath shaky as she inhaled.

110

"I can do that." She forced a smile. "I go to parties all the time. What's one more? And you'll be there, right?"

"Right."

"I like parties," Jackson said. It was a lie. He wasn't much of the party type but no way was Dani going without him.

Reign's eruption was restrained but intense. His eyes changed and he bent forward, his words low and threatening.

"Not happening, puppy. Safety first."

Jackson leaned in to meet him, dropping his voice to match Reign's tone. He wasn't going to be intimidated by a pussycat. "If it isn't safe for me, it isn't safe for her."

"I'll make it safe for her."

"How do you plan to do that?"

"None of your business."

"But it's my business," Dani said, inserting herself into the conversation.

Reign sat back, flicking his hair away from his face. Dani's gaze bounced between the two of them. They kept talking in this secret language. She understood the words but obviously not the meaning these boys were giving them.

"Listen, both of you, I understand that you're trying protect me and I appreciate that, but despite appearances, I'm not a bimbo and I'm not stupid."

"No one thinks you're stupid."

"Or a bimbo," Reign added. "This is just complicated and private."

"Private? I saw a guy get killed. I'm not worried about someone's privacy issues."

"It's not that." Reign looked at Jackson for help. Dani turned her attention to Jackson. He'd just met Reign. How did he know more than she did?

"The people at this party are a little different."

"Different how?"

He met her gaze dead on and she could see the serious glint in his eyes. It was the same look he'd given her last night. She could believe him. But she wasn't sure she wanted to.

"They have...heightened senses."

"Like?'

"Smell, sight."

"Touch," Reign inserted.

Jackson glared across the table then turned back to her.

"And they don't like strangers. They believe anyone not like them is fair game."

The term made Dani laugh uncomfortably. "Fair game for what?"

"Whatever they can get away with." Jackson's words sent a shiver down her back. She looked to Reign, waiting for him to deny the comment. He sighed.

"Jackson's right. They'll see someone like you—gorgeous and sexy—and they'll be all over you. But—" He silenced Jackson with glare. "I'll be there and everyone will know you belong to me."

"How do you intend to do that?" Jackson asked. His fingers tightened briefly on her leg but even when that grip relaxed, every other muscle in his body remained tense.

"How do you think?"

"Not happening."

"That's up to her."

"You're not marking her."

"Mark me?" she asked, hating that she felt out of the loop. There wasn't a chance for either man to answer. The waitress appeared with their order. Plates landed on the table, crushed together until the white Formica tabletop was almost invisible. She looked at the plain, low fat meal in front of her. Then glanced at the boys' plates.

112

They'd ordered everything meat on the menu. And went at it like they hadn't eaten in a month.

Must be nice, she thought with a sigh. If she ate half that, she wouldn't be fit into her costumes for a week.

She took a few bites and let them make small gouges in their food piles before she asked the question again.

"Mark me?" she finally said. "What does that mean?"

Jackson tensed next to her but didn't say anything. Reign took a bite of his omelet and finally answered.

"It means that you'll have my scent on you. Like Jackson said, these people have very strong senses, primarily sense of smell. If my scent is on you, they'll know you belong to me."

"You're kidding right?" She looked at Jackson. He shook his head. "I'm almost afraid to ask, but how do you put your scent on me?"

"By touching you."

"Touching me," she repeated. She glanced at Jackson. He had his head bent down, concentrating on his food. She didn't know if he was angry or trying to keep out of the conversation completely.

"Yes." Reign opened his mouth like he was going to speak, stopped then started again. "Sex is the best way."

Jackson's head snapped up and a low snarl rumbled from his throat. Reign didn't react. He met her stare with blatant hunger in his eyes.

Dani squirmed. Images of her in bed with Reign filled her brain. It wasn't as if she hadn't thought of it before. Maybe it was Jackson's presence or the fact that she'd been fucked into oblivion last night but today the pictures in her head seemed real. She could feel his hands on her skin, his lips on hers.

She took a soothing breath and ignored the heat moving through her pussy. And tried not to think about her nipples pressing through her thin bra and into her shirt. Jackson's eyes glowed, as if he knew she was soaking the ugly panties he'd wanted to her wear.

The fire in her sex spread through her body. Her mouth opened, just a little, letting in more air, her body desperate for the oxygen which seemed to have gone missing. Too hard to breathe. The pictures slammed into her brain, relentless. Her and Reign. And Jackson. Male bodies surrounding her. One beneath her, the other behind her, both males penetrating her. Fucking her. The strong sexuality of Jackson balanced by the animal lust of Reign.

"You three want anything else?" The pop of the waitress's gum yanked Dani from her fantasy and she automatically shook her head. Neither man answered. The other woman shrugged and slapped the bill on the table.

Once she'd walked away, Dani forced more air into her lungs, calming herself and focusing on what Reign had truly said.

"You aren't really expecting us to have sex, right?" *Please. Yes. No.*

He shook his head but there was a glint of a smile in his eyes. "Unfortunately, no. I don't expect you to agree to that." He glanced at Jackson almost daring him to interrupt. "But it needs to be skin on skin contact," Reign continued. "As naked as you'll let both of us be."

She gulped her warming ice water and thought about what Reign said. It made no sense.

She put down her spoon and stared Reign down.

"You want me to rub up against you so people can *smell* you on me? You realize how insane this sounds, right?"

Reign's head moved in what could be called a nod but there was no commitment to the movement.

She looked in Jackson's eyes. "You don't have anything to say about this?" She expected some protest from the man she'd spent the night with. He'd said he was jealous of Reign but when the man starts talking about getting naked with her, Jackson says nothing.

"I hate the idea, but I agree with Reign that if you're going to that party, you need to have his—*and my*—" Another pointed glance to Reign. "Scent on you. I don't trust these people but they usually have the sense not to go after something that clearly belongs to a stronger animal."

She gulped at the term "animal". That's how it sounded. Like when a cat marked its territory.

"It will make tonight much more safe."

If Jackson hadn't been sitting there, she would have dismissed it as a joke. Or that Reign was trying to get into her pants this way. But Jackson seemed to believe, even agree with, everything Reign said.

She looked from man to man. There was no hint of humor, not a twitch of lips trying not to smile. They were freakin' dead serious about this.

And neither of them seemed inclined to share any more information. Later she was getting some answers. Like who these people were at the party and how could they smell the remnants of skin touching skin?

She sighed. "When do we do this?"

It was subtle but she saw Reign's jaw relax, like he'd been worried she'd reject the idea or decide to bail on the whole project.

"Tonight, before the party. I'll make the arrangements for a car and come by your place about eight."

She nodded. Her insides trembled, a strange mass of fear and lust—which hadn't dissipated even through the strangely clinical discussion about Reign putting his "scent" on her. Jackson seemed to recognize the jumbled emotions and rubbed his hand across her thigh. There was little sex in this touch. More comfort.

115

"You're going to be there too?" she asked. It wasn't that she didn't trust Reign but Jackson was so solid she wanted him there.

"Yes."

"Maybe," Reign corrected. He looked at Jackson and there was that weird silent communication between them. Neither man moved and Dani was about to speak, something to break the tension before the two of them started breaking dishes. Then Reign announced, "We'll talk about it."

When I'm not here. This whole protective, macho guy crap is getting a little annoying. She shook her head, irritation making it difficult to find phrases that didn't start with "listen assholes—" Her gaze caught the clock on the wall.

"Oh, damn. I'm going to be late. I've got to go." She nudged Jackson with her knee. Rehearsal started in twenty minutes. She waved her hands, hurrying him up. He looked a little offended then slid out of the booth. She hooked her heel over the end of the bench and pulled her body down into the aisle. Jumping up, she kissed Jackson on the cheek. "I've got to get to work." Then she included Reign in her stare. "Figure this out for tonight, but I'd really like Jackson there. If it won't, you know, get me killed or anything."

"We won't let anything happen to you," Reign vowed. The intensity in his words soothed some of Dani's fears.

"He's right." Jackson put his arm around her and cuddled her closer. Her body reacted, molding to his, wanting to be pressed against him, without their clothes. "Hmm." Jackson rubbed his cheek against her head. "Don't worry, baby. We'll take care of you." Neither the movement nor the words were sexual but that didn't stop her body from responding, heat sinking into her pussy and the desire to climb him like a stripper's pole almost too much to ignore. He bent down so his lips were against her ear. "When you get back from rehearsal, baby." This time his words were pure sex and she had no doubt about his meaning. "As soon as you get back."

She lifted her head and smiled. If nothing else, this lust was distracting her from her fears about the party. And the party was distracting her from the lust. Great, she was just a big ole mess.

"I should go." Another quick kiss to Jackson and she forced her legs to carry her out the door. She had work to do.

Jackson watched her walk away. Men and women stopped and watched as she passed by, the sweet flip of her ass too intriguing to ignore. The human male in him wanted to jump up on the table and pound his chest, declaring that she belonged to him and challenging any male who wanted to even look at her. The wolf, strangely, had a different reaction. The animal whined when she left, but it wasn't jealousy or fear. The wolf was confident that she belonged to him. Jackson did a quick scan of the wolf's reactions in the past few minutes and while the animal hadn't been serene, he'd felt safe, even sitting across from a Cat.

Made no sense. Jackson sighed. But he'd never completely understood his wolf.

The door closed behind Dani and she walked by the window, waving as she headed toward her car. Once out of sight, Jackson swung around and sat back down, facing the Cat who was still plowing through his breakfast. Jackson followed suit. Despite their differences of opinion about the party tonight, they both needed to eat.

They ate in silence. Jackson tried to ignore the spicy male scent that came from the Cat. The smell of the cooked meat on his plate was enticing but part of his hunger came from the desire to bite the man across from him.

It was strange. Not necessarily that he was attracted to a guy—he'd had those feelings before—but the fact that Reign was a Cat. Jackson had met a few Cats in his day and he'd never found their smell remarkable. It hadn't been offensive but never before had he had the urge to lick another's skin to see if the intriguing spice translated into taste. His cock gave an insistent twitch.

Oh good. His dick was trying to join the conversation.

Wasn't this perfect? His friend Gideon, back home in Anchorage, would think it was fucking hysterical. For much of the past year, Gideon had teased Jackson about his sexual orientation, swearing that Gideon's "gaydar" was going off like crazy. In truth, Jackson knew Gideon was just trying to get into his pants but still he couldn't deny the attraction to some males. He'd never acted on it. The attraction had never been intriguing enough to pursue.

Now he'd found a male who his cock really wanted and he had to be a Cat and a bit of an asshole to boot. Perfect.

And even better, what Reign really wanted was to fuck Dani.

Finally Jackson had enough and pushed his plates away. It was time to move on with the conversation. Reign followed suit moments later. Jackson sipped his coffee and waited. This was the pussycat's show as far as he was concerned. He wasn't changing his mind. He was going to that party tonight.

Reign drained his water glass then set it on the table with a firm click. That seemed to be the opening shot.

"You can't go to this party tonight."

"I'm going." This wasn't defiance or irritation. He wasn't going to let Dani go to that party without double protection.

"You can't. They'll kill you. Literally."

"How uncivilized," Jackson mocked.

"Exactly. I don't know what wolf gatherings are like but Cats? They'll tear you to pieces."

"If I don't go, Dani's not going."

"Fuck, Jackson, you're worse than your brother." Reign sagged back against the leather cushions. "I'll be there. I'll protect her. Trust me. That's a hell of a lot safer than a wolf showing up at a Clowder."

Jackson played with his coffee cup for a moment. "I believe you're sincere about protecting Dani, I really do." He could at least give the Cat that. "But what happens once she points this guy out? Are you really going to just walk away? Let *him* walk away?"

Reign turned his head, looking at the dingy tile on the floor.

"Face it. If you have a chance to catch this bastard, you're going after him. And what will you do with Dani?"

"Fine. I'll have one of my friends look after her. I'll have one of the other cops come."

"A human?"

"Better than a wolf. A fight will break out the minute you step on the floor. It would never work." Reign shook his head. Then made a puffing noise like a chuckle suppressed deep in his chest.

"What's funny?"

"Oh, I just thought of a way you *could* attend the Clowder and *maybe* not get killed." The Cat's eyes sparkled with undisguised glee and Jackson felt his gut clench.

Whatever was going on in Reign's mind, Jackson wasn't going to like it, but what the hell? If it got him into the party and protected Dani, he'd do it.

"What is it?"

Again Reign shook his head. "Shouldn't have even brought it up. It's not going to happen, so just forget about it."

"What is it?"

The smirk on Reign's mouth wasn't comforting as he leaned forward, reaching almost to Jackson's side of the table. "You could probably go in..." He let his words trail away. "As my lover."

"What?" Jackson jerked back. Had Reign seen Jackson's interest?

119

Reign's smirk turned into an all out, arrogant "gotcha" grin. Smug bastard.

"That's the only way. If you walk in there marked with my scent then the other Cats would be curious but they probably wouldn't touch you." He grimaced. "My reputation would be shot—for fucking a dog—but I can live with that."

Jackson considered the idea. Reign clearly expected him to balk, to reject the idea as he ran for the door. But Dani wanted to go to this party, wanted to point this asshole out, do her part. And Jackson knew he needed to be there.

Besides, it would be kind of fun to call the Cat's bluff.

And you'd get a chance to have that hot body against yours. Oh, good. His conscience had to join into the conversation. But once the image came to mind, he couldn't let it go—him in bed, naked, his cock rubbing against Reign's, hard masculine hands squeezing his ass as they pumped against each other. His fingers curled into a fist. He shook head his trying to clear the fantasy but before it disappeared, the mental movie changed and Dani was there, her body behind his, her tits teasing his back, her wet pussy pressed against his ass.

He groaned.

Reign chuckled. "Yeah, I didn't figure you'd go for that, so, I'll take Dani—"

"I'll do it."

"What?" All expression left Reign's face.

Jackson was rather proud of himself that he didn't smile at shocking the Cat.

"I said I'll do it."

"You'll go as my lover?"

"Yeah. You need to mark me, I can handle that." *I think.* He was just going to have to find a way to hide his body's response. Somehow he didn't think Reign was going to appreciate Jackson's hard-on.

"You're serious," Reign said.

"Yes. Were you?"

"Sure."

"Fine."

Jackson stared at Reign, who stared back. He couldn't even imagine what the other male was thinking. His own mind had slowed down until one single thought filled his brain—*what the fuck have I done?*

Chapter Eight

ဢ

Dani fiddled with the sandwich Jackson had made for her, knowing she needed to eat but unable to put anything in her mouth without her stomach rebelling.

The day had been a total goat rope. Rehearsal had sucked. The director had been late, then pissy. And then because he kept changing things and they were less than a week away from opening, they'd called another rehearsal. Instead of being home at five for a nice leisurely round of hot sex with Jackson before Reign showed up, she'd walked in at eight twenty. Both men waiting for her, her hair still damp from her shower at the theater.

She sighed and tried to wrap her tired mind around what was next.

"You okay, baby?" Jackson asked, rubbing his hand across her shoulders. She leaned into his hip, needing the physical support, and nodded. She would be okay. She'd just been thinking about this all day long. When she wasn't thinking about sex. Between the fear and the lust, her body was a complete mess, not sure how to react.

She scraped her hair away from her face. "I'm fine." She looked at Reign. "Let's just do this, huh?"

He nodded and Jackson stood back, giving her room to stand.

She looked at him as she started toward the stairs. "Are you going to be there? I mean here?" She wasn't sure which she wanted. Did she want her current lover watching while another man touched her? Or would it be better if he wasn't around?

Jackson shook his head and a self-mocking smile moved his lips. "Probably not a good idea."

She nodded, the smile easing some of her tension. She grabbed his hand and pulled him in for a quick kiss.

"I won't be far, baby," he said as she pulled away.

Again she nodded, finding it hard to speak. She barely glanced at Reign as she started up the stairs, her body stiff and tight. Each step she mentally shored up her resolve. It wasn't like she hadn't done this sort of thing before. She wasn't even going to have sex with Reign. They were just going to touch a bit and hell, she liked Reign. Wanted Reign.

An awkwardness existed between them. Reign followed her into the bedroom.

"Are you okay?" Reign asked the question and Dani took a tight breath before nodding. "You don't have to do this," he assured her. "We'll find another way to get this guy." She knew how much that offer must have cost him.

That made Dani feel even worse. The fact that she couldn't describe Winston, couldn't help the sketch artist, had kept her awake at night.

"But your best bet is tonight and the only way I can go to this party tonight is if I'm wearing your scent."

Reign nodded.

This time when she breathed in, she forced her lungs to expand and take in the full volume. She could do this. It wasn't like the idea of touching Reign was appalling. Just the opposite. It was intriguing. Seductive. And maybe that's what stopped her. She was still trying to adapt to the fact that she'd fucked Jackson last night. After knowing him for less than a day. Despite Jackson's assurances, it seemed a little slutty.

And now she was planning to get naked with another man. While her lover waited downstairs.

Not that Reign was going to fuck her—he'd been very clear about that—but it needed to be skin on skin contact.

She looked at the gorgeous man before her. His tawny eyes were captivating—not only with the rare color but the heat. Only one other man had looked at her with just blatant hunger. And he was sitting in her living room waiting for her to finish. She shivered just thinking about Jackson. And Reign. Ooh, both of them.

Her nipples tightened as she imagined being wrapped between them. Temptation sizzled in her stomach.

She could do this. *Think sex Goddess. Think sexy. He wants you. He made that clear.*

But before she could become the sex goddess sensual enough to carry her through the rest of this exercise, she had to overcome one hurdle.

"Let's do this." Without letting herself think, she whipped off her t-shirt and dropped it to the floor. Leaving her bra alone, she undid the button and zipper of her skirt and pushed the material down.

She was confident in her body. She kind of had to be—going topless five nights a week—but still, there was the normal trepidation of being naked with a new guy.

She pushed her shoulders back and forced herself to meet Reign's stare.

His gaze held hers for a moment and then he released her eyes, following the line of her throat down to her torso. He looked at her breasts, still bound and compressed in her lacy bra.

"Damn," he whispered, the sound so soft she almost missed it. Heat radiated off his body and sank into her core. Liquid fire warmed her pussy and she fought to shift beneath his hungry stare. Oh yeah, she could do this. His perusal continued, going lower, lower, pausing at her waist. A strange look crossed his face and he blinked, the lust shifting into confusion.

Age-old insecurities reared up and grabbed Dani by the throat.

124

"What's wrong?" Was there something wrong with her body? Wasn't she sexy enough?

"Nothing, it's just I—"

Unable to stand it any longer, she looked down...and saw the ugly panties Jackson had insisted she wear. And she'd put back on after her shower.

"I'm going to kill him. These were Jackson's idea."

So much for her sex goddess routine.

"They're nice." The words were strangled by Reign's laughter.

"They're hideous."

"No," he said between suppressed chuckles. She had to give him credit. He was trying not to laugh. "They're just so...cotton." He couldn't hold it back any longer and laughter escaped.

"That's it. Jackson!"

Jackson leaned against the front door, staring at the stairs. It was as far away as he could get without actually leaving the condo and he wasn't prepared to do that. At least not yet. If it got too bad, he'd probably have to run. His wolf was clawing inside his brain, demanding he return to his female and...what?

Fuck her? Watch Reign fuck her? Let Reign fuck you?

Knowing his wolf needed the release, earlier in the day Jackson had driven into the desert, found a little patch of isolation and shifted. He shook his hair, pretty sure he'd never get the sand out of his paws and fur. Still, it had done him good. The wolf was calm. He would almost have said resigned but the animal didn't think in those terms. It didn't seem to mind that Reign was upstairs with Dani, touching Dani. If anything, the damn beast acted excited.

Made no sense. He'd called his father's Beta, Byron, and asked if he'd ever heard of a werewolf who'd claimed a mate but didn't mind another male touching her. Byron had hemmed and hawed, muttering that Jackson really needed to call his father. But his dad would ask questions. Questions Jackson wasn't ready to answer.

He tapped his fingers against the wood door, the tension pulling his muscles coming from the human's stress and the wolf's excitement. He knew what was happening upstairs was necessary for Dani to go to this party but he didn't know if he could handle it.

If he heard too much—if he heard the cry she made when she came—he'd have to leave. It would be the only choice. Killing a cop was a bad idea. He had to keep telling himself that. It gave him something to think about besides what was going on upstairs in that bedroom. Dani's soft curves pressing against Reign's hard muscles.

And he knew what Reign had planned. The best way to mark her was to come in her, on her. It would be the safest thing for her but Jackson wasn't sure he could handle it.

Maybe it would be best if he left. He could go hang out by the pool until it was done. *And then you're going to have to get marked as well.* Jackson's stomach clenched at the thought. Had he really agreed to this? He looked at the phone and thought about calling Max but decided against it. How was he going to explain to his twin that he was going to willingly crawl into bed naked with another man? And a Cat. And why didn't the idea freak him out more?

He thumped his head back against the door, the pain a minor distraction. Between thoughts of Dani, he'd thought about what would happen tonight—he and Reign would be naked together, bodies against each other, and damn, there had been no moments of panic. Even his wolf had stayed calm. Except maybe to get a little excited. Like the beast wanted it. Yeah, that was perfect. His wolf wanted to get fucked by a Cat. That was one for the werewolf psychologists.

Still it was strange not to have the instinctive panic he was expecting. Maybe his wolf was—

"Jackson!"

His head snapped up and he growled, lunging for the stairs, his wolf coming to life. What had that bastard done? He'd kill him. He'd rip his throat out. The bloodthirsty personality that lived beneath his skin snarled its approval, wanting the kill. The fact that Reign was a Cat just made it sweeter.

Jackson slammed open the door, keeping a leash on his wolf as he stormed in, ready to defend.

And immediately turned on the defensive. Dani stalked toward him, her lips peeled away from her lips.

"I'm gonna kill you," she growled.

"Me? What did I do?" His wolf recognized the danger of a pissed off female and retreated, leaving Jackson to face her alone.

"It's these panties."

"What?"

"These damn panties that you insisted I wear. Here we are, all ready to get down to business..."

Reign scoffed — in between chuckles.

Jackson ignored the sound.

"I'm trying to feel all sexy, act like some freakin' sex goddess and I pull off my skirt to reveal *granny panties*."

Jackson didn't know whether to laugh or scream. It was obvious which route Reign was taking.

"That's what this is about? Your *panties*? I thought he'd attacked you or something."

"Hey!" Reign's protest was again dismissed.

Dani rolled her eyes, ending with a glare at him. "Reign would never hurt me but how can I be sexy in huge cotton panties?"

Jackson skimmed his eyes down her body, his cock twitching at the sight of her in those panties.

127

"Baby, you're sexy in anything."

She flinched, as if she hadn't been prepared for that.

"You could wear a cardboard box and Reign and I would both still be begging to fuck you."

"Oh."

That set her back on her heels and her anger seemed to dissipate, leaving behind the natural sensuality.

"Come here, baby." The command pulled her forward. Two steps and she was right in front of Jackson—the tension in the room shifting from anger to sex with one simple instruction. He turned her around so her back was against his chest, putting her on display for Reign.

Jackson notched his thumbs into the waistband of panties, the soft cotton warm from her skin. He leaned and scraped his teeth across her neck, a gentle punishing bite. "I'm going show Reign just how sexy you are." He whispered the words against her skin, her hips pressed back, meeting his erection. This was better, even knowing the Cat watched, it was better that Jackson was here, that *he* was the one to strip off the last bit of her clothes.

He dragged the cloth down, aware that Reign watched. He inched the soft material over her hips, revealing her beautiful sex. The material cleared her thighs and fell, forgotten on the floor.

All laughter disappeared from Reign's eyes as he stared at Dani's almost bare pussy. Jackson's cock twitched at the blatant inspection, proud and aroused just from watching another guy get hard by looking at her.

"See, baby. He's hard." Jackson brushed a kiss along her neck. "He wants to fuck you."

He raised his chin, calling the other man closer.

Reign hesitated, catching Jackson's eyes to confirm he was okay with this. Jackson nodded and Reign stepped forward, stripping off his shirt as he drew near. He reached up and cupped Dani's neck in his hand, bending down and placing his mouth on hers. The urge to overwhelm her, to dominate pounded through his brain but he forced himself to move slowly.

Vividly aware that Jackson stood behind her, Reign teased Dani's lips, his head swirling at the sexual taste of the woman and the hot scent flowing from the wolf. A low hum of arousal rippled through her body but Reign wanted more than that. He wanted her screaming, begging to have him fuck her. Not that he was going to get the chance to fuck her. He didn't think the wolf was going to let him penetrate Dani, but that didn't mean he wouldn't have his hands and mouth all over her.

Months of fantasies flooded his brain—of having Dani before him, bent over the end of his bed, his cock in her pussy, riding her hard. He knew Jackson would never let that happen but he was seizing the opportunity now to indulge all his Cat senses.

He flicked his tongue out, teasing her upper lip. She sighed and opened her mouth, just a little, reaching for him, giving him a taste. Sweetness saturated the tip of his tongue as he delved between her lips, tempting him with more. The male wolf standing behind her should have crushed his arousal but damn, he was ready to pound nails with his dick. Having Jackson watch just made Dani's flavor more intriguing. Reign pressed forward, sliding his hands to her waist, rubbing his lips across her mouth. The natural sensuality he'd sensed in her rose to the surface and she tipped her head to the side, opening to him, accepting the shallow dips of his tongue into her mouth.

He purred, letting the sound rumble into her. Her lips curved in an open-mouthed smile. The smile faded as she moaned, arching her neck to the side. Reign watched the wolf smooth his lips along her throat ending with a tiny bite where her neck and shoulder met. The pale pink mark drew a growl from inside his chest, wanting his own mark on her.

But distraction followed, taking the Cat's attention.

Dani turned her head, seeking his lips and Reign complied, blocking out the wolf and focusing on Dani. His head swirled, drowning him in sweet hot female and the delicious natural scent of her skin. He twirled his tongue around hers, teasing and sucking. The Cat's urge to play came through even with so much on the line.

Intense heat poured from Dani and the wolf — both sensations too fascinating to resist. Warmth radiated from Jackson and Dani like a sunbeam, just waiting for him to drop into, curl up and stay.

She reached up and draped her arms around his neck, dragging him closer. The lace cups of her bra abraded the tight peaks of his nipples, the lightest touch, just enough. He grabbed her ass, feeling her hips roll back, away from Reign. His lips twitched, fighting to pull up in a snarl. Then the Cat realized she wasn't pulling away from him — she was rubbing her ass against Jackson's dick. His cock pushed on the seam of his jeans, damn well demanding freedom.

He lifted his head for just a moment and her eyes slowly drifted open. Desire and hunger flared in the seductive gray depths. She looked drunk on the sensuality. Needing to share in that, he cupped her head in his hand and held her in place, his lips covering hers, his tongue drinking deep.

A new heat brushed against his chest and he pulled back enough to look down. Jackson reached between their bodies, his hands sliding between Dani's breasts. He worked by touch and with a clever flick of thumb and forefinger, the front clasp gave way and the delicate lace cups spread apart. Jackson stripped the material away when it would have clung to her nipples, leaving her bare.

"Damn," Reign whispered, the reverent sound echoed by Jackson's humming agreement. Jackson tipped her head, scraping his white teeth along her neck, arching her back, and pushing her breasts forward and up. It didn't make sense. Why would the wolf be offering his woman's tits to another man? But Reign ignored the question. The Cat didn't worry about consequences.

He cupped her breasts in his hands, his thumbs zeroing in on her nipples, rubbing slow circles around the tight peaks. He glanced up. Dani watched him, her body still trapped in the sexual nature of their contact, but there was no new heat. *Damn, she doesn't like to have her breasts played with.* That was too bad because she had some luscious tits but if only one of them was getting anything out of it...

Unable to resist one more squeeze, he started to pull back but Jackson's voice stopped him.

"Harder."

Reign lifted his head. The wolf's eyes glowed red. The hair on the back of Reign's neck stood up but he rejected the fight or flight instincts.

"Harder," Jackson repeated, a sharp nod following the instruction.

Reign slid his thumb and forefinger of Dani's nipple and pinched, just a shade stronger than he normally would have. A tiny whimper escaped her lips and she rolled her hips forward. Harder. The wolf was giving him advice on fucking his woman. Strange. Maybe the wolves were much more open than Reign had been led to believe. But he didn't think so. There was just something strange about this particular wolf. And the woman between them.

He bent down and placed his lips over the tight peak, stroking first, loving the feel of her nipple against his tongue. Her chest rose in slow deep pants. Yes, she liked a harder touch but she could enjoy a softer caress, once her body was humming. He groaned, just imagining being inside her, fucking her hard and sucking on her pretty tits. She'd scream. He'd come.

He swirled his tongue around the nipple, warning her moments before he pressed down light with his teeth, not pain just a pinch. She moaned and pushed closer. He opened his mouth and sucked, hard.

"Reign!" It was the first time she'd said his name in passion. He purred and sucked again, even as he wrapped his hand around her hip and pulled her closer, sliding his knee between her legs. Wet heat coated his thigh, soaking the material of his jeans.

"Oh fuck." He growled the words against her skin and once again he heard the wolf's response. Reign looked up. Dani's back was arched, one hand digging into his shoulder, one draped around Jackson's neck. The other male curled around, holding her body up as he plunged his tongue into her mouth. Every thrust of his tongue brought a slow roll of Dani's hips, rocking her clit against Reign's thigh.

He skimmed his hands down her hips, cupping her ass, holding her still. She could come easily this way but he wasn't missing what might be his only chance to taste her. With one final lick to her breast, he sank down, landing on his knees with the innate grace of a Cat. He rubbed his lips against her smooth mound, the sleek skin devoid of hair except for a thin strip right about her slit. He hooked his hand beneath her knee and lifted, draping her left leg over his shoulder, opening her. The juices from her cunt painted her inner thighs, tempting him. The sweet sexual perfume that always surrounded her was stronger here. Potent.

He lapped at the slick liquid, groaning as the mellow flavor landed on his tongue. He took another taste, rubbing his cheek against her thigh, indulging himself for just a moment, knowing he couldn't linger as he'd like. He mentally tracked the time. The party started in less than two hours. He smiled against her skin. No, that wasn't enough time to do everything he wanted to Dani.

He looked up, the wolf still claimed part of her attention, long drugging kisses that looked delicious. Part of him wanted to stand and join in but the stronger side couldn't resist the temptation before him. Or the chance to tease her away from Jackson.

Reign trailed his fingers up the inside of Dani's thigh, higher, delicate flutters to her pussy lips. She groaned and pumped her hips forward, silently begging for more. *That's it, kitten. Purr for me.*

He pushed closer, spreading that pretty cunt open with his fingers. Unable to stop the sound, a purr rippled from his throat. He leaned forward and stroked his tongue up the full length of her slit, savoring every drop of liquid.

Dani dragged her mouth away from Jackson's, needing oxygen, needing to slow the spinning in her world. She gasped in a few breaths but it did little to clear her mind. She glanced down. Reign's blond hair brushed her thighs, teasing little strokes sending shivers across her skin. He raised his eyes, drilling her with his gaze as he dipped his tongue between her pussy lips, a slow stroke to her clit, then deeper, slipping the tip into her opening.

Dani gripped Jackson's arms, using his strength to support her. Reign swished his tongue around her clit and gave a little suck. Heat rushed from her body and she groaned, sure she was drenched.

She couldn't find the strength to be embarrassed—not with Reign licking her and Jackson behind her kissing and biting. She felt like a sensual meal offered up to two ravenous beasts.

Reign slid his tongue into her pussy and fucked her, shallow fast thrusts, working that sensitive first inch of her cunt until she wanted to scream. Until she did scream.

"Reign," she gasped, sinking her fingers into his hair, gripping his head and holding him as she arched into him, trying to get him deeper, needing more. A wicked purr rose from Reign's throat and the shimmering vibrations surrounded her clit. It was just enough. She cried out and froze as the bright jolt rippled through her cunt. Her knee wobbled and she grabbed at Jackson for support.

Reign lifted his head but his stare moved past her to the man behind her. Some kind of male telepathy must have occurred because Jackson nodded and they moved together — Reign standing, Jackson easing her into his arms.

Reign scooped her up and spun around carrying her the few feet to the bed. He set her on the mattress, her heels resting on the edge. She placed her hands at her hips, preparing to slide into the center, he stopped her, his hand on her hip holding her in place.

"You taste too good for just one time," he murmured. "Lie back."

Drunk on the sexual energy in the room, she looked at him and then up to Jackson. He'd backed away, not leaving but standing at the door, his fingers gripping the frame as if physically holding himself apart. Her chest tightened. Was this — whatever this was with Reign — going to screw up what she and Jackson were building?

She opened her mouth to ask Jackson if he wanted this to continue. He shook his head, stopping her question.

"It's okay, baby," he said, the gravelly voice barely audible. "Let him have you."

Reign looked over his shoulder, glancing at Jackson before turning back to her. "I'll stop if you want me to." He slid his fingers between her knees and pressed them outward, opening her thighs. Pulling her gaze away from Jackson, she stared at Reign and found herself locked in his eyes. His hands stroked the insides of her thighs, soothing and seducing with each caress. He pushed closer, never touching her pussy but teasing her upper thighs. "Do you want me to stop?"

Chapter Nine

ഔ

Dani couldn't resist one more glance at Jackson. His eyes glowed but he nodded, giving her permission.

She took a deep breath and relaxed back, letting her knees fall open and her head drop back on the bed.

Reign murmured nonsense words as he lowered himself to the side of the bed, leaning and spreading her pussy lips with his hot fingers, baring her for his tongue. A kitten's purr rumbled from his throat as he lapped at her cunt, like a cat tasting the sweetest cream. She didn't know how he made that sound but every time he did, she felt it, on her pussy lips, in her core. It made her want more, need more.

"Come for me again," he whispered, barely taking his lips from her skin. "Let me taste your sweet cream, kitten."

She wanted to tell him she couldn't, that it was too soon for her to come again, but the hot swirl of his tongue on her clit, teasing the sensitive flesh sent a shot of renewed need into her pussy. Maybe she could...

He kissed her clit, rewarding her for her reaction, then returned to the luscious long strokes of his tongue. He took his time, not driving her toward some hard orgasm, as if he was tasting her to please himself. His purrs and whispers tantalized her flesh and she couldn't hold still. She rocked her hips up, seeking more, needing him...but this time he held back, tasting her as his pleasure, until she was begging, pleading for him to let her come.

"Please, Reign, let me..." Her voice sounded strange to her own ears, low and sexual.

He lifted his eyes, watching her as he floated another caress across her clit. She cried out. So close. She wanted to beg him to do it again but her voice was gone.

"I'm going to lick this pretty cunt, kitten, until you scream and cream in my mouth."

"Yes," she moaned.

"Then I'm going to come on those beautiful tits. Mark you so every male knows that I belong between your thighs."

Her nipples tightened as he growled.

"That's it, kitten. I know you want this."

"Please!"

He dipped his head and gave one long wicked stroke of his tongue, as if he wanted one last taste. His lips slipped over her clit, rhythmic sucking that compelled her hips to move, to rock with him. God, it was so good but she needed more. She needed…

As if he heard her thoughts, two fingers pushed hard into her passage. She groaned and punched her hips up, meeting his thrusts. He fucked her with his fingers, timing each stroke with the sweet suction of his lips until she couldn't fight it any longer, until the need to come overtook her senses. He tickled her clit with his tongue and sent her flying.

Her scream caught in her throat as another shocking wave flowed from her pussy and washed into her limbs draining them of strength, energy.

An animalistic roar, like a giant jungle cat, echoed through her sensation-clouded mind. Pressure compressed her chest and she opened her eyes. Reign knelt over her, his knees straddling her ribs, his cock, hard and deep purple, cupped in his hand.

"You taste so good, kitten, I'm ready to come just from licking you." He stroked he fist up and down his shaft.

Yes. She reached up and placed her hand on his cock, curling her fingers around the part he couldn't reach.

"Oh, Dani, that's too sweet. Damn, kitten, I need to fuck you."

"Yes." Her moaned agreement ignited his climax. Hot streams of cum splattered across her breasts. He pumped his hand hard, drawing out the last traces.

He reached out, placing his palm on her chest and rubbing his cum into her skin. The slow sensual caress was like nothing she'd ever felt before. He was right...she was marked. Claimed.

Reign shifted, sliding down her body, bending until his mouth hovered over hers. The scent of her pussy surrounded him and she smiled knowing that she'd marked him as well.

"Thank you," he whispered against her lips.

A low, dangerous growl shattered the seductive energy of the room. Dani felt her eyes pop open and she looked up at Reign. Tension ripped through his body, the warning inherent in the animal sound.

Slowly, as if Reign didn't want to startle whatever was making the noise, he rolled off her. His scent still clung to her skin but there was nothing to be done about that.

Blinking, she looked toward the door, knowing that Jackson was somehow making that foreign noise. She gasped as she saw him. The low light in the room made his eyes glow red. His lips were peeled back from his teeth — teeth that looked strange, almost like an animal's. His fingers gripped the drywall as if he held himself still by the sheer strength of his fingertips.

His glowing eyes zeroed in on her pussy. Protective instincts came to life and she closed her legs. The growling grew louder and she thought she heard the tear of wallpaper.

"I don't think that's a good idea," Reign whispered. "He probably won't hurt you but hiding from him is just going to piss the animal off."

She wanted to ask what Reign meant but knew now was not the time. Taking his advice, she spread her thighs, opening herself.

Still Jackson didn't move, didn't release the violence that gripped his body. He licked his lips, as if imagining the taste of her flesh but somehow she didn't think he was interested in a slow tongue fuck.

"Jackson?"

His head snapped up and canted to the side, staring at her as if he didn't recognize his own name. Something had a hold of her lover.

Moving with a sexual instinct she didn't understand, she rolled away from Reign, not going far, but just enough, turning onto her stomach. She raised her hips and separated her knees, offering herself to Jackson.

She glanced over her shoulder. He didn't move, frozen, his chest rising and falling in tight breaths. She arched back and lowered her head into her arms.

"Fuck me, Jackson," she whispered. "Please, fuck me." Hunger poured from him but still he didn't move. Not sure if she was tempting the beast or soothing it, she slipped one hand between legs, spreading her pussy lips, opening her cunt to him. "Please. I need you. Come inside me."

His growl vibrated the pictures on the wall and she heard the sound of material tearing—not a zipper opening but actual cloth ripping. Hot strong fingers gripped her hips and she had only a moment warning before he thrust into her—hard, deep, his cock stretched long, almost too much. She cried out and buried her face in the blanket, biting the thick material to hold back her whimper. The heavy penetration shook her body but God, she didn't want it to stop.

He pulled out and slammed back in, each stroke claiming and marking her pussy. His fingers dug into her hips, holding her in place as he fucked her.

"Dani, is he hurting you?" Reign's question barely made it through the sensations surrounding her. She shook her head.

"No. Good. Feels good."

It was such a weak word for what was happening to her body. He kept on, hard and deep, like her body was designed for his cock. Her cunt fluttered, tightening as he filled her again. The shock turned her groan to a gasp and she heard Jackson scream, the wicked pulses of her climax massaging his shaft.

He moved, leaning over her, his hips still pistoning into hers, as if he couldn't stop the motion. His teeth scraped her shoulder, sharp, almost painful. She waited, somehow knowing what would follow.

"No!"

Reign's sharp cry snapped Jackson's head back and he growled, fury lancing his chest that someone, something would dare interfere.

A hard brisk smack on his cheek followed.

"No biting. Not tonight."

The command in Reign's voice reached into Jackson and yanked his conscious to the surface. He looked down. Dani was bent before him, his cock buried deep in her cunt. The hot compelling scent of her pussy filled his nose. He blinked, coming back to himself. His teeth were stretched long, taking the wolf form.

With a deep breath, he willed his incisors to retract. As his heart calmed, his memory returned. He'd been fucking Dani — hard, pounding into her.

He groaned and started to pull out, horrified that he might have hurt her. All he could remember was the need to claim her, to blend his scent with Reign's on her skin. To spill inside her pussy. Fuck, he wasn't wearing a condom. He'd never fucked a woman without a condom before. It was too dangerous.

His cock slipped out of her passage until only the head was still inside. He ground his front teeth together and willed himself to pull out, but fuck, the heat was incredible, the sleek grip of her walls, soft against his cock. His hips rocked forward, his body fighting the mental commands to withdraw. Clamping down on the wolf that howled in his brain and the furious demands of his cock, he placed his hand on her hip and eased back.

"No." Her moan was soft and low. "Don't leave me."

"I don't want to hurt you, baby."

"Not hurt. Good. So good." She dug her fingers into the blankets and lifted her ass, pressing back, sliding him into her. Her cunt eased for him, practically begging him to push inside while honor demanded that he pull back. "Fuck me, Jackson. Please, I need you."

Her plea was too much to resist and the sweet sound clouded his mind. He thrust forward, controlling the power just a little more. She moaned and pushed back, sending him deeper. Damn, she wanted to be fucked. Hard.

He looked up. Reign watched, the tension in him melting away, his hand wrapped around his cock, long, lazy strokes that called to Jackson to match.

"Ride her, Jax. She wants that cock of yours."

The words curled around Jackson's dick and he sank into her pussy, groaning as the slick heat fully penetrated his senses. Damn, he was naked inside her. He had to pull out. He couldn't come inside her. The dangers were too high. They'd be bound together if he came inside her. It would be painful for her if he didn't fuck her again, and again.

But as he eased his dick back along the soft sexual path of her passage, he couldn't remember why that was a bad idea.

Natural instincts won and he thrust back into her, groaning as she gripped him so sweetly.

"Yeah, that's it," Reign encouraged. "Let her feel it."

Dani moaned and pressed back, taking him hard and deep. Her cunt eased for him, slick and wet. Damn, she was perfect. Every time he penetrated her, she met him, slamming her ass back against him.

A long high feminine cry filled the room as her pussy contracted, massaging his cock. More, he wanted more. Needed to feel that again.

His hips pounded against her ass. He was about to climax but he wanted her to come one more time, feel the delicate squeeze to his cock before he pulled out.

"Help me," he said to Reign, half command, half plea. He gritted his teeth together, fighting the urge to spill inside her. "Help me make her come."

Reign's eyes flashed and he rolled over, stretching out beside Dani. He slid his arm beneath her body, his fingers sliding between her legs. Her whimper wove through his chest, wrapping around his heart and drawing him closer as Reign stroked her, his fingers brushing Jackson's cock as he plowed through the tight flesh of Dani's cunt. The blankets muffled her cry as wicked contractions of her pussy rippled down Jackson's cock, squeezing and pulsing.

Years of self-preservation and lectures from his father and older brother had ingrained themselves into his muscles and he yanked back, pulling his cock from the warmth of her cunt. The wolf in his head screamed its displeasure but it was too late. He came, his cum splattering across her ass. His shout tore through room.

He looked down and saw his seed on her back. His wolf didn't like that he'd been denied coming inside her but seeing his cum marking her…the wolf howled. Jackson smoothed his hand across her back, smearing his semen into her skin, adding his scent to Reign's.

The three scents blended perfectly, a mixture of sweet and spice. Jackson closed his eyes and licked his lips, wanting their tastes on his tongue.

* * * * *

Dani slid off the end of the bed and stood. Her legs wobbled and the world swooped and spun for a moment. Instantly, two male bodies surrounded her, caging her, supporting her. She blinked and looked up into Reign's concerned eyes. "Are you okay?"

She flashed a weak smile. "A little dizzy. Lightheaded I guess." He didn't smile back so she did the next best thing. She kissed him. "I'm fine." With Jackson behind her, she slipped between their bodies but the need to taste him, to offer what she'd given to Reign was strong. She placed a lingering kiss on his lips then forced herself to walk away.

The room smelled like sex, the scent surrounding her.

"You can jump in the shower," Reign said.

A shower sounded good. She was a little sticky. "Won't that kind of defeat the purpose?"

"You can rinse off." Reign winked. "Just no soap."

She nodded. The two men stood side by side, watching her. Jackson shifted, dragging his shirt down to cover his still hard cock. His gaze jumped from her to Reign and back. Reign's jaw tensed and he folded his arms over his bare chest. The sexual atmosphere in the room took on a masculine flavor. This wasn't lust directed at her.

"Are you two okay?"

Reign nodded. "Fine. We just need to do a couple more things before we're ready to go." He looked at Jackson, his lips compressing at the edges. Jackson nodded as well but he looked away before Dani could read his eyes. "Go take your shower. This won't take long."

Felling a little like she was throwing Jackson to the wolves, she turned and walked into the bathroom. This whole evening verged on the completely weird and she needed a few minutes on her own.

Closing the door behind her, she looked into the mirror and tried to catch her breath. The image before her did nothing to calm her pounding heart. Her cheeks were flushed red and her lips swollen. She looked like a woman who'd been fucked—long and hard. She locked her elbows and leaned on the bathroom counter, giving her trembling knees extra support. Despite the blatantly sexual aspect of her job, she'd never lived the wild exotic life people associated with Vegas showgirls.

Until tonight. Two men. She rubbed her hand across her stomach. The dried traces of Reign's cum lingered. Despite the fact that she was going rinse off, she felt as if she'd been well and truly marked by him. And by Jackson. Even once the traces of semen were washed away, she'd feel the imprint on her soul.

Low voices rumbled through the door and spurred her to action. She didn't know how long she had and she wanted this shower, needed a few moments to herself. She started the water and climbed under the stinging spray, letting the water cascade across her skin. Her nipples—rarely sensitive— puckered as the sharp droplets fell across her breasts.

She didn't linger—something inside her didn't want to erase the traces of these men from her body. She killed the water and let the air swirl around her. Even that shadowy caress made her body ache for more.

A crash followed by a grunt and a series of heavy thuds which Dani recognized as her books hitting the floor stopped her thoughts cold.

Dani wrapped a short robe around her and hurried from the bathroom.

Reign and Jackson faced off in her bedroom, practically growling at each other. A bottle of lube lay on floor between them, an obvious casualty of their battle. Her neatly stacked hardcovers were mangled in a huge pile.

"What's going on?"

For a long time, neither man moved. The strain in his body didn't change but finally Reign straightened.

"Wolf-boy has changed his mind."

"You said you'd mark me," Jackson snarled.

"I said you had to become my lover. That means *I fuck you*." He folded his arms across his massive chest—a look that could have been described as casual if Dani hadn't seen each muscle pulled tight. "So if you want in on this, bend over and spread—"

He never got a chance to finish his sentence. Jackson's growl filled the room seconds before he launched himself across the small space separating them. He hit Reign hard in the chest and both men went down. Dani screamed and jumped out of the way as they rolled toward her. They crashed into the foot of the bed but neither man seemed to even notice.

"Stop it." Feeling like a schoolteacher, she clapped her hands together. Neither man reacted. "If either of you ever wants to fuck me again, you'll stop this now."

That the boys heard.

They both froze. Looked at her. Then back at each other.

Great, they had a unifying desire—fucking her. It might have thrilled her if she hadn't had to use the threat to stop them from killing each other.

"Get up and let's figure this out."

Reign—currently on top—jumped up as if he'd suddenly realized he was on top of another naked man. Jackson was a little slower but he finally got to his feet.

"Now, what's the problem?"

"The agreement was," Reign began, "that if Jackson wants to attend tonight's party, he has to become my lover. That's a condition of going." He glared at Jackson. "It's nonnegotiable."

"If I don't go, she doesn't go," Jackson replied, stepping forward.

The electricity crackled between the two men and Dani knew she had to diffuse it before they ended up at each other's throats.

"Stop." She stepped between them. "I don't quite understand—hell, I don't understand at all—why all of this is necessary but you two assured me that it was." Reign nodded, Jackson glared at him.

"You can just mark me the way you did her," Jackson announced.

"No. Because when we walk into that room tonight, we're declaring ourselves lovers and *these people* will see through a lie." Reign pulled back and once again crossed his arms on his chest, glaring at Jackson. "And you agreed to it, puppy."

"Fine," Jackson said, picking up Reign's challenge. "Then let's just do this." Though Jackson made the announcement, he didn't move. He looked furious and Reign wasn't far below him on the pissed off scale. His eyes did a quick scan of the room with all the enthusiasm of a death row inmate choosing his execution site.

Anger vibrated between them as Jackson moved toward the bed.

Dani held her breath. This wasn't going to work. Physically it might happen but no one was going to be happy with the result.

"Wait. Why don't you try it a different way?" Neither man responded but they didn't turn away. Now if she could just explain what she meant. "You know, instead of just fucking, try making love." Both men scoffed and Reign rolled his eyes. "You know what I mean. Kind of like what you did with me." That got their attention. "Make it sensual instead of just one body pounding into another."

Neither man looked at the other or at her. They stared at different patches of carpet.

"Let's try this. Come here." She took each of them by the hand and led them to the foot of the bed, urging them to sit on either side of her, Jackson on her right, Reign on her left. "Okay," she said after a moment. She turned her head and kissed Jackson. For a moment his lips were unresponsive, then he returned the caress, turning and matching her, his tongue whispering tiny flicks to her upper lip. She pulled back and turned to Reign. He met her, his tongue sinking immediately into her mouth, commanding a response. Breathless at the two sensual but so different kisses, she turned again to Jackson.

"Dani, it needs to be my scent on him," Reign said. "We've marked you."

She looked at him. "Tonight, when we go to this party, I'm trusting both of you to keep me safe, right?"

Both nodded.

"Then you need to trust me now."

Chapter Ten

ഌ

Reign looked like he was going to protest again but after a long pause, he nodded, once. She turned back to Jackson, offering her mouth, open. He growled at her blatant invitation and accepted, driving his tongue between her lips. Reign's teeth nipped the tight muscle right below her ear and she moaned, dragging herself away from Jackson's intoxicating kiss. She had to stay in control. For this to work, she had to keep thinking. She turned her head, holding her arm around Jackson, not letting him withdraw as she kissed Reign. She cuddled him close when it was time to pull back and turn her attention to Jackson.

A few more kisses and she'd worked them close, so close she barely had to turn to taste each man. The tension in Jackson's shoulders warned her he knew what she was up to but Reign seemed unaware. Or maybe he didn't mind.

Drugged on their kisses, she pulled her mouth away from Jackson, biting his lower lip as she retreated, knowing he would follow. He growled and pursued her, trying to capture her mouth. She moved just out of reach and with her hand at the back of his head, urged him...to Reign.

She nudged Reign forward, guiding him toward Jackson.

Then she waited, breathless. Would it work?

They were close. Their mouths only an inch away from each other. Eyes open, they stared at one another.

Jackson was the first to move. He leaned forward, just enough—a mere whisper of lips against lips, giving Reign space to run if he wanted. Dani saw the glint in his eye. He'd been prepared for an impersonal fuck. This would make it more real.

147

But he didn't retreat. He shifted, turning his head to meet Jackson. For a moment, their lips just touched, nothing more, no movement or caresses, then slowly they adjusted, tilting and sliding until their mouths fit together. She watched, unable to pull her gaze away, captivated by their strong masculine lips moving against one another.

A flicker of a tongue caught her attention. Jackson drew back—but not far. He grabbed in a quick breath and then returned his opened mouth to Reign.

Unexpected heat welled up inside her. She wanted to be a part of it, wanted more, but knew she shouldn't break up this moment. Knew she shouldn't—

She must have made some sort of sound because they pulled back, turning away from each other and looking to her.

"I don't think she likes being left out," Reign said. Laughter and heat returned to his eyes.

"No, it's not that—" Her protest was stopped by Jackson's lips on hers, Reign's mouth on her throat. She groaned and tipped her head back, trying to remember why she couldn't lie down and let them fuck her. Oh, right, they needed to fuck each other.

Gathering strength she didn't know she had, she ripped her mouth from Jackson's seductive kiss and pushed Reign back.

"Wait." Her command came out more of a plea. The fact that she was panting and somehow her robe had opened and both men had their hands inside didn't help her distraction level. Jackson eased his palm between her legs, his fingers teasing her pussy and oh, it would be so easy to just spread her legs and let them fuck her. It wouldn't take much to push Jackson over the edge.

Or Reign for that matter.

But no, she was on a mission.

She wiggled backward and after a moment's hesitation, both men let her go. She squirmed until she was lying in the middle of the bed, her robe open, her pussy displayed. Neither man stared at her tits — they were both fascinated by her cunt.

"Come here," she said, offering one hand to Jackson and the other to Reign. Without a glance toward each other, they reached for her. As they crawled up beside her, she turned so she faced Jackson. There was a method to her madness. It might drive her insane but hopefully it would accomplish what they thought needed to be done.

Reign cuddled up behind her, his cock sliding against her ass. He was hard again. So was Jackson. She wiggled a little closer, his cock bumping against her pussy. The delicate pulses rocked against her clit and she fought the pleasure.

Temptation surrounded her. The seduction intended for the men seduced her. She wanted them both, fucking her. Later. Once this was over. Holding that promise in her mind, she leaned down and kissed Jackson. He let her lead for a moment then seized control. God he tasted good. His tongue swirled around hers, teasing and tempting until she wanted to crawl inside him.

Forcing one little bit of her mind on the task at hand, she reached behind her and grabbed Reign's arm, wrapping him around her. She started him slow, guiding his hand up to her breast. His fingers slipped quickly to the tight nipple and he pinched, hard. Dani cried out and used the moment of freedom to gasp in a breath.

Lights swirled behind her closed eyes. Jackson's kiss overwhelmed her even as Reign nibbled on her neck. Heat pulsed inside her pussy and she rolled her hips forward, rocking against Jackson's erection. He groaned and shifted, sliding his cock between her legs. Oh, that's what she wanted, wanted him inside her, but no, she had to do this. She picked up Reign's wandering hand and guided it, sliding it down her hip and forward — onto Jackson's thigh.

Tension crackled in the air and Jackson pulled back from their kiss...but she didn't let go. Her hand on his, she eased Reign into the caress, leading him up Jackson's side, across his ribs, the tight muscles straining with the first light strokes. She let her fingers skim along beside Reign's, soothing until Jackson relaxed. Then she let go and waited, meeting Jackson's piercing stare. He watched her as Reign's hand paused and then began a slow return stroke, his fingers brushing Jackson's skin. For a long time, there was no other movement besides Reign's hand on Jackson, both men adapting to the caress.

Vaguely aware that time was passing, she leaned forward, urging Jackson onto his back. She rolled with him, pausing on top, savoring the heat of his body beneath hers, letting him feel her, before she slipped onto the other side, leaving Jackson between her and Reign. As she lay beside him, she offered her mouth, hoping Reign would follow her lead.

One long drugging kiss later, she forced herself to retreat. After being fucked so well, it should have been impossible to want more, but she did. The tastes and scents combined inside her to make her pussy clench, aching to be filled. Dragging in a harsh breath, she leaned away, opening the space between Jackson and Reign.

Nothing happened. The two men stared at each other, each waiting for the other to give in.

Seconds passed and Dani's heart sank. It hadn't worked. She'd just wanted to add a little heat to their practical necessity. But it had failed.

Then Reign moved.

Jackson stared at the male above him, over him. He clenched his hand into a fist and fought the instinctive urge to rise up, to conquer instead of submit. Not sure how he'd found himself in this position, he silenced the demands of his pride and waited. Waited.

The anger in his chest was subsiding. Despite his attraction to Reign, when the moment had come and Reign had explained he intended to fuck him, Jackson had lost it. Probably not for the reasons Reign and Dani believed. Jackson might have been able to go through with it if Reign had kept it clinical but the damn Cat hadn't been able to resist teasing Jackson about taking it up the ass. Almost like he'd wanted Jackson pissed.

Dani had managed to calm them down but was this really going to work? He took a breath, ready to tell Reign they'd figure out something else, but before the words could make it from his brain, Reign leaned down and brushed his mouth across Jackson's. They'd kissed moments ago. This was different. This was freely offered—a prelude to fucking.

He couldn't believe he was going to do this. He was going to let Reign fuck him. To actually have him penetrate his ass. The wolf in his head didn't rebel. The damn thing practically purred, urging Jackson to take more.

Letting the animal's instinct lead him, he turned his head and opened his lips, offering Reign a taste. He hesitated, just a moment, before he pushed his tongue inside.

Jackson crushed a groan before it could escape. He closed his eyes and fell into the kiss. It was different from kissing a woman. Reign was used to being in charge of a kiss. He stroked his tongue, commanding Jackson's submission. For a moment, Jackson let the other male take the lead, matching his licks and caresses. The wolf rebelled, wanting Reign's mouth but hating the passive nature.

Delicious wet heat pressed against Jackson's thigh and more warmth slid across his chest, tickling his nipple. It took him a moment to catalog the sensations—Dani's pussy draped across his leg, her mouth on his chest. Reign drew back. Jackson pushed up, chasing him, missing the male's taste as he pulled away. Reign smiled—arrogant bastard—and returned long enough to bite Jackson's lower lip, trailing away with a fast lick to the same place.

Jackson waited, almost expecting Reign to grab the lube and get this moving but the Cat, like Jackson, seemed willing to go where Dani led. And she wasn't finished with the seduction just yet.

She pushed herself up, her breasts teasing Jackson's chest, her pussy pressing down on his hip. Her heat covered his skin as she leaned across him, offering her mouth to Reign.

Jackson watched as they kissed, their lips and tongues blending and retreating. Again his wolf's reaction surprised him, growling low, not in anger, in hunger. He licked his lips, wanting to be part of the sexual kiss.

Dani retreated, leading Reign down. She placed another hot kiss on Jackson's chest. Reign watched for a moment then mimicked her caress. Jackson hissed as they both kissed and licked, their hands and mouths teasing his skin. He closed his eyes but that made it worse. God, the erotic anticipation of never knowing when, where the next stroke would come made his eyes roll back.

He lifted his head and watched. Dani's black hair spilled across his chest, teasing his skin as her tongue trailed down his pecs. Reign, blond and male. His strokes came harsh, biting caresses to the tight lines of Jackson's stomach, just enough pain to make him want more.

Reign's eyes were closed — either he was totally into this or he was imagining that he was fucking a woman.

As if he heard Jackson's thought, Reign looked up, meeting Jackson's stare. Fire flowed from the male's eyes and he bent down scraping his teeth across Jackson's skin, leaving a red streak.

His cock twitched — hell, the damn thing had been hard all day, even fucking Dani hadn't been enough to ease it. Now this.

Slim sleek fingers curled around his shaft and Jackson moaned. Reign's eyes widened then he turned and looked, watching as Dani slid her hand up and down Jackson's cock. Feeling strangely like an observer, though his cock was throbbing in her hand, he couldn't pull his eyes away from the scene before him.

Dani looked at Reign as she placed the tip of her tongue along the underside of the head and licked. Heat shot through Jackson's cock and he grabbed whatever was near. His right hand gripped the blankets. His left hand landed on Reign's back. The male didn't seem to mind the sharp bite of nails into his skin.

Reign watched Dani's tongue trail up Jackson's cock and licked his lips. He knew where this was leading. In moments, Dani was going to pull back, offer that thick erection for Reign's mouth. He'd fucked guys before—not often but he'd done it—just quick hard ass fucking usually during a Clowder. Never had he considered sucking another man's dick. Except seeing Dani's mouth on Jax—yeah, he wanted that. Something about the wolf made him want to do more than an impersonal fuck up the ass—which was probably why he'd been such a dick about it—but he wanted Jackson's cock in his mouth, wanted to know what it was like to lick the long, hard shaft.

Even as he thought it, Dani eased back, her lips wet, her eyes hazy with lust. She blinked as if to remind herself they had another purpose and looked at him, asking him to join her. Knowing what she expected, he hesitated, not quite ready to let the wolf know how much he wanted this. He leaned forward and flicked his tongue out, one tentative lick up the side of Jackson's cock. The reaction that shot through the male's body was subtle, a mere tightening of his thighs, a soft hiss. Damn, he could do better than that. Tasting Dani as he licked, Reign tried to remember what he liked when others sucked his cock. He bent his head lower and lapped at the base of his shaft, teasing the spot before he moved up, flattening his tongue against the thick rod and slowly working his way to the head.

This time, Jackson's response was less controlled. His hips pushed up, a convulsive thrust that Reign recognized. He lifted his head and smiled at Dani.

"I think he likes this."

She nodded.

"Help me." It seemed easier, more natural to have Dani joining him. She leaned forward, licking her tongue out, a kitten's stroke to Jackson's cock. The sight drew a groan from Reign. He could practically feel her mouth on his dick. He stretched over and kissed her, enjoying the way her flavor mixed with Jackson's.

Dani let his kiss linger then drew back, leaving him to face Jackson's cock on his own. Reign thought about every woman who'd ever sucked him off and tried to recreate the sensations. He slid his hand between Jackson's legs and cupped his balls, squeezing lightly. Another male would recognize the threat. Jackson groaned and froze, as if waiting to see what Reign had planned.

He had this male in his hands. Power and pleasure zipped through his skin and he opened his mouth, accepting just the thick head of Jackson's erection. That earned him a grunt and another shallow thrust of Jackson's hips. Reign smiled as he pulled back and went to work, determined to drive Jackson crazy.

He wasn't sure when he realized that Dani had shifted away—and he was alone, sucking Jackson's cock. He'd been lost in the sensation and taste, fascinated by Jackson's responses and the way Reign controlled them with little licks or long strokes. He'd learned that Jackson liked having his balls squeezed, harder than Reign would have imagined. And loved it when Reign rubbed his tongue on the underside of the head.

Jackson moaned and rocked his hips up in a restrained thrust. Reign lifted his head. Dani's leg was curled up, her knee resting on Jackson's stomach, leaving her pussy open and visible. His cock twitched wanting to invade that tight hole. Dani lay half across Jackson's chest, their mouths fused in hot, deep tongue kisses.

A wicked part of his mind protested that his efforts were so casually dismissed. He opened his lips and pushed down, sinking half of Jackson's cock deep into his mouth. Jackson cried out and arched, punching his shaft a little farther. The head hit the back of Reign's throat and he almost choked but he fought the sensation, pulling back, sucking, maybe just a little too hard, as he retreated.

"Oh fuck." Jackson's groan filled the room and Reign resisted the desire to smile. He had Jackson's attention. And he understood why women found such power in sucking a man's cock. He eased Jackson's dick back into his mouth, a little slower this time, beginning a distinctive rhythm, designed to make him come.

Jackson grabbed at the sheets below his hips, not allowing his fingers to sink into Reign's hair. Fuck, it felt good. He could tell that Reign hadn't done this before—or if he had, it hadn't been often—but intent and energy made up for special skills and Reign was intent on making Jackson come.

"I like watching you," Dani whispered against his ear. She rubbed her hand across Jackson's chest, her fingertips teasing his nipples, flicking the hard tiny peaks. "It's so hot watching your cock slide in and out of his mouth." She bit his earlobe and Jackson groaned. Her words floated in and out of his head, his mind centered on the hot mouth working his cock. "Don't fight it, baby." She snuggled closer, pressing her breasts against his chest, rubbing her tight nipples across his skin. "Come." She brushed kisses across his jaw. "Come in his mouth." As she whispered her command, she covered Jackson's lips with her own, a strong sexual kiss.

Jackson's senses overloaded. The scent and taste of Dani, Reign's powerful sucking and the wickedly sexual atmosphere combined and consumed him. Jackson grabbed the back of Reign's head and held him in place as he pushed his cock up, meeting Reign's downward thrust. His wolf howled and Jackson's cock released, pouring his cum down Reign's throat. A quiet voice in the back of his head tried to warn him it was wrong, he shouldn't be doing this, that he never came without a condom, but God, he couldn't pull away.

He came back to himself to feel Dani's hot tongue licking his throat, nuzzling her face into his shoulder, soothing him. His muscles began to function again and he cupped the back of her head and pulled her up to his mouth needing her taste. After a too-short kiss, she leaned back, her eyes encouraging, almost sympathetic. Fuck, it was time to, well, get fucked.

He looked down his body and saw Reign standing beside the bed, his eyes serious, his body holding a tension that hadn't been there moments ago. The sexual fun atmosphere that Dani had worked to create had thinned to an almost unbreathable space.

Swallowing deeply, Jackson did what he had to do. He rolled over onto his stomach. He knew he needed to assume the position but everything in his being rebelled at the thought. Well, his body wasn't rebelling. It was anticipating. His cock began to harden again and his back was aching with the need to arch, to present himself to the man who would fuck him. It was his mind that tried to reject it.

He would never be the Alpha wolf like his brother Mikhel but he'd never considered himself submissive. And the thought of being topped by another male, and *a Cat*, sent his instincts into high fight or flight response. But he'd agreed to this and he knew it needed to be done.

Sensing the energy coming from his lovers… *Fuck, Reign is already your lover, the man sucked you off. You can do this. Do it.*

The mental pep talk gave him the strength and he pushed his hips up, opened his knees and lowered his head to his elbows.

Dani's fingers drifted across his back and the scent of her cunt filled his head as she snuggled closer, pressing her body to his side, silent support.

Hot rough hands slid down his back, joining Dani's delicate caresses. God, Jackson wanted to hate it, his mind thought he should, but damn, Reign's hands felt good on his skin. Without looking he knew when Reign crawled onto the bed, kneeling behind Jackson.

A cool, slick finger teased his rear entrance and Jackson had to force himself not to flinch.

Reign took his time, easing his fingertip around the tight hole, then slowly pressing forward, just a shallow penetration until he felt Jackson's body ease and accept him. He drew back and added a second finger, keeping his movements as gentle as he could. The tight squeeze made him want to groan but he swallowed the sound. They were doing this for a reason. He shouldn't be this into it but fuck, he wanted to drill Jackson's ass, wanted to feel that tight hole around his cock. Reign licked his lips, remembering the almost sweet taste of Jackson's cum. It hadn't tasted at all like Reign had expected. It had been good and he wanted more.

The thought jolted him and he thrust his fingers in. Jackson tensed at the heavy penetration and Reign mentally apologized. He didn't say the words aloud, afraid that if he did, he'd explain what had distracted him and telling another man he liked the taste of his cum was a bit too much for his brain. Still, he didn't want to hurt Jackson.

Dani lifted her head and stared at him—her eyes glittering, warning him to go slow. He nodded, sending his apology to her. That seemed to satisfy her and she kissed Jackson's shoulder. The tiny caress had a remarkable effect on the wolf's body. Muscles relaxed, the grip on Reign's fingers eased just a bit.

"That's it, kitten. Distract him." He chuckled, unable to resist teasing the wolf just a little. "It will give him something to think about besides my cock sliding in and out of his ass."

Jackson lifted his head and glared at the Cat. Reign laughed again and Jackson knew he was doing it deliberately.

"Just get on with it," Jackson commanded, needing to move this along.

The sound of a bottle opening grabbed his attention and Jackson fought the instinctive tension. So far, he'd been able to take it but he knew Reign's dick was a lot thicker than the fingers that he'd pushed inside him. He eased his grip on the sheets beneath him, feeling the tips of his fingers ache as his claws threatened to return. He'd already torn Dani's wallpaper. No need to destroy her sheets as well.

The thought had barely left his mind when the broad head of Reign's cock pressed against his opening and Jackson tensed.

"Relax, man. We'll take it slow."

He took a deep breath and allowed his body to follow Reign's instruction.

Heat, pain and wicked pleasure emanated from the slow penetration.

"That's it." Warm hands ran over his hips, easing him. Reign's voice crept inside him, teasing his cock like a caress. "Fuck, that's good. Let me in." As he spoke, he pushed deeper. The burning overwhelmed the pleasure for just a moment. "Almost there, Jax, you can take me." It was a lover's voice, a lover's call.

"Yes." Jackson took a deep breath and tried to relax. Reign slid in a little deeper, going slow, letting Jackson's body adapt to each stretching inch until Reign's groin was pressed against Jackson's ass and his cock was buried inside.

Jackson grunted, feeling stuffed and wondering vaguely why anyone—man or woman—enjoyed this. Then Reign pulled back. The sensation sent pleasure shivering up his spine. Okay, that was a little better. His body resisted again as Reign thrust back into him but it was easier the second time.

Jackson dug his elbows into the mattress and shifted, pushing his ass back as Reign came forward. Both men groaned as his groin hit Jackson's ass.

Reign continued to move, keeping his thrusts slow and steady. So slow Jackson wasn't sure the man would be able to come like this. He wiggled his hips and Reign groaned. The next penetration was harder and rocked against a point inside

Jackson. The unexpected jolt drew a gasp from his throat. A lightning shiver zipped up his spine.

"Oh fuck," he moaned, his cheek pressed against the cool sheet. "Do that again."

Reign froze. "What? This?" He repeated the thrust and hit that place again.

"Fuck yes. Right there." He tipped his ass, trying to guide Reign's strokes. Now he understood why guys did this. Oh, damn, that felt good. His cock was hard again and he moved against Reign, driving him a little harder each time.

Reign seemed to understand and picked up the pace and pressure. Fingers gripped his hips, holding him in place, forcing him to be still while Reign fucked him. Jackson's instincts resisted the show of dominance but he couldn't fight the pleasure.

"Dani, help me, baby."

For a moment Jackson didn't understand Reign's request. His mind was locked on the cock sliding in and out of his ass and the wicked pleasure jolting him each time Reign nailed that place deep inside him.

Dani shifted, easing her body away from his. He regretted the loss of her heat but seconds later her slim fingers gripped his cock and began to pump.

The dual caresses—to his dick and his ass—were almost too much. He fought the need to come, wanting to feel it just a little longer. But his body and his lovers had different opinions. Reign continued his solid thrusts, not too hard, just enough that Jackson knew he would feel this later.

Dani's fingers found the perfect beat matching the steady fucking in his ass. Jackson groaned, unable to decide which he needed to fuck more—the hand curled around his cock or the shaft sliding into his ass. He tried to move but Reign held him in place.

"Fuck, come on, man. You gotta come," the Cat groaned, breathless, his hips still working the rhythm. "Just let it go."

Jackson tried to ignore Reign's command but his body gave it up. It felt so fucking good.

"Come on, baby," Dani whispered. Her words were that final caress he needed. The orgasm jolted through his cock and slammed into his gut, the hot spurts of his cum pulsing from his dick and slipping through Dani's fingers.

"Oh fuck!"

His orgasm seemed to trigger Reign's and the Cat slammed into him one final time. A long loud roar ripped from his throat as he held himself locked in Jackson's ass, pouring his cum inside.

Jackson's arms gave out and he collapsed forward, drawing flat out on the mattress, his body drained, his mind fuzzy. Vaguely he became aware of low voices and a warm wet cloth wiping across his skin, cleaning away the traces of lube and cum.

Dani stretched out next to him, her fingers scraping back the front strands of his hair.

"How you doing?" she asked, her voice low and concerned. She had to be confused by all this but she seemed to trust him and Reign enough go along with it. And the scent of her arousal told him she wasn't freaked out by what she'd seen. She'd liked it.

He blinked his eyes open and looked up. Did he tell her that he'd enjoyed it? Or continue with the freaked out, homophobic attitude he was sure she expected?

"I'm good," he said, knowing his satisfaction flowed through his words. In the background he heard water running, Reign cleaning up. Jackson shifted. He was going to need to rinse off as well. Wearing Reign's scent was one thing—smelling like a brothel was another. "How about you?" he asked, rolling to his side and rubbing the ends of Dani's hair between his fingertips.

She blushed but nodded. "I'm good. That was—" She shook her head. "Wow."

"Yeah." He wrapped his hand around her back and pulled her forward, cuddling her body close. Dani allowed the gentle manhandling, sliding her knee between his and tipping her head back, giving him access to those perfect lips.

Something shifted inside him, soothing him, calming him. The wild fuck from Reign had been, well, wild, but this — this connection — tugged on his heart.

Reign stepped out of the bathroom and looked at his lovers — oh, he hadn't technically fucked Dani yet but he didn't doubt that moment would come. Sooner rather than later if he had his way.

And he'd sure as hell fucked Jackson. His cock twitched at the physical memory of sliding into that tight hole. And the sheer power of it — to have that strong body beneath his, submitting in such a fundamental way.

He walked closer to the bed. They lay on their sides, facing each other, cuddled close, whispering. The intimacy between them could have excluded him but Dani's shy smile as he approached welcomed him.

The problem came with deciding which body to snuggle up to. His instincts told him to slide in behind Dani, let his cock slip between her ass cheeks. It would put her luscious tits within easy reach.

But then he thought about it. Dani had been right — it had to be more than just one body pounding into another. Reign smiled. And wouldn't it freak Jackson out to be cuddled by a man?

Reign crawled up from the end of the bed and lay down behind Jackson, moving close, letting hot flesh meet hot flesh. Jackson tensed but the strain lasted only a moment and the intuitive sensuality seemed to allow the caress of Reign's skin against his.

"You okay, baby?" Reign asked his voice filled with mock sympathy. He placed a chaste kiss on Jackson's shoulder. He followed it up with a sharp kitten bite that elicited a grunt. "I hope I didn't hurt you." As he spoke he petted the male's hip, teasing him with the possibility of wrapping his fingers around Jackson's cock.

Dani looked up, her eyes twinkling with barely contained laughter. Jackson growled and shook his head. "I'd watch yourself, Cat. Paybacks are a bitch."

"I can handle it. I'm a big boy."

"I *know*."

Laughter trickled out of Dani's lips and dragged a chuckle from Reign. He dropped his head onto Jackson's shoulder and put his arm around the other male, hugging him.

The little bit of teasing changed things between them. Reign lifted his head and realized he'd been kissing Jackson's neck. Real kisses, meant for pure pleasure—given and received. Jackson had tipped his head giving Reign the space he needed.

Reign looked up and saw Dani's knowing gaze—as if she saw and understood the strange vibe that passed through the men. It wasn't like Reign didn't want to fuck her. He did, but damn, he wanted Jackson too. He licked his lips, unable to stop himself, remembering Jackson's cock pushing into his mouth. It had been strange and seductive—having a man's pleasure so much in his power. He wanted that again. Wanted to feel that power again.

And then damn, he wanted to fuck Dani.

Reign purred low and long—his Cat nature overwhelming the human attitudes, seeking pleasure from both people. Though his Cat wasn't a separate creature like Jackson's wolf, the Cat genes tended to strengthen during intense moments and right now, Reign's Cat side didn't understand why Reign couldn't just fuck. Now. Again. All night. He had to remind himself that he had a bigger mission than sex.

He looked at the clock and sighed. Time to think like a cop.

"The car will be here in forty-five minutes." Hating to lose Jackson's heat, Reign started to roll away.

"Wait." Dani's voice stopped him. She lifted her upper body and try as he might, sexual harassment training or not, he couldn't not look at her tits. Of course, in sexual harassment training they never used a woman like her as an example—at least not a naked one.

He didn't need to look down to know Jackson was staring at her tits as well.

The Cat inside him purred and his mouth watered. Yes, he could have her. Suckle those pretty tits and then fuck her. Slide into the wet heat he could smell.

Reign shook his head and blinked, hoping the interruption of his sight would give him a chance to focus—on something besides her tits. It helped. A bit.

"We need to go." There was no time for more fucking because if they started again, he wasn't going to stop until he was inside her.

"This won't take long." A hint of steel bracketed Dani's voice, warning she wasn't going to be denied. She nudged Jackson's shoulder like she wanted him on his back. As he started to roll over, Reign realized how close he'd been to Jackson—close enough that his cock had slipped between his legs.

Their three bodies shifted until Jackson lay flat on his back, Reign rested beside him and then there was Dani. She crawled on top of Jackson, her naked pussy spread against his rib cage.

Reign gulped and tried to find his voice.

"Uh, honey, we don't really have time for you to—"

She shook her head. Defiance and a blatant challenge flashed in her eyes and Reign was smart enough to concede.

"I just thought..." Dani said as she slowly spun her hips in a circle. Heat followed the movement and Reign wanted to scream. "That since you've both marked me." She pressed forward her knees and started to hump the hard muscles of Jackson's stomach. The scent was incredible—pure aroused woman.

Reign saw Jackson lick his lips and knew both males were hungry for the hot liquid dripping from her cunt.

"I thought it was only fair—" Breathless she took a moment. "Only fair that you wear my scent as well."

She pressed and swirled, marking Jackson's stomach with her pussy juices, leaving hot trails to brand themselves into Jackson's skin.

Jackson growled and grabbed her ass like he was planning to lift her up and impale her on his cock, but she pulled back, easing her hips up and out of his grip.

Reign sensed the impulse in Jackson—to grab her and fuck her, claim her no matter what she said—but both were too civilized to do that. Jackson released his hold on her ass and she smiled.

"I like the idea of you wearing my scent," she whispered against Jackson's mouth. After a long leisurely kiss that made Reign's balls ache, she pulled back. "And you..." She turned her lust-filled gaze to Reign and he thought he'd come right there. "You need to be marked as well."

He tensed—not sure he had the restraint Jackson had shown. If she tried to mount him like that, he was going to fuck her—and they'd never get to this stupid party.

Dani didn't move toward him. Instead, she slipped her hand between her legs, her fingers dipping into her slit. She moaned as she moved against her own touch, a few discreet pumps into her cunt, then she removed her hand. Her pussy juices coated her skin. She reached out and placed one finger on Reign's stomach and slowly began to trace a pattern. Light glinted off the slick juices on his skin as she burned her name into his flesh. Pausing to dot the "I" at the end, she looked up and smiled — wicked and feminine.

"Now, they'll know you belong to me."

With that announcement, she leaned down and kissed Jackson. Reign watched, wanting his turn. She sat up, though it was obvious Jackson was reluctant to lose her, and crawled over Reign, granting him a slow, sexual kiss before she moved away.

"I guess I'll go get ready."

She slipped off the bed and disappeared into the bathroom.

Reign collapsed back onto the bed, his heart pounding and his breathing fast and shallow.

"I think I'm in love," he muttered.

"Me too," Jackson agreed.

The two males lifted their heads and stared at each other.

"Fuck," they said in unison.

Chapter Eleven

ॐ

"You can't be serious." Dani stared at Jackson but he didn't move, didn't react. Didn't laugh and say it was all a joke. "Have you seen what I'm wearing?" She pointed to the skimpy outfit hanging on her closet door. There wasn't much to it. The dress was fire-engine red, glittered and would cover her ass but just barely. The top was a halter top that dipped low between her breasts. Her breasts would be free to sway and move with every step she took. Since they were going to this event as an upscale party crowd, the outfit was perfect, sexy and exotic.

Which made Jackson's request even more insane.

"You want me to wear granny panties underneath that outfit?"

"Yes."

She looked at the underwear Jackson held in his hands. They were pale yellow and almost full briefs. The legs were cut a little high but the waistband would land right at her waist and everything would be fully covered. What was sexy about these?

"They aren't even mine." At least she didn't think she had anything that ugly in her drawers.

"Yes they are. I told you I would replace the ones from last night."

She squinted and glared. "And you bought granny panties?"

He nodded.

"Jackson..."

Reign stepped out of the bathroom rubbing his hair dry with a towel. Another towel hung low around his waist, leaving his chest bare and so delectable she wanted to run her tongue across the distinct lines of his muscles. Heat swelled into her pussy and she pressed her lips together to crush a groan.

"You're supposed to be getting dressed."

Surely Reign would be an ally in this.

"Reign, you decide. Jackson wants me to wear those—" She pointed to the frumpy yellow underpants. "When we go out tonight." Knowing she had to tip the scales in her favor, she picked up the pair of panties she'd been planning to wear. "I want to wear these." She stretched the waistband and showed the sexy lace confection. Barely there, the panties hung on her hips and were cut high, leaving large amounts of skin uncovered.

Reign's eyes tightened and he looked at both pairs of underwear. Then he looked at her. "Are you planning on showing anyone your panties tonight?"

She scoffed. "No."

The eyebrows on both men rose and they stared pointedly at her.

"Well, except for you two."

"And we already know that your pussy is gorgeous. Wear those." He nodded to the pair Jackson was holding. Dani felt her mouth drop open. "If something does happen and your skirt gets flipped up, no one can see your pretty cunt."

Jackson didn't say anything but he nodded and held out the panties—not giving them to her, but opening them. With a sigh, she leaned one hand on his shoulder and lifted her right foot, stepping into the silky material. He supported her while she put her leg through the other hole but she never got a chance to pull the waistband up. He did that, sliding them up until the high band slid around her waist.

Warmth followed the path of his hands as he ran his palms over the whole area covered by the silk—down her ass, across her stomach and down between her legs, cupping her pussy. He placed a kiss on her neck.

"This belongs to us, baby." She shivered at the possessive tone. She wasn't sure if he even recognized that he'd claimed her pussy for both men. "Only we get to see it."

He stroked his fingers along the top of her mound, sliding down until he held her in his palm. Heat rushed into her sex.

"Jax, get your hand off her pussy," Reign said as he dragged his trousers on.

Jackson just raised his eyebrows.

"Why?"

"Because if you don't, you two will end up fucking again and we'll never get out of here."

Dani giggled. It was insane. She'd just done wild, sexy things with two guys, neither whom she knew very well. And she was going to a party to point out a murderer.

She should be completely freaked out. Instead, she felt like laughing. Somehow with Jackson's strength and Reign's power around her, she felt safe. And sexy. She didn't let herself imagine for a moment that this was a permanent thing—somehow she couldn't imagine either man accepting both men in her bed—but it had been fun, sexual and she liked the idea that, at least for tonight, they belonged to her.

"Get dressed, baby. We've got to go."

Jackson's prodding sent her into action. She spun out of his arms and grabbed the dress she planned to wear. With the high panties on, she couldn't feel any of the silky skirt against her skin. That had been one of her favorite things about this outfit. Well, that and the reactions she got when she wore it.

Knowing that she wasn't going to win this battle and she was the one who'd asked Reign to decide, she turned her back to Reign and Jackson and let the robe fall to the ground. Both men continued to get dressed themselves but she knew they watched. She grabbed her top and slipped the thin strap around her neck, adjusting the front over her breasts. The tight peaks of her nipples immediately appeared, pressing against the silk.

Her guys would to love that. She reached behind her and tied the straps that kept the front panel in place. She bent forward, feeling her skirt pull up, hoping the granny panties didn't show, and slipped her feet into her red four-inch heels. With the added height, she'd be almost as tall as Reign and Jackson. Their cocks would fit perfectly against her pussy.

A new rush of moisture flooded her sex and her pussy clenched. Her fingers fluttered with the need to reach into her panties and touch herself. She drew in a long slow inhale and released it.

Finally she turned around. Jackson and Reign stood side by side—light and dark.

Her knees weakened at the hunger she recognized in their eyes. She also felt a surge of power. These two men—strong, powerful, sexual animals—were captivated by her. As a unit, they started forward, stalking her. Her pussy trembled with the need to be fucked but she knew it couldn't happen.

"Wait." She held up one hand. Both men jerked to a stop, heat flashing in their eyes. Neither man responded well to commands. "Isn't it getting late?"

They paused and for a moment it looked like they were going to ignore her. Reign nodded, his eyes going dark.

"She's right. Let's go." The words came out hard and crisp. All cop.

The three of them headed downstairs.

"I've called for a car," Reign warned as they approached Dani's front door. "From the minute we get inside the limo, we'll be observed." Dani nodded then followed Reign's stare. His focus was trained on Jackson. Jackson grimaced and nodded as well.

"I get it."

"These people aren't going to like having you there in the first place so don't do anything that gives them the idea we aren't lovers."

"I *got* it."

The delicious sexual tension from moments ago had evaporated in a heartbeat and pure tension remained. Would she be able to recognize this guy if she saw him again? Maybe that was why she hadn't been able to help the sketch artist. *What if we went to all this trouble and I don't recognize him?*

"Then we'll have had a night of really hot sex," Reign whispered against her ear.

She jerked and looked at Reign. He smiled. Oops, she'd said that out loud.

"Don't worry, kitten, you'll be fine." He placed a quick kiss on her lips. "Just remember, when we get there, stay by me or Jackson and under no circumstances approach this guy. And don't drink—"

"She gets it, Reign. Chill." Jackson grabbed her hand and pulled her out the open door. She breathed deep, not realizing how claustrophobic she'd been feeling. Jackson was right. She was starting to panic just a little.

Jackson locked the door behind them and led the way down the path to the parking lot and the waiting limousine. The driver nodded as he came around to open the back door. Trying to keep her breath steady, hoping it would calm her heart, which had decided to start racing, she focused on the sleek lines of the limo, the discreet black shine of the paint.

The door opened and she bent forward, raising one leg to climb into the back of the car, knowing there was no elegant way to get into a limo.

A low, snarling growl rumbled from behind her and she froze, pausing for just a heartbeat before she looked over her shoulder. Jackson stood almost behind her, his eyes glowing red as he stared at her ass.

And she realized her skirt had ridden up.

Needing something to break the tension, to ease the strain in her chest, she wiggled, sliding her skirt a little higher until the elastic edge of her granny panties showed.

The growl deepened until Jackson's words were almost unrecognizable.

"Get in the car."

Fighting a giggle, she climbed inside and crawled to the far side of the cabin. Jackson entered after her, his face a dark glower. Wow, where had the gentleman who opened her car door gone? He'd disappeared and been replaced by this powerful, dominant lover. But somehow the sense of safety remained.

Reign climbed in, nudging Jackson over. Dani sat in the corner, stretching her legs out in front of her, letting her skirt sit high on her thighs.

Jackson growled and she could have sworn she heard Reign snarl.

She chuckled quietly to herself. Oh, this was going to be a fun evening.

The drive across town was mainly silent. On Jackson's part, that was because if he said anything it would be to tell the driver to turn around so they could drag Dani's ass back into the house and fuck her until she knew better than to tease a wolf. And a Cat.

Remembering what Reign had said about them being observed from the time they climbed into the car, Jackson slid his hand around Dani's hip and pulled her close, shifting her so her knee rested on his and her ass was in his hand. Teasing her just a bit, he slipped his finger under her skirt and scraped his fingernail across the elastic of her panties.

Dani's eyes flashed with irritation and Jackson chuckled. Reign reached over and lifted Dani's hand off Jackson's and carried it to his lips, biting down on the tip of her finger before sucking it into his mouth.

Hmm. Reign and Dani. Lovers. This was something he needed to consider. He'd never heard of a werewolf who shared his mate. He glanced at the woman next to him, her smile making him want to kiss the smirk off her lips. She would be a good mate. Strong, sexual. Loving.

His family was going to love her. Well, once they got over the fact that he'd taken Max's woman. That thought put a bit of a damper on his future plans but before he could think about it too long, the car pulled to a stop.

"We're here," Reign announced quietly.

Jackson pushed away all the shit going through his head — the future and mates and why he considered Dani his mate yet accepted Reign fucking her — that would all have to wait. Now he needed to focus on Dani and protecting her.

The driver came around and opened the door. Reign climbed out, Jackson followed and they both turned to help Dani from the car. She slid across the bench seat until her feet hung out the door, the hem of her tight skirt riding up, high. Pale yellow panties appeared beneath the glittering red material that was supposed to be covering her ass. She paused, as if giving them a moment to look.

Dani put one foot on the ground and eased herself to standing, taking their arms and stopping between them.

"Oops." Her eyes widened and were as innocent as a Siren's.

Reign growled.

She patted his chest, like a woman calming a big dog — or Cat as it were. "Good thing I'm wearing those granny panties," she said, her voice lazy and teasing.

"Good thing." Jackson couldn't stop his laughter. She might have conceded to wearing the panties but she was clearly letting them know it had been her decision in the end.

"Let's go," Reign commanded, taking Dani's hand and leading her forward.

Jackson followed, scanning the building entrance as he walked forward. This was it. He was entering a Clowder. He'd never known a wolf to attend one of these Cat gatherings. Too dangerous. Rumors abounded in the wolf world. The tales always ended with the wolf disappearing and a warning to young wolves to stay away from the Cats.

Reign nodded to the doorman standing in the elevator lobby. The guy seemed to recognize Reign and pressed the call button. A line of humans waited extending around the lobby, all eager to be allowed access to the club. Jackson shook his head. No daughter of his would ever end up at a Cat party.

The thought created a flurry in his brain. First that he would have a daughter. He looked at Dani. They hadn't discussed anything so forward thinking as children. Hell, she didn't even know she was sleeping with a werewolf. And a Cat. And God knew what their children would be.

Fuck. Jackson clenched his fingers into a fist. None of it made sense and really he didn't have time for this now. It was times like these he wished he was more like Max. Max was great at focusing on the present.

Reign turned and looked at Jackson as he approached. He raised his eyebrows as if to ask if everything was cool. Jackson nodded. Everything was fine. He just needed to pay attention to tonight and later, tomorrow or the next day he'd worry about the future.

He moved in close, standing a little behind and between Dani and Reign. Heat radiated from the Cat's body and the wolf's nature was to snuggle up to anything warm.

Jackson didn't want to cage the wolf in his brain. He needed the animal's instincts but he also needed to be able to think. He mentally nudged the wolf and waited for the elevator to open.

Dani looked around, her eyes hopping from the bouncer to the crowd. She started to turn. Jackson grabbed her arm and stopped her, pulling her close. Reign crowded in as well.

"Everything's okay," Jackson whispered. He pressed his lips against her ear hoping to muffle the sound so the Cat working the door didn't hear. "Reign and I have it covered. Trust us."

She gave a slow nod and licked her lips. Reign moaned beside them and Jackson understood the sound.

The elevators opened and the bouncer waved them onboard.

Dani took one bracing breath which Jackson didn't think anyone would notice and stepped inside.

Reign followed and Jackson went in last. They formed a little group in the corner.

The elevator closed and Reign turned, curling his body toward Jackson's. Even knowing he needed to keep up the pretense, Jackson resisted for just a moment then he relaxed into the embrace leaning in, clamping his lips down on Reign's, taking the opportunity to control the kiss. He could feel Reign's urge to fight, but after a tense moment, he opened his mouth and accepted Jackson's tongue. Their groans became real as they moved closer, hips pressing against each other.

The elevator rose smoothly, taking them closer to danger. Jackson lifted his head, fighting the lust and fog that threatened. Reign's eyes burned with a matching need. Jackson glanced at Dani. She stood, locked against Reign's body, her eyes focused on their lips.

"Feeling left out, baby?" he asked, bending down and taking her mouth in a long drugging kiss, amazed at the way her taste blended with Reign's perfectly, making it a powerful temptation. Addictive.

It was like hot chocolate and whipped cream. Each good alone. Incredible when mixed together.

The door chime announced their arrival and Jackson forced himself to leave the seduction of Dani's mouth, pleased to see she looked a little unfocused when he pulled away. Good. He liked knowing he wasn't the only one on the edge.

"Let's go, boys and girls."

* * * * *

Reign took a deep breath and stepped off the elevator. He didn't much like being in the lead, preferred to take up the rear, watch for covert attacks but tonight he'd have to leave that to Jackson. The first scent off that elevator had to be Cat, particularly when a wolf was accompanying him.

The club manager was there to greet him. He smiled when he saw Reign, greed glittering in his eyes as he bowed his head in welcome.

It wasn't often Reign hit the clubs. And usually those nights when he did appear, he was in need, *heavy* need, of entertainment. He'd been willing to pay well for PussyCats able to take his cock for the night.

The manager sniffed the air and the edges of his mouth bent down and his nostrils stretched long, as if something foul had been left to die at his feet.

"Good evening, sir." He looked over Reign's shoulder. "I see you've brought...guests — " The word was more curse than welcome. "With you tonight."

Reign tipped his head back and looked down. "Yes. Friends. Good friends." He didn't look away, drilling the manager with every ounce of menace he possessed. "I wouldn't be happy if anything happened to them."

The threat was more than implied and definitely received. He could see the manager's throat work as he gulped.

"Of course, sir. Any friend *of yours* is welcome."

"That's what I want to hear." He glanced around the room. "Table?"

"Yes, sir. We have one in the front." He waved toward the dance floor. Reign didn't even bother to react. "Or we have a lovely place right over there along the wall."

"Better. We'll go there."

He didn't even look to see if Jackson and Dani followed. He had to trust that Jax understood Cat politics. The Cat led, others followed. A low rumble spread through the room as they wove through the tables. It would be common knowledge within moments that a wolf was in their midst. Reign would be ostracized for fucking a dog for a while but Cats had short memories. Hell, they'd probably never know he was doing it to save them from addiction and death.

The mocking voice in his head that might have been called his conscience, if he thought Cats had a conscience, laughed. Right. He'd fucked Jackson because of the case. For no other reason. Not because of the delicious smell that coated his skin or the sleek muscles stretching and straining. Even the hot ass open and spread before him. His cock twitched in the tight leather pants and Reign groaned. Fuck. He needed to focus, think like a cop but his dick had other plans.

The club manager stepped out of the way and opened his hand toward the table, situated against the wall. It was a booth and blocked a little too much of the entrance for Reign's comfort but he didn't think he could be that picky. That would cause too much suspicion in his direction and having the wolf with him was dangerous enough.

"Can I get you—" The manager sniffed. "And your friends anything?"

"Tanqueray and tonic," Jackson announced, his voice hard and just a little snide.

Reign nodded. "I'll have the same. Dani?"

"Wine." Her hand fluttered. "White wine. Uhm, pinot grigio. Anything is fine."

Jackson grabbed her hand and pulled her down onto the bench, putting her between them.

The manager bowed and walked away.

"It's okay, baby," Jackson whispered. "You're going to be fine."

Dani nodded but her eyes kept snapping to the crowd. Time to take action.

Reign wrapped his hand around her neck and turned her head, forcing her eyes to focus on him. "When we're done tonight, I'm going to take you home, spread those pretty legs and fuck you blind." His cock twitched as Reign said the words. He lifted his chin. "And the wolf's going to drill that tight ass of yours."

Dani's eyes widened and he knew the instant she was listening to him. Fear forgotten and lust taking control.

"I've never..." She glanced over her shoulder to Jax.

He could almost see Jax's assurances, ready to soothe her nerves with promises of never doing more than she wanted. But she was living in the Cat world now and he needed her aroused, not frightened.

"You'll like it when he fucks you, kitten." Jackson's eyes flashed red but the light was immediately crushed. "I'll be inside your cunt and you'll love the slow fuck to your ass."

The sweet scent of her pussy juices burst into the air and Jackson growled. Reign leaned forward, his cock throbbing against the tight pants. God he hoped Winston appeared early in the evening or he was going to be permanently damaged.

Their drinks arrived and with a silent toast they all took a sip. Reign was pleased to see neither of his companions took big gulps. They were taking it slow. Just had to look like normal patrons. Until their killer appeared.

Dani put her glass back on the table, her fingers trembling just a little. Jackson must have seen the nervous twitch as well. He reached up and curled his hand over hers, picking it up and raising her fingers to his mouth. With a smug smile toward Reign, Jackson kissed the backs of Dani's fingers. Some of the tension slipped from her body as she watched Jackson's mouth on her skin.

Reign licked his lips. Wanting the same taste. His cock pressed against the line of his zipper, just a bit too painful to be fun. He pressed the heel of his hand against his erection, trying to ease it down in some way. Nothing seemed to work. Except fucking. Yeah, that's what he needed. He glanced around the room. There had to be some kind of private rooms here. Or they could slip downstairs and use the back of the limo. Yeah, the three of them would fit nicely.

He groaned knowing he couldn't leave just to have sex but damn his body wanted it.

He reached under the table and slid his fingers over the smooth skin of Dani's thigh. The short skirt didn't cover much, left long lovely inches of flesh bare before he had to lift her skirt. Her knees were squeezed together. Very ladylike but not what he wanted.

"Spread your legs," he said, his voice low but strong enough so that both his lovers heard the command. Dani gasped and hesitated, glancing at Jackson as if seeking permission. That wasn't going to work. "Just a little, kitten. No one can see."

The tight press of her thighs relaxed enough that he could slip his fingers between her legs. The heat was incredible, almost burning him. Moments later, another set of fingers joined his—Jackson. The backs of his fingers brushed against Reign's and somehow that translated into a squeeze around his cock. Damn, they needed to go somewhere where they could fuck.

Intent now, he flipped through his memory. He'd looked at building plans earlier in the day and mentally laid the plans over the room. The door on the far side of the dance floor led to their storage room and loading bay. That might work. At worse there was a wall he could lean Dani up against and fuck her—or have Jackson on his knees, his cock sliding between those lips. Fuck, he'd take them both.

His eyes tracked the crowd as he looked back, opening his mouth to suggest they disappear for a few minutes. It wouldn't take long. He'd save the leisurely fuck for later. When he wasn't ready to pound nails with his dick.

The top of his thigh tingled, jolting him from his thoughts, close enough to his cock to feel the vibrations through his groin. He shifted over and dragged the cell phone out of his pocket.

He didn't recognize the number but there was something familiar about the area code. He flipped the phone open and held it to his ear, music pounding in the background.

"Reign," he answered. "Who's this?"

"Uh, this is Detective David Banner with the Anchorage Police Department. Who's this?"

A cop. From Alaska? Reign turned his head and dropped his voice. "Detective Alastair Reign, Las Vegas PD. What's up?"

"I'm calling about Max Haverstam. He says he's worked with you before."

Max? Reign glanced over at Jackson. Even with the stronger werewolf senses there was no way he could hear, not with all the music and people.

"He in some kind of trouble?"

"There's been an incident. He's involved." Reign laughed. Of course there was an incident. It was Max they were talking about. "He used you as a reference," the cop said.

Reign laughed again. Max must really be in a bind.

"As much as I'd like to put his ass in a sling, he's a good guy. I'm guessing he's telling you the truth."

"So I can trust him?"

There was just enough amusement in the cop's voice to push away any remaining stress. Jackson wasn't going to have to take off to bail his brother out of jail.

"Is there a hot brunette with long legs involved?" Reign asked, not wanting Max completely off the hook.

"No."

"Then you're good. He's had my back on a couple of jobs. I'd believe him."

"Okay. Thanks."

Reign looked up. His spine tingled with awareness. If the other cop had anything else to say, Reign didn't hear it. He flipped the phone shut and placed on the table. He turned his head and looked at Jackson.

"We are about to have a visitor."

Dani tensed but took a slow breath, calming almost as quickly. She flipped her hair back, a nervous gesture that looked sexy as hell. Jackson nodded and sat back, looking cool and calm and dangerous. Good enough to eat.

"Reign, haven't seen you here in a while."

Reign dragged his gazed across Dani and Jackson before turning to face the tall Cat standing at the edge of the table.

"James." He nodded but didn't get up. Most Cats weren't that formal. And despite the phone call and his best intentions, the hard-on in his jeans hadn't abated. At all. Dani's knee pressed against his didn't help. He leaned back in his chair, letting his muscles relax, draping one arm around Dani's back. He noticed Jackson shift as well, subtly blocking her from his side. Two predators protecting their prey. "This is an honor. You don't usually pop out of your cage this early in the evening," Reign said, keeping his tone light.

The corner of James' mouth kicked up in a cynical smile.

"I like to know who's in my club." He looked deliberately at Jackson, barely glancing at Dani. "Particularly when they seem a little out of place."

Jackson smirked and turned his eyes to Reign, clearly letting Reign lead.

"He's a friend of mine." Heat echoed between them. "A *good* friend."

"Well, there are some who aren't going to be happy that he's here." James leaned a little closer. "I don't want my club torn up." There was a plea to his voice that he was sure Jackson recognized.

Reign smiled. "We'll be good. Just want a few drinks and show the puppy how the real half lives."

James straightened and nodded. "Think about calling it an early night, huh?"

"I'll think about it." That was all Reign was willing to give. James sighed and walked away.

"And that was...?" Jackson asked in a low voice.

"James Blayat. Manages the club."

"Friend?"

"Friendly enough."

"Do you trust him?"

Reign scoffed. "I don't trust anyone." He glanced around the room. He recognized dozens of Cats, wouldn't call any of them friends. Sure as hell wouldn't let one of them guard his back — not like he was Jackson. Reign didn't try to explain it. He could trust Jackson, knew it, believed it. Any male who'd let himself be fucked just to protect his woman was loyal beyond measure.

He tapped his fingers on the table, wondering what it would be like to have that kind of devotion directed toward him. He shook off the thoughts. The main goal tonight was catching Winston. Then Reign could worry about the fact that he wanted to fuck a werewolf's mate — and the werewolf himself.

Chapter Twelve

Jackson scanned the crowd, surreptitiously searching for Dani. She'd run to the restroom. Or that had been her excuse. He didn't doubt she was searching the crowd for this guy. They'd been at the club for almost an hour and a half and her nerves had stretched tighter with each passing minute.

He leaned against the wall and monitored the room. They'd abandoned the table about an hour ago when Reign had decided they couldn't see enough of the room. He'd positioned them near the wall, able to see the dance floor and the entrance.

Jackson hoped Dani appeared soon. He wasn't too worried about her in this crowd—not with his and Reign's scents on her. She was so well marked she could have been wearing a neon sign that flickered with their names, but he liked having her close.

He did a slow sweep of the room and noticed a few glances directed back at him. Cautious, very clearly trying to appear *not* to be looking.

He took a sip of his G&T and turned, easing closer to Reign, his chest brushing Reign's arm. His free hand he slid around the other male's back.

Reign looked over, his curiosity silent but visible in his stare.

"People are watching," Jackson said under his breath as he leaned in, brushing his lips across Reign's.

"Then let's give them something to see." As he finished speaking, he opened his mouth. The growl of the wolf in Jackson's head overcame any lingering phobias he had and Jackson met Reign's kiss, driving his tongue into the other man's mouth. The foreign sensation of kissing a man the same height with hard muscles instead of soft breasts pressing against his chest was countered by the seductive taste and power. Reign met him, stroke for stroke, battling for control, each man letting the other lead for moments at a time before nature demanded they command.

Sexual instinct took over and Jackson turned, easing their bodies face-to-face, pressing close. Reign planted his hand on Jackson's hip and held him in place as he rocked his hips, cock rubbing against cock. Reign's purr dragged a groan from deep inside Jackson. The lights started to sparkle behind his closed eyes and he yanked his mouth away, gasping in a desperate breath.

"Think they're still watching?" he asked, fighting the urge to rip open his jeans and free his cock, grind it against Reign's.

"Who the fuck cares?" Reign responded, biting Jackson's neck, just a shade too hard. Reign's sharp teeth were going to mark his skin but damn, the thought only made him harder. Heat enveloped his cock and he realized Reign had slid his hand between them and was cupping his erection, rubbing it. Oh God, just a few more strokes and he was going to come. Right here, in this crowded room.

Reign didn't seem to care. He covered Jackson's mouth with his, his tongue going deep.

The intensity alerted the lust-crazed portion of Jackson's brain. This wasn't right. Something was off. The change had been subtle, shifting over the last hour. The clearheaded cop faded and left behind a creature consumed with sex. Not that Jackson minded having his dick massaged but it seemed out of character for Reign to be doing it public.

Jackson snapped his head back, ripping his lips away. A warning snarl roared from Reign's throat. The satisfied Cat who purred when he was stroked was gone. And another creature was fighting to take his place.

"Reign?" The Cat didn't respond. "Reign," Jackson tried again. "Are you okay?" He kept his voice low, aware that they were still being observed.

Reign blinked, shook his head as if to clear it, then blinked again.

"Damn," he whispered, inching back, his hand falling from Jackson's groin. Despite the fact that he knew it was best, Jackson couldn't help but miss the other man's touch.

"Are you okay?" he asked again.

Reign swallowed and nodded. "I think so. Fuck, I don't know what's wrong with me." He eased back but stayed close, well within the touch of an intimate friend. "All I can think about is fucking—you, Dani. Damn..." His grip tightened on Jackson's shoulder. "I've got to focus. God, this isn't normal." He looked up, his stare communicating more than his words. As if he wanted to assure Jackson that he wasn't normally a sex-crazed fiend. "I shouldn't want to fuck you this badly."

Jackson raised his eyebrows, a tiny portion of him offended. After the last few hours, he was somehow more adaptable to the idea of fucking another man. Reign hadn't quite gotten to that point, it appeared. Feeling...miffed, was the best word he could come up with, was insane but that didn't stop the strange sensation.

Reign shook his head. "Because really, all I want to do is walk out of here—" His voice dropped to an almost unrecognizable rumble. "Find the nearest flat surface, bend you over and slide back into your tight ass."

Jackson felt his cock twitch, reacting to the strong sexual words. The way his body reacted was one part shocking and two parts exciting. He'd never been this attracted to another male, but with Reign he wanted to fulfill the explicit image that Reign created. Then he wanted to take Reign in the same manner. To claim his lover in the most dominating, basic way.

Reign grabbed Jackson's hip and pulled him close, rubbing his cock hard against Jackson's erection. "We need to fuck. Now."

Golden light flickered in Reign's eyes, warning Jackson that the Cat was making its presence felt. That was dangerous. In any setting but particularly around other Cats. If he shifted, the others would follow suit and God, what a melee that would cause.

Jackson gripped Reign's shoulder and eased him away, trying to capture the human's attention, giving him strength to beat back the Cat's demand for air time.

With a shake of his head, Reign's eyes cleared. He took a shallow breath and Jackson could see the control return to his friend.

"Fuck, I don't understand this." He dropped his gaze, embarrassment turning to anger.

Jackson stared at him for long seconds and then swore.

"What?" Reign asked, his eyes curious and hungry at the same time.

"I think I know what's causing this."

"Causing what?"

"This." He made a quick swipe with his hand down Reign's groin. He told himself it had a dual purpose—giving their watchers something to see and passing along his message—but that didn't explain the pleasure he got out of it. "This need to fuck."

"Well?"

"You sucked me off."

Jackson glanced at Reign and even in the dark light of the club could see the male's blush.

"Yeah, so?"

"There's something...it's some compound in our werewolf semen..."

"Yes?" Reign prompted when Jackson didn't continue.

"From what we can tell, it's designed to make human females better able to accept us. They heal faster and they get aroused. Or stay aroused."

Reign glared at him. "Why the fuck didn't you warn me?"

"Because when someone's got his lips wrapped around your dick the last thing you want to do is stop them. Besides, I never thought it would affect a male. I've never had *a male* suck me off before."

"Well it was a new experience for me too."

An unexpected jolt surged through his chest. The thought that his was the only cock that had ever been inside Reign's mouth made his dick twitch.

"How long will this last?"

"No idea." Reign looked at him, irritated that Jackson didn't know the answer. "You're male and you're a Cat. I don't know how it's going to affect you. For human females, it's about twenty-four hours."

"Great, so I'm going to be ready to fuck anything that moves for twenty-four hours." The corners of Jackson's eyes got tight and he felt his lips tremble, like a snarl was begging to come out. The sound echoed through his head from his wolf. Neither of them liked the idea of Reign fucking someone else. Reign didn't seem to notice. He turned his head away and scanned the bodies around them. When he finally turned back to Jackson, the irritation hadn't abated.

"Look at it this way," Jackson said, leaning close and placing his lips against Reign's ear. "When I fuck your ass later tonight, you'll recover quickly…" He nipped Reign's earlobe. "And then I can do it again."

"You can try."

Jackson took a deep breath.

Dani.

As if they both scented her at the same time, he and Reign looked up and turned. Jackson felt the groan that rumbled from deep in Reign's chest.

Dani strolled through the crowd, capturing the eyes of every male she passed. She walked with a slow, hip-swaying gait that made every cock hard. But her lust was for them alone.

The crowd parted before her and she came forward, the short skirt flipping up with every step. The glittery top did nothing to restrain her breasts so they swayed and shimmied.

Reign's purr harmonized perfectly with Jackson's growl — both animals coming alive at the sight of their mate.

She walked forward and the heat enveloped them like a blast. Jackson grabbed her hand and pulled her between them. Her delicate gasp just added fuel to the fire. Needing her taste, needing to be inside her, Jackson tipped her head back and plunged his tongue into her mouth. She gasped but he knew it wasn't for him alone. Vaguely he was aware of Reign pressed against her back. The slow subtle pulses as Reign rubbed his cock on her ass.

Damn, to have her between us as we both fuck her.

As if Reign was thinking the same thing, he whispered, "Will you take us, baby? One of us sliding in that sweet cunt, the other fucking your tight ass."

"Yes," she moaned, tipping her head back, giving both males access to the sleek line of her throat.

"Have you ever taken it up the ass before?" Jackson snarled. For some reason having former lovers fuck her cunt didn't bother him, but her ass — that belonged to him and Reign.

She shook her head, her eyes glazed over with the heady seduction.

"Good. Because we'll take you. That sweet ass belongs to us."

187

"Damn straight," Reign growled. He scraped his teeth across her neck. The mark sent a spike of need into Jackson's groin. They needed to get done so they could go home and fuck.

Damn. Forcibly fighting his wolf, he pushed Dani away. Her mouth opened and she stared at him like he'd taken away her favorite toy.

"Uh, we need to find this guy."

"Damn, you're right." He watched as Reign physically peeled his body away from Dani.

Dani nodded. "Right." She was breathless as she spoke and her words did wicked things to her breasts as she reported. "I didn't see him. I tried to hit most of the corners of the room but I didn't see anything."

"What now?" Jackson asked, keeping his body tight against Dani's. The possibility of someone watching them gave him a good excuse.

"Let's dance," Reign announced.

"You sure that's a good idea?" His cock ached, hard and in need to fuck something. Someone. At this point, he didn't care if it was Reign or Dani, but he needed to come. The thought of bodies twisting on the dance floor, rubbing together—damn, he wasn't sure he could keep his control.

"Better than fucking one of you in the corner."

"Besides, I like to dance," Dani said. For a brief moment, he almost thought she didn't feel the tension between them. Then he saw the sparkle in her eyes. She knew what would happen on the dance floor. Little tease.

With her hips swinging in a blatantly seductive rhythm that called to both him and Reign, she walked off, clearing a path through the crowd to the dance floor.

Drawn by the sweet noose that pulled them forward, both men stumbled after her. Her feet hit the raised dance platform and she started to move, her hips rocking in time to the beat.

Her breasts swayed unrestrained beneath that nothing top she wore.

"Fuck," Reign moaned.

"Yeah."

Though they both knew that this was a bad idea, neither man could resist. They joined her, Jackson covering her front, Reign pressing against her back.

Jackson pressed close, bending his knees until his cock was positioned right at her pussy. Reign's hands lifted her ass, raising her until she was perfectly situated against his erection.

Dani's laughter trickled through the room as they moved with her, against her. Two hard cocks. Two delicious men. They wanted her. Jackson rocked his hips deeper, sliding along her clit. Oh, yes, that's what she needed. If she couldn't have them coming inside her, she at least wanted to come.

"Oh yeah, fuck her, man. Rub that sweet cunt." Reign's voice was harsh against her ears as he massaged his cock against her ass. Their promise to fuck her—at the same time—made the seductive pressure of his cock even stronger.

She let the music fill her and raised her arms, letting the sound curl through her body, creating delicate caresses.

"Fuck me," she moaned, needing their cocks inside her.

For a moment, both men moved with her, then Jackson, the strongest of all of them, pulled back.

"We've got to focus. Let's find this asshole so we can go home and fuck."

Dani nodded. He was right. They were here to find—

"That's him." She could barely contain her scream as her gaze landed on the man they'd been looking for. Both Jackson and Reign froze for a heartbeat then they moved. Their bodies rocked to the music but their attention had shifted off sex.

"Where?" Reign's voice was low, near her ear.

Tipping her head back as Jackson crowded closer, she whispered. "Tall guy, dark hair, wearing the gray suit."

Jackson pumped his hips connecting with her clit and eliciting a groan. She forced her eyes to remain open, trying to lock the man's image into her brain. "Talking to your friend."

Reign didn't even flinch as he looked up. "Got him." He straightened, easing Dani into Jackson's arms. Though his body still carried with it that sensual power, his eyes were all business. "Let's go." He grabbed Dani's hand and led her to the edge of the dance floor, still cloaked in the darkness of the club. Jackson followed close behind. A new kind of tension shuttled between them.

Without looking toward the killer, Reign said. "You're sure that's him."

Keeping it as subtle as possible, Dani scanned the corner of the room, not stopping when her eyes landed on him. He was in deep discussion with James, Reign's friend. "That's him. I'm positive."

"Okay, Jackson…" Reign shifted, like he was pulling something out of his pocket. The handoff was discreet but whatever passed between them was now in Jackson's pocket. "Give me a few minutes, then get her out of here. I'll call you later—"

"No." Dani shook her head. Reign looked like he might protest. "Come by. Let us know what happened."

He nodded, then bent down, placing his lips on hers. She savored the warm kiss, letting his lips press against hers, soft but strong. Finally he drew back, licking his tongue across the peak of her upper lip.

"I'll see you later, kitten."

He looked at Jackson. Energy bounced between them. He leaned forward, pressing their open mouths together. Heat flared between them so strong that Dani felt it in her core.

Reign grimaced as he drew back. "Got to keep up appearances."

Jackson smiled. "Right." His eyes grew serious. "Stay safe."

"Always. I'll see you at her place later. Take care of her."

As Reign walked away, Jackson put his arm around her waist, pulling her back against him. "He'll be okay," he comforted.

She nodded and tried to believe it. Trying not to follow him with her eyes, she tracked Reign through the crowd, watching as Winston and Blayat slipped through a side door. Seconds later, Reign followed. The door closed behind him and Dani's heart began to race.

It was strange that after such a short acquaintance both these men could mean so much to her. Of course, they had been pretty intense hours spent together. Jackson nuzzled her neck, his lips hot against her skin, his body pressed tight against hers. She could feel the hard line of his erection pressing against her ass. Her pussy responded, clenching, growing wet, preparing to take him.

Despite the danger and the fear, somehow her body could still lust. She never would have thought it was possible.

How long they stood there, Dani didn't know. Her mind couldn't track the passage of time. Her senses were consumed and dominating all her thoughts.

"Damn."

Jackson's low curse grabbed her attention. She looked up and followed his gaze. He was watching the doorway through which Reign had disappeared. Three large men — bouncer types — went inside.

Dani started in that direction, her mind already on what they had to do. Jackson's hand stopped her.

"What do you think you're doing?"

"We've got to help Reign."

"No, I'm getting you out of here."

"Three, very big, very mean men just followed him. We've got to at least warn him." The edges of Jackson's mouth turned down and she knew he was weighing her safety against saving Reign. "I'll be okay. I'll stay in the background but we can't let Reign get hurt." She waited as long as she could. "Please. We could call for backup for him."

"I'm not sure that's a good idea," Jackson muttered, his eyes monitoring the area around them. "Come on." With his hand firmly on her upper arm, like he was restraining her from taking off on her own, he walked closer toward the door. Another quick scan of the room and he nodded. Dani took that as her signal and opened the door, slipping inside. Jackson followed.

Her shoes clanked against the metal floor. The door had opened onto a stairwell. She inched forward, giving Jackson room to follow her onto the landing. No sounds echoed from above but voices rang below.

She tipped her head down, raising her eyebrows in silent question. Jackson nodded. Not sure which she wanted more — Jackson in front of her or behind her — she tried to quiet her steps by moving on tiptoes. They followed the voices down one full flight, pausing at the landing.

"Stay here," Jackson commanded as he stepped in front of her.

"No way." Partly because she didn't want to be left out but mainly because she didn't want to be left alone. The dark stairwell was kind of creepy.

He glowered at her for a moment but then sighed. Grabbing her wrist, he guided her down the next flight. The stairs ended opening up into a warehouse of sorts. Cardboard boxes filled the small area, leaving narrow pathways.

Voices rang from the far side of the room.

Jackson held his finger to his lips, warning her to stay silent. Then he silently told her to stay put. Nodding, because she really didn't want to interfere, she grabbed the stair railing and held on.

While she watched, Jackson crept forward, peering around the corners of stacked boxes. He moved closer to the voices. She stretched up, not releasing her grip on the railing, but enough to watch him as he explore. His head bobbed down like he was swearing but there was not sound. Strange noises echoed around the corner but Jackson's body blocked her and she couldn't see. It didn't sound like a fight—there were no grunts or groans. The sounds of fists hitting flesh was noticeably absent. It sounded more like animals—feet padding across the concrete floor, low snarls and growls.

Jackson backed up. As he returned to the base of the stairwell, Dani whispered, "What did you see?"

Jackson didn't reply. He shook his head and began unbuttoning his shirt. She stared as he stripped off the black silk and dropped it to the ground. He reached for his belt buckle before she stopped him.

"What are you doing?" He couldn't seriously be thinking about sex right now, could he? Reign was in danger and this room was just too creepy for any sexual thoughts. Again Jackson ignored her question.

Before he dropped his trousers, he pulled a gun out of his pocket and handed it to her.

"Do you know how to shoot?"

She shook her head.

"Just squeeze the trigger. The safety is off. Point it at the chest and squeeze. If it's anyone or *anything* but me or Reign, shoot it."

The weight of the gun pulled her arm down—or maybe it was the fact that her muscles were shaking.

"Jackson—"

"I'm going to go help Reign. I need you to do me a favor." She nodded, knowing she would do whatever he asked. "I need you to put your hand over your mouth."

"What?"

"Just do it. Hand over your mouth, hard. You're going to want to scream. Don't."

She didn't understand but knew she wasn't going to get an answer. Not now. She slapped her free hand over her mouth and watched.

Jackson pushed his briefs down and stepped out of them. Having seen him naked, Dani was still impressed by the hard male body.

"Ready?" he asked.

Not moving her hand, she nodded. He flashed her a weak smile. The smile stretched, long, no, wait, that was his face stretching. The soft sounds of bones breaking and muscles rippling filled the tiny space and covered Dani's gasp. The scream that Jackson had warned about lodged in her throat and struggled to get free. She gulped, trying to force it back as she watched his body change and shrink, falling to the ground. He landed on all four...paws. Paws? He was a wolf. Jackson had just turned into a wolf.

A tiny bit of the scream escaped and she was glad her hand was over her mouth muffling the sound. The wolf shuffled closer, running his nose across the ground around her feet. Dani froze, her mind trying to catch up with what she'd just seen, her body trying not to flinch at being so close to a wolf. Instinct made her want to run but she fought it with every bit of her strength.

Jackson ran his nose up the inside of her leg. His tongue flicked out and licked her thigh, right at the edge of her skirt. With that greeting, he turned and ran, heading back toward Reign.

Reign? Was Reign a werewolf—God, the word was even hard to think—too?

A loud roar, like a lion calling its challengers, rang through the warehouse and Dani backed up, putting herself against the wall. With hands that still trembled she raised the gun that Jackson had given her and pointed, ready for whoever or *whatever* might come toward her.

* * * * *

Jackson ran around the corner, pausing only long enough to determine which of the five large mountain cats before him was Reign. His arrival was like a blanket of ice. All bodies froze for two heartbeats. Then the leader of the Cats screamed his challenge. Jackson met the sound with a growl of his own and lunged, heading for the leader, aiming for his throat. Cats liked to circle their prey, play with it. They weren't prepared for the prey to attack. Reign reacted, taking down the Cat next to him, using Jackson's arrival as a perfect distraction.

Jackson's teeth sank into the Cat's throat. He bit down hard and fast, knowing he didn't have long before the others were on him. A Cat's claws could do a lot of damage to a wolf. Blood rushed over him as he ripped through the jugular. His wolf demanded that he stay and finish the kill but Jackson forced himself to move on.

Claws grabbed at his back and Jackson leapt away. The speed and claws of the Cats made them deadly opponents. Jackson's only advantages over the strong animals were his teeth and the fact that he could stay on control during the shift. The Cats tended to be consumed by the animal. They reacted instead of planned. Jackson circled around, feeling the burn through his left side. Only three Cats remained standing. The one Jackson had gone for wasn't dead yet but he was down.

Reign jumped over the leader's body and took the space next to Jackson. The other two Cats squared off with them, growling and roaring. Reign responded to their warnings, voicing his own challenge. After thirty seconds of the posturing, Jackson had had enough. He growled one time and went for the Cat in front of him. His attack spurred the rest and suddenly there were bodies and teeth, claws and bites. The roars turned to whimpers.

Jackson allowed his wolf's instincts to lead and clamped down hard on the Cat's throat. The killing instinct wouldn't let him release his prey. His paws gripped the rough concrete surface as he bore down on his bite and moved inexorably backward.

A heavy weight landed against his side knocking him free of the kill. He growled and scrambled to his feet, his body locking down in attack mode. He bared his teeth to the attacker before him then realized the Cat was Reign. Reign had knocked him off his kill. Probably for the best. The two animals turned side by side and faced the carnage. Blood was splattered and smeared across the floor and some of the boxes. The Cat bodies were mostly alive. At least one was in danger of dying. Somehow Jackson couldn't come up with any sympathy.

Silently moving together, they changed, their bodies straining and shifting, pulling back to human form. Blood covered their hands and smeared around their mouths.

"How are you going to explain this?" Jackson asked.

Reign recognized the curiosity—not aggression—in Jax's question.

"I'm working on it." He looked around. "Where's Dani?"

"Oh fuck." Jax turned and jogged off toward the entrance. Reign followed. The Cats weren't going anywhere, and if they did, it made it easier. At least one would die. The others would have a short brutal captivity. Any time in a cage was too much for a mountain cat but maybe it would teach them not to work for asshole drug dealers.

They came around the corner of some boxes and skidded to a stop. Dani crouched in the corner of the stairs. Under any other circumstances, Reign would have thought the position was incredibly sexy—the shadow between her legs promising slick hot flesh. But the gun gripped tight in her hands ruined the image. Her eyes were so wide Reign didn't think she could blink without help. Her stare shifted to them. The tip of the gun moved with her gaze.

"Dani? It's okay, baby. We're here."

She didn't move, didn't seem to hear them.

Reign inched forward. Dani jerked and seemed to come awake. She lifted the gun and clenched her jaw.

"Dani. Put the gun down." This time his voice reached her. The energy drained from her body and the gun dribbled from her fingers. Reign lunged forward, grabbing the weapon before it could fall. "That's it, baby. We've got you." He put his arms around her, holding her tight, trying to wipe away some of the terror in her eyes.

"Reign?" She looked up. Her eyes went into overdrive, blinking and tearing up. "Are you a wolf too?"

Reign smiled. "No, Dani." He almost left it at that. Did she really need any more horror in her life? But he couldn't. "I'm a Cat."

"A cat?"

"Yeah, I'm a shapeshifter but my other form is a cat. Something that looks like a mountain lion."

"A mountain lion," she repeated. The laughter that burbled from her throat bordered on the hysterical. "That makes perfect sense."

He bent down and placed a kiss on her slack lips. "I'm sorry you had to find out this way."

She nodded but the tight grip on his arm told him she wasn't done processing it.

"We need to go," Jackson announced. Reign looked over his shoulder. Jackson had dressed and was looking around the warehouse like other bad guys might appear at any moment. And he was probably right.

"Yeah." Though he hated to do it, he eased Dani away from his body. "You going to be okay, kitten?"

Dani nodded but he knew the reaction was society's training. Her mind was somewhere else and he needed Jax to get her away so he could call the cops. At least now he knew what Winston looked like and he knew which Cats were working for him.

"You'll take her?" It wasn't so much a question but Jackson nodded.

"I've got her." Jax started toward Dani but stopped, pausing long enough to turn his face, slam his lips against Reign's. It was a hard toothy kiss. Reign opened his mouth and snagged Jax's tongue, taking, commanding just for a moment. Their growls matched in the air and they both pulled back.

"Take care of her."

"I will."

Reign nodded, trusting Jackson, knowing the wolf would do anything to protect this mate. He watched as Jackson took Dani's arm and eased her up to standing, leading her away through the back hallways, avoiding the main club.

Reign waited until they were safely positioned in the elevator before he flipped open his phone.

"Charlie? I've got the weirdest thing in front of me. Maybe you could come by and help me out."

Charlie responded as Reign had expected him to, vowing to be there in moments. Reign wandered back into the main fight room. The Cats were still there in Cat form, teeth marks marring throats and bellies.

Serves you right, you bastards.

He had a scratch on his face and some claw marks on his ass. They wouldn't heal quickly but it shouldn't leave a scar.

He flipped open his phone and called the zoo's emergency line. A groggy zookeeper answered.

"This is Agent Alastair Reign with the Las Vegas PD and I have a couple of mountain lions...at least that's what it looks like," he said, adding a touch of confusion to his voice. "Looks like some kind of cat fight club. They're injured and bleeding. Can you come get them?"

He gave the address and smirked as he closed his phone. Perfect. Those bastards would be trapped while the zookeepers observed them. And maybe, just maybe they'd become part of the exhibit, locked forever in their animal forms in a cage. That was the perfect revenge.

He crouched down and watched the Cats. One would probably die. He was bleeding pretty badly. One other just looked stunned. The other two had scratches and some deep bites from the wolf. Reign nodded to himself. Jax had been good in the fight. He owed the werewolf his life.

Reign had slipped into the storage room and gotten there in time to see Winston slip out the far door. Led away by James. Bastard. The Cats had jumped Reign before he'd had a chance to follow.

"Stupid assholes," Reign said to the Cats. "The guy is killing your own people." He stood up and walked around the scene. Charlie and the others would be here any minute. He needed to get his story straight and it couldn't include Dani or Jax.

Chapter Thirteen

ಬ

Reign rolled his shoulders back as he stepped onto Dani's front porch. It was late, or early, depending on how he wanted to look at it. Going on four o'clock. He stared at the door but didn't knock. He shouldn't be here. He was tired. It was late. Jackson and Dani were probably asleep. Naked. Together.

His lips pulled back in a snarl. The potent rush of sexual desire had smoothed out over the last hour but that still left the original lust for Dani. And now that he'd had a sampling of her, he wanted more. Wanted to play and fuck.

And there was Jackson. The few men Reign had fucked before had been random encounters, usually at the sexual peak of a Clowder. No one he'd ever cared to meet with again. Something about the wolf intrigued him. He gave the impression of being buttoned down, the conservative accountant his brother had described, but he'd let Reign fuck him and come hard from it.

But things were different now. He couldn't expect that kind of welcome. Earlier in the evening Jackson had been willing to let Reign fuck him *and* Dani because it had a purpose. Somehow he couldn't imagine the wolf letting him back in their bed. Even just seeing them together for the few hours tonight he could see they were much more solid than Dani and Max had ever been. Dani was sleeping with the right brother now.

Too bad wolves don't like to share.

He sighed and rubbed his finger over the screen of his phone. He wasn't in the mood to be rejected. He'd just call and tell them everything was fine, leave a message on Dani's cell phone so he didn't have to interrupt.

Before he'd dialed the first number, the door swung open and Jackson filled the open space. Reign's cock gave a little twitch, renewed interest in once again having the wolf beneath him.

"Going to stand there all night?"

Damn dog hearing. He looked so calm and distant while all Reign wanted to do was bend him over and push inside him again. *Wolves heal fast, his ass could probably take another round.* The smug voice in his head wasn't helping his dick quiet down at all. Of course, Reign doubted Jackson would be willing to take it again so easily.

"Did your pointed little ears perk up when I walked up?"

Jackson didn't react to the doggy slur. "Yeah." He nodded and stepped back, indicating that Reign should come inside. He couldn't imagine why but he followed Jackson inside. "How did it go?" Jackson asked as he closed the door.

He was dressed casually, bare feet which Reign found surprisingly sexy, loose pajama bottoms and a T-shirt that was a bit too big. Seemed like unusual fucking clothes to Reign.

"Fine. I acted confused and like it was something I stumbled on. Turns out the drug is a bastardization of a cat tranquilizer. Has a really nasty effect on Cats and luckily for me, it's also becoming a popular drug among humans." He shrugged at Jackson's questioning look. "If it was just a cat drug there's nothing illegal about that."

"So what did you do?"

"I called in Charlie."

"Charlie?"

"My partner." His lips curled up in a smile. "His name's not really Charlie. It's William Tuna."

Jackson chuckled, getting the joke. "You call him Charlie."

"Yeah. He helped me clean up. Made it look like I stumbled on the situation while I was out with friends."

"But you didn't get the main guy, Winston?"

"No, but I know where to find him." The back of his eyes ached as he thought about it. "At least I know one of the guys who is working for him. One who didn't end up dead or in a zoo."

Jackson's eyes popped wide open. "You called the zoo?"

"Teach those assholes to work for drug dealers." The grin on Jackson's face sent a warm shaft of tension into Reign's groin. He brushed the sensation aside. He'd be home soon enough. "How's Dani?"

Jackson winced. "A little freaked."

"Can't blame her."

"No." He tipped his head toward the stairs. "You should come see her."

"Ahh, don't know. She's probably asleep."

"Her eyes are closed but she's not sleeping. She's been worried about you." Jackson closed the space between them, the steps slow but deliberate. He stopped inches away, allowing Reign to feel the heat spiraling off his body. "So have I." As if they'd done this hundreds of times, they moved together, leaning in, turning heads to match up mouths. Reign groaned as his lips met Jackson's, soft and strong. A surge of lust that matched the insane need to fuck from earlier pounded through his cock but he reined it in, savoring the kiss. Taking it for what it was—a welcome, a greeting and glad you're safe.

He moved in, meeting Jackson as he pressed forward, close enough that he could feel Jackson's erection pressing against his. He rocked his hips forward, enjoying the friction for a moment but instinct urged him back. Not because it was another man or even because Jackson was a wolf. But because this wasn't about fucking. That kiss had been a lover's kiss.

Reign put a hand on Jackson's shoulder and took a step back, putting inches between their bodies. It really didn't make sense to start thinking of Jackson as his lover. Even if the wolf was willing, Cats didn't form relationships. Not permanent ones. Not without a lot of scratching and clawing. His parents had been like that and Reign didn't even want to go there. He was fine on his own with the occasional fuck.

The smirk on Jackson's face indicated he recognized Reign's retreat and for some fucking reason found it amusing.

"Come upstairs." Jackson seemed to believe that Reign would follow because he turned and walked away. Reign watched for a moment, his eyes locking on Jackson's ass as he ambled up the stairs. Fuck it had felt good pressed up against him. He resisted the urge to reach down and thump his erection. *It has to be some kind of lingering effect from the freaky wolf spunk.*

Jackson disappeared around the corner at the top of the stairs and moments later, Reign heard the murmur of voices — masculine and feminine. Dani was awake.

Reign rolled his shoulders back and put his first step on the bottom stair. Every instinct he had told him to leave. Now. Before he got any more entangled. Reign recognized the voice in his head not as the Cat's solitary nature but the male side of him. He could already see it forming. Despite Dani's appearance and her job, she was a nest-er. And she'd taken up with the king of nest-ers — a conservative werewolf.

They seemed to be inviting him inside.

He found himself at the top of the stairs, not realizing he'd moved, his body drawing him forward even as his mind still debated.

But he couldn't leave. Couldn't *not* see Dani after she'd had the shock of her life. Of course, he could blame that on the wolf. *He* hadn't changed forms in front of her.

He pushed open the bedroom door and saw them, snuggled in the big bed, Jackson's body wrapped around Dani, his front to her back. Faint scents of their earlier lovemaking clung to the air. Blankets covered them but it was easy to see their legs were intertwined. He paused for a moment. They were clearly a couple and if he disappeared right now, they'd go on together.

Maybe that was for the best.

Then Jackson looked up, his eyes locking with Reign's. Somehow the wolf managed to imbue that stare with a challenge, daring Reign to come forward. *Why?* Jackson was wrapped around one of the hottest bodies in Vegas, she appeared content with him and he seemed to be inviting Reign to join them. If she belonged to him, he'd have her hidden away from other predators.

But she didn't belong to him.

He sighed. Fuck this. He was just going to go with what his body wanted and deal with the emotional crap later. And what his body wanted was to be cuddled up against the two bodies in that bed.

His first response was to get naked but considering neither of them was naked he just kicked off his shoes and crawled up the mattress, stretching out next to Dani. As he got close, he could see the red in her eyes, the dried streaks of tears. Damn, they'd made her cry.

"How are you doing, kitten?"

The endearment made a lot more sense now and for the first time in hours, Dani felt like smiling.

"I'm okay." Or she was heading that direction. Jackson had brought her home, shock holding her together until she'd arrived safe in her own home. Then she'd lost it. The meltdown hadn't been pretty but Jackson had withstood it. She cringed at the memories, hoping they weren't even worse than what her mind retained. Finally, she'd cried and screamed and cried it out and all that was left was silence as she tried to accept it. Jackson had turned into a wolf. Reign turned into a cat. She hadn't actually seen it but she'd seen the claw marks on his hip.

She ran her finger next to the scratch mark along his cheek.

"Does this hurt?"

"Stings. Cats aren't like werewolves. We don't heal when we change form."

Werewolves. Changing forms. Cats. "Oh."

That brought a half smile to Reign's lips. "Kind of hard to deal with, huh?"

She took a deep breath and tried to quell the new rush of panic. Jackson's fingers squeezing her hip helped calm her. He'd been with her all night, comforting, strong, unmovable even when she'd shouted at him to get out. He'd held his ground and let her hysteria run its course.

Wanting to return some of that comfort, she stroked her fingers over the back of his hand.

"It's a lot," she finally answered. She shook her head and then included Jackson in her gaze. "I'm not really sure what to believe right now." He raised his eyebrows, questioning her statement. "Well, it's pretty unbelievable, right?"

"That's just your mind trying to convince you what you saw wasn't real," Jackson said. He kissed her shoulder. "It was."

She gave a little shiver, almost wishing she could go back a few hours and skip the whole scene. Suddenly Winston seemed minor.

Reign lifted his head. "Do you want to see me change?"

She hesitated then nodded. Jackson hadn't offered to turn back into the wolf but Dani didn't need the reminder. She could still hear the creaking and popping of bones and muscles as he'd shifted. Reign looked over her shoulder to Jackson, seemingly waiting for an approval. Jackson nodded as well and Reign rolled away, landing lightly on the floor.

It was strange but now that she knew he was part cat, she could see the catlike mannerisms and movements.

He stood up and pulled off his shirt, the muscles of his back stretching and pulling. Jackson squirmed behind her and smiled. The two of them had looked hot earlier in the evening, masculine hands moving across masculine skin. Despite the gravity of the situation, she felt a little heat between her legs. It was hard not to being with these two guys.

Reign pushed his jeans down, giving both her and Jackson a nice view of his ass.

"Wow." Her comment was barely audible but Reign heard it, looking over his shoulder, arrogance glittering in his eyes.

"Come on, pussycat," Jackson said, his voice taunting. "Just get on with it."

Reign's eyes dropped down to slits and he muttered something that Dani couldn't hear. She looked at Jackson and he shrugged. She wasn't sure if that meant he didn't hear what Reign had said or he just didn't care.

Reign turned around. Dani gasped, first at the semihard erection that he was sporting. Then she saw the marks—four long scratches running from his hip down his thigh.

She sat up. "Is that from tonight?"

"Yeah, one of them got a claw on me."

"What about you?" she asked Jackson. He hadn't been moving like he'd been hurt and there hadn't been any blood but they also hadn't been naked since they'd gotten home. She'd been a little too freaked out to think sexy.

"I got clawed but as Reign was saying, when I come back to human, minor wounds disappear."

She turned back, feeling like she was watching a horror movie, waiting for something to jump out and startle her into screaming. Reign's golden eyes met hers and she nodded, giving him permission to do whatever he was going to do.

He took a deep breath and shimmered, the air around him turning gold as his body morphed, shrinking down, skin changing. There was no bone snapping or muscles creaking. He just changed.

"That was different from what you did," she said not taking her eyes off the mountain lion standing in her bedroom. The eyes were the same—Reign's golden stare not changing even though the form around them was totally different.

"Yes. Cats and werewolves are different kinds of shapeshifters. He is always a Cat. Even in his human form. And in his Cat form, he's still very human." Jackson chuckled. "He might even come when you call him."

A low growl that sounded nothing like a cat's purr rumbled from the deep inside the animal's chest.

"Will you change?" She wasn't sure she *wanted* to see it again, but it might help her mind process everything.

Jackson shook his head. "Probably not a good idea. My wolf is a separate animal from me. We just share a body. So when I become the wolf, I really am a wolf. He can tell who is a friend and who isn't but he might not like being this close to a Cat." He chuckled. "He might chase Reign up a tree or something."

The growling turned into a full roar and the Cat leapt onto the bed, making the mattress dip. Dani's muscles locked up. She knew it was Reign and Jackson had said Reign was still inside the animal but still, that was a lot of muscle and teeth and claws.

The Cat opened his mouth and roared again.

Dani flinched.

"You're scaring Dani," Jackson snapped, the command and protection in his voice easing her. She snuggled backward, savoring the warmth of his body even as the big cat stretched out in front of her, head hung down, almost as if he was apologizing for roaring at her. It was really kind of sweet. If she could get over the idea that there was a man inside that big cat body.

"Can I touch him?" she asked Jackson, keeping her eyes locked on Reign.

"Sure. Good little pussycats like to be petted."

The Cat growled and his eyes narrowed but he nudged her hand with his head, encouraging her to stroke him. Her mind told her fingers to move but she still hesitated, taking a deep breath before brushing the tips of her fingers across his coat. The top hairs were rough against her fingers but a soft undercoat drew her attention.

Reign wiggled into her touch, rolling onto his back, baring his belly—and the hard kitty cat erection. Her hand froze as she stroked his stomach.

"Oh."

Jackson chuckled. "Like I said, he's very much the same man in this form." He leaned in close and put his lips against her ear, whispering the almost silent sounds. "And I'm pretty sure the human gets hard whenever he's near you as well."

The Cat purred and Dani continued her petting, even as her mind worked through Jackson's words. He didn't seem to mind that Reign wanted to fuck her. He'd actually sounded excited about it.

And she wasn't completely sure how she felt about that. Earlier had been one thing. There had been a purpose to it. And yes, she'd always been attracted to Reign. But then Jackson had appeared and their relationship seemed so permanent, even after just one night.

"I'm not going anywhere, baby," he said, nipping her earlobe, speaking as if he heard her thoughts. "We're both going to have you until you scream."

Somehow that simple affirmation gave her confidence. It reminded her of last night and the solid steady statements that convinced her he would never lie to her.

He placed another hot kiss beneath her ear. "The kitty cat and I will both have you." A lick. "Enjoy you."

Her fingers clenched in Reign's fur. The Cat's chest rumbled and she felt the purr. The sound seemed to rumble through her hand and into her pussy.

It was insane, completely insane. The man behind her turned into a wolf, the mountain lion in front of her turned into a man—or at least she thought he'd eventually turn back into a man—and her mind kept turning back to sex.

Made no sense.

Jackson chuckled behind her as if he could sense the heat moving through her pussy. He pressed his hips forward, rubbing his erection against her ass, promising more. A delicious zing zipped through her pussy.

"That's it, baby. So sweet."

She heard Jackson's words even as Reign shifted. The body beside her changed. The hand that had been stroking fur now touched flesh—hot, hard male flesh. Her hand drifted down, moved by instinct. Her fingers spread out, sliding across the rippling muscles, the tight bumps of his abs teasing the pads of her fingertips.

"Yes. That's it." She heard Jackson's voice in her head as she reached forward, her hand wrapping around Reign's cock. Heat pulsed through her palm as she slowly stroked him. Just like a cat, he rolled and stretched, moving into the caresses, letting her tend to him. He pressed his hips upward, urging her hand down his cock.

Hot kisses and murmurs of encouragement whispered across her skin as Jackson watched, his body surrounding her, protective and sexual at the same time.

It was a slow realization that she was wet, aroused. The touches and kisses had been comforting and the shift to sexual so subtle that she found herself rocking her hips back against Jackson's cock. The edge of Reign's mouth kicked up and he eased his hand down, cupping her pussy through the thin shorts, his fingers fluttering, thumping little pulses to her entrance.

As if they were in silent communication with each other, Reign and Jackson each reached for her shorts and pushed them down, taking her panties along as well, leaving her bare.

Jackson shifted away and moments later when he returned, he was naked, the rough hair on his legs tickling her sensitive skin.

He moved in, snuggling back up to her, his hands sliding around and cupping her breasts, teasing her nipples under the t-shirt she still wore. He knew just how much pressure to apply, strong and firm, just on the pleasure side of pain. She skimmed her hand up Reign's chest, running the pads of her fingers over his nipples. The tiny peaks perked up and he moaned, rolling into the caress.

Jackson chuffed behind her. She could feel the humor rolling off him. He didn't seem to mind indulging Reign. She glanced over her shoulder. Jackson's eyes met hers. Heat and light, humor and lust flared back at her.

She cocked her head to the side, asking silently—not for permission but for agreement—to continue. Jackson bent down and put a light kiss beneath her ear.

"Touch him, baby. Let the two of us love you the way we were meant to."

The words swirled around her head. It wouldn't be her making love with Reign, it would be both of them. More confident that she wouldn't be screwing up what she had to with Jackson, she leaned forward and pressed a kiss on Reign's shoulder, licking to taste the taut skin. She continued to pet him, letting her hands and lips wander across his chest and stomach.

As she touched Reign, Jackson touched her, his hands sliding up her hips, teasing the flesh between her legs, dipping his fingers into her pussy, his touch delicate and strong. Reign cupped her head in his hand and pulled her down, taking her lips in a lazy kiss, swishing his tongue inside her mouth, drawing her into his to play.

The sensations piled on her, overwhelming rational thought. Holding herself in place for Reign's kiss even as her hips rocked against the slow finger fuck from Jackson. God, it was happening again. She was having sex with two men and it seemed natural and right. A brief moment of clarity jolted through her brain, reminding her that she didn't do things like this. Desperate and a little panicked, she drew back gasping for breath, reaching back to stop Jackson.

"Wait, we should—"

"Fuck." Reign said the word against her lips, distracting her with another kiss. She moaned into his mouth, trying to remember why this was a bad idea.

"It's okay, baby." Jackson eased his fingers deeper and she released his wrist, wanting that touch. "We need you. Both of us. Let us love you."

That special quality of Jackson's voice that made her trust him pushed through the filter of panic, calming her.

That's what it felt like—love. She knew it was too soon. She'd known Jackson only a few days. And her conversations with Reign had been few and mainly focused on Winston. But this felt right. Being between them felt right. And if she regretted it later, she would at least know she went into it with her eyes open.

"Yes," she whispered, turning her head and meeting Jackson's kiss. Reign's lips and teeth moved across her neck.

It was slow and languid, sexual but with no rush, no urgency. Before when they'd been in bed together, there had been a specter over them. Time and reason. Now it was just pleasure. Every stroke, four hands moving across her skin, lying on her back with both men over her, sucking and biting her nipples until she felt every kiss in her pussy, her hips pumping the air, seeking relief. Fingers slipped between her legs, brushing against her clit, a whispered caress before moving on, deeper, sliding into her cunt. Sensation surrounded her, filled her and she needed more.

"Please." She moaned the word, begging her lovers to ease the wicked tension they'd created.

Vaguely she was aware of masculine murmurs, instructions and guiding hands, lifting her and positioning her hips. She looked down. Reign lay stretched out beneath her, his hands cupping her breasts, thumbs worrying her nipples. The gold from his eyes gleamed in the weak light of the room.

"Fuck me?" she asked.

Heat flared in his gaze. "Yes, kitten." He pressed up and she bent down to meet him for a hot, deep kiss that burned through her body, making the ache between her thighs worse. Breathless, they pulled back. Dani turned her head, knowing Jackson would be there. Even as his mouth devoured hers in a kiss that made her head spin, Reign shifted her body, drawing her down, the round head of his cock easing into her opening. She moaned into Jackson's mouth, sucking on his tongue and savoring the sweet groan from him.

Heat stretched her pussy and she drew away from Jackson, her focus on the hard cock filling her. Her fingers clenched, one hand digging into Jackson's palm, pulling the tension away from her pussy as she forced her body to relax, to let Reign push inside in her.

"Fuck that's pretty, baby." Jackson sucked on one her fingers, stretching out beside them, watching Reign's cock penetrate her. Stunned and overcome by the sensation, she stared at Jackson. Any lingering concerns about looking like a slut disappeared as he stared back at her, that serious sexy gaze filling her with confidence. Without even asking she knew that for some reason he was okay with Reign and her fucking but no other man would be allowed near her. She belonged to them.

Would belong to them. They'd promised. At the club. They were going to both take her at the same time, both men inside her. She trembled a bit, her mind zigzagging with possibilities.

Once again, Jackson was there with solid comfort.

"Not tonight, baby." He kissed her fingertips, a seductive mixture of sex and strength. "Tonight you're just going to ride him." His hand stroked up her arm. "Show him how delicious it is to be buried in your hot, pretty cunt. Show him what it's like to have you on top of him."

As if he were giving her instructions, she nodded and turned her attention back to the man who filled her. She pressed down, letting the final inches sink into her pussy. A low groan escaped her throat as she rested down, her ass against his thighs, her legs spread wide.

Still conscious of Jackson beside her, she concentrated on Reign. The arrogant glimmer that usually lived in his stare was gone and all that remained was heat. Hunger. For her.

She placed her hands on his shoulder, her breasts swaying as she rocked forward, lifting up and sliding that glorious cock from inside her. She watched Reign's eyes, fascinated by the desire. His gaze didn't glow red like Jackson's did when he was aroused but it was no less obvious that Reign wanted her. She drew back until just the tip was inside her then she pushed down, the movements long and slow. Dreamy. Reign skimmed his hands across her thighs, twirling random circles on her skin.

The Cat personality radiated through him, the indulgent way he guided her hips, up and down. There seemed to be no rush, despite the rising urgency inside her. She circled her hips, gasping at the subtle brush against her clit.

Reign groaned and held her in place as he thrust up, the first hard push inside her. Shivers raced across her skin, sparking from her pussy.

"God, that's beautiful." She heard Jackson's words, felt him beside her, his fingers teasing her breasts, sliding down across her stomach to her pussy. He curled around her, applying his lips to her nipples, sucking and biting, adding delicious layers of sensation. As Reign slipped out, Jackson wrapped his fingers around Reign's cock, stroking her pussy lips as he caressed the point where their bodies met.

Reign growled but there was no threat in the sound. Only desire. His fingers tightened on her hips and he pulled her down, driving up into her.

Her head dropped back and she moaned, digging her nails into the tight muscles along his ribs. The tiny scratches seemed to send Reign over some invisible edge. He punched his hips up, slamming into her at the perfect angle.

Her orgasm came up like a surprise storm, rippling through her pussy, drawing the breath from her lungs. And it didn't stop. Her lungs constricted and she felt her eyes widen, staring at the man below her. She'd come before, she knew how to make herself orgasm, but never had it just been a surprise. He lifted her up and drove his cock back into her passage. The heavy thrust sent off another wave of tiny shocks.

Two masculine, competing growls filled the air. Her head was turned and Jackson claimed her mouth, as Reign pumped his cock in and out of her again, holding her hard against his hips as he came inside her. The growls turned to groans and Dani's eyes drifted shut, colors swirling inside her head.

Her lovers continued to stroke, calming caresses to ease her from the radical high. The world shifted and she let her eyes open to watch Reign and Jackson turn her, splay her out on the bed, every ounce of strength gone.

Both men leaned over her, Reign on her left, Jackson on her right. Jackson.

"What about you?" she asked, letting her fingers drift across his stomach, though she wasn't sure she had the energy to be fucked again.

The corners of his mouth pulled up. A shy smile that made her heart ache. "I'm fine, baby. I came when you did." He grinned at Reign. "All over the puddy-tat."

214

Chapter Fourteen

ဢ

Reign listened to the steady breathing of the woman beside him and tried to keep his heart from pounding. What the hell was wrong with him? The fact that he was still next to her, faking sleep, was strange enough but he had the urge to pet and cuddle her. Made no sense. He was the Cat. *He* was the one who got stroked, when he wanted it.

The fact that he was willingly in bed with a wolf also freaked him out.

He forced his head up, looked over Dani's shoulder and Jackson's head toward the clock. It was almost time for him to get up anyway. He had to do follow-up on last night.

Keeping the mattress still, he rolled off the side of bed, his feet landing on the floor with a quiet patter. Both bodies on the bed shifted, filling in the space he'd abandoned.

Reign grabbed his jeans and headed toward the bathroom. A quick shower would wake him up, clear his mind. He stepped under the stinging spray and moaned, letting the heat wash over his body.

He heard the bathroom door open and kept his head down, water dripping down his head and back, even when Jackson pushed aside the shower curtain and climbed in. Reign waited. He'd basically agreed to let Jackson fuck his ass and it appeared the wolf wasn't going to let him leave without that happening. He tried to stay relaxed. He'd never allowed another man to fuck him. Wasn't sure he was going to like it but he wasn't backing out on the deal.

Jackson moved behind him, their bodies brushing together as the scent of strawberry filled the shower stall. Strawberry lube? Bracing himself against the wall, he waited

215

for the first penetration, trusting Jackson enough to take it slow.

Slightly scratchy warmth tickled his back as more strawberry burst into the small space. Reign flinched. Jackson was washing him? The slow rub of the sponge across his skin confused the hell out of his mind.

"Relax, man." Jackson followed the command with a kiss to Reign's shoulder. "Just enjoy."

Reign inhaled and tried to do just that. He'd been mentally preparing for being fucked, instead he was being pampered. The warmth and caresses sank into Reign's muscles. If Jackson was trying to loosen him up to be fucked, it was working. The only part of him that wasn't relaxed was his dick. It stayed hard, waiting.

Jackson knelt down, sliding the sponge along the backs of Reign's knees, down to his ankles. His fingers stroked the same skin, lingering on the curve of Reign's ass, teasing the split between his ass cheeks. A low purr rumbled from Reign's throat before he'd even realized it.

"Nice," Jackson whispered as he stood, his kisses hotter than the water that poured over Reign's skin, rinsing away the bubbles. "You've got the best ass." Jackson moved close, his hard cock pushing against Reign. "Well, except maybe for Dani."

"I hear that." They both chuckled, males united in their lust for the female.

"Turn around." Jackson followed up his request with more kisses. Reign briefly wondered if that was how he got women to do what he wanted. Command and then kiss so they didn't really notice they were following orders.

Of course, none of his thoughts kept him from turning, facing Jackson, shifting until their cocks pressed against the other. He turned his head and met Jackson's kiss, hard and deep, even as they pumped against each other, the wicked friction sending hot shocks down his spine. He clamped one hand around the back of Jackson's head and the other to his hip, holding him in place when he would have pulled away. God, he could come from this and then he probably wouldn't care what Jackson did to his ass.

Jackson sucked on his tongue then pulled back just enough to whisper. "I'm not done."

"Neither am I," Reign pointed out with a growl and another thrust of his hips.

"It's my turn, right? Let me finish."

Reign relaxed his hold on Jackson's hip. He was right. They'd agreed to this. And really, if anyone was going to fuck his ass, he'd bet Jackson would do a damn fine job of it.

Waiting for Jackson's next instruction, no doubt to turn around and get himself ready, Reign was shocked again. Jackson brought the sponge back up and rubbed it over Reign's chest. When Jackson pinched one of his flat nipples, Reign knew he wasn't expected to totally relax. The hard caress sent a shock to his dick. He propped his shoulders against the shower wall and inhaled. The strawberry scent wasn't too strong and blended nicely with the male arousal that flowed between them.

Even as Jackson washed him, bubbles clinging to both their chests, he stroked and touched, kissing bare skin. Reign closed his eyes and let himself be seduced, just as they'd seduced Dani earlier.

Jackson went to his knees, the shower spraying the soap from Reign's stomach. As the bubbles disappeared, Jackson ran his tongue across the tight ripples, loving the subtle reactions in Reign's body, the way he moved into the caresses. He's such a Cat, Jackson thought, giving Reign's abs another lick.

Reign's cock twitched like it was trying to get Jackson's attention.

"Jax, man, what are you doing?"

217

He tipped his head back, water dripping across his cheeks. "I thought it would be obvious." He smiled. "Guess I'm not doing it right." Just so Reign would get the idea, Jackson took his erection and did a long slow lick from the base to the tip. "That better?" A low grunt-growl combination broke from Reign's throat—almost like a purr that had been cut off.

Oh no. Jackson wanted that purr.

He'd never done this before but he had a feeling Reign would forgive his inexperience. Being male, Jackson knew that a bad blowjob was still pretty good.

The wolf in his head seemed to agree, yipping and growling.

He took Reign's cock in his hand and pumped it, testing to see how tight to grasp. He knew he'd found the right touch when Reign started thrusting against his hand. He kept up the steady pumping, not too fast—he didn't want Reign coming before he'd had a chance to taste him properly—while he pressed up on his knees and returned to the ripples of muscles marking Reign's abs. Dani's fingers had traced these lines earlier, now Jackson followed the same path with his tongue, finding a sensitive spot just below Reign's bellybutton. A faint shiver ran across the tight skin. Jackson returned, scraping his teeth, biting down just enough to make Reign jump.

"Jax." The name was a mixture of warning and need. Good but not the sound he wanted. He stroked his tongue over the tiny red mark left by his teeth and moved away, tasting and kissing the smooth skin, almost hairless. He smiled thinking of Reign as one of those scary-looking hairless cats. That was something else to throw into his pocket for later. When he needed to tease the Cat.

For now, he had things to do. He turned his head and lapped at the base of Reign's cock. It was a strange sensation but something he could get used to. The scent was delicious. Not sweet and sexual like Dani but compelling, intriguing. An essence of Dani's pussy juices remained on Reign's skin, combining the two scents, flavors.

He stopped the pump to Reign's dick and let his mouth wander, open lips, tongue, tasting. He trailed the tip of his tongue up the underside of Reign's cock. That elicited another shiver. Jackson shifted on his knees, the hot water still pouring down on them. He reached down and wrapped his free hand around his own dick, pumping a few times, not wanting to come just yet but needing the touch.

Reign shifted, his hips pressing forward, a silent nag to Jackson to get back to what he was doing.

He smiled. Reign wasn't one to miss out on his pleasure. Jackson could understand that.

He looked up. Reign was staring down at him, those golden eyes blurry with hunger and confusion—like he didn't understand why Jackson was on his knees sucking him off. That just made Jackson's smile wider. Poor little pussycat. Didn't understand giving pleasure without expecting it in return. But he'd learn. Jackson was going to teach him.

He took a deep breath. He wanted this, wanted to know what it was like but it was still a defining moment.

He opened his mouth and let the thick head slip inside. He moaned as his mouth was filled, Reign's muscles fighting to keep still as Jackson took as much as he could, fighting his gag reflexes to take Reign deeper. He tightened his lips, sucking as he pulled back.

A low purr rumbled from deep in Reign's chest and Jackson growled, the sound muffled because of the cock in his mouth. That was it. He wanted the Cat to purr for him. Redoubling his efforts, he pushed forward again, first slowly, then faster as he learned how hard to suck, how to make Reign purr. He grabbed his own cock and began to stroke in time to his sucking.

Fingers gripped his head, not guiding him, holding him.

"Jax, man. Oh fuck." Reign's hips pushed forward just a touch too deep and he came, spilling his cum deep into Jackson's throat.

He swallowed what he could but had to pull back, the cum still pulsing from Reign's cock. He pumped his hand up and down Reign's shaft, drawing out more, the water washing it away as it splattered on his shoulder.

Jackson rested his forehead against Reign's hip, his breathing hard, his cock even harder. Hands urged him to stand and he forced his legs to move, his knees stinging from the shower floor. Reign pulled him up into his arms, their bodies pressed together.

Reign's hand curled around his Jackson's cock, replacing Jackson's hand, a good hard pull that grabbed deep inside him. Jackson braced a hand on the wall and moved with Reign's strokes, pushing his cock through the tight grip. Just a hand job, like he'd given himself thousands of times, but fuck, this was somehow better.

"Come on, man. Let me have it." Reign's words and an almost painful bite to his shoulder pushed him over the edge. Jackson cried out and came, his seed pouring through Reign's fingers.

"That's it." They turned, facing each other, each holding the other up.

"So good."

"Fuck yeah."

Jackson wasn't even sure who said the words. Both voices echoed in his head. *So good.*

* * * * *

"Heading out?" Jackson drawled from the bottom of the stairs. Reign's head snapped up as if he hadn't known that Jackson had been standing there, watching him. Even with their short acquaintance that seemed unusual for the Cat. Reign was very aware of his surroundings. The fact that he hadn't been prepared for Jackson's approach meant his mind was somewhere else.

Reign shrugged off his surprise. "Uh, yeah. I've got to go make some kind of report."

"And find Winston?" Jackson didn't like that there was a killer out there who might find out that Dani was the witness to put him away.

"Yeah." A merciless gleam filled Reign's eyes. "Now I know who's working with him. I can beat it out of him."

That soothed the vicious streak his wolf needed satisfied.

"What should I tell Dani?" She was still upstairs, asleep.

"I'll call her."

Jackson nodded and tried not to smile. Reign was a typical Cat. He didn't do commitment.

Too bad for him the wolf had already made his claim.

Reign tugged on his jacket and started for the door. Damn, Jackson thought. He was in full escape mode.

The wise thing to do would be to let Reign go. Hell, it had been a night of great sex. They could leave it like that. Dani had gotten a night with Reign and that might be enough. She'd admitted to the attraction and maybe one night had satisfied her curiosity and Jackson could have her to himself.

But that didn't feel right. Not that having Dani was bad or wrong but the three of them just seemed better together.

And damn but Jackson was pretty sure he was going to want to feel Reign's cock inside him again. And that shower upstairs had been enough to leave them both panting. No, he wasn't ready to let the Cat go, not just yet.

Keeping pace with Reign's steps, Jackson met him at the door, grabbing the frame as the Cat opened the door. This time Reign knew Jackson was there and paused, looking back over his shoulder.

"Take of yourself," Jackson said. It was strange letting him go, knowing he was going out on his own to find and confront a killer. Reign nodded and started to turn away but Jackson couldn't let him leave. Not like this. He stepped close and hooked his hand around Reign's neck. He didn't have to pull hard to draw the Cat to him, as if Reign needed this as well. Jackson brought him close and covered his mouth in a hot kiss. They didn't waste time on preliminaries. Both moved hard and strong on the other, their tongues tangling. It was a fast hard kiss that left Reign's lips red and Jackson's teeth aching.

"Kiss Dani for me," Reign said, turning away.

"I will." Jackson didn't even try to keep the laughter out of his voice.

"I'll bet."

"You'll call us later, right?"

Reign paused and Jackson could see his mind working, already trying to find his escape route. He looked up, meeting Jackson's stare and for a moment, Jackson could almost see Reign's body move toward him but the Cat managed to pull back.

"I'll call you."

He took another step and stopped. "By the way, that call last night. At the club?" Jackson nodded. "It was about Max. Cops were checking to make sure he wasn't an axe murderer or something."

Jackson felt his stomach drop.

"You're just telling me now? Is he okay? Where is he?"

Reign shrugged and there was a hint of a smile bending those beautiful lips. Arrogant asshole. "I think he's fine. Cop who called me was from Anchorage."

Jackson stared at the empty space, barely aware that Reign had disappeared. *Anchorage? What the hell is Max doing in Anchorage?*

He looked around and remembered he'd forgotten his phone. He grabbed Dani's off the wall and dialed Max's cell. It was still early in Anchorage but damn it, if his brother was in trouble, he could be awake enough to tell him about it.

It rang four times before Max picked up.

"This is Max."

"Hey."

"Jax? Man, where are you? Are you okay?"

Relieved laughter rumbled from his throat. Max sounded like his usual self. "I'm fine. I hear you're in Alaska. And you got arrested? What the hell are you doing?"

"I didn't get arrested. I was helping the police."

There was a pause that warned Jackson that was only partially the truth. What was his twin up to? Before he could ask, Max jumped in with questions of his own.

"And where the hell are you? I fly all the way up here and you're MIA."

Jax chuckled and rolled his eyes. "Yeah. Guess where?"

"Where?"

"Vegas."

"What?"

"Came to see you."

Max's laughter rang through the phone line. Despite their differences, they were definitely twins. After a moment, Max said, "What's going on? What have you been doing in Vegas without your little brother to take care of you?" Jackson straightened up. There was a lot he needed to discuss with Max but he didn't want to do it over the phone. This was a conversation they needed to have face-to-face. "Jax?"

"I'm here." He cleared his throat. "Stuff's been going on. I'm okay," he said knowing Max's protective tendencies. "I was with Reign last night, that's how I found out you were in Alaska."

"What were you doing with Reign?"

"It's a hell of a long story. And something we should talk about later. You know, face-to-face."

"I hear that." He could almost see his brother's thoughtful face. "When are you coming home?"

"Uh...don't know yet. I could hang around here for a few days, wait for you here." He wasn't ready to leave. He sure as hell wasn't going to leave Dani until Winston was caught.

"Uh yeah. I'm actually going to stay in Anchorage for a few days." He laughed. "I'm not sure the cops want me leaving town just yet."

Jackson shook his head. "What did you *do*?"

"Nothing. Much." Jackson didn't believe that for a minute. His brother was up to something and he'd only been in Anchorage for three days. *Of course, you got up to something in Vegas in three days.* He pushed aside the annoying reminder from his conscience. "It's another face-to-face conversation that we have to have."

"Well, don't think you're getting away from telling me *everything*," Jax warned. If nothing else, Anchorage was a small city. He was going to run into the people Max might be pissing off.

"Max?" The feminine voice was faint but distinctive through the phone line. That made more sense. This involved a woman. He could believe that. Soothed his own guilt just a little bit about taking Dani so soon after they'd broken up.

As if his thoughts conjured her, she appeared, walking down the steps, wearing nothing but a long t-shirt. She leaned against the wall and smiled shyly.

Dani bent one knee and raised it, curving around so the edge of the t-shirt pulled up, revealing one bare ass cheek.

"Listen, I've got to go."

Jackson heard his brother speak but the words had no meaning.

"Yeah, that's good," Jax replied. "We'll talk later."

"Yeah, later."

He hung up the phone, dropping the receiver on the couch before stalking across the room.

Dani lifted her chin and looked up at him. "Who was that?"

"Max."

Her eyes widened. "Where is he?"

"Anchorage." He shrugged. "He flew up to see me."

Dani smiled, her eyes lighting up with the grin. "That's funny." She looked over Jackson's shoulder. "Where's Reign?"

"Gone to work. He said he'd call us."

She laughed and tipped her head back, reaching up and draping her arms around the back of Jackson's neck. She pulled him close and placed a quick kiss on his lips.

"Don't you know boys never call when they say they will?"

* * * * *

Twelve hours later when Reign hadn't called, Jackson started to pace. He really didn't want to have to hunt down that pussycat but he wasn't going to let him go. The Cat and Dani belonged to him. And Reign was just going to have to get over his panic.

Jackson looked at Dani. Her cheeks were flushed and her eyes a little dreamy from coming twice. She'd been home from rehearsal for two hours or so. The connection between them was new enough that his wolf had felt the need to stake its claim so Jackson had carried her to bed almost as soon as she'd walked in the door. Her cries and moans had soothed the wolf and made Jackson hard enough to pound nails.

The sex had left them both sated and lazy. They'd discussed dinner but neither of them had made a move to do anything about it.

It wasn't until Dani asked if Reign had called that Jackson's instincts went on alert. Was the Cat just being a pussy or had something gone wrong?

To fill the silence, Jackson turned on the TV. Unable to settle, he listened to the canned music of the evening news and the anchor's lead into breaking news.

"A shooting in downtown Las Vegas has left one person dead and one police officer injured. The suspect is still on the loose."

Dani and Jackson froze, their attention drilled into the television.

"James Blayat, part owner of Spirits, a popular nightclub here in Las Vegas, was found shot to death early this afternoon. Witnesses say a man was seen running from the building moments before. When police arrived they found Blayat's body and the wounded officer. The name of the police officer has not been released pending contact with his family but we do know he is in serious condition at a local hospital."

Chapter Fifteen

ဢ

Jackson followed Dani down the hospital corridor, scanning the hallways as he kept up with her long strides. Dani was focused. Wasn't thinking about her own safety. If this bastard had gotten to Reign, he might have found out about Dani. She didn't seem to care. She was thinking only about Reign.

A little twinge of jealousy inserted itself into Jackson's brain but he slapped it aside. He was worried as well. He just didn't have the societal luxury of showing it the way Dani did.

His phone calls to the hospital had yielded no information. Unable to stand not knowing any longer, they'd come down.

She stalked up to the Emergency Room desk. He didn't hear her request but he saw the nurse shake her head.

"I'm sorry, miss, but I'm not allowed to give out any information."

Dani's fingers twisted together then she propped her left hand on the counter.

"Not even to his wife?"

The nurse flinched at the sharp question.

Jackson managed to keep his surprise hidden. He glanced down and saw that she'd slipped the thin ring she'd been wearing on her right hand to her left, and turned it around so it looked like a simple wedding band.

The nurse flipped through the file in front of her. "We have Agent Reign listed as unmarried."

"It's a recent development."

"Uhm, if you'll just wait here for a moment."

She walked down the corridor and spoke to a stern-looking man standing with another guy, hair cut short, serious eyes. The shorter one wore a lightweight coat that Jackson assumed was used to hide his weapon. The two of them just screamed "cop". Funny, he would never have looked at Reign and thought "cop". Thug, Cat, sexy. All those terms applied but not cop.

The two men talking to the nurse looked down the hall, their eyes focusing on Dani and Jackson.

"You think this is going to work?" Jackson said quietly.

"I hope so. It is Vegas after all."

The nurse left the two cops and walked away, disappearing down the other end of the hall, as if she didn't want to get involved in what happened next. The older of the two men turned and came down the hall, stopping before Dani, nodding to Jackson. Jackson sniffed the air to check. The guy was a human.

"May I help you?"

His question contained more suspicion than the desire to be of assistance. The aggression that lurked underneath made the hackles on the back of Jax's neck rise up. His wolf growled low and long, muddling Jax's ability to concentrate.

"And you are...?" Dani replied with arrogance that matched his tone. The agent's lips tightened but he didn't back down.

"I'm Detective Tuna. Now, how can I help you?"

Dani had insisted Jackson tell her what Reign had said before he'd left—he'd mentioned the "Charlie" Tuna comment. She used that now, smiling like she was relieved to have an ally. It was fascinating to watch Charlie melt then shake it off. "You're Charlie." This time "Charlie" flinched.

"Yes."

"Reign's mentioned you. I'm Dani." She held out her hand.

"Nice to meet you." The suspicion was now laced with confusion. "The nurse said you're claiming...I mean, that you said you're Reign's wife." With each word, Charlie seemed to grow more confident. "Reign's not married."

Dani smiled and Jackson could see Charlie fight not to melt under the glow.

"He is now. It was kind of a spur-of-the-moment thing." The soft, feminine way seemed to blind Charlie. Jackson watched, reminding himself to be aware of her power. She could be tough as nails, strong, even bitchy but damn, she did bimbo really well. "Reign and I haven't gotten around to telling people yet." Damn, it looked like she was actually blushing. "It's kind of embarrassing that we got married on a Friday night by a very bad Elvis impersonator. We were sure that people would think we had to be drunk."

"Uh..." Charlie's mind had clearly been blanked by Dani.

"Could I see him? Is he all right?" Tears appeared in her eyes and Jackson knew they weren't faked. Conscious of the role she was playing, he still had to touch her. He placed his hand on her shoulder and squeezed.

Charlie didn't seem to notice. He was captivated by the tears tripping over her lower lids.

"He was shot — three times."

Dani gasped and Jackson couldn't stop his reaction to her response. He stepped close, putting his front to her back, letting his body heat comfort her. She leaned into him.

"Will he be all right?" Jackson asked, speaking for the first time. Dani needed his support.

Charlie's lips pinched together until they turned white. "They don't know. He's in a coma right now. One of the shots was to his head. It just grazed his skull but enough to put him out of it."

"Can I see him?" Charlie looked ready to deny her question but then she said, "Please?"

The tough grizzled cop wilted under the weight of a pain-filled woman and nodded.

He led them back down the hall, speaking softly to the cop who'd been in the hall and again to the officer who stood outside his door.

Charlie opened the door and indicated Dani started forward, Jackson right behind her.

"Wait. Who are you?" Charlie demanded.

"Our priest," Dani snapped, her anger returning. Jackson tried to look pious as she grabbed his hand and pulled him in behind her.

Dani took two steps into the room and stopped, her heart skipping several beats before racing to catch up. Reign lay in the bed, his blond hair gone, shaved along one side.

She looked at the nurse who stood near one of the machines. "Can I touch him?"

"Of course. Talk to him. It might help."

Dani looked at Jackson, her eyes filled with fear and uncertainty. He joined her at the bedside, urging her closer.

"Talk to him."

"What if I'm not the voice he wants to hear?" she whispered. Now that she'd bullied her way into the hospital room, what if Reign didn't feel the connection that she had? Admittedly it had only one night of sex but it had been really hot sex and it had been one *long* night. "I mean, shouldn't his family be here? And what if he really has a wife somewhere?"

"I'll worry about finding his family. You talk to him. Remind him of what he'll be missing if he stays away."

Jackson's eyes twinkled.

"I'm supposed to have phone sex with a guy who's in a coma?"

"It'd make me come back from the dead."

"Is there a problem?" Charlie asked from the doorway.

"Uh, no. Just receiving some spiritual guidance." Bracing herself for rejection from an unconscious man, Dani leaned down. "Reign?" What to say next? Jackson's hand covered hers, encasing her and Reign's fingers in his palm. The warmth gave her strength. "Come to back to me, Reign." She lowered her voice. "Come back to us." Yes, that sounded better.

She took a deep breath and just started to talk, hoping her words would slip through the darkness and find him somewhere.

* * * * *

The silence in his head transformed, music infiltrating the calm. He fought to hear it, needing it to pour over him. The sound was soothing, soft and delicate, with hints of bass, pulses that matched the beats of his heart.

Conscious of his frozen state, Reign savored the sounds, tracking the minutes, focusing as time became clearer. The music evolved into a voice. His beleaguered mind took a moment to connect the tone with the face. Dani. Whether his body moved or not, his soul smiled. She was here. With him. Whispering to him. Asking him to come back to her.

Then her voice drifted away and panic tried to seize him but before it could take hold, the bass returned and this time he recognized the timbre. Jackson. He was here as well, his voice low and steady. The words didn't make sense but he felt the compulsion to return just as he had with Dani's pleas.

He wasn't sure how long he drifted, his mind fading in and out, his body fighting the wounds and the human drugs they'd put in him.

Slowly he fought his way to the surface, needing to return — to Dani and Jackson.

It was light when his mind broke through the surface and he was able to react, to move just a little. Just enough to open his eyes. For a moment he stared up in silence. Dani sat beside him, looking tired, her fingers clutched in his. She was reading to him. Harry Potter if he wasn't mistaken.

Focusing all his concentration on his hand, he squeezed her fingers. She squeezed back but didn't look up and he realized his body had probably been reacting to hers even while his mind was blanking.

"Dani." Damn his voice was hoarse but she heard. Her head popped up and the book tumbled to the floor as she jumped to her feet.

"Reign?"

"Hey, kitten."

"I need call the nurse."

"Not yet."

Tears welled in her eyes and her grip tightened on his.

"How do you feel?" she asked, her fingers stroking his hair.

"Tired. Beat up." He struggled to lift his head, knowing something was missing. "Where's —" Even as he started to ask the question, he saw the answer, lying five feet away, curled up uncomfortably in a chair. A dark shadow dusted Jackson's cheeks, like he hadn't shaved in days.

As if he sensed Reign's stare, Jackson opened his eyes and blinked, looking around. His gaze landed on Reign and Dani and his mind cleared. His body tensed and Reign thought for a second that Jackson would lunge out of the chair. Instead he just smiled.

"You're awake."

"Yeah." The energy to keep his head up was too much and Reign dropped back on to the pillow.

"I'd better call the nurse."

This time Reign didn't protest except to say, "Don't let them give me any pain meds."

Dani smiled and shook her head. "Jackson's already got that covered."

Reign didn't get a chance to ask what she meant. Nurses and doctors arrived and he was caught in checkups and medical details.

Jackson and Dani stayed out of the doctors' way but they didn't leave. Jackson watched closely. From the way the nurses and doctor included Jackson and Dani in their conversations, Reign had to believe they'd firmly established themselves with the medical staff. No one put anything into his IV without telling Jackson what it was and what it would do.

Reign relaxed, letting his wounded body heal, drifting off to sleep. He was safe. Dani was here and Jackson was watching over both of them.

* * * * *

Reign shifted, trying to get comfortable. Damn, he needed to get out of this bed. One day since waking up and his body was well on the way to recovery. From what Dani had said, Reign had been out of it for two days. The medical staff said he'd been in a coma. He knew it had taken that long for his body to throw off the effects of the human drugs. From what he'd been told, Jackson had stopped the painkillers immediately after he'd arrived. Only then could Reign begin to heal at his natural rate. His metabolism didn't work like a werewolf's to heal him almost instantly but it would be faster than a normal human. He needed to get out of the hospital before the docs noticed.

"Is it safe to come in?"

Reign looked up and saw Charlie in the door.

"Sure. Come on in."

Charlie tipped his head toward the chair. "Where's your guard dog?"

Reign hesitated. "Jackson?"

"Yeah."

"He ran home to clean up." Forcing a laugh, he asked. "Why do you call him that?" Surely he couldn't know about Jackson's tendency to get furry. The wolf wouldn't be careless with that kind of information.

"Well, damn, he wouldn't let anyone in the room. Even questioned the doctors and nurses, demanding to know what they were giving you. You had to pass inspection before he'd let you close."

Reign chuckled. "He's a little protective."

"Is he really a priest?"

The chuckle turned to a choke. "Uh, sure."

Charlie's eyes squinted down. "I didn't think so. Does that mean Dani's not really your wife?"

"Is that what she said?"

"Yeah."

"Sure, she's my wife." The words had a strange, calming effect. Calming for a moment. Then the panic set it. He didn't plan to marry. Not to Dani, not to anyone, ever. Cats didn't mate for life. Unlike wolves. No doubt Jackson had already laid his claim to Dani's future. The thought created a weird mix of emotions. He craved the sight of Jackson fucking Dani, his tight ass pumping as he rocked between her thighs. And the way she screamed when she came. Fuck that was sweet.

But while one part of him wanted Jackson to be the one fucking Dani, the thought that he might be left out, not there, made his chest ache in a way that had nothing to do with the bullet wound in his side.

"Where's she at? She hasn't left your side for three days."

"She's missed a lot of rehearsals being here. I told her to go." Charlie nodded and looked like he was going to ask more questions. Questions Reign wasn't sure he wanted to answer or even think about. "Enough about that," he said, pushing himself up in the bed. "What about the bastard who shot me? No one's taken a statement. I haven't given you a description. Are you even looking for this guy?"

"We already got him."

"What?"

Charlie shrugged. "Day after you were shot. This guy Winston calls up, confesses, tells us where the gun is, tells us where he is. Practically begs to be arrested. We walk in and the idiot's surrounded by illegal drugs. Doesn't even try to hide them. Confesses again and then starts telling us about every illegal thing he's done since he was sixteen years old."

"Is he trying to get a deal?" Reign wasn't quite sure how he felt about that. He wanted the bastard to pay, not only for what he'd done to him but because of the damage he'd caused the Cats' society.

"No. Doesn't want a deal. Practically begged to be taken to jail. He's a weird bird. When we found him, he kept asking us if the wolf-man was gone and pleading for us not to let the wolf-man get him."

"Wolf-man?" Reign hadn't meant to repeat the words but they just slipped out. Fuck. What had Jackson done?

"That's what he said. Thought he was going for an insanity defense but everything else about him is completely sane."

Reign forced a laugh. "Well, maybe he's been using some of his own product."

"That's what we figure."

* * * * *

Jax glanced around the corner before he walked in. Reign was asleep, his eyes closed, his head tipped to the side of the hospital bed.

Jackson stepped inside, approaching the bed, preparing to check the IV. He wanted to make sure they hadn't given Reign any painkillers. The human drugs were death to a Cat's metabolism. As he squinted to read the tiny words written on the bag, Reign's eyes snapped open.

"What the fuck were you thinking?" he demanded.

"What?" Jackson snarled back, his wolf instinctively responding to the attack.

"You went after Winston. In your wolf form? What were you thinking? What if he tells someone?"

Anger, irritation, rage—the emotions combined and boiled up inside Jackson. He felt his teeth extend. "He won't." The words came out more growl than spoken.

"He might."

"Trust me. He's so freakin' scared, he won't be able to talk without babbling for years."

"He's already talking. What if someone decides to believe him? What were you thinking?"

The rage, the fear at seeing Reign in the hospital bed, at seeing him so close to death bubbled to the surface. All the emotion he wasn't allowed to show because it wasn't permitted by society erupted.

"I was thinking about, *imagining,* what it would feel like to rip his throat out and eat his heart. I was *thinking about* killing the man who'd hurt my mate."

The word seemed to surprise both of them.

"I'm not your mate." Reign sat up, his lips pulling back.

"Fuck that. You belong to me and to Dani. Just accept it."

"Fuck you. I belong to no one. Not you. Not Dani."

Dani stood in the doorway and tried to ignore the pain that ripped through her chest when Reign declared he didn't belong to her. And Jackson...mates? What the hell did that mean? Sounded like some weird werewolf ritual that she probably should know about.

But that was for later. Now she had to face Reign and Jackson.

A pissed off Reign and Jackson. Male anger. The convenient reaction to all things frightening or irritating.

She stormed inside, exhausted from a grueling rehearsal. Preparing to break up a battle between her lovers.

"Both of you stop it."

Neither man—uh, male—reacted.

"Bullshit," Jackson snapped. "You belong to me and you sure as hell belong to Dani. Tell me you can walk away from her."

"Who I can walk away from and who I can't is my business," Reign snarled. "And you're not involved, so keep the fuck out of my business. I don't need..."

This was going nowhere. Dani thought about screaming—that would get their attention but it would also get the attention of every person on the floor and given that neither male looked particularly human at this point, she didn't need others to come running.

She grabbed the bottom of her shirt and yanked it up, baring her breasts.

Both males stopped and stared, mouths dropping open, eyes popping wide.

She pulled her shirt down, snapping them out of their breast-induced trance.

"Good to know that works." She blinked her eyes, refusing to let the tears fall. So both men were already planning their escape. "Now, the first thing we have to do is get Reign healthy enough to go—" *Home.* Except he would be going to his home. Not hers. "To leave the hospital. The doctor said he'd be stopping by this afternoon and if you're well enough, you can go home."

The furious blinking of her eyes wasn't working but there was no way in hell she was going to cry in front of these two men. Not now.

She pulled her shoulders back.

"And both of you should consider that maybe, just maybe I don't want to 'belong' to you. I don't want to belong to anyone. Before you start laying claim to me, you'd better check with me first."

She looked around the room. She'd planned to stay with Reign for the afternoon, wait for the doctor. *Screw it.* She flashed another glare at the two men then spun on her heel and stalked out.

"Assholes," she muttered as she hit the doorway.

"Fuck."

Reign nodded, agreeing with Jackson's pithy assessment.

"I should go after her." Jackson said it but he didn't move.

"Probably best to let her calm down a bit."

"Yeah. Besides, you're the one who needs to apologize."

Reign sat up, the sheet falling between his legs and baring his thigh. "Me? What about you?"

"Me?" The shock on the wolf's face was almost laughable. "I'm the one who wants to keep her."

"Yeah but you wolves have to realize that not everyone is meant to be mated and that human women like to be asked." It was impossible to keep the smug tone out of his voice. It wasn't often he was in the right about relationships. Jackson looked at him and seemed to come to the same realization.

"Fuck."

"Exactly."

That drained the fury from the room. Reign stared at the empty doorway. He was better but he wasn't up to chasing after a pissed off woman. And God, what would he say when he caught up to her? He sagged back on the bed. His energy was returning and it was time to get back to life.

Jackson leaned his forearms on the railing, his head hung down. Before Reign realized what he was doing, he reached up and scraped his fingers through Jackson's hair, pulling it away from his face. His sensual nature came through and he repeated the caress, enjoying the way Jackson's hair felt on his skin, sliding through his fingers. Jackson leaned into the touch, almost purring.

You'd think the man was part Cat. Reign decided not to voice that sentiment. He didn't feel like another snarling fight. He'd leave it for later when he could do something with the wolf's irritation…like get him bent over the bed.

"What are we going to do?" Jackson asked, lifting his head.

* * * * *

Dani stormed out of the hospital, the heat hitting her as she left the building. After a moment to get her breath back, she let the warmth settle back into her bones. It had been too damn cold in the hospital anyway.

She started toward her car — her feet aching from five hours in high heels — intent on going home, drinking a glass of wine and snarling at the TV. That would make her feel better. Arrogant assholes. Both of them. They weren't going to decide who she slept with. She decided that.

Her phone began playing Duran Duran's *Notorious* as she shoved the key into the lock. Her front teeth snapped together and her head dropped back. *Max.*

Max, it turned out, had gone to Alaska, hoping to see Jackson. Somehow the two had crossed in the skies. She kept expecting Max to call and say he was home but for some reason, he didn't appear in a rush to leave Alaska.

Probably found some woman.

The song started up again and she hit the screen. Since they'd made contact, her phone was the way the twins were connecting with each other. Normally, she didn't mind but *normally* she wasn't pissed at one twin. Usually she'd been pissed at the *other* twin.

Taking a quick breath, she lifted the phone to her ear.

"Hi, Max."

"Hey, Dani. How are you doing?"

One lover wants me, one doesn't. I'm exhausted, confused and pissed.

"Fine," she said instead of letting Max enjoy that little rant. She didn't ask how he was in return because at this point, she wasn't sure she cared.

Max must have read the irritation in her voice because he went straight to the point.

"Is Jax around?"

She looked up at the hospital, four floors up, where Reign's room faced the other way.

"He's inside with Reign."

"Oh." Disappointment chimed through one word. "Could you have him call me?"

Dani's messaging service. "Sure."

Not really caring that she might annoy Max, she pressed her thumb against the "end call" portion of the screen. She and Max hadn't talked about the fact that she'd made their breakup final by leaving him a voice mail. Neither seemed to want to bring it up and she was good with that.

She glared back up at the hospital. Max hadn't said it important or urgent. But still…despite the fact that she was pissed, she wanted to see Jackson and Reign. Going home didn't fit her style. She didn't back down from fights. She wanted to have it out, even if she had to do it in a hospital room.

All the better. They'll be close to medical help if I deck one of them. She shoved the phone into her purse and stomped back into the hospital. The elevator was thankfully empty so she didn't have to fake being pleasant to anyone. She nodded to the nurses—well familiar with her now—and zigzagged through the halls to Reign's room. She stopped just outside the half-closed door and took a breath.

"What are we going to do?" she heard Jackson ask.

"About Dani?"

"Yeah."

"I don't know."

Despite the fact that they seemed to once again be planning her life without consulting her, she held back, wanting to hear this great plan.

"I'm staying," Jackson said. "Until she kicks me out, I'm staying."

"You've only known her —"

"Less than a week. I know. I knew that first night. Knew something was different."

"So, if she's your mate, why would you want to share her with me?" Reign's voice held the confusion that Dani had felt when Jackson seemed to be pushing her to make love to Reign. Good to know she wasn't the only who found that strange.

Jackson's chuckle was almost too low to hear. "There's something between the two of you, and let's face it, between us. It feels right when we're together. The three of us."

"Cats don't mate for life." Reign's determination rang through his words.

Jackson laughed. "We'll see how long you keep thinking that."

"Listen, wolf-boy, it's not in our nature."

"Whatever." Jackson seemed unwilling to concede. He just laughed off Reign's protest. Dani realized it was time for her to go in, face the boys, though she had no idea what she was going to say.

She looked up, reached for the door and saw Reign's doctor heading toward her. Wouldn't be a good idea for him to hear the boys discussing cats and dogs. It would just add to the confusion.

"Doctor's on his way," she announced as she walked in the room.

Jackson's head snapped up. Reign's eyes widened for just a moment. Good to know she could surprise the guys with the super senses.

"Dani." Jackson reached for her and her body responded, putting her hand in his and letting herself be pulled into his embrace, his arm around her back, his hip pressed against her stomach.

"I'm okay." She realized the truth behind the words. They hadn't meant to be assholes. They were just men after all. She'd have a chat later with Jackson about what being his "mate" might mean. Not sure that she was opposed to being his mate but she needed more information.

Reign reached up and took her left hand in his. She glanced down. Concern flickered back at her through his eyes. She squeezed his fingers letting him know she was fine.

That's how the doctor found them minutes later, Jackson's arm around her, her fingers entwined with Reign's.

"Good morning, Mister Reign."

Reign grimaced and Dani shared a smile with Jackson. Reign did *not* like to be called Mister Reign and heaven forbid someone call him Alastair. Dani had barely contained her shock when she'd found out that was his first name. He *so* didn't look like an Alastair.

The doctor, also used to her and Jackson's presence, looked at the chart, asked a few questions, including where Reign was going when he left the hospital?

"He can stay with me," she blurted out. The doctor blinked and got this confused look on his face. Oops. They thought she was Reign's wife. Where else would he go? She giggled and shrugged, doing her perfect imitation of a bimbo. "Silly. I mean, of course, he'll come home with me. We're married." She looked at Reign, silently begging for confirmation. He nodded but the corners of his mouth were squeezed tight. They hadn't discussed this and, based on what she'd overheard between him and Jackson, Reign might not want to stay at her place.

"And I can be there," Jackson added. "When Dani has to go to work." He tipped his head and somehow managed to look pious. "To offer spiritual guidance as well as physical assistance."

Jackson looked at Reign, practically daring him to counter the offer. Reign's lips quivered like he was trying to suppress a chuckle...or a growl. "That would be fine," Reign said.

The doctor went through medications which Dani was pretty sure Reign wouldn't take and gave him final instructions, including no strenuous activities. That made Reign's eyes darken and she almost expected to hear him growl.

"For how long?"

"I'm sorry?" Doctor Robins asked.

"For how long can I not do any strenuous activity?"

"Oh! Until the stitches come out. Probably a week."

With a final pat to the bottom of Reign's bed, the doctor left saying he would give the discharge information to the nurses.

He pulled the door shut behind him and then Reign released the growl.

"I'm asking my own doctor," he said.

Jackson laughed, squeezing Dani's hip and holding her close. "I'm pretty sure even a Cat doctor is going to say no sex for a few days."

"It's already been a few days," Reign groused.

Dani shook her head and looked up at Jackson. "He's going to be a pain in the ass, isn't he?"

"I just about guarantee it."

Chapter Sixteen

&

Music rose through the hall—the canned orchestration that accompanied most Vegas shows. This was no different, except Dani was performing. So far, they'd seen her in half a dozen different numbers, some dancing, some simply posing. But this was the finale.

Dani walked on stage, the full flight of feathers surrounding her ass, making her look like a large silver peacock. A silver peacock with perfect tits. She smiled—that vague, distant smile that comforted Jackson. No emotion lingered behind her smile. She felt no connection to the humans—particularly the males—who watched. This was her job. She came closer, stopping at the edge of the stage. She stood, waiting, allowing the adoration but gaining no pleasure from it.

"Yeah, baby." The lecherous whisper came from two seats over—from the young man sitting on Reign's left. Jackson was on the aisle but he heard the kid's comment.

A fierce growl rumbled from beside him and Jackson tensed. Reign had heard the kid as well. Jackson looked over. Reign's eyes were squinted low and tight and the points of his fingers were stretched into claws, gripping the arms of the theater seating.

"Down, boy," Jackson whispered.

Reign looked prepared to ignore Jackson in favor of ripping the throat out of the guy sitting next to him. The young buck was practically drooling, his eyes locked on Dani's tits. Jackson felt a reflected aura of jealousy. Those tits belonged to them—him and Reign. Later tonight, Dani would beneath him — them — and those perfect breasts, tight nipples would be hard and ready for their mouths.

The finale continued and Dani sauntered across the stage, her breasts swaying slightly as she took each step. The kid sitting next to Reign leaned so far forward his face was almost buried in the toupee of the man sitting one row in front. Tension raked Reign's body and damn if those claws weren't going to leave permanent damage to the theater seat.

"Ease back," Jackson said in a low voice. "Just remember who she's going home with." Reign nodded and his lips pulled away from his lips. Any moment he was going to turn and lunge for the stage. Jackson put his hand on Reign's knee. He flinched but didn't look away. Jackson could tell Reign's possessive instincts — despite his assertion that Cats didn't claim mates — were split between their woman and the pitiful male beside him. Reign's Cat wasn't a separate presence in his mind the way Jackson's wolf was but the Cat reacted to the tension of his host human and was obviously fighting to be free.

Maybe it was time to give the kitty something to think about besides killing the human next to him. Keeping his movements slow, almost subtle, Jackson skimmed his hand up the inside of Reign's thigh. As he drew closer, he moved faster until his palm rested on Reign's cock. He was already hard — not surprising.

Reign jerked and looked around, like he didn't know what was happening. Then he froze, his tension in his body shifting from attack mode to sex.

Even as Reign recognized Jackson's hand between his legs, Jackson went deeper, cupping his hand around Reign's balls and squeezing gently.

The sensation shot through his groin, making his cock harder, ready to burst. But the caress did the trick. He was no longer intent on killing the puny human but damn, if Jackson kept this up, they were going to have a bigger problem on their hands — like Reign throwing the werewolf to the ground and fucking him right there in the theater. The past five days had been brutal. No sex. After he'd been released from the hospital, one of the doctors in the Cat Community had checked him out and given him the same advice the human doctor had — rest, heal. No strenuous activity.

But as of three o'clock today, he was cleared. For whatever.

And he had a night of very strenuous activity planned.

He wanted to fuck, to make love to Dani all night. And he wanted Jackson.

He wasn't sure how he felt about that — or how Jackson felt about it — but he was sure that if the three of them ended up in a bed together, he was going to take his turn on Jackson. His cock tightened as he thought about it, the hard male body beneath his, taking him inside. The fact that Jackson wasn't a submissive made it even more arousing — that he would open himself, make himself vulnerable to Reign's penetration.

Dani strolled to their side of the stage. She smiled down, looking directly at them. Reign knew that with the bright lights blasting down on her, she couldn't possibly see them but it felt as if she was smiling just for them. It was a secret, seductive smile. One that promised so much more. Jackson's hand tightened on Reign's cock. He'd seen it too. The strokes to his cock became less about distraction and more about pure sex.

He dragged his coat down, hiding what was happening. His hips rolled up, convulsively pressing into the tight grip of Jackson's fingers. God, he had to stop this. He couldn't, wouldn't embarrass himself like this, wouldn't come in his trousers. Not like this.

He grabbed Jackson's hand and yanked it away from his cock, hating the loss but knowing now was not the time. The days of restraint tore at Reign's control, weakening his ability to control the Cat that was currently clawing at his insides, demanding release. And fuck that would be a bad idea. A wild cat loose on the Vegas Strip. Stupid for a multitude of reasons.

He had to get out of here. Thankfully the show was almost done. He needed to move, to work off some of the energy.

Of course, the only true release was going to be sex and a lot of it.

Applause surrounded him and Reign looked up. The dancers were taking their bows. Dani and the other two topless women paraded to the middle of the stage and posed. The noise in the room grew deafening, which was actually a good thing because couldn't Reign control the growl that tore from his throat.

The curtain went down and the lights came up. The audience voices dropped to a low rumble.

"Damn, did you see the rack on that dark-headed chick?" the punk next to Reign said with a nudge. "How'd you like suck on those babies?"

"How'd you like to crawl out of here on broken knees?" The threat was barely out of mouth and Reign had just enough time to mark the kid's reaction before Jackson dragged him into the aisle. Reign's body fought the forcible retreat even as his mind knew it was for the best. He wanted to go back and gouge the guy's eyes out for daring to look at Dani's breasts.

"Keep it under control."

Jackson's warning just echoed what was going on in Reign's head.

They approached the stage door. Groups of twos and threes were approved by the guard and allowed access. Dani had given them instructions and a pass. She would be waiting for them backstage. Jackson glanced at Reign. The tight line of his shoulders, the constant rolling, almost twitching of his muscles. And Jackson was sure that if Reign looked up, his eyes would be glowing. This was one pussycat who was not fit for human company at the moment.

"Why don't I go check on Dani? You wait here."

Reign raised his head and just as Jackson suspected, the Cat's eyes were staring through Reign's gaze. His lips quivered and Jackson could see his teeth—long and sharp, definitely not human.

"You're close to your change, aren't you?" Reign didn't respond. He snarled and jammed his fists into his pockets, looking away. Yeah, he was close. "Do you need to go for a run?" Taking on the animal's form usually helped release some of the tension. At least that's how it worked for his wolf.

Reign shook his head. "I don't need to run." He glanced at Jackson and a shiver scraped down his spine. "I need to fuck." The words were growled low and muffled and left no room for error.

"Will you be okay here? I'll go get Dani?"

Reign nodded. His shoulder rolled back and his head tipped to the side. *Damn*, Jackson thought, *he's on the edge*. But he seemed to be controlling it. He had to trust Reign knew his own limits.

"Hang in here."

With that warning, Jackson flashed his backstage pass to the guard and was allowed entrance.

The hall was crowded, half-dressed women slinking by him with no concern in the world. He appreciated the view but found it a little strange that they would walk around with their breasts showing. He didn't like the idea that Dani might be one of these women. Determinedly he kept his eyes focused up, above the neck if possible as he navigated the hallway. He tried to remember the instructions Dani had given to find her dressing room. She'd explained it to Reign and he'd nodded wisely.

Jackson had listened but hell, he couldn't drive well-laid-out city streets. There was no way he could manage the maze of back stage.

He was lost. Bodies passed him, some half naked, until he felt surrounded and his wolf started to panic. He gave in and asked for directions. He was close and within two left turns was in front of her dressing room door. She'd warned him that she shared with three other dancers so he wasn't surprised that another feminine voice called for him to enter when he knocked.

He opened the door and two female bodies appeared, one wearing nothing but a tiny thong that left her ass nearly bare. And Dani. A yelp followed as he stepped inside and she shrugged her robe around her shoulders. She relaxed when she saw who it was.

"Ooh, welcome," the other woman said, her words more of a theatrical moan than anything else. She slithered to her feet and arched her back giving him a clear view of her surgically perfect breasts. "And who do you belong to? Say no one and I'll put you in my stable." The blatant, flirty sexuality amused him but he had no interest.

When Dani was near, it was impossible for him to notice any other woman.

"Sorry, Jess, this one belongs to me." Dani's possession eased something deep inside Jackson's heart. Dani was his mate, his lover. They hadn't known each other long enough to verbalize the sentiment but Jackson didn't doubt that they'd get to that place. The element he didn't know, couldn't predict was Reign.

"Ooh, so is this the twin?" Jessie's eyebrows crinkled. "Damn, you're right. He looks just like the other one—but without the playboy glint in his eye."

Dani's cheeks turned a delightful shade of red.

Jackson looked at her. "You think Max has a 'playboy glint'? I'm sure he'll be thrilled to know that."

"That's not something you have to share with your brother," she said with a warning. Jackson waited for the jealousy and discomfort to follow but there was none. Dani wasn't even thinking about Max.

"Well, you certainly have an eye for hot-looking men."

"Yes," Dani said with a smile. She turned to her friend. "But that's not why I slept with him." She threw one arm around Jackson's shoulder and neck. She leaned in and scraped her teeth across his neck. "It's because he's so freakin' sexy I can't stand it."

Joy and energy seemed to radiate through her body, penetrating his. He caught her against him, pressing her hip to his. She squirmed like she was trying to get closer.

"But what about the cop? I thought you said something about doing a cop."

She shook her head and looked up at Jackson, wrapping her other arm around his neck so he faced her. "She makes me sound like such a slut when she says it like that." A giggle burbled up in her chest.

"But we know better."

Her smile stretched wide. "Yeah." She sighed, happy to be in Jackson's arms, happy that the performance had gone well. Just happy. "Did you like the show?"

"It was great. You were amazing."

"Yeah?" She'd been complimented before but it was different hearing the admiration coming from Jackson.

"Amazing. You're an incredible dancer, sexy, gorgeous. I thought I'd come just watching you," he whispered as his hand tightened on her ass, pulling her closer, shifting their bodies so she could feel his erection pressing against her mound. Reminding her that it had been five days—five very long, sexually frustrating days—since they'd made love.

"Did you like the end?" She couldn't resist rubbing her breasts against his chest to remind him that she'd been topless.

The edges of Jackson's eyes tightened just a little. "It was fine."

She tipped her head back. "You knew going into it what I did and that I'd be topless tonight."

"I know. And I'm okay with it. Or I thought I was until the kid next to Reign started drooling."

She smiled and shrugged. "It happens." She glanced over her shoulder. "Where is Reign?"

Dani pulled back. She couldn't stop her lower lip from curling out in a low pout. After all, he'd come to the show to see her. A visit backstage was part of the fun of opening night.

"Uh, I left him outside."

She looked up and saw the truth in Jackson's eyes. She didn't understand it but for some reason, it was best that Reign hadn't come backstage.

"Hey, sorry to break up this little, uh, sex-fest the two of you have going..." The teasing in Jessie's voice soothed any ruffled feathers Dani had. "But are you going to the party? Opening night? Free booze? Hot guys...oh wait, you have one of those."

"I have *two* of those."

Jessie laughed. "Ooh, willing to share?"

"Not on your life. They're mine." She turned to Jackson, sliding her fingers through his hair. "*All* mine." She might have felt a little panic at such a public declaration if she hadn't felt Jackson's cock twitch against her pussy. Needing to taste him, she pushed up on her toes and licked the soft peak of his upper lip, gently calling him out to play, demanding her lover's attention.

And Jackson was there, strong, loving. He cupped the back of her head and covered her mouth with his, his tongue sliding between her open lips. The warm heady rush of flavor she'd come to associate with Jackson flooded her senses, zapping the strength from her knees. She leaned into him, using his strength to keep herself upright.

"Okay, well, I'm going to leave now. I'm going to the party because I don't have two delicious men to fuck."

Jessie's snappy farewell was enough to pull Dani back. Without releasing Jackson, who seemed intent on tasting every inch of her neck and shoulder, she looked at her friend.

"G'night, Jessie. See you tomorrow. You did a great job tonight."

Jessie winked. "Have fun," she mouthed more than spoke.

Jackson scraped his teeth across her skin just at that moment. She moaned and smiled at her friend. "I will. Don't worry."

Jackson kissed and licked his way back to her mouth. It would be so easy to just let him overwhelm her. The thin threadbare couch would work as a perfectly good horizontal surface but no, she wanted more than that. She wanted both her lovers tonight. Dragging her mouth away, she dragged in a breath and forced her legs to take a step back.

"We should go. Find Reign."

Panic seemed to land momentarily on Jackson's face. "Good idea."

She reached for the tie of her robe. A low, sexual growl erupted from his chest as if he sensed or smelled her body's response. Unable to stop herself, she licked her lip then traced her tongue across his.

"Why did you leave Reign outside? I thought he'd get a kick out of seeing the backstage world. Half-naked women traipsing around seems like his kind of thing."

"Normally, yes. Uh, he's a little...stressed."

She could tell from Jackson's emphasis on the word that Reign was a hell of a lot more than stressed. And even though her experience with this sort of thing was limited, she was pretty sure a stressed out Cat on the Vegas Strip was not a good idea.

252

"How stressed? I mean, is he cranky or is he pissed?"

Jackson flashed her a wicked smile. "Different kind of stress. I think the last five days of no sex have finally gotten to him."

"It's *only* been five days," she pointed out. "You'd think he could survive."

"The Cat's constitution is a little different. They aren't used to denying themselves something they want."

"Ah." She strolled back to Jackson's side, letting her hand wander up his chest. "What about you? It's been that long for you." Her own body had been vibrating with the need to come for days but it just didn't seem right—to fuck when Reign couldn't.

"I'm about to come in my jeans just standing here." He wrapped his arm around her waist and yanked her close, guiding his erection into the notch between her legs. "And as much as I'd love to bend you over that makeup counter and fuck you until your knees give out—" She shivered as her pussy responded to the sexual promise. "I'm not sure it's a good idea to leave Reign alone for too long. The doctor cleared him for sex this afternoon, so get dressed, baby, and let's go home and get naked." He punctuated the sentence with a sharp smack on her backside.

She laughed and stepped back. "Well, if that's what we're going to do, maybe I should get started here."

She untied the silky robe and revealed the high full briefs that Jackson had tossed in her gym bag this afternoon before she left.

With Jackson's hot gaze tracking her movements, she hooked her thumbs into the waistband of her panties. She didn't really mind wearing the granny panties. It actually made her feel sexy.

But tonight, she wanted to be a little wicked—to push her men to the edge.

She slid the slick briefs down her legs and dropped them back in her bag. A low growl from Jackson made her smile. Seemingly ignoring him, but in truth, concentrating on his reaction, she tugged her skirt off the hanger and eased it up, over her thighs. The waist band hung low on her hips, dipping belong her bellybutton.

Deciding to go all out, she skipped her bra and tugged on the thin, cropped tank top, sighing as the material caressed her tight nipples. She smoothed her hands down her body, making sure the right amount of skin was showing.

Done with her show, she finally looked up at Jackson. Heat came off his body in waves. His fingers twitched like he was considering reaching for her.

"Ready to go?" she asked with as much innocence as she could muster.

Jackson scoffed. "You're playing with fire, baby." She smiled and started toward the door. "And you're going to be lucky if you don't get fucked in the taxi on the drive home."

"Hmm, think so?"

He laughed as he took the gym bag from her hand and put it over his shoulder. Dani brushed her fingers along his arm, wondering if he would take her hand. He reached up and intertwined their fingers. It was a simple caress but something about it seemed so powerful. A public acknowledgement that they were together. Not exactly part of a "normal" couple but they were bound together.

As they reached the stage door, it opened and a breeze fluttered past her legs, tickling up under her skirt.

She said good night to the guard at the door and stepped outside, expecting Reign to be waiting. She scanned the area quickly then looked in askance at Jackson.

"There." He lifted his chin to the shadow at the corner of the building.

If Jackson hadn't pointed him out, she wouldn't have seen him. Her feet slowed, the instinctive reaction to approaching a predator. Reign stepped out of the shadow and Dani gasped. He looked almost feral. The strange tension of his body twisted his muscles until he looked like something inside him was trying to break free.

"You'll be fine. He won't hurt you." Jackson's low comment eased her panic enough that she could make herself step forward.

Reign came at her in a rush, grabbing her and carrying her against the wall. His hips pressed against hers, seeking and finding a space between her legs. Heat invaded her pussy and she gasped as he made a slow, hard thrust— as if he was trying to get inside her. Here. Now. The hard line of his cock teased her neglected clit, sending a shiver up inside her sex.

Reign purred and buried his face in her neck, his lips, tongue and teeth moving across her skin. The edge of her skirt fluttered and she felt the warmth of Reign's hand slide up her leg, lifting her thigh and curling it around his hip. She tried to care that they were in public, but it was difficult to concentrate as Reign's steady purrs roared through her head.

Two hundred pounds of hot sexual male surrounded her, wanting to consume her. She glanced to the side and saw Jackson watching them, his eyes heated, focused on the place where Reign's cock pumped against her pussy.

Reign's hand continued its upward glide, cupping her ass, sliding down between the slit in her backside and stroking the open wet flesh of her pussy.

She groaned and moved into the caress, wanting more. Needing more.

Reign's head snapped back and he stared down at her. Confusion, irritation, desire—the three emotions flickered through his eyes in rapid succession. The animalistic glaze to his stare cleared and Reign returned.

"Where are the panties I saw Jackson put in your bag?"

Myriad replies came to mind and Dani picked her favorite.

"I had to take them off—" She blinked her eyes innocently. "They were *wet*."

Reign's eyes flashed and she felt his cock rock against her, as if he couldn't stop the movement. But then he straightened, putting two too many inches between their bodies.

"Nice try, but I think the panties are a requirement."

His glower broke the seductive mood and she rolled her eyes upward.

"Oh, God, not you too."

He ignored her and looked over at Jackson. "Did you know she was naked under this?"

"Yes."

"And you let her out like this?"

"It was a special occasion. It won't happen again."

"Do you have them with you?"

"The panties?"

"Yeah, they're in the bag."

Reign held out his hand and Dani yelped. She scanned the area to see who was watching.

"You can't be serious."

But Jackson was already unzipping her gym bag and reaching inside. His fist appeared, the panties crunched in his fingers. He put them in Reign's hand.

Using his body to block what was happening, he stretched the elastic waistband, his eyes glittering with a wicked dominance that drenched Dani's pussy.

"See, kitten, that's why you need to wear these. So no one but us knows that your pretty little cunt is wet and ready to be fucked."

Every nerve in her body seemed to trigger at once.

"Now, come on. Let's get you properly dressed."

"We're on the street. The guard is staring at us."

"He can't see anything. Jackson is blocking his view." He bent down a little, holding the elastic leg open.

She made a sound that was a mixture of a groan and a hiss, raised her right leg and slipped her foot, shoe and all, through the hole. She glared at Jackson and tried to stand as normally as possible as Reign opened the other leg and she stepped into it. Damn, she wanted to be irritated—she *was* irritated—but something about the situation was still making her pussy cream. Maybe it was the blatant possession and lust that shone in both men's eyes.

"There you go." Reign's voice was low as he straightened, pulling the underwear up her legs, his fingers created a fire trail across her skin. He paused when he reached the edge of her skirt and she saw both men position themselves around her, completely blocking her from anyone's sight. A person on the outside might know something was happening but they wouldn't be able to tell what.

His hands continued to climb until he met the waistband of her skirt. He stopped, letting the elastic snap against her skin. Then as if to assure himself that she was "properly" covered, he ran his palm down her ass and around, sliding between her legs, cupping her pussy, his fingers tapping lightly.

"Yeah, she'll have these drenched by the time we get home."

Somehow her irritation had disappeared and the hunger had returned. Reign bent down and covered her lips with his, a gentle warning kiss—promising her that she wouldn't be wearing the panties for long. When his mouth retreated, Jackson's took its place. Yes, this is what she needed. Her lovers, both touching her, loving her.

She groaned as he slid his tongue between her lips, deep into her mouth.

"Let's go, kids." Reign's interruption drew a growl from Jackson and Dani smiled. He'd been so cool and restrained tonight—a calming force—but she couldn't forget that he was part animal as well. And it appeared both her lovers were showing their beast side tonight. "Down, boy," Reign said. "There's a bed and food just a taxi ride away."

The words seemed to be slow in penetrating but finally Jackson backed up.

Dani ran her thumb along her lower lip. She could still taste both men. Familiar but so different. Both decadent in their own way.

"You're right. Let's go." She grabbed each man's hand and started off, pulling them behind her. She had plans for these two. She led them around to the taxi stand and almost immediately a cab pulled up. Donnie, the bellman, smiled and reached for the back door as she approached.

"I'd better sit up front," she said. He nodded and opened the front passenger side door, helping her in. Jackson had warned about her getting fucked in the taxi home. If she sat in the back with those two, they'd have their hands on her, maybe even fingers inside her before the taxi had made it out of the hotel parking lot.

And while that sounded like fun, she knew the boys were anticipating it.

This would be a little punishment for putting the granny panties back on her.

The cab shifted as the two big males climbed into the back. Dani smiled at the driver and gave him directions to her condo complex.

Jackson and Reign remained silent behind her, steady, heaving until it became a physical presence in the car. She wasn't going to be the one to break it.

She flipped down the passenger visor, pleased to see there was a mirror. Using the task of checking her makeup as an excuse, she tipped the mirror so she could see the backseat.

Jackson and Reign sat, staring benignly forward. Neither man looked at her and a small spiral of hurt built in her chest.

They didn't even care. They weren't even going to tease her about distancing herself or warn her that it wouldn't make any difference. The urge to pout rose up inside her. Childish, she knew but still...

Jackson shifted, his shoulders rolling back as though he couldn't get comfortable. He rested for a moment, then moved again.

Dani's mouth dropped open and she tilted mirror farther down. Drat, she couldn't see. The muscles along Jackson's jaw clenched and he took a sharp fast inhale. What the hell? She sat up taller, trying to see into the backseat but the cab's front bench was too high.

Jackson leaned back, dropping his head onto the rest behind his, staring up at the ceiling, his chest rising and falling in tight pants. She looked at Reign. His body was tilted toward Jackson but his eyes were trained forward, staring right at Dani through the reflection. His lips quirked up in a confident smile. Lust poured from his stare into her, sinking down, swelling in her pussy. She squirmed in her seat. Even without seeing, she knew Reign was touching Jackson, his hand rubbing that hard cock. Dani shivered. She could practically feel the caresses to her own flesh.

Jackson closed his eyes and the muscles along his jaw rippled as he fought the pleasure.

"That's it," Reign whispered.

"Don't make me come," Jackson begged, their voices so quiet the cabbie couldn't hear them.

"I won't," he said, sliding his hand between Jackson's legs and rubbing his balls. A low groan escaped Jackson's throat and Reign couldn't resist leaning in, putting his mouth next to Jackson's ear. "Can you smell her? She's wet and slick. Ready for you to fuck her." Damn, he'd meant to just taunt Jackson a bit, to push at his control and tease Dani. Reign hadn't expected it to make his dick hard enough to pound nails.

He'd been hard, all night, all day. Since the doctor had approved him for sex, he'd been imagining the night. Dani. And Jackson.

Hell, he'd been so horny after a week of not coming, Reign had almost fucked the nurse at his doctor's office but something stopped him. Maybe it was the fact that Jackson would recognize a foreign scent on his body. Or maybe it was just the thought that fucking Dani and Jackson would be better than anything he could find with anyone else.

Dani licked her lips and Reign's grip tightened on Jackson's cock.

They'd be lucky if they got inside her house before she was penetrated by one or the both of them.

"Stop, Reign. Please."

Reign almost ignored Jackson's request. A desire he wasn't sure he recognized swelled inside him. *He* wanted to be the one to make Jackson come. To make him punch his hips up, driving his cock into his fist.

Yeah, he would make Jackson scream and then he'd fuck Dani. She was waiting for her Cat lover to mount her. Waiting to be fucked, hard and long. With a groan that had more to do with regret than pleasure, Reign pulled his hand back, letting his fingers trail away, slipping across Jackson's hip.

He wasn't done with either of them. Not by a long shot.

Chapter Seventeen

℠

Jackson dropped his head back on the seat, his eyes closed, his chest rising and falling in tight hard breaths. The tight line of his body grabbed Reign's attention, wrapping the sensation around his dick like a fist, making it hard to remember they were in public. He cocked his head to right and saw Dani watching them. Her eyes flashed in the tiny reflection. Her mouth hung open, wet and ready to be filled. Even if she couldn't see what was going on, she knew what had happened.

Knew that Jackson had almost come with just the stroke of Reign's hand.

Fuck. He curled his fist and looked away, staring out the window. His body and his mind fought two different battles — wanting and needing, knowing that he shouldn't but still craving, wanting the hard feel of male flesh against his and hungering for the sweet scent of female pussy, wet seductive cunt that would hold him as he rode between her thighs.

The scent of her pussy filled the cab until it consumed his every sense.

He ignored time as it passed. His world turned from the cerebral experience to a purely sensual one — Dani's scent, Jackson's need, Reign's own hunger. Even the touch of his clothes against his skin served to make him hard. The heat from Jackson's body. The delicious perfume of Dani's cunt. Yeah he was going to have them both.

The cab pulled up in front of her building and Jackson tapped Reign on the arm, warning him that they'd arrived. The Cat came alive. His eyes popped open and he came erect, sitting upright, staring at Dani, his eyes barely tracking beyond her form.

As the cab stopped, all three bodies waited—as if they were frozen.

Dani blinked and looked up into mirror. Whatever had caught her attention still held it.

Jackson reached into his wallet and pulled out the forty dollars, throwing it over the seat. The cabby grabbed it as if it was a lifeline. His hands shook as he reached into his pocket to get change. Curious at the man's panic, Jackson glanced at Reign. His breathing continued in the hard shallow pants but it was the teeth that were probably freaking the man out. Reign's lips were peeled back, his teeth long and sharp. Definitely not human.

"Keep the change," Jackson snapped. Now wasn't the time to quibble about money. He needed to get Reign inside.

Reign bounded out of the cab, climbing over Jackson to get out, as if he was a cat that had spotted an escape, slipping through its owner's legs to find freedom.

Reign didn't go far. He stalked to Dani's side, sniffing her neck, rubbing his jaw against her shoulder. His hand caught the back of Dani's leg and lifted, easing her thigh around his waist. The soft sigh that escaped Dani's lips reached Jackson and spurred him forward. It seemed like he was the only one thinking at the moment—which was something considering the way Reign had been rubbing his cock for most of the trip— and if he didn't get them inside, they'd be fucking on the front grass of Dani's condo complex in a few minutes. Reign rocked his hips forward, like he was trying to get inside her.

Make that a few seconds.

The sound of the cab driving off registered in Jackson's mind and he dismissed it. One less thing to worry about. Now he had to get his lovers inside.

"Let's go."

Dani looked at him over Reign's shoulder. Her eyes glittered with undisguised need. He could see she was trying to regain some sanity but it was equally obvious that Reign was pushing her hard and fast to an orgasm. Almost afraid to interrupt—the Cat's control at a dangerously low point—Jackson put his hand on Reign's shoulder.

"Let's get her inside. Then you can have her."

Tension rippled through the muscles beneath his palm but Reign seemed to regain his power. He lifted his head. The golden light in his eyes tightened down to a low fire, then came to life, sparkling with blatant desire—and a touch of humor.

"I intend to. Several times." His body shifted and he moved away, easing his body from Dani's and crowding close. Jackson held steady, intrigued that he felt no masculine instinct to back up. Reign kept coming until the hard bulge of his erection pressed against Jackson's. "And after I've spilled inside her, fucked that pretty little cunt, when she's too sore to take me, I'm going to have you." Jackson's cock twitched at the sensual threat. "Hard and deep." He knew his eyes must have widened because Reign chuckled, leaning in close, his lips a breath away from Jackson's. "You didn't really think you were going to escape having my cock in your ass after the way you've been teasing me for the last three days."

Reign punctuated his words with a firm bite to Jackson's lower lip. The subtle pain made it impossible for him to formulate a reply. Hell, he knew he'd been taunting Reign, teasing him, almost tempting him to fuck him. Looked like he was going to get his wish.

"Don't get too excited." Jackson forced the lust from his voice and went for mocking. "Sure you can get it up after you've fucked Dani?"

The Cat's eyes squinted down to a glare. Cats took their alley cat reputation very seriously.

A deliberate throat clearing brought their attention back to Dani. She'd backed up, her high heels empty on the concrete walkway.

"All this talk about fucking me—maybe you want to ask me about that."

Reign smirked and looked at Jackson, shaking his head. "Baby, we can smell how much you want it. You'll let us have you. Your panties are soaking wet. Again. I felt them when I had my thigh between your legs. You want us." He took one step forward, like he was going to physically demonstrate.

She matched his motion, retreating. "Maybe." She held up the pale blue panties they'd slipped on her at the theater. "But you'll have to catch me first."

She dropped the silky material and turned, accelerating into a full-out run in seconds. She ran around the first building, her white legs flashing like beacons in the night.

Reign froze, his body gathering tension into each muscle. "She didn't..."

"Tease and run from two predators. Yes, she did."

With a laugh that was part growl, Reign took off. Jackson followed. The two males moved like the animals that inhabited their bodies. Both hunting their prey, confident in the end result of the chase. They turned the corner, both pausing long enough to scent the air. She hadn't turned toward her condo. The trail went off to the left. Toward the pool.

They ran, shortening her lead until they were close.

"I'll go in the far entrance," Jackson offered. Reign nodded and headed for the first gated entry. She was in here somewhere. Hiding? Not likely. Not for long. Reign pulled the metal gate shut behind him, hearing the latch click quietly. Her scent was near. The soft perfume of her shampoo, the delicious scent of her arousal teased his nose. The far gate opened and closed. Both predators were in place now.

To human eyes, she might have been barely visible. But Reign could see her clearly, crouched behind a stack of deck chairs. He looked across the pool and saw Jackson nod.

Moving with the animal instincts that lived in them, they stalked her. Reign moved closer, watching as she scrambled away. Jackson shifted his path to intercept. She looked back and forth, the panic of being the prey coming to her. Her breath came in short, harsh pants. But the sweet liquid of her pussy still creamed her thighs. Reign licked his lips, tasting her on the air.

Jackson moved in, herding her toward Reign's position.

He leapt over a reclining chair and landed softly on the loafers he'd slipped into for the show. Positioning himself behind her, he crept close, waiting for her to realize she was trapped between them. With Jackson approaching from the front, she stepped back.

Reign straightened and waited, placing himself in her path, blocking her escape. She glanced over her shoulder but probably didn't see him in the dark. She placed her foot behind her, inching her retreat from Jackson, into Reign's waiting arms.

She hit his chest with a quiet thump. Her gasp made Reign's cock pulse. He needed to slide into her, fuck her but the desire to play with his prey a bit before devouring her was an instinct he couldn't deny.

"We've caught you, kitten. That means we get to have you." He scraped his teeth across her earlobe, finishing with a sharp nip that made her cry out. "Shh, baby, you don't to wake the whole complex." He licked her neck. "Unless you want them to watch while we fuck you."

She shook her head. "Reign, my place is just—"

He made a disappointed clicking sound with his tongue. "You should have thought of that before you ran from us." He trailed his teeth across her skin, a subtle warning. Jackson came closer, his eyes burning red. The little chase had brought out the wolf in him. "What do you think, Jax? We're going to have to teach our little kitten that it's dangerous to tease wild animals."

Jackson nodded and leaned down, covering her mouth with his. Reign watched, knowing that Jax had his tongue deep inside her. Reign pressed closer, rubbing his cock against her ass. Dani pushed back, moving into the caress. He slipped his hands up under her short skirt, finding her bare, remembering that she'd stripped of her panties on the front walkway.

Heat and liquid coated his fingers as he teased her thighs open. He flicked his fingertips across her pussy lips and felt the groan deep in her throat.

"Poor baby, that sweet pussy's been aching for some cock for days, hasn't it?"

She ripped her mouth away from Jackson's and moaned, "Yes."

Five days of doing without, of wanting her cunt, of needing to be inside her swelled in him and he couldn't fight the ache any longer.

He lifted her out of Jackson's grip and spun around, easing her down on one of the reclined deck chairs. Her skirt fluttered up high on her thighs, promising a glimpse of her pussy. Totally focused, he flipped her skirt out of the way and spread her legs, opening her. "Fuck, Jax, look at her."

He felt the wolf beside him, his warmth making the fire inside Reign burn even hotter.

"No, Reign, someone might come out here." She tried to protest, easing the hem of her skirt down. "Someone might hear." Moonlight landed on her pale skin and illuminated it, outlining her sleek legs.

"Then you'd better be quiet." With no other warning, he buried his face in her wet cunt, driving his tongue into her opening. Her cry rang loud and ended with a strangled gargle as she clamped her lips together. The sound turned into a low moan. Reign purred against her pussy lips, letting the rumble vibrate into her sex. Wet flooded her passage. And Reign lapped it up. He still wanted, *needed* to fuck her, but having her flavor on his tongue soothed the ragged edges of his hunger.

He lifted his head just as Jackson knelt beside them. And Reign moved, craving a connection to the male wolf. The urge to fuck Jackson had become a constant but this was different. He wanted to kiss him, share Dani's flavor. Jackson turned his head and met Reign's kiss, accepting this attraction between them.

Jax drew back. "Damn, she tastes good."

"Yeah." That ache satisfied, knowing that Jax was with him, hungry for the same things he wanted, Reign returned to her sex, lapping and tasting. His senses opened wide and he savored each reaction, the way her body vibrated and twisted, wanting more but fighting the pleasure.

Material tore and Reign lifted his head, blinking as he stared at the sight before him. Dani's top was in pieces, rent by Jackson's hands. Her breasts arched up as Jax leaned down and sucked the tip of one into his mouth. His hand raked across her skin, wolflike caclaws erupting out of his fingertips and leaving pale pink scratches across her stomach.

Reign purred at the sight. The wolf wasn't as in control as he liked to think. Keeping his eyes on his lovers, Reign lapped at her pussy, little kitten licks designed to drive Dani wild. Her cunt clenched, as if wanting to be filled. *Don't worry, little one, you'll get your share of cock tonight,* he vowed silently. He twirled his tongue around her clit, capturing the subtle shifts in her body, finding the place that made her scream, made her want to come.

She groaned and rolled her hips up, physically begging him to fuck her.

"Don't come," Jackson warned. He bared his teeth enough so Reign could watch as he bit down, teasing her nipple in a slow sensual bite. Her cry echoed through the condo complex. He followed the bite with a slow sensual lick that sent shivers across her skin. "Reign's been five days without your cunt. Let him enjoy it enough before you come."

"No, please, I can't…" Her pleas drifted away as Reign stabbed his tongue into her pussy, rubbing the hard tip on her inside walls, stretching deep. She dropped her head back, arching up, pushing her nipple against Jackson's lips, begging for more of the almost painful caresses. Her body was lost to her, wrapped in the sensation. Whispers in the corner of her mind tried to tell her to stop this, to make them take her back to her house, but she couldn't bear a break in the intense pleasure. It was too wicked, too compelling for her common sense to invade.

Jackson suckled one nipple before transferring his attention to the other. Each strong, powerful pull of his mouth was like a jolt to her sex, making her twist and shiver against Reign's mouth. She couldn't take much more, not if he wanted her to follow his order not to come.

"Jackson, please…"

He lifted his head, the red in his eyes locking the breath in her chest.

"You might show these tits to half the world but no one but us touches them. They belong to us. Do you understand?"

"Yes." Her agreement was more moan than spoken word.

Reign growled his approval but didn't stop his strokes. He pulled back and twirled his tongue around her clit, one long sloping sweep before slipping his lips around the tight bundle of nerves and sucking ever so slowly. The rhythm he set up was like a deep, hard fuck. Jackson seemed to feel the same beat and joined in, sucking her nipple in time. God, she couldn't take any more. It was too much. They were too much.

Opening her mouth, she screamed, the sound shattering the quiet night.

Vibrations shot through her cunt, sliding into her core and swelling until her body melted.

Hot lips kissed her neck, whispering up her jaw, teasing her lips. Warmth encased her body as Reign stretched out beside her, nibbling on the side of her throat.

"Baby, you know you weren't supposed to come until Jax said you could."

She ignored the warning reprimand. Her mind and body were locked in one accord. She turned her head and captured Jackson's mouth with her own, driving her tongue in deep, letting his taste expand inside her. Gasping for breath, she shifted and turned her attentions to Reign, covering his lips and growling her command into his mouth.

"Fuck me. Now. Both of you. Fuck me." She couldn't stand it any longer. The orgasm that had leveled her body only made the desire worse. She wanted them both.

"Is someone there?" The curious masculine voice rose from the other side of the pool. Dani recognized the sound and took immediate stock of her situation. She could *not* be found half naked with her skirt thrown up over her pussy.

"It's just me, Michael. *Security guard,*" she whispered to her lovers. For a moment she thought they would ignore her urgent tone but then as one unit, they stood up and pulled her to her feet, smoothing her short skirt down. Reign's hand lingered overlong on her ass, as if warning her that they weren't done with her. *Good.*

The metal gate creaked open and a flashlight swung across the water and onto the concrete. It swept in a low arch until it encountered their three pairs of feet. The light bent upward, almost blinding them.

"Dani?"

Michael had worked in the condo complex for three years and pretty much knew everyone by name.

"Hi."

"Are you okay? I heard a scream." As he lowered the light, more figures filled the space behind him. Dani looked down and saw the torn material of her top. With a move that

269

she hoped was subtle, she crossed one arm across her chest and curled the other up, tugging the ripped sides closer together.

All the while trying to think of an answer.

"I...uh...I—"

"She tripped over the deck chair," Jackson explained in that calm, commanding voice of his. Dani did her part by giggling and shrugging with feminine embarrassment.

"Are you okay?"

"I'm fine. They caught me."

"But we should get something on that ankle," Reign added. He winked toward Jackson as Reign turned and scooped her up in his arms. The material of her skirt fluttered down, leaving her ass bare. Cool air rushed across her skin.

"Reign!" Her gasp only made him chuckle.

"That's what you get for stripping your panties off in public." He said the words so low she knew no one but her and Jackson could hear him.

The small crowd that had formed around Michael shifted as Jackson stepped forward, gently easing them aside. His presence also served to shield her, protecting her modesty.

Reign followed Jackson through the group of onlookers, heading toward Dani's house. Licking her had been delicious, her taste sweet on his tongue and he didn't doubt that before the night he'd be there again, but now his cock was about to burst. Seeing her lying there, legs spread, that beautiful cunt open and glistening, wet, just for them. He looked at Jackson's back and wondered again about this strange threesome they found themselves in.

The first time it had been from necessity but now he knew his words to Jax earlier were the truth. He was going to fuck Dani and then...he'd fuck Jackson. God, just the thought of having the two of them spread and waiting for his cock made him ready to come inside his jeans.

He snarled, needing to release some of the energy inside him. Needing to free the animal that lived within him.

Dani turned her head and ran her lips up his throat, her breath hot against his ear as she whispered. "Fuck me." She bit down on the soft lobe. "I need you to come inside me."

Her mouth continued to tease him, with words and kisses, until they reached the front door of her place. Somehow Jackson opened the door. Reign didn't care how, only that it was done and he was free to fuck her. Part of his mind told him to hold back. Punish her for coming when Jax had told her not to, but Reign wasn't in the mood for games. His cock wasn't in the mood for games. He needed to fuck. Needed to be inside her.

Peripherally aware of her surprised noises—damn the woman was deliciously verbal—Reign flipped Dani over, catching her as she fell forward, his arm tight around her waist, holding her ass to his groin.

Heaving in a deep breath, she flipped her hair back and straightened.

"I haven't prepared you yet, so I'm not taking your ass tonight but don't ever think I'm not going there. And soon."

Dani nodded.

"You want that? Want my cock in your ass? Jax riding your cunt."

She tipped her head back and cried out. "Yes!"

He scraped his teeth across the back of her neck, capturing the taste of her. Her moan warned him that he'd bit down hard, probably too hard, but he couldn't stop. The animal inside him was alive tonight.

"Bend over, kitten. I'm going to have you. Now. Hard."

There wasn't a breath of hesitation in her, as if she wanted exactly what he did—hard, deep fucking.

She leaned forward, grabbing the arm of her recliner, bending deeper, lifting her ass, the long sleek lines of her dancer's legs stretching out from beneath the tiny skirt. The material covered her ass and the sight offended him. Reign ripped it aside, not sure if he'd torn the cloth or not. Not caring. Only aware that her ass, her pussy was bare and wet.

He tugged down his zipper, freeing his cock. The shaft sprang out, hard, long. He wrapped his hand around it, squeezing the tip so he didn't come. He didn't want to spill on her. He wanted to be inside her. Wanted his cum flooding her pussy.

Yeah, that's what he needed. He fitted the head of his cock to her opening. Slick, wet heat grabbed him. Something inside him told him to slow down but the Cat and the need and the five days of thinking but not having became too much and he surged into her. This time her scream was muffled by the seat cushions but he felt it, heard it. Every last decibel.

The tight squeeze of her cunt around his cock told him she'd come just as he'd plunged inside her. But there would be more. She was wet and slippery. She'd take him. Hard.

With that thought in mind, Reign pulled back and began to fuck her. His mind clouded over, the animal in him screaming to be released. Reign fought it and welcomed it, using the Cat's strength to hold back his orgasm. She felt too sweet. The slick ride of her cunt was perfect. Made for him.

His balls pulled up close to his cock but he held back. God, he wanted to more.

A masculine scent crept into the room. Though he recognized it, Reign couldn't stop the scream of warning.

"We're cool," Jax said. A low, muffled thump followed and Reign had just enough awareness to see Dani's shoes and panties hit the floor. He peeled his lips back from his teeth, hoping for a smile, knowing it was more of a growl.

Jax chuckled and the sound was enough. It dragged Reign's attention back to his fucking. His hips pumped against Dani's ass, his cock shuttling in and out. God, it was so hot. So tight. He needed to stay inside her.

"Reign."

The soft feminine whimper snagged his attention.

"I need to come. Please, Reign."

He wrapped his hand around her waist, zeroing in on her clit, loving the way her cunt grabbed him as he teased her. He licked her throat. The intoxicating flavor of her skin coated his tongue.

The urge to bite her, to make his mark on her was almost too powerful to resist. He pushed the impotent craving aside. Unlike the wolf, his bite wouldn't change her, wouldn't transform her. It would only kill her.

Roaring into the night, Reign grabbed her hips and began to thrust, hard and deep. His cock drilled into her, feeling her cunt grab him and pull him deeper. Damn she could take him. She would take him. The sweet contractions and muffled cries told him she'd come and Reign let out a scream of his own, demanding that the world acknowledge his power, his ownership of the female who lay beneath him. With a roar that shook the walls, he came, flooding her with his seed, filling her. The act of coming on her earlier paled in comparison to putting his cum inside her. She moaned as the pulses filled her.

Reign smiled, knowing he looked smug and arrogant but how could he not? When your woman came that hard, held you that tight, a male had to feel some satisfaction.

He nudged his hips forward, his cock still hard inside her. It would take a few more fucks to calm the thing down but that raucous orgasm helped. He breathed in, fascinated by the scents of the room—Dani's cunt, his cum, Jackson's desire.

Reign glanced right. Jackson watched, his eyes glowing red and locked on the place where Reign's cock penetrated Dani.

"Fuck her," Reign commanded, pulling out, savoring Dani's whimper as his cock slipped from her pussy. His cum trickled down the inside of her thigh, spilling across her skin.

Jackson shook his head and almost made a step back, like he was fighting the temptation.

"She's wet and hungry. She wants to feel both our cocks inside her. Fuck her," Reign said again.

Jackson stumbled forward, his hands moving to the waistband of his trousers as if he wasn't precisely in control. Reign didn't quite understand it, but he wanted Jackson to have her now, while his cum was still inside her, blending the very essence of each man in her body. He reached forward and ripped the material of Jackson's fly, tugging it open. The wolf growled but the sound changed as Reign gripped Jackson's cock, stroking it. "Fuck her. Take her."

"I can't," Jackson groaned but even as he protested he moved forward, taking her hips in his hands, positioning his cock to her opening. The lessons trained into him from his father and older brother filled his head. But even those voices weren't strong enough to fight the instinct to claim his woman. Dani's whimper as he slipped the head into her pussy made the decision for him and Jackson thrust forward, deep and hard. Dani cried out, grabbing the chair beneath her.

"That's it. Fuck that sweet cunt. She is so hot, so wet. Fill her, Jax. Come inside her."

His hips continued to pound against her ass but he held back, fighting the tingling in his spine, the need to come.

"You need this, man. Fill her."

"No." The word was low and soft. He barely had the strength to force the response from his mouth.

If he came inside her, he would be claiming her, binding her to him. Since Reign had left the hospital, Jackson had explained to Dani what being his mate would mean and how it would happen but she hadn't agreed. He couldn't do this to her.

Reign leaned close, putting his mouth against Jackson's ear.

"Can you imagine not fucking her? Not having her?"

Jackson's neck stretched long and his lips pulled back, baring teeth that were stretching, dangerous.

"Or having some other man fuck her?"

With a snarl that reverberated through the room, Jackson shook Reign away and turned his full attention to Dani. She slammed her hips back, meeting his hard thrusts. Reign groaned and moved close rubbing his hard cock against Jackson's hip, moving with them as they fucked.

Jackson tried to fight the wolf's desire, tried to regain control but the animal was strong, spurred on by Reign's words. The wolf wasn't letting him back down. The sweet contractions along his cock and Dani's muffled scream told him she'd come but he couldn't stop. He needed to be inside her just a little longer.

"Please, Jackson." She dropped her head down between her hands and pushed back, shoving him back into her. "Please." The hunger in her voice was too much.

With a shout, he came, pouring into her in steady pulses. The wolf howled in his head. He'd done it. He'd claimed her.

Reign purred beside him, his hips pumping as he came on Dani's back and Jackson's hip.

The scents of all three blended in the air, keeping Jackson hard. The wolf paced inside his brain and he couldn't calm the beast. His heart pounded. Coming inside her had started the transition, turning her into a werewolf but the animal still needed to lay claim. The wolf needed to finish it, mark her so the world would see.

Feeling his teeth stretch long, almost painfully, he bent forward and pierced the slim line of her neck. She cried out and he felt the contractions of her cunt as she came again. The wolf inside him rumbled his pleasure and the Cat followed suit, purring and growling.

The reality of what he'd just done, of what he'd done to Dani slammed into his brain. The human side of him rebelled but the animal rejoiced. She belonged to him. There were ways to reverse it but they would be painful for both of them.

Jackson forced his hips back, sliding his cock out of her. Her whimper and the slight pump of her hips as if she didn't want him to leave her comforted him.

He opened his mouth, the apologetic explanation forming on his lips. He never got a chance to speak the words. Reign approached, slipping his hands under Dani's collapsed body and lifting her until she stood, held upright between his and Jackson's body. Her head dropped back, landing on Jackson's shoulder, openly revealing the bite mark on her neck. The wound would heal quickly, probably by morning. The sight of his possession made him hard again and he couldn't resist pumping his cock against her ass. She smiled and wrapped her arm behind his head, pulling him close, dragging him down.

Unable to resist, he kissed the four puncture wounds and savored each shiver as she responded. She moaned and turned, wrapping her arms around Jackson's neck, pressing her breasts against his chest, her pussy rubbing against his hip.

"You came inside me." Her voice was lazy and sexual, more pleased than scared.

"Yes."

She smiled and leaned back, letting Reign support her weight. "Does that mean I belong to you?"

"Yes."

"And you belong to me."

"Yes."

She pulled him forward and stretched up, meeting him with a hot open-mouthed kiss. She pumped her hips forward, rubbing her clit against his hip. Reign was pressed up against her back, no doubt his cock slipping between her ass cheeks, tempting her with both of them. Gasping, she pulled back, one hand going behind her to reach for Reign.

"That's it. She's ready for more," Reign said. He cupped her head and turned her face so he could kiss the other side of her neck. "You want more cock, don't you, baby? You want more cock inside you." Reign's gaze met his over her shoulder, intent and heat. The two of them would fuck her, claim her together.

The werewolf bite and his cum would make her crave sex. And he and Reign would be there to satisfy her.

"Please," she moaned, her body squirming like she couldn't get enough of their touch. "Fuck me."

The light in Reign's eyes flared with pure lust.

"Oh, we will, baby. We will."

Chapter Eighteen

ର

Jackson awoke, his cock hard, hot, a fiery streak moving up the long length, his eyes rolling into the back of his head. The low moan that escaped his throat was impossible to contain.

The hot mouth that encased his cock retreated.

"Shh. You don't want to wake Dani." Reign's laughing words barely had time to penetrate Jackson's half-sleep state before he swallowed Jax's cock. Jackson grabbed the empty sheet beside him, fighting the urge to thrust and to growl. Fuck!

"What are you doing?" Jackson asked softly, keeping the words as low as his breath would allow.

Before he answered, Reign lashed his tongue across the head of Jackson's cock. He retreated with a slow sexual lick. Reign raised his eyes, staring straight into Jackson's gaze.

"Pretty obvious." He flicked his eyebrows up and down. "I'm going to fuck you," he said. "Thought I should make sure you come before I sink into that hot—" *Lick.* "Tight—" *Swirl, stroke.* "Ass."

Conscious of the body asleep beside them and the way they'd put her to hard use through the night, Jackson tried to hold back his noises but damn, Reign was good. His mouth was strong, sucking with just enough pressure as he pulled back. Unable to stop himself, Jackson slid his hand into Reign's hair, holding him, touching him as he sucked him off.

He pushed his head back into the pillow, trying to keep still but unable to resist the steady suck and wicked release of Reign's mouth.

"God."

Reign snapped his head back. "Not even close. But thanks for the compliment."

He grinned and winked and drove Jackson's cock deep into his mouth. The Cat's tongue swished and flicked across the underside of his shaft, somehow adding suction as he retreated.

Jackson bit down, grinding his teeth together. Needing more. Just needing.

His teeth stretched long and he knew that urge to bite was more fundamental than a human craving. Dani wore his mark but the wolf wouldn't rest until Reign had been claimed as well. He didn't have to worry about turning Reign into a wolf but he needed to mark him. Unable to stop himself, he grabbed Reign's arm and yanked it up, turning the wrist into him. Jackson leaned toward the pale flesh that appeared before him and bit down.

Reign groaned but didn't release his cock.

Jackson turned his head toward Reign. The two male stares met, realizing what had just happened, what was happening between them. Jackson licked the wounds, his teeth still extended, ready to make a more permanent mark on Reign's neck so everyone would see his claim.

With a groan that rumbled through the room, Reign swallowed Jackson's cock, taking him deep, pumping his mouth up and down, sucking hard as he pulled back, every stroke reaching into Jax's core.

Jax's cry filled the room. There was no way to hide it. The taste of Reign's flesh on his tongue. The vital memory of marking him was too much to handle. He'd claimed the male, marked him for the world to see. And he was a Cat. The trouble that situation would cause for *both of them* was incredible but Jackson couldn't worry about it now.

With a single upward thrust, he came, spilling into Reign's mouth. Oh, fuck. He hadn't meant to do that. Hadn't meant to come in him again. Like Reign needed any help being aroused. The man was an alley cat. He'd fuck anytime, anywhere.

Thinking Reign would come up pissed, Jackson looked down, ready to offer a grudging apology. He would only take so much of the blame considering Reign had woken him with a blowjob. Instead of irritation glaring back at him, Reign grinned, his eyes laughed. He'd intended Jackson to come in his mouth.

"Bastard," Jackson muttered.

"Now I'm going to being able to fuck you long and hard."

Jackson's muscles clenched at the thought of the fuck that was coming his way but he couldn't refuse. Didn't want to refuse.

"Roll over. It's your turn now, wolf-boy."

Long sleek legs shifted beside him and the scent of warm aroused woman filled the air. Both males took a moment to breathe deep. Reign crawled up between Jackson and Dani, crouching over both their bodies. Dani opened her eyes and smiled.

"Did we wake you?" He kissed her quickly. "I'm thinking it was hard to sleep through the wolf coming." He flashed his eyes at Jackson. "You scream like a girl."

"Fuck you."

"Maybe later." The Cat leaned down and placed a kiss on Jackson's lips as well. "I get to do you first."

Dani giggled and Jackson shook his head. The Cat was in a playful mood. Strange, during the day, away from bed, Reign was all mountain lion—focused, dangerous. But when it came to sex, he liked to play. Like a kitten. Jackson held that revelation to himself, ready to pull it out when he needed it the most.

"Actually I woke up before that." She ran her hand across Reign's shoulder. "But you two looked so hot together, I didn't want to disturb you."

"Our kitten is a voyeur, Jax."

"Yeah."

A hint of red tinged her cheeks but she shrugged, not at all ashamed of watching.

"Nice. Since you're awake, you can help me fuck our boy here."

Dani's tongue appeared between her teeth. "Goody, what do I get to do?"

"Give him something to do with his mouth so he doesn't wake the neighbors." Reign balanced himself on his hands, hovering over her. Jackson's cock grew hard. Watching Reign, seeing his muscles move, pure animal power and strength, knowing that he had the right to reach out and touch, made his wolf growl.

"I can do that."

Reign nodded and bent down, opening his mouth and rubbing his lips across her nipple. It wasn't a kiss, just a caress of lips to skin. The tight peak stretched even further and a wicked little catch broke from Dani's throat.

He stroked the flat of his tongue over her nipple, like a cat lapping at cream.

Jackson moved, turning his body, laying claim to her other nipple, loving the way she arched up, pressing deeper into his mouth. He sucked hard and the hot scent of her pussy juices filled the room.

"Yeah, that's what he needs." Reign turned his head and met Jackson in a deep kiss, tongues twined around each other, the taste of his own cum mixing with Reign's unique flavor. "Make her scream," he commanded as he pulled back. Crawling back down to the end of the bed, brushing kisses across Dani's stomach, Jackson's hip, light caresses that he got the feeling were more to pleasure Reign than either him or Dani. The Cat just liked to touch. He guided Jackson onto his hands and knees so he straddled Dani.

"Good morning," Jackson greeted her, placing a quick kiss on her lips.

"Morning."

"How do you feel?"

She smiled, her cheeks turning a delightful red as she stared up him. He could see the memory of the previous night in her eyes. And the things they'd done. To her. With her. There wasn't an inch of her body that hadn't been touched, loved, fucked. It had been early morning—near four o'clock—before they'd showered, changed the sheets and collapsed back on the bed, all three of them exhausted and too fuck-addled to do any more.

"Good." She squirmed.

"A little sore?" The blush deepened and she nodded. "I'll go easy on you, eh? Let me know if you want me to stop."

"Hello? Fucking? Let's go." Reign smacked Jackson's ass.

Dani giggled and Jackson rolled his eyes. "Impatient pussycat, isn't he?"

"Yes, but he's ours." If Reign heard her, he didn't respond.

"He is that." He kissed her again and then inched down the bed, positioning himself between her legs, the deep pink of her pussy glittering with her liquid. He licked his lips, tasting her on the air. He moaned and bent down teasing the tip of his tongue to the upper edge of her slit. The hot sweet taste of her cunt tantalized his senses, begging for more. He nudged her thighs wider, opening her completely. She hissed in a quick breath and Jackson watched her to make sure it was surprise not pain that drew the sound from her.

She nodded and lifted one foot, draping her knee over his shoulder, inviting him in. With a groan, he leaned forward, opening his mouth and kissing her pussy, dipping his tongue into her passage, rubbing lips and tongue against her sensitive flesh, sucking on her pussy lips, loving the way she creamed and rocked her hips, guiding him to where she wanted more.

"That's it. Fuck that looks sweet. Smells fucking great."

Jackson moaned his agreement but didn't take his mouth away from her delicious pussy. Even when cool slick fingers teased his opening, he lapped, relaxing as Reign started with one finger and moved up to two, pumping in and out. The sensation was still foreign enough that Jackson had to pause and breathe, reminding his body to relax.

Reign scraped his teeth across Jackson's back. "That's it, man. Let me in. You know it'll feel great." The words and their subtle caress allowed his ass to ease. "Oh, yeah. One more. Take one more and then I'm going to fuck this sweet ass."

The burning grew as Reign pushed three fingers in. Jackson turned his head, pressing his lips against Dani's thigh, and grunted, fighting the instinctive protest. Dani didn't speak but she ran her fingers through his hair, comforting him, giving him another focus as Reign began to finger-fuck him, the slow steady thrusts too much at first but then his body eased and he found his hips moving, pushing back against Reign's hand.

"Yeah, you're ready."

Reign pulled his fingers out, wiped them on a towel he'd placed beside them and picked up the bottle of lube. The distinctive click of the bottle opening echoed through the room.

As Reign slicked up his cock, Jackson had the revelation that Reign had done some planning for this. He'd obviously gotten up and gathered all the supplies they needed while he and Dani had slept. The man moved as silently as, well, a cat.

That thought kept him amused long enough to fill the time until Reign placed the thick head of his cock to Jackson's ass. He'd been stretched and had done this before but still Reign's cock was thick. He pushed the first few inches in and waited, giving Jackson time to adjust before pressing deeper.

The burning returned, straining his muscles to hold still as Reign filled him.

Jackson lifted his head, gasping for breath, fighting the pain-pleasure that assaulted his ass. It felt good, so good. There was a corner of his mind that felt like he should rebel, that he shouldn't want this so much but damn he couldn't resist the need to feel Reign inside him. His body was primed to fuck.

"Oh, fuck you feel good," Reign groaned, sinking in. He kept his penetrations slow, almost tormenting.

"So do you," Jackson felt compelled to admit. He looked up. Dani watched, her eyes twinkling with a mixture of sexual pleasure and laughter. "And you, baby, taste delicious." Deciding he'd been too long from her cunt, he lowered his head and licked a long single stroke up the center of her slit. Breath caught in her throat and Reign's cock twitched deep inside Jackson.

"Oh, yeah, lick her, man. God, she is so sweet."

Agreeing silently with the male buried balls-deep in his ass, Jackson buried his face in her cunt and sank his tongue into her passage, stretching deep before drawing back and licking the sensitive opening.

Distant noises tried to penetrate Jackson's mind but he brushed the intrusions aside. All that mattered was Dani and Reign.

Reign lifted off his back and grabbed Jackson's hips.

Jackson braced himself, digging his elbows into the mattress, knowing that Reign's slow thrusts were going to change. A cautious fuck wasn't on the agenda. Reign pulled back. A wicked retreat before the hard penetration. The shock made Jackson tense but Reign's hands and soothing words eased him and he relaxed, letting Reign sink into him. Reign's cock pressed against that sweet spot inside Jackson's ass and he cried out.

Dani squirmed beneath him and Jackson smiled. He didn't want to neglect her. He dipped down and lapped at her pussy, teasing, tasting strokes, using her seductive scent to calm his pounding heart.

Reign retreated and drove in, harder, deeper.

Jackson fought back the moan, his body easing to take the thick cock. It felt so good.

"Oh fuck, that's—"

The door popped open.

Jackson snapped his head to the right. Breath locked in his lungs.

Max filled the doorway, his mouth open, his eyes so wide he looked like a cartoon character.

"Uh...uh..." His head twitched back and forth as he seemed to be taking it all in. "Damn. Uhm, I'll be back. Later. Much later. Think I'll go for a walk."

Before Jackson could protest, Max had backed out of the room and pulled the door shut.

For a moment, no one moved.

Then Dani draped her arm across her eyes and sighed. Red washed over her cheeks.

Jackson took a deep breath and tried to contain the exploding neurons in his brain. Max. Had seen him. With Dani and Reign. "I need to go talk to him."

He squirmed, trying to break the hold his lovers had on his body. Reign's cock shifted inside him and both men groaned. Even with his brother's arrival, his need hadn't subsided.

Dani looked at him then her gaze shifted and she stared over his head to Reign. Some sort of silent communication passed between them.

"I should go," Jackson protested again, but he heard the wavering conviction in his voice.

Reign's hands tightened on his hips. And Dani's fingers slid through his hair, subtly guiding him back to her cunt. The captivating perfume of her sex lured him closer and he couldn't resist. He flicked out his tongue. The flavor exploded in his mouth.

Even as he groaned, Reign sank back into his ass, filling him.

"Wait. No. I need to go—" Hot teeth bit into his shoulder, followed by a slow stroke of Reign's tongue.

"Let me fuck you," Reign whispered. His voice compelling in its power. "Let me have you." He pumped his cock again into Jackson's ass. "And you can't leave Dani desperate. Needing your mouth."

"Max."

"Later. Now you belong to us."

Jackson couldn't resist—the pleasure of Reign's cock and the sweet taste of Dani's cunt. Blocking his brother from his mind, he let his lovers captivate his senses, pressing back as Reign fucked him, driving his tongue into Dani's pussy, savoring her taste as she cried out, coming against his lips.

He groaned as Reign's large hand closed around his cock, pumping in time to his thrusts, until Jackson couldn't hold back. He cried out, coming on the bed sheet. Reign moaned moments later, his cock buried deep inside Jackson, hot spurts filling his ass.

* * * * *

Jackson scraped his wet hair back from his face, using his fingers to comb through the longish strands. His body was buzzing—alive with good sex and emotion. He needed to find his brother. Needed to explain. It wasn't going to be a fun conversation but it needed to be done. And the sooner the better.

He picked up the phone and hit Max's number. His twin answered almost immediately.

"Where you at?" Jackson asked.

"Downstairs. By the pool."

"I'll be down." He clicked the phone off and took a deep breath. It was time to face his brother.

But first he had to face his lovers.

He walked out of the bathroom, stopping when he saw Dani and Reign still lying on the bed, the scent of their loving filling the room.

"I need to go talk to Max."

Dani nodded but she snagged her lower lip with her teeth.

Instead of turning toward the door, he knelt beside the bed and kissed her, sinking his tongue into her mouth, needing her taste with him.

"It'll be okay, baby."

Again she nodded but he could tell she didn't believe him.

Reign watched as well, his eyes shuttered and dark.

Jackson pushed himself up and headed for the door. "I'll be back." His foot had landed on the top stair when Reign's voice stopped him.

"Jackson." The Cat approached cautiously. "Tell your brother whatever you need to."

"What?" Jackson turned and shook his head, not sure what Reign meant.

"You know, tell him you were drunk or that I coerced you or that it was a one time shot. Sexual exploration. Tell him whatever you need to." He grimaced and in the light, it almost looked like he blushed. "It won't hurt my feelings or anything, I guess, is what I'm trying to say. Just tell him it was a one-off."

Jackson pushed back up onto the landing, crowding Reign with his body.

"That would work." He leaned in and kissed the other male, driving his tongue deep into his mouth, commanding a response before he pulled back. "But what will I tell him the next time he recognizes your scent on me? And the time after that." He placed another fast, hard kiss on Reign's mouth then ran down the stairs, strangely lighthearted. As if Reign's reluctance to reveal their relationship made Jackson's desire to do just that much stronger. Cats had a tendency to be very casual about their relationships but if Reign thought he was getting away without a fight, he was in for a surprise. Jackson's wolf growled his agreement. The Cat had been claimed, marked. He belonged to Jackson now. And Jackson planned on keeping him.

Jackson walked out the front door and down the zigzagging paths. It was early—damn early for Max—so Jackson didn't run into anyone on his way.

The pool area was quiet. Max reclined on one of the deck chairs, his face tilted up to the sun. Jackson remembered the night before and Dani spread out on one of those chairs, her skirt kicked up, her breasts bared and tight. His cock twitched inside his jeans and he hoped this conversation didn't last long. He wanted to get back to his lovers. The desperate need to fuck would ease a bit, but now, so recently after he'd marked them both, his body, his wolf needed to reinforce the claims.

Max's eyes popped open as Jackson approached.

"Hey."

"Hey."

A strange distance appeared between them that Jackson hadn't ever experienced.

He sat down, taking the chair next to this twin but not reclining back.

"You okay?" Max asked.

Jackson smiled. Max was always trying to take care of him.

"I'm good. You?"

"Good."

Silence filled the space and Jackson knew it was up to him to fill it. His brother wasn't going to cross the abyss.

"Listen, about upstairs—"

"Don't worry about it."

"No, I want to explain."

But Max interrupted again. "You and Dani?"

Of that whole scene upstairs, the part he notices is Dani and me? He must be avoiding the other third of the situation.

"Uh, yeah."

Max nodded. "I guess I can see that." He laughed. "God, now that I think about it, I'm not sure why I didn't see it before. You're what she needs. She's what you need. Damn, I bet you guys'll be great together."

"Thanks." It was good to have his brother's blessing. But that was only part of the equation. "About Reign—"

"No need to explain."

"No, I have to—"

"Really you don't."

Jackson crushed his wolf's growl. He was the sane, calm twin. He had to remember that. Max sat up, swinging his legs to the side so their knees bumped into each other.

"Listen, it's—"

Max's hand covered Jackson's mouth.

"You don't have to explain. Trust me. I understand."

Jackson tried to pull away but Max only followed him, his palm clamping down on Jackson's mouth, inhibiting any sound.

Max grimaced. "While I was in Alaska I met Mandy and Gideon." Jackson nodded—because he sure as hell couldn't speak. "And I'm sleeping with both of them."

"Mmm?" The answer came out muffled.

"Yeah. Both of them. Not really sure how it happened but it did so I completely understand you and Reign. Though it's going to take awhile to get that picture out of my head." As if both men had forgotten that Max had his hand slapped across Jackson's mouth, Max kept talking. "I mean, it must be something that runs in our family, with Mik and Taylor and Zach."

"Mmm?" Damn, he sounded like Scooby-Doo.

"Oh yeah, you haven't talked to Mikhel?"

Jackson shook his head.

"Well, that's what he's going to warn you about. I guess their wedding is going to be a three-way affair." Max sighed and offered a self-defeated smile. "Well, I guess we all came by it honestly."

Jackson's mind churned but it took a moment to catch up with Max's last comment. *Came by it honestly?*

He yanked Max's hand away. "What?! Wait. You mean Mom and Dad and..." He thought about all those years, growing up in his father's house. Who...? "Byron?"

"Oh, yeah. Guess you haven't talked to Dad either."

"No, I've been dodging his calls."

"I was too. He caught me just as I was leaving Alaska. I guess with Mik's wedding they've decided to come out."

Jackson sank down, not sure how he felt about that. This was his parents after all and while he knew they had sex — obviously since they had five children — the idea of them having a *sex life* was a little too freaky for his mind to handle. And the fact that another male had entered in that relationship. Wow. It was going to take a bit of time before he could adjust to that reality.

He looked over at Max. There was a foreign serenity — for lack of a better word — that hung about his brother.

"You're happy." It wasn't a question.

"Yeah."

"Mandy and Gideon, huh?" He didn't know why the idea should shock him. After all, he was mating with a human female and a Cat. "Mates?"

He nodded. "If they'll have me. I haven't quite broached that subject yet."

Jackson laughed. Max was the impulsive twin yet he was the one waiting to claim his mates. Jackson had just plowed forward.

"What about you? Dani and Reign?"

"Yeah."

Max's eyes squinted down. "He's a Cat. How's he dealing with the fact that you're his mate?"

"He's having issues but he'll come around."

"You sure?"

Jackson shrugged. "He'd better or I'm pretty sure Dani will kill him."

Epilogue

℘

"I'm going to kill him," she muttered under her breath, watching Reign move through the crowd.

Dani tapped her foot and swung her knees to the music. The crowd on the dance floor was an interesting mix of bodies. Or maybe an interesting concentration. The bride was dancing with both her grooms and her best friend was out there with her two lovers as well. Dani and Jackson had danced to the last song while Reign prowled the outside of the room. She glanced over, her eyes tracking his path. The feral heat to his stare made her heart flutter. He looked like a caged animal, searching for a weakness in the bars, ready to make his escape.

"It will be all right," Jackson whispered. He leaned close and put his hand on her leg. The tension in her body eased. His touch smoothed the rough edges of her nerves. And there had been a lot of them lately. She'd gotten vacation from the show so she could attend the wedding with Jackson. It hadn't been strictly necessary but he'd wanted her to meet his family. The stress of that was bad enough—the stage manager wasn't inclined to let dancers leave, not three weeks after the show had just opened.

Then there had been the weirdness of meeting Jackson's parents. Just three weeks after being engaged to their *other* son. The first meeting had been a mixture of tight smiles and confused looks.

And on top of all of that, Reign looked like he was ready to bolt. He'd flirted with every female in the room. Jackson's assurances helped a bit but she was going to rip Reign a new one once they got back to the hotel.

If he even came back to them. What if he chose one of the cute female werewolves to go home with? The little bitches seemed more than eager.

"Trust me, baby," Jackson said, his voice calm and almost amused. "He's fine."

She looked at Jackson, trying to take strength from his steady gaze.

"If he puts his hand on one more woman…"

She let the threat linger in the air.

"Make him shower before he touches you. That will get him."

The twinkle in Jackson's eyes made her smile. "And what will you be doing while he showers?" She leaned down and placed her lips against Jackson's ear. "Fucking me?"

"Yeah."

"Licking me?"

"Oh yeah."

She felt his answer deep inside her cunt, making it clench and shiver. God, she needed him. Wanted him. He was solid and strong. A man she could rely on. Someone to hold onto.

"Loving me?" she asked again, pushing just a little, needing his strength to keep her steady.

"Yes."

His soft, serious voice drilled through the sexual teasing, straight to her heart. She snapped her head back and she stared down. Lovers had told her before that they loved her but it was usually during or right before sex. Never just while they were playing.

"Really?"

The right edge of Jackson's mouth pulled up into an arrogant, confused smile.

"Of course, baby. I love you."

The center of her chest fell away, leaving for a brief moment the empty hollow with purely sexual need, then the emptiness was filled — with love.

"I love you too."

Their smiles matched as Jackson nodded.

"Good."

"What are we going to do about Reign?" she asked, tipping her head toward their wayward lover.

Jackson shook his head. "Don't worry. He's just freaking out because he's a Cat but he'll be back. They always return."

About midnight, Dani realized that Jackson had been right. Reign had scouted the crowd, scanning, sniffing, sampling the available females. But even when he'd disappeared, he'd returned, moments later, his face set in a disgruntled visage, like he hadn't found what he was looking for.

Dani tried to keep her nerves under control, she really did, but seeing Reign flirt and seduce all those women...

Strong arms surrounded her pulling her back against a solid, hard chest.

"Don't worry," Jackson assured her again.

"Are you sure?" she asked. "He's disappeared with three different women and I'd really hate to have to rip their lips off at your brother's wedding."

Jackson chuckled and cuddled her closer, easing her against his cock. "Yes, he left the room with three different women but did you notice how fast he returned? And without the woman?"

She shook her head. She'd been too annoyed to see Reign leaving with a strange woman. She wasn't about to watch the return, to see the flustered, flushed, satisfied look on the woman's face. She'd seen the look on her own face too many times in the past three weeks. She didn't want to see it on another female.

"We both know Reign isn't that fast of a fuck—not even for a quickie."

"Really?" She hated the hopeful sound in her voice.

"Really." Jackson tightened his arms around her. "I've seen him ride your slick cunt for hours, filling you, fucking you. He takes his time."

Every word was like a thousand tongues on her clit. She grabbed his hands and gripped them, using his strength to keep herself upright.

"That's it, baby. I'm going to take you home and fuck you, have you. Fill that sweet cunt, ride between your thighs, spilling my seed into you."

Unable to resist, she dropped her head back, not caring who might see. "Yes." She rubbed her ass against his cock. "Fuck me."

"Soon. Soon, baby. I'm going to have you."

A low growl rumbled from behind them. It was familiar and Jackson chuckled when he heard it.

"I think we finally got the kitty cat's attention."

"Are we leaving soon?" Reign said by way of greeting. "Being around all these dogs is starting to irritate me."

Dani tilted her head to the side and blinked her eyes. "Funny, that didn't stop you from *pawing* every available female in here."

Reign's cheeks actually turned red as he turned and looked at the almost empty dance floor. The party was winding down. At least here. Jackson was sure that the real fun was beginning in rooms nearby. Jackson's parents had offered him his old room but he'd declined. He wasn't bold enough to fuck his two lovers in his parents' house.

"Let's go," Jackson said.

Jackson made plans to meet up with Max, Mandy and Gideon for brunch the next day and there was a family barbecue planned for the next evening. It was comforting to be at home again. He'd left after college, needing to be away from his father's pack. Being the son of an Alpha could be a pain in the ass.

But now it was different. Made him think about moving back.

He led the way as they said goodbye to the bride and grooms. He hugged his brother and Zach. It still shocked him that the two men were lovers. He wasn't sure why except maybe it was the "I don't want to think about anyone in my family having sex" instinct.

Reign held out his hand to Mikhel. Mikhel looked at it, not responding in kind. It didn't bother his brother that Jax was sleeping with another man. He just didn't like that he was sleeping with a Cat. Said a human would have been preferable.

After a long moment, Mikhel stretched out his hand and met Reign's palm.

"Congratulations."

"Thanks, Cat."

Reign's jaw clenched and Jackson rolled his eyes. Just what he needed—a brawl at his brother's wedding.

"Mikhel, he does have a name."

Mikhel shrugged with the deliberate arrogance of an Alpha wolf.

"Why do they bother? Cats never come when they're called."

Jackson watched Reign's shoulders pull back and stepped forward. What the fuck was he going to do if his brother and his mate started to fight? Tension became a palpable force around and between the two male bodies.

"Mikhel!" The female voice ripped through the air with enough power to make every male flinch. Taylor stepped forward, her white gown swirling around her feet. "Back off."

Mikhel had the grace to look sheepish. "Ah, I was just playing with him, baby. You know how Cats like to play."

"Not at my wedding."

The words were crisp.

Mikhel straightened and looked down at his bride. "*Our* wedding."

"Right and if you want to have *our* wedding night, you'll back off."

Mikhel's mouth spread into a wide smile. Damn, Jackson couldn't remember seeing his brother smile like that—not since they were kids.

Mikhel tipped his head back and laughed. He grabbed Taylor, pulling her to him. "God, I love you." He snuggled her up against his hip, holding her in place as he looked over her to Reign and Jackson.

"Reign, you must be a pretty fine pussycat if you've caught my brother. Welcome to the family." Mikhel looked down at the gasping woman in his arms. "Was that nice enough, baby?"

"Very nice." Taylor stroked her hand down his cheek and he took the cue, bending down and kissing her.

Reign sniffed like the whole thing offended him and walked away. Laughter followed his exit and Jackson tried not to groan.

Dani sidled up to him and slipped her arm through his.

"Problems?"

"I don't know. Cats don't play well with others."

"We should go after him."

Jackson nodded and waved to his brother who was currently kissing his bride and had his hand wrapped around Zach's back, pulling the male into their embrace, so didn't notice.

They made it back to the hotel in relative calm, Dani and Jackson discussing the wedding and reception. Reign concentrated on driving. He was too horny to talk. He wanted to fuck.

He was the first out of the car, needing air that wasn't infused with the scents of Jackson and Dani. The fresh breath didn't help much. He followed them up to the room. Jackson pulled Dani to the side of the bed and wrapped his arms around her, kissing her, sliding his hands up and down her sides.

Reign started to move in then stopped. Usually there was some kind invitation, some indication that he was welcome. Hell in the three weeks since they'd gotten together, he'd never once not been welcomed. But somehow there was a wall between them now.

It only took a moment to figure out why. The women. Damn, it wasn't like he'd fucked any of them. And what did they expect? He was a Cat. It was his nature.

Reign folded his arms on his chest, feeling like a spoiled child sent to bed without dinner. Fuck, he hadn't touched any of them. Much. Hadn't been able to. His cock just wasn't interested.

It was that damn werewolf bite. Erotic as it had been when Jackson had sunk his teeth into Reign's skin, now it was a damn nuisance. If it hadn't been for that bite, he could be off with one of those hot little werewolf chicks. Several had approached him, liking the danger of fucking a Cat, but when he'd followed them into the hall...nothing. He'd tried kissing the first one but the taste hadn't been right. Like something sour had invaded his mouth.

So he'd avoided the whole mouth-to-mouth contact after that one but still, nothing seemed to work. His cock stayed brutally calm. Damn werewolf bite.

"So, what? I'm being punished?" He heard the snide tone to his voice but couldn't stop it. The scent of Dani's cunt had filled the car making him hard the whole drive back to the hotel.

But he was being sent to bed without any sex because he'd been a bad boy.

Dani shook her head. "Not punished. You just get to watch."

"How long?"

The confusion in her eyes comforted his soul just a bit.

"How long, what?"

"How long do I have to watch?"

She smiled and the wicked seductress came through. She reached up under her dress and pulled down her panties. The scent of her pussy filled the room and he heard Jackson's groan joining with his. She stepped out of the pink underwear.

"Until you can't stand it anymore."

She turned and climbed onto the bed, her body stretching and elongating like a cat's, wickedly sensual. The soft flowing material of her dress spilled cross the bed, draped across her ass, giving him the perfect view of the indent between her ass cheeks. His cock pressed against the smooth placket of the dress trousers he'd worn to the wedding. Damn, was she ready to have that sweet ass fucked?

He watched as she crawled forward, straddling Jackson's legs, her hands working the button and zipper of his fly. Jackson's groan and Dani's gasp of appreciation signaled the release of his cock. Damn, if he was going to be forced to watch, he wanted a good view. He shifted to the side, the small hotel room not giving him much space but needing to see it all — Jackson's cock, Dani's red lips as she sucked him off.

Dani's mouth hovered over Jackson's cock and Reign groaned, knowing the sweet heat from her breath, that moment of anticipation before she actually licked — her tongue flicked out and swirled around the thick head of Jackson's cock.

Reign groaned and grabbed at the air, keeping himself back, fighting the urge to step in and rip Dani away — torn between wanting Dani's mouth on his cock and wanting his mouth on Jackson's cock. The werewolf was a seductive fuck partner that was sure. He liked everything, loved to have his body stroked, willing to take it hard in the ass, willing to give it hard.

Dani opened her mouth and swallowed, taking Jackson's cock deep into her throat. Reign's dick jumped, wanting the same treatment, needing something.

She groaned as she deep throated Jackson, giving him a few extended moments in her mouth before she pulled back. She'd done that a few times to Reign and he knew how sweet it was. Jackson's hips pumped up, like he couldn't resist fucking a few more inches into her mouth. Temptress that she was, she retreated, petting him and soothing him though she didn't allow him back in her mouth.

She turned her head and stroked her tongue across the base of his cock.

Jackson's hands slid her dress up, baring her ass, revealing her pretty cunt. Reign found himself wandering in that direction, needing to see her pussy as she sucked Jackson. Tiny streams of liquid trailed down the inside her thighs.

He strode forward, grabbing Dani's hips and holding them still, grinding his cock against her bare ass.

"That's as much as I can stand."

She glanced over her shoulder, a wicked smile on her swollen lips.

"You sure?"

"Don't tease me, kitten. You're already going to get your ass fucked tonight. It's just a matter of whether it's slow and as gentle as I can make it or hard and fast so you can't walk tomorrow."

She laughed. Reign bent down and bit her ass. The laughter turned to a groan.

He leaned forward, wanting a kiss, the need to be grounded with them too strong to ignore. He moved toward

Dani but she drew back, the laughter in her eyes turning serious.

"Did you fuck any of them?"

"No."

"Did you want to?"

He looked at her and the man beneath her, both staring at him intently waiting for his answer. He knew all he had to do was leave. If he was that unhappy with the situation he could leave. Leave Dani and Jax. Eventually the influence of the bite would fade and he'd go back to what he'd been. Fucking whoever he wanted. If he stayed, the bond between them would grow stronger.

He shook his head, going with the truth. "Not really. I guess I was just feeling a little cornered."

Dani smiled, sympathy glowing in her eyes. "That's okay. We all feel like that sometimes."

Reign shrugged, wanting to lighten the mood, get them back to their original goal—fucking. "I guess if I can put up with wolf-boy howling at the moon, you guys can handle my little quirks."

"Asshole," Jackson said though Reign could hear the affection behind the word.

"But you love me anyway." He said the words and then froze. He hadn't meant them that way. It was just something that he said.

"I guess I do," Jackson said with a sigh.

"Me too." Dani's admission was much nicer. She leaned over and pecked him on the cheek. "Now, weren't you saying something about fucking?" Her eyes sparkled with lust and laughter.

His heart fluttered. He wasn't ready to admit it, wasn't sure there would come a time when he could accept it, but he wasn't going to leave these two. They all belonged together.

Also by Tielle St. Clare

ﬔ

Wolf's Heritage 3: Maxwell's Fall
Wolf's Heritage 4: Jackson's Rise
Wolf's Heritage 5: Shadow's Embrace

Print Books:
Christmas Elf
Collective Memory
Ellora's Cavemen: Dreams of the Oasis III *(anthology)*
Ellora's Cavemen: Jewels of the Nile IV *(anthology)*
Ellora's Cavemen: Legendary Tails II *(anthology)*
Ellora's Cavemen: Tales from the Temple II *(anthology)*
Enter the Dragon *(anthology))*
Feral Fascination *(anthology)*
Irish Enchantment *(anthology)*
Shadow of the Dragon 1: Dragon's Kiss
Shadow of the Dragon 2: Dragon's Fire
Shadow of the Dragon 3: Dragon's Rise
Shadow of the Dragon 4: Dragon's Prey
Through Shattered Light
Transformations *(anthology)*
Wolf's Heritage 1: New Year's Kiss
Wolf's Heritage 2: Summer's Caress
Wolf's Heritage 3: Maxwell's Fall

About the Author

🔊

Tielle (pronounced "teal") St. Clare has had life-long love of romance novels. She began reading romances in the 7th grade when she discovered Victoria Holt novels and began writing romances at the age of 16 (during Trigonometry, if the truth be told). During her senior year in high school, the class dressed up as what they would be in twenty years—Tielle dressed as a romance writer. When not writing romances, Tielle has worked in public relations and video production for the past 20 years. She moved to Alaska when she was seven years old in 1972 when her father was transferred with the military. Tielle believes romances should be hot and sexy with a great story and fun characters.

🔊

The author welcomes comments from readers. You can find her website and email address on her author bio page at www.ellorascave.com.

Tell Us What You Think

We appreciate hearing reader opinions about our books. You can email us at Comments@EllorasCave.com.

Why an electronic book?

We live in the Information Age—an exciting time in the history of human civilization, in which technology rules supreme and continues to progress in leaps and bounds every minute of every day. For a multitude of reasons, more and more avid literary fans are opting to purchase e-books instead of paper books. The question from those not yet initiated into the world of electronic reading is simply: *Why?*

1. *Price.* An electronic title at Ellora's Cave Publishing runs anywhere from 40% to 75% less than the cover price of the exact same title in paperback format. Why? Basic mathematics and cost. It is less expensive to publish an e-book (no paper and printing, no warehousing and shipping) than it is to publish a paperback, so the savings are passed along to the consumer.

2. *Space.* Running out of room in your house for your books? That is one worry you will never have with electronic books. For a low one-time cost, you can purchase a handheld device specifically designed for e-reading. Many e-readers have large, convenient screens for viewing. Better yet, hundreds of titles can be stored within your new library—on a single microchip. There are a variety of e-readers from different manufacturers. You can also read e-books on your PC or laptop computer. (Please note that Ellora's Cave does not endorse any specific brands.

You can check our website at www.ellorascave.com for information we make available to new consumers.)

3. *Mobility.* Because your new e-library consists of only a microchip within a small, easily transportable e-reader, your entire cache of books can be taken with you wherever you go.

4. *Personal Viewing Preferences.* Are the words you are currently reading too small? Too large? Too... ANNOYING? Paperback books cannot be modified according to personal preferences, but e-books can.

5. *Instant Gratification.* Is it the middle of the night and all the bookstores near you are closed? Are you tired of waiting days, sometimes weeks, for bookstores to ship the novels you bought? Ellora's Cave Publishing sells instantaneous downloads twenty-four hours a day, seven days a week, every day of the year. Our webstore is never closed. Our e-book delivery system is 100% automated, meaning your order is filled as soon as you pay for it.

Those are a few of the top reasons why electronic books are replacing paperbacks for many avid readers.

As always, Ellora's Cave welcomes your questions and comments. We invite you to email us at Comments@ellorascave.com or write to us directly at Ellora's Cave Publishing Inc., 1056 Home Avenue, Akron, OH 44310-3502.

ELLORA'S CAVE
Romanticon

Annual convention
for women who
refuse to behave

www.JasmineJade.com/Romanticon

For additional info contact: conventions@ellorascave.com

Discover for yourself why readers can't get enough of the multiple award-winning publisher

Ellora's Cave.

Whether you prefer e-books or paperbacks,

be sure to visit EC on the web at
www.ellorascave.com

for an erotic reading experience that will leave you breathless.

CPSIA information can be obtained at www.ICGtesting.com
Printed in the USA
LVOW07s2359101215

466287LV00001B/88/P